AGA1NST GRAVITY

Also by Gary Gibson

ANGEL STATIONS

GARY GIBSON

AGAINST GRAVITY

TOR

First published 2005 by Tor
an imprint of Pan Macmillan Ltd
Pan Macmillan, 20 New Wharf Road, London N1 9RR
Basingstoke and Oxford
Associated companies throughout the world
www.panmacmillan.com
www.toruk.com

ISBN 1 4050 3446 7

Copyright © Gary Gibson 2005

1 3 5 7 9 8 6 4 2

A CIP catalogue record for this book is available from
the British Library.

Typeset by IntypeLibra Ltd.
Printed and bound in Great Britain by
Mackays of Chatham plc, Chatham, Kent

AGAINST
GRAVITY

LABRATS

13 October 2096
The Armoured Saint Pub, Edinburgh

It began on the day when Kendrick Gallmon's heart stopped beating for ever.

The pain crashed down on him suddenly and he sagged, unable to prevent his legs crumpling at the knees. He looked down at the stained interior curve of a toilet bowl and gripped its cool ceramic sides with shaking hands, his ears full of the sound of his own laboured gasping. He vomited noisily, bright agony rushing through his every nerve ending, like wildfire surging through a tinder-dry forest. He watched his knuckles turn white where they gripped the porcelain, and he wondered if he was going to die.

And then, mercifully, the pain began to ease off, leaving him gasping and shivering in the chilly cubicle. He could feel his knees turning damp through his thin cotton jeans. His mouth tasted acid and foul.

Reaching inside his shirt with a couple of fingers, Kendrick touched the bare skin of his chest. It felt cold and smooth, like a marble statue. Next he applied them to his wrist and tried to find a pulse. Finding nothing there, the knowledge sent a chill sweeping through him, so intense that it made his teeth chatter. He moaned in horror, convinced he must have somehow got it wrong.

But he knew the truth. Something had changed inside him, for ever.

Kendrick stumbled to his feet, triggering a series of vivid, dizzying flashes behind his eyes: until it passed, he had to lean with one

1

shoulder against the cubicle's graffiti-stained door. He sucked in air through his nostrils, calming himself steadily.

As suddenly as it had come, the pain washed away, like some Pacific storm leaving a devastated village in its wake. Random, dis-associated thoughts tumbled through his mind like flotsam. He glanced down into the toilet and grimaced, before hitting the flusher.

Two long months without a seizure, and now this.

He turned and pushed the cubicle door open. In front of him stood a row of washbasins, under a dirt-streaked mirror mounted on the wall above. The door opened suddenly, admitting loud music mixed with the sound of booze-filled conversation. A man stepped in, letting the door swing shut again, reducing the noise to a low murmur mingled with the muffled thump of bass.

There was something familiar about the other man's face; he looked about late forties, with a black beard turning grey. Kendrick noted the bags under his eyes, which were a pale, watery brown, and how he wore a long woollen coat still damp from the snow.

Those somehow familiar eyes settled on Kendrick, still leaning uncertainly against the cubicle's door frame.

Kendrick experienced a brief bout of dizziness, convinced that there was something important he needed to remember.

"Ken, what the fuck happened to you?"

Peter? Peter McCowan. How could he have forgotten? His thoughts felt muffled, obscured, as if a veil had been hastily drawn over his memories.

Kendrick could see his own reflection in the mirror and realized he looked like shit. He stepped past McCowan and ran water into a washbasin. He splashed some across his cheeks, but it didn't make him feel any better.

"Bad seizure," he replied shakily. He didn't feel up to elaborating.

"How bad?"

"*Very* bad." Kendrick coughed. "Don't use that name," he added.

"So, what name should I be using?"

"Never my real name, for a start." He leant over and sluiced a jet of water around his tongue, trying to get rid of the lingering taste of acid. He spat the water back into the sink and pulled himself upright, again catching sight of himself in the mirror.

Short-cropped head, narrow face: the same gaunt, fleshless aspect of so many Labrats. Still, he had coped a lot better than most of them, given that most of the Labrats were dead.

In the mirror he could see McCowan behind him, gently shaking his head. "Malky's still out there in the bar, wondering what's happened to you."

"I'll get back to him." Kendrick noticed that his hands still shook slightly. Perhaps that was only nerves and not, as he suspected, indicative of augment-related nerve damage. "It's just something I have to be prepared to deal with," he added over his shoulder.

He glanced up again at McCowan's reflection in the mirror. *What is it that feels so wrong here?* The longer he paused, the more he was filled with a tremendous sense of unease.

Kendrick closed his eyes against a fresh twinge of nausea. He should just make his excuses, go home, sort something out with Malky another time.

"I'll be frank, you look in bad shape. I don't think Hardenbrooke's treatments have been doing you any good."

Kendrick turned slowly, studying the other man's face. Bright coruscations slid across Kendrick's line of vision, followed by another wash of dislocation. With it a snatch of knowledge: a memory suddenly revealed, as if it had been temporarily locked away in some dark closet of his mind, only now returning with all the subtlety and grace of a drunken punch.

As he almost lost his balance, McCowan stepped forward as if to help. Kendrick backed up against the washbasin and put out a warning hand that stopped him.

"I'll take it you're not okay," said McCowan.

"Something's happening to me." It was starting – he was losing his mind at last. Any notion of finding a cure for what was inside him suddenly seemed far-fetched, laughable. How could he have fooled himself for so long?

"You're going to have to tell me what's wrong," the other man insisted.

Dead man, dead man – the words kept spinning through Kendrick's mind like a mantra.

Peter McCowan, staring up with vacant eyes at the dark ceiling of a lightless storage area, as if that gaze could penetrate the many levels of the Maze to see the sun beyond . . .

McCowan had moved further away from the door leading back into the bar area. Kendrick lurched past him and gripped the handle, began turning it.

The familiar sound of the bar beyond increased slightly. He paused with the door fractionally open.

"You're not here," he murmured, turning to see if the dead man *was* still there. McCowan still gazed back at him with calm eyes.

"It was a long time ago."

"I'm sorry."

McCowan cocked his head. "What for?"

"For letting you die."

The other shook his head. "They were never going to let both of us out of there – you know that for a fact. We both knew your family might still be alive out there somewhere. But there was no one who needed me, so I looked like the obvious choice."

This was too much. Over the years he'd imagined what it would be like, to be able to talk to Peter one last time, to find a way to understand what had happened between them. Now it appeared that he had the opportunity, and suddenly he didn't want it. He wasn't ready for it.

It came to Kendrick that he must be caught up in some particularly vivid form of hallucination generated by his augmentations:

4

fantasies that imposed themselves on the real world. How much longer did he have left, then, before he could no longer distinguish the imagined from the real? Was this what it was like for other Labrats when they got close to the end, when their augs consumed first their nervous systems and then their bodies, from the inside out? Did they imagine their pasts literally coming back to haunt them?

If that was the case, then perhaps he would be better off dead.

"I'm here to tell you something. I need to go soon, so are you listening to me?"

Kendrick stared down at the door handle. Sanity lay on the other side of it. "All right, I'm listening."

"Don't trust Hardenbrooke. He's a dangerous bastard. Do you hear me? He's dangerous."

Kendrick pulled the door open. Before he could step through, he sensed the ghost of Peter McCowan coming up close behind him. He saw its shadow darken the inside panel of the door, and felt as if his blood was about to freeze over.

"One last thing before you go." Kendrick could even feel the ghost's warm, beery breath on the back of his neck. "So that you know I'm here to help you. The leather suitcase sitting near the front of the bar – look inside it."

"I don't understand."

"Near the entrance."

The shadow shifted, and Kendrick imagined a pallid hand reaching out to pull him back. He stepped through quickly and slammed the door shut behind him, loud enough to attract one or two stares from some of the Saint's other clientele. He ignored them, turning back to the door he had just stepped through. He reached out and gently pushed it open again.

Nobody was there.

But there never had been, had there? He was sure of that.

*

5

The Armoured Saint pub was long and narrow, with wide windows facing out onto the street at one end and a bar extending from near the entrance all the way to the dark alcoves in the rear. Kendrick now turned left, towards the front section.

Between the bar itself and the tall windows looking out over the street, Kendrick could see a raised area of floor with a few tables and chairs on it. Business was quiet this early in the evening so it was currently deserted. A leather suitcase rested on the floor by a table next to the windows. A half-finished drink stood on the table as if someone had left in enough of a hurry to forget about their luggage.

This is crazy. Suffering an unpleasant delusion was bad enough, but paying this much attention to it was a step beyond. Kendrick turned away from both the table and the suitcase and found his way back to Malky, who was at the very rear of the bar. The air there was hot and thick with the stench of smoke and booze, in pleasant contrast to the bitter cold outside.

He found Malky staring vaguely into space, his arms folded over his stomach so that his checked shirt was rucked up over his pale rotund belly, exposing the elaborate design on his cowboy belt buckle. This buckle was something that Malky treasured and one of the bioware dealer's favourite stories revolved around his first and last visit to Los Angeles, only days before that city abruptly ceased to exist. Small and round, with his thinning blond hair brushed into an untidy side-parting, Malky was hardly the image of a frontiersman.

He raised his eyebrows as Kendrick sat down beside him. Malky smiled. "Well, I was beginning to think you'd gone home."

"Please, Malky, I feel bad. Really bad." He'd surely only imagined that his heart had stopped beating. A ridiculous notion: if it had, he'd be dead. He subconsciously reached up again and touched fingers delicately to his chest. Malky again raised his eyebrows questioningly, and Kendrick shook his head.

"Don't ask." He ducked his head a little, resting his elbows on the table top, briefly massaging his temples with his fingertips. He glanced back up at Malky and managed a faint grin. "I think I'm starting to hallucinate."

Malky sat up a little straighter, and Kendrick was pleased to see a look of genuine concern sweep over the little man's face. "What happened? Have you had another seizure?"

"Yeah – now I'm seeing ghosts." Kendrick leaned his head back against the nicotine-stained wallpaper and shrugged amiably, as if to say that it really wasn't any big deal.

Malky looked even more alarmed. "You need to see Hardenbrooke *now*. This is serious."

"It's not like I'm in the final stages or anything," he replied. "Look." Kendrick pulled down the collar of his T-shirt and leaned closer, eyeing the people around them. But nobody was looking.

The lines and ridges marking the flesh over his ribcage were visible, but only barely. There was no sign of the overwhelming striation that indicated a Labrat in the final, terminal stages of rogue augmentation growth. "Okay? So take it easy."

Malky glared at him, while Kendrick let his own gaze pass over the bar's other inhabitants. Most of the accents around them were, unsurprisingly, American. When he'd first come here to Scotland it had been easier to keep track of faces, but in recent years that had become impossible, as even more refugees escaped from the US and its civil war.

"What do you mean, 'seeing ghosts'?"

"Just what I said." Kendrick remembered his malt whisky and picked it up. He fingered the thimble-sized glass, wishing he could find a more satisfactory way to numb the memories that the ghost – no, he reminded himself, the *hallucination* – had dredged up.

Malky shook his head. "I'm telling you, we shouldn't just be sitting around talking like this. You need medical treatment." He reached out and touched Kendrick's hand as he lifted the whisky to his mouth. "And no more of that stuff might not be a bad idea while we're at it."

"I still need those papers," muttered Kendrick. "That's why I'm here."

The "papers" in question would give him the identity of a lawyer who had died in the LA firestorm and so was therefore not in a position to complain about this misappropriation of his life.

"Don't worry, that's all sorted out."

"Thanks."

"My pleasure, really." Malky shot him a pitying look.

Kendrick drained the last of his whisky, a comfortable heat settling in the pit of his stomach. "Look, I'm seeing Hardenbrooke tomorrow anyway, so it's not going to make any difference if I see him now or then."

"Fine, I admit defeat. So . . . whose ghost did you see?"

Kendrick made an exasperated noise. "Malky, I didn't see anything. I *imagined* I saw something." He could feel the alcohol softening the edge of his thoughts. Nonetheless, he realized that he was on the verge of a serious panic attack. Perhaps talking about his recent experience would objectify it, help put it outside himself.

"I imagined I was talking to someone who died back in the Maze. When I turned around, there he was, like I'm speaking to you now." Kendrick winced. "Trouble is, it felt real enough."

Malky put a hand to his mouth as if appropriately appalled. "Fuck, I'm sorry. That can't have been easy."

"It was a long time ago," replied Kendrick, echoing the ghost's own words.

Delusions, seizures . . . what else could they be but the precursor to a long-drawn-out death for him?

As he closed his eyes, the hubbub of the bar became abruptly muted, distant. In this artificial hush he searched for the sound of his own heartbeat.

He could hear nothing.

Yet, on opening his eyes again, here he was, still breathing, thinking, patently alive. Another hallucination, then; imagining that he was dead, hollow, silent on the inside.

Barely a moment had passed, and the world flooded back in on him. Delusion or not, Malky was right: he should go and see Hardenbrooke immediately.

So why didn't he? Why would he trust the word of a dead man, a phantom?

He suddenly remembered the suitcase sitting unattended at the far end of the bar.

". . . Won't say anything more about it, then," Malky was saying as Kendrick stood up. Malky looked up at him with a perplexed expression. "Where are you off to now?"

"I'll just be a second." *This is stupid*, thought Kendrick. Even so, he hurried to the far end of the bar, making a casual study of the people around him. Faces he'd seen a hundred times before but had never spoken to.

The unfinished drink was still sitting on the table. The suitcase still sat next to it on the floor. It couldn't have been there for long before he located it, or Lucia or one of the other bar staff would have noticed it by now.

Kendrick sat down on a seat nearby and glanced around him. What if the owner of the suitcase came back and found him poking through its contents?

The suitcase looked expensive, its leather soft and creamy, the silver clasp glowing brightly under the overhead lights. Feeling like a thief, he leaned down and opened it.

Kendrick found himself gazing down into a jumble of wires and electronic paraphernalia, all bunched around several lumps of putty-like explosive. That this might itself be part of some extended hallucinatory episode crossed his mind.

The best thing to do was to see what someone else thought they saw. He stood up and stepped over to the bar.

"Lucia."

She glanced over at Kendrick from behind the bar with a nodded greeting. Then she frowned, as if noticing something in his expression. She finished serving her customer, then stepped out from behind the bar. Lucia was tall, imposing; in a previous life she'd been a military engineer, adrift in Cuba with the UN peacekeeper forces there while the unrest back in the US spiralled into civil war. After that some chain of circumstance had brought her here, to the Armoured Saint. Apart from her work as the bar manager she helped Todd take care of any security requirements on behalf of the Saint's owner – who, it so happened, was Malky.

She looked down at Kendrick. "What's up?" she asked, in a voice deep enough to be baritone.

"I need you to tell me if I'm imagining things." He gestured at the open suitcase.

Lucia stepped over and glanced inside. Her eyes grew large, almost saucer-like, and her dark Hispanic skin visibly paled. She headed back behind the bar and flipped a switch to shut down the sound system. Customers stopped in mid-conversation as the lights came up.

"Bar's closed," she yelled. "Everybody out – now!"

Some regulars merely grinned at her, as if some great jest was being played. Other customers just looked confused. Kendrick glanced down the entire length of the Saint and saw Malky jerk upright, confusion and anger chasing each other across his features.

"Out. Now. Everybody," she bellowed again, clapping her hands thunderously above her head. Kendrick eyed the open case nervously. He could hear Malky yelling something similar, a look of panic on his face as he slammed open the fire doors at the rear.

Malky hurried over to join Kendrick while Lucia chased the rest of the bar staff outside, along with their customers. Grumbling and questioning, they went wandering out into the icy night.

"In the bag." Kendrick pointed.

Malky stepped up to the table and sat down heavily on a stool. Leaning forward, he looked as if he was about to push his head right inside the case. His angry frown turned to a gasp of horror.

"Oh shit," he whispered, "we're going to have to call the cops." He looked back up at Lucia, who rejoined them. After her efforts the Saint was silent and empty.

"Come on," said Malky, leading Kendrick away by the arm. "If I'm calling the cops, you sure as hell can't afford to stick around."

"But my ID—"

"—Will be safe against most police checks. But there's no reason to tempt fate, is there?" said Malky. "Once we're out of here I'm phoning the cops so somebody can come round and defuse that thing before it blows my livelihood to bits."

"If I'm even so much as questioned—"

"I just said, I know. We'll go out the back way. Lucia, get upstairs and check if anyone's there. Get them out into the street if they are."

Kendrick still had his Euro Citizenship card, of course, but that had been illegally altered to disguise his Labrat past. Otherwise his movements would become severely restricted. Carrying this card wasn't even mandatory; in fact, citizens of the European Legislate were not obliged to carry them at all. But in the right circumstances – like a bomb scare – background checks might go a lot deeper than normal. Even if he'd possessed the LA ID that Malky had been promising him, there were no guarantees that it would survive the full scrutiny of some Legislate investigative committee determined to root out terrorist activity.

As they reached the empty rear of the bar, Malky leaned over the counter-top and grabbed a long broomstick from its mounting on the wall. A hook was attached to one end of the implement. Next he pushed a table and a couple of chairs to one side, till Kendrick could see that there was a trapdoor set in the floor. Malky spun the pole around to insert the hook neatly into an iron ring fitted to one edge of the trapdoor, then, with a clatter, pulled it up and to one side.

"What about cameras?" persisted Kendrick. "Is there anything the police might be able to use against me?"

"There are, and there is. But as soon as you're out of here I'm going to have Todd alter the security system's memory pronto. Believe it or not, he works fast when he needs to." The open trapdoor revealed a ladder leading down into darkness.

11

Malky climbed down rapidly, Kendrick following without hesitation.

They stepped off onto a cellar floor several feet below. Although it was dark here, Kendrick's surroundings instantly became clearer to him as his Labrat-augmented senses compensated. He saw roughly plastered walls, bare floorboards underfoot, and large metal casks piled up against the walls. The smell of stale hops assaulted his senses as Malky unlocked a door at the far end of the cellar.

"Through here." The pub's owner stepped through, into darkness. Kendrick followed him, traversing a floor that was sticky with rivulets of beer. He passed through the door to find himself in an unkempt garden backing onto a narrow alleyway glistening with frost.

A chill wind sliced at Kendrick's face. Since the Gulf Stream had been cut off a few decades ago the summer in Scotland barely lasted six weeks; global warming had altered the flow of air currents over the tropics so that they no longer carried equatorial warmth towards Northern Europe. Temperatures in the higher northern latitudes had plummeted, and there were people muttering about whether or not they were sliding into a new Ice Age.

Malky stood waiting for him. "Tell me what just happened there," he asked, his expression agitated.

"There was a bomb in the bar."

"How did you know? You didn't put it there yourself, did you?"

"Oh, come on, I . . ." But what could he possibly tell him? Certainly not the truth. Malky would assume it was a lie, and Kendrick would be the last to blame him.

"I knew the same way any Labrat would," Kendrick improvised. It was, after all, an entirely valid explanation.

Malky gaped at him with an incredulous expression. "You're telling me you sensed it – right from the other end of the bar?

C'mon, Kendrick, not even a Labrat could do that. Someone must have warned you, yeah?"

"Look, I don't have the time for this. I'm going to get myself out of here before anyone arrives. Okay? Let me know what happens." Kendrick raised a hand in farewell and hurried away, Malky's suspicious gaze burning between his shoulder blades.

Kendrick didn't see a figure peel away from the shadows near the parked cars, but he knew immediately that he was being followed. He turned a corner at the end of the block and waited there till, a second later, his pursuer appeared. Kendrick grabbed him by the shoulder and spun him around.

"Easy!" said the other man, his accent making it clear that he was an American. "Easy, I just want to talk to you."

"What about? Did you leave that bomb in the bar?"

The stranger stared at him, bug-eyed. "Is *that* what it was? Christ, I wondered what was going on."

"You were in there too?"

"Yes, trying to find you. Then everyone got thrown out." He smiled. "You don't remember me, do you?"

"No, I don't." Which was a lie. There was something familiar about the man's face. But it wasn't like seeing the ghost back in the bar – this time there was no nausea, no sense of impending dread; none of the symptoms that usually preceded a seizure. Whoever he was, he was no apparition.

"The Maze, y'know? Though it's been a long time."

"I'm afraid I don't recall."

The other man laughed. "Well, we never actually spoke before. My name's Erik Whitsett."

"But you were—"

"In a coma, yes. Well, I recovered about a year after they brought me out of the Maze. When you didn't appear outside in the street, I figured you must have headed out the back somewhere, so here I am."

13

Kendrick shook his head. "Mr Whitsett, I'm sorry I didn't recognize you. It's just that—"

"It's been such a long time. Yeah, I know. Look, I haven't been spying on you or anything. It's just that I really need to talk to you."

The sound of sirens drifted through the night air, a few streets distant and coming closer.

"I think we should take a walk first, Erik."

They crossed the street and kept moving, Kendrick leading the way, Erik hurrying beside him. Kendrick cut diagonally across Parliament Square and stopped Whitsett with a palm against his chest once they were on the other side.

"Erik, I don't know why you're here or what you want from me, but you should know I'm not happy at being discovered." He kept his voice low as people wandered past them on all sides, slipping in and out of brightly coloured 3D air projections that reached out from shop windows to dance and shimmer for their attention. The air was filled with the gentle cacophony of sales jingles just barely on the edge of perception.

Whitsett shook his head. "I'm not here to blackmail you. I'm just hoping I can help you. Buddy sent me, and I don't think you've forgotten *him*."

"All right, you've got my attention. What do you want?"

"Have you heard about the deaths? All the deaths of Labrats?"

Kendrick opened his mouth, then closed it. There had been some news reports about the deaths of one or two who had testified many years before against the Wilber Regime, particularly against Anton Sieracki, although that trial had been posthumous.

"I heard something about Adams and Gallagher, that they were murdered. Nobody knows who by, right?"

"That's true, but there are others you might not have heard about: Perez, Sachs, Hauptmann, Stillwell – all dead."

14

Kendrick studied Whitsett as he spoke. Small, rotund, with a full beard. He'd been little more than an inanimate shape in Kendrick's memories, the next best thing to dead himself. But here he was, alive and well, which gave Kendrick a sense of hope. If Whitsett could get better, then perhaps so could any of them.

"I remember them," said Kendrick slowly, "but I hadn't heard from any of them in years. Are you saying that somebody's killed them?"

"That's exactly what I'm saying. But they're not targeting all Labrats, just those from the same experimental programme you and I were placed in. Something's definitely happening."

"You're saying somebody planted that bomb in order to kill *me*?"

"I can't see any other explanation, can you? So if you've been trying to lead an incognito life, maybe somebody's noticed."

"That doesn't explain how you knew where to find me, Erik."

"You're still using the same contact details from the last time you saw Buddy, yeah?"

"So *he* told you where to find me." Whitsett nodded. "But you should know that I haven't seen Buddy for a few years. We don't really keep in touch that much any more."

The sirens sounded very close now. The two men weren't yet far enough from the Saint. By some unspoken agreement, they began walking again, side by side.

They cut down another alley and crossed over a wide street beyond, always moving in the general direction of the city centre. Kendrick had noted how Whitsett kept the collar of his jacket pulled up high, a scarf wrapped tightly about his neck. It was a colder night than usual, but Kendrick suspected that Whitsett had other reasons for covering himself up so carefully.

"You and Buddy were both in Ward Seventeen, the same time as me. I barely remember any of it, so I guess that makes me one of the lucky ones."

"The lucky ones were the ones that weren't there at all. If you or Buddy think you know who would want to plant a bomb, it would be nice if you could tell me just who."

"It's— Ah, shit." Lights flashed at the far end of the street and they watched as an unmanned police car cruised slowly past, its low upper surface bristling with lenses and sensors. They kept to the shadows and moved on, quickly turning a corner and getting out of sight of the robot vehicle.

"What's more important right now," Whitsett continued, "is knowing you're not the only one who's been seeing strange things."

"How do you—?" Whitsett stopped in a darkened doorway and unwrapped his scarf. Kendrick saw now the dozens of dark ridges reaching up from under the man's shirt, like shadowy branches converging towards the base of his skull. His chin and cheeks looked swollen, distorted.

How long Whitsett still had to live Kendrick couldn't guess, but by the looks of things probably less than a year.

"Look, I'm sorry for what's happened to you," Kendrick said, the words coming not at all easily. "My augmentations have turned rogue too. I sympathize."

Whitsett laughed with a low, throaty chuckle that shook his small frame. "I've made you uncomfortable. I'm sorry about that. I've had a long time to come to terms with what happened to me – as we all have. What comes, comes. Look, maybe this isn't the best place, so is there anywhere else we can buy ourselves a drink? There's a lot we need to talk about."

"Maybe you can answer my question first. If you know – have *any* idea – who planted that bomb, then you need to tell me."

Whitsett glanced around and shook his head. "All right. It's almost certainly Los Muertos, but don't take that as a definite."

Kendrick laughed. "This far from the Maze? Why on Earth would they want—?"

"Look, perhaps this isn't the best time and place to be discussing such things. Let's say we arrange to meet some other time – and soon. How about tomorrow?"

"Maybe."

"Just maybe?"

"I don't understand why Buddy couldn't come and speak to me in person."

Whitsett sighed, and produced his wand. "Look, before anything else I'd like to make sure we can get in touch, before any more of those cop cars come rolling by."

Kendrick hesitated, then shrugged and produced his own wand. They keyed the devices, allowing them to link to each other and share communication details.

Whitsett was smiling, but his expression had become more guarded. He buttoned his coat back up, after carefully wrapping the scarf tightly around his neck. "I'm glad it's cold, or this would be a lot more difficult to hide. In answer to your question, Buddy's got a lot on his mind, arranging . . ." He hesitated. "Things. I think it's more a case of . . . he's surprised *he* hasn't heard from *you*."

Whitsett paused for a moment, then continued. "What did you see – in your visions?"

Kendrick paused, forming his reply. "I'm sorry, I'm just not ready to talk about that yet. I saw *something*. What does it matter?"

Whitsett persisted. "A green place, then? A winged—"

"Please. I'll be happy to discuss it with you some other time, but not now."

Kendrick wondered if the fear showed on his face. Whitsett studied him with calm eyes, making him feel like he was being judged in some way. After a moment Kendrick turned away.

"I'll speak to you soon," he said to Whitsett, the words sounding more abrupt than he intended. "Goodbye."

Whitsett nodded. "I'll be in touch."

Kendrick walked rapidly away, not wanting to turn back and see there was nobody there.

Going back to his own place wasn't an option – at least, not for

17

tonight. If Malky and Todd failed to wipe him from the Saint's visual records, if somebody knew who he was and wanted to kill him for some obscure reason, then simply heading home really wasn't going to be a good idea. Kendrick slowed, realizing he had nowhere else to go.

After a moment, some instinct made him head for Caroline's place. She might not be happy to see him, but where else was there? Besides, he now wanted someone familiar, someone who'd been through the same experiences that he had.

After only half a block, he turned around and saw that Whitsett was gone. He studied the spot where they'd last spoken together, his fingers flexing unconsciously. *He's real*, he decided. *He's real.*

It took Kendrick thirty-five minutes to make his way by foot through the city centre, heading for Stockbridge. The brisk pace and the cold air helped to sharpen senses that until now had been dulled by barely faded nausea. He palmed his wand and stepped up to the entrance of a refurbished tenement building in which Caroline Vincenzo owned a flat, on the top floor. The entrance stairwell visible beyond the reinforced glass was brightly lit. He carefully, steadfastly ignored the voices in his mind, yelling out all the reasons why he shouldn't be here.

He could use Caroline's cryptkey – still stored, even after so long, in his wand's memory – to gain access, but he didn't think she'd react well to that. Instead he touched the wand to his ear and waited for her to answer.

Pain flickered brightly in the back of Kendrick's skull, sending him reeling and collapsing against the vestibule side-wall.

Not again, he thought. *Not twice in one night.*

He started to hyperventilate, on the verge of panic, letting himself slide down until his back pressed against the door. Bright flashes now strobed and flickered at the edge of his vision as he settled his buttocks onto cold concrete. Bile forcing its way to the back of his throat, he gagged.

Kendrick looked down at the wand nestling in the palm of his hand as it pinged faintly. *Come on*, he thought. Perhaps she simply wasn't at home. Perhaps—

A tsunami of agony bore down on him and he yielded to it as the street around him disappeared from sight. Then the strangest thing happened . . . the pain was gone, in an instant.

He was somewhere else, a soft, warm wind buffeting his head. The air around him was as thick and sweet as honey. It was the same as before: a figure, born of some inner recess of his mind, floating there in the breeze on wings that shone and glistened under golden light.

Its wings sprouted impossibly from the shoulders of a tiny homunculus figure, perhaps a hand-span in height. The wings were wide, shimmering things whose surfaces seemed to drift and flow as if caught in some invisible current. Its blank face – so disturbingly human – gazed back at him with an expression of amused contempt.

Kendrick felt as if he had been reduced to a point of simple awareness, somehow suspended in the air as though his thoughts were trapped in some dense, liquid amber. The boy with the gossamer wings suddenly appeared to grow bored – then darted away from him with shocking speed. Kendrick's non-existent eyes stared after the tiny figure as it flew across a landscape born of dreams.

He was now in some kind of garden that surrounded a group of low, office-like buildings whose pale walls glowed as if they radiated some inner light. Beyond and surrounding this garden were tall trees. Above his head, on either side, the ground curved upwards to meet itself far overhead, so that he appeared to be trapped on the inside of a vast cylinder.

He had been here before, always in the throes of a violent seizure that tore at his body and his nerves, always leaving him feeling ruined, sick and distraught. He had seen the same gossamer-winged boy before . . . and this strange garden, and the building it surrounded.

Kendrick could see the boy-creature, wings flapping lazily to carry it above the long untended grass.

He looked up, studying the walls encompassing his world, wondering why he would dream of this place of all places . . .

And then he was back in Edinburgh, the breath ragged in his throat, staring up into Caroline's face, realizing in an instant that she must have dragged him inside from the vestibule to where he now lay at the bottom of the stairs. Worry and anger warred with each other across her face as he closed his eyes, waiting for the pain to go away.

13 October 2096
Caroline Vincenzo's flat, Edinburgh

Kendrick pulled the T-shirt over his head and studied his bare chest in Caroline's bathroom mirror, noting the lines that traversed his hips, curving across his ribcage, continuing under his left arm and around his back, and culminating near the base of his skull before burrowing even deeper into his flesh. They had been there since his days in the Maze but, now that his augments had turned against him, there would soon be more – it was only a matter of time. The lines felt hard under his fingertips, as if steel cables criss-crossed beneath his skin.

Next he touched two fingers to his wrist and found a pulse but, instead of the familiar rhythm he had known all his life, there was a steady throb more like that of a machine.

He leant closer to the mirror, studying the fine flush of red in his cheeks – he could see with far greater detail than any unaugmented human. Something was keeping his body going, keeping the blood pumping through his arteries. But it wasn't his heart. Not any more.

"Kendrick?" Caroline's voice from outside the bathroom door. "Are you okay in there?"

"I'm fine."

He pulled his T-shirt back on and walked into her living room. Not so long ago, it had been *their* living room, but that had all ended several months before. He watched as she rolled a cigarette, an act of folly since her augs would sweep the active agent from her bloodstream before it got anywhere near her cortex. But for Caroline it was a carefully crafted eccentricity. She told people she liked the taste.

Thick dark hair spilled in heavy curls down the back of her shirt. Kendrick noticed that she was still wearing a suit, and the eepsheets and papers scattered around the floor in wild abandon suggested that she'd only just returned from meeting clients, and had been busy in locating suddenly necessary notes and reference materials.

"Thanks for letting me in," he said.

Caroline shrugged lightly, an expression of cool distance on her face. She reached out with one foot that was still clad in an expensive low-heeled shoe, and hooked an ashtray lying near her on the floor. Then she tapped ash into it. The cigarette was still her shield, its smoke a mask over her thoughts.

"I could have left you there, Kendrick, but you know how my neighbours are." She sighed heavily. "What happened to you tonight?"

"I had another seizure."

She shook her head. "So you came to me? What am I supposed to do?"

"It's not that." He then told her about the earlier events in the Armoured Saint.

"Christ," Caroline muttered once he'd finished. "Did you have to speak to the police?"

"I left before they arrived."

Kendrick sat down across from her and smiled half-heartedly. "The seizure only hit once I actually got here. It was the second one today, and the first hit a couple of hours ago."

"Two seizures in one day?"

He nodded.

"I'm sorry, Kendrick." She looked confused. "I had no idea. I . . ." She trailed off, her features wreathed in blue smoke. He studied the faint, raised lines in her flesh just barely visible where the top buttons of her shirt had been left undone. When she was out in public, habit made her keep the shirt buttoned up. Behind her, he could see the city's rooftops under a moonlit sky.

He could almost read Caroline's thoughts. They were both of them Labrats, and what was happening to him could happen to her too, any time. She was probably scared because there was every chance she would end up the same.

Going to a regular hospital for medical treatment was out of the question, and they both knew it. What they carried within their bodies was, by definition, unpredictable. That was a good enough reason for many of the Labrats to be locked away without trial for the rest of their short lives, as soon as their augs showed signs of turning rogue. If you went to the wrong country and they found out you were a Labrat, they just shot you and burned your corpse.

Caroline appeared to make up her mind about something. She stubbed out the remains of her cigarette and stood. "You can stay here tonight on the couch," she said briskly. "I'll get some stuff for you." She disappeared into the bedroom and returned with a couple of blankets and a pillow.

As she went back into the bedroom, Kendrick stared morosely after her. Then he turned to the window, not wanting to get absorbed in some maudlin reflection about something that was long finished. He stared out over the slate rooftops of the city. Beyond them the vague bulk of the Castle loomed high over everything else. The tarmac far below was grey and shiny in the freezing rain that had begun to slant down.

Tomorrow he would have to go back to Hardenbrooke's Clinic. He had no choice, really, as Hardenbrooke was the only one who might help him.

Kendrick spoke quietly into the air to find if Caroline had changed the voice-access code on her windowscreen software. Then he stepped back as the sheet of glass became opaque, the

Edinburgh skyline disappearing behind a corporate logo that rushed towards him on a swell of electronic music.

He heard her step back into the room behind him.

"That logo . . ."

"The TransAfrica Corporation," she replied. "I'm sure you remember."

"So you've been doing all right?"

She arched one eyebrow, reading between the lines: *Without you, you mean?* "Better than okay. You know how much time I spent on this stuff." Kendrick switched his attention back to the screen, where an image of a spinning globe had now replaced the logo.

Caroline had won the design contract for the TransAfrica project only a few months before she had abruptly ended their relationship, without explanation, a few months after his seizures had first manifested. Feeling abruptly uncomfortable, Kendrick sat down on the couch. So she was doing better than okay? He watched the show, glad for the distraction from everything that had happened so far in a single evening.

The animated globe resolved itself into a recognizable image of the Earth as seen from near-orbit space, this viewpoint spinning rapidly downwards, through dense clouds until the continent of Africa became visible below. As this viewpoint now shifted, the southern tip of the Iberian Peninsula became visible above the North African coast. Then a thin, glistening line connecting both continents appeared, zooming in yet closer until this line resolved itself into a huge bridge.

The main part of its span consisted of four great pylons, the middle two bedded in the watery depths of the Straits of Gibraltar. The sea around the pylons became suddenly transparent, like blue-tinted glass, and a voice-over began to explain the engineering difficulties of trying to construct something so huge. All that was impossible, of course, without the lessons learned from the construction of the *Archimedes Orbital*.

He turned to Caroline.

"What do you think?" she asked him.

"I'm impressed. You've done good work. I'm really impressed."
He turned back to the images unfolding on the screen.

The *Archimedes Orbital* – Max Draeger's great white elephant,
his downfall – still up there somewhere, far above the Earth.
Kendrick stared at the images, his thoughts far away.

Caroline left Kendrick alone to make up his bed on her couch. He
was trying to ignore the misery washing over him now that he was
back in a place he'd never thought he'd see again. He hadn't even
told her about Peter McCowan, or his meeting with Whitsett.

She had a right to know, but in some way he wasn't ready to
talk. He still couldn't quite believe he was in any kind of real
danger. Perhaps Whitsett was just some lone crank who had constructed this fable on the spur of the moment, inspired by the
events in the Saint an hour or so before.

Kendrick switched off the light, but sleep wouldn't come easily.
There was just too much to think about. It wasn't only that he'd
spoken to a ghost, but that this ghost, this hallucination, had told
him something that he would never have found out otherwise.

That was too much to think about. He spoke quietly into the
air again, reactivating the windowscreen, but kept the sound off
this time, aware of Caroline sleeping in the next room.

The presentation she had long worked on doubled as an interactive environment so that, once the logo had faded away, he was
able to cause the viewpoint to zoom away from Earth and out into
space. It didn't take long for him to locate the *Archimedes*. It had
been there all the time, but now, seeing the enormous space
station there on the screen, Kendrick remembered something.

As the great cylinder of the *Archimedes* hove into view, studded
with lights that twinkled in a touch that had more to do with
artistic flourish than reality, a half-formed idea began tingling in
the back of his mind.

He directed the windowscreen to zoom in closer to the

computer-generated image, and recalled all the stories, all the speculation. A lot had happened up there.

Although it was only reasonable to assume that Caroline would have spent some time on programming the *Archimedes* into its environment, Kendrick could not fail to notice the remarkable attention to detail. Perhaps this was purely down to her professionalism, but Kendrick found himself wondering. After all, although undoubtedly Draeger's greatest engineering achievement, it was far better known as a catastrophic failure. And although it clearly contributed to the project Caroline was now peripherally involved in, why would she spend so much time getting the *Archimedes* so correct in every detail?

Exhaustion began to overcome curiosity, however, and Kendrick felt sleep finally overtaking him. As he lay in the dark, he grew aware that he was frightened to close his eyes; frightened he might wake up to find his body changed in some less-than-subtle manner – thick ropes of half-sentient machinery, with its own unfathomable desires, burrowing under his flesh like eels.

Anything was possible, and Kendrick had long since discovered that there was nothing so terrifying as the unknown, the unpredictable.

10 October 2096
Angkor Wat

The heat seemed even more unforgiving than usual as Marlin Smeby ascended a short flight of ancient stone steps before stepping, with considerable gratitude, into the air-conditioned reception area. He stopped to savour the chill before moving on. After a nod to the security guard sitting at the main desk, he continued onwards to Max Draeger's private elevator.

Less than a minute later he entered Draeger's office, registering the vast stone-built mural that took up most of one wall. His gaze then moved on to the teeming jungle visible through the panoramic windows that formed the wall opposite. Draeger was standing there, hands in his pockets, staring out across the jungle and beyond. With his bleached hair and leathery copper skin, he looked the perfect image of the tanned Californian billionaire.

An air projector displayed an image above the smooth expanse of Draeger's desk, and Marlin recognized it instantly as the *Archimedes*, a dull grey tube that belied the reality of the space habitat's enormous size.

"Marlin, welcome. I hope your journey was comfortable." Draeger followed Smeby's gaze to the image of the *Archimedes*.

"The journey was fine, sir." Smeby took a seat by the long obsidian desk, removing an eepsheet from his jacket pocket and placing it on the polished surface between them.

"This is everything I've been able to find out about the inmates of Ward Seventeen." Draeger removed one hand from a pocket and placed it, fingertips down, on the desk. As Smeby scooted the eepsheet across the slick desktop, Draeger halted its progress. His fingers danced briefly across the document and reams of information scrolled rapidly under his hand.

Draeger nodded as if satisfied, and tapped at a coloured panel. The edges of the sheet strobed red in response, indicating that its contents were currently being uploaded to a data bank contained within the databand bracelet that Draeger wore.

"Very interesting, this. Los Muertos have clearly established the link between the surviving Labrats and the *Archimedes*." Smeby waited in silence as Draeger's fingers thoughtfully tapped out a light rhythm on the desk. "Interesting, but not quite as satisfying as I had hoped."

"There have been difficulties."

"I'm already aware of those." Draeger took his seat across from Smeby and studied him, one hand half-covering his mouth. "How are your treatments progressing?"

That could have been an innocuous question but, in the several months since he had entered Draeger's employ – or, rather, since Draeger had paid the bribes necessary to extricate Smeby from the Chinese jail in which he had been languishing – Smeby had learned to sense the inherent threat in every such discussion they had. Smeby nodded carefully, keeping his features deliberately neutral as he framed his reply.

"The spurts of growth in my augmentations appear to have been stopped, but it may be too early to decide if this is permanent." He swallowed. "I'll need further treatments, further observation, and Dr Xian thinks it'll be a while before they'll know for sure if I'm in the clear."

Draeger nodded. Smeby had fully expected to die in that Chinese jail. He'd had his augmentations surgically implanted only a few years before, in a Bangkok clinic that took only cash – anything but US dollars. For some reason it had felt like a good idea at the time. It had been getting harder, a lot harder, to find mercenary work without possessing that extra edge. And if you didn't take that one vital step further, maybe you'd find yourself caught in a mountain pass while some guy who could see in the dark, and with reflexes three times as fast as your own, crept up behind you with a knife. With odds like that, the surgery had seemed a reasonable gamble – for a while.

Draeger nodded towards the *Archimedes* image, still hanging in the air. "Tell me, Marlin, what you know about the station."

"Only what I've read up on it over the past several days, sir."

Draeger waved a hand. "So tell me what you've found out."

"The original project was handled by three of your subsidiary orbital development firms, working in tandem with the United States government – while there still was a United States." Smeby shrugged briefly. "The work on it started in the early 2080s, and it was intended to demonstrate the scientific superiority of the United States at a time when it was coming under almost constant attack by unknown forces utilizing biological or genetic weapons. This was at the same time that President Wilber instituted the Emergency Government, suspending the Constitution. And discontinuing the electoral process."

"But there were other reasons too for building the station, Marlin?"

Smeby cast him an appraising look before continuing. "Yes, there were. I am a religious man, Mr Draeger, and I think Wilber was wrong. He believed that he could reach out to God by using the *Archimedes* – a sin of pride. God sundered the United States and scattered its people with plagues and fire. That was our punishment for our hubris. Now the *Archimedes* itself is inaccessible."

Draeger's expression remained serene. While Smeby was speaking, he had been staring again out over the treetops rising beyond the ancient temples. "You were there, weren't you, Marlin? At the end?"

"Excuse me, sir?"

Draeger turned back to him. "During Wilber's flight, you were one of his . . . they called you the God Squad, didn't they?" Smeby could feel his face redden. The term that Draeger had used was uncomplimentary at best. "You were there, trying to smuggle him out of the White House before the Senate could have him arrested." Draeger touched his data bracelet and the edges of the eepsheet flashed again. Smeby could see new information displayed there now, and didn't need to look too close to know what it would be.

Draeger turned the eepsheet around and slid it back over to Smeby, who ignored it. "Don't you remember your old name?" asked Draeger. "Or does that stir up too many bad memories?"

"Lots of bad memories, sir. But what's the point of this? You've already got me working for you."

"I want you to understand how much is at stake here . . . your plastic surgery is excellent, by the way. What I'm about to tell you is intended for only a few people's ears, so you should feel privileged that I've decided to share it with you. I'm sure you'll appreciate the risks otherwise."

Oh, I do, Smeby thought to himself sourly.

Draeger continued: "Much of the research carried out on board the *Archimedes* primarily involved molecular engineering. The station itself is partly a result of nanotech, using materials farmed from robot lunar mining operations. Some of that research, particularly into developing bio-organic technologies that could fuse with living bodies, was later developed still further through covert military experimentation." Draeger smiled, but Smeby could see no humour in the other man's eyes. "Research which included experimenting on members of the American public."

Smeby shrugged. "Dissidents, enemies of the state – the kind of people who welcomed our worst enemies inside our borders with open arms."

Draeger cocked his head to one side. "You approve, then?"

"That's beside the point. What's the purpose of all this, sir?"

"What if I told you that Wilber was right to think that he could find God through the *Archimedes*?"

Smeby was silent for several seconds as he sought an appropriate reply.

Instead, Draeger pre-empted him. "Let me fill in the rest of the details, then. There was a containment breach on board the *Archimedes* before it was even half completed. Self-organizing molecular machinery invaded the substance of the station, and the *Archimedes* was subsequently abandoned, under World Court jurisdiction." Draeger smiled, crookedly. "Do you know precisely what went wrong?"

For some reason that he couldn't quite fathom, Smeby's throat had become very dry. "No, I don't, sir."

"Your beloved President wanted to find God. He interpreted my theories in such a way that he believed *I* could help him in that. The heart of the *Archimedes* consists of self-learning, self-motivating artificial-intelligence routines embedded in nanite machinery designed to function in cooperative colonies. Hard-wired to specific tasks such as decoding the structure of space" – Draeger smiled more broadly – "or finding God."

"You're crazy."

"Quite possibly, yes, but my definition of God is not quite the same as Wilber's was. If there is a God, Mr Smeby, he's not Jehovah or any other of an endless pantheon of crude tribal deities that are still worshipped even today. God is . . . intelligence seeking to sustain itself. If that intelligence exists it would leave traces, in the structure of our universe itself. The cooperative intelligences on board the *Archimedes* were designed to find those traces, the evidence."

"And have they?"

"Oh no, Mr Smeby. They've done much, much more than that."

21 April 2093
Venezuela

Kendrick woke again a little while before darkness fell, his mind still half-full of scattered dream-images, to feel a hand brush against his shoulder like the caress of a ghost.

"*Jesus,*" he yelled, jumping up, suddenly wide awake. Dull red lines of text glowed faintly on his databand, a weather feed detailing the hurricane skirting St Lucia and moving south-west, scattering fishing boats across the northern coast of South America and tearing through villages as it went.

Finding a secure landing spot before the winds really hit hadn't been easy. Then came a lot of waiting, and a growing certainty that João wasn't ever going to appear, that they were on some kind of a wild-goose chase that just might get them killed if they weren't careful.

"Sssh, it's me, João." He crouched at the entrance to the tent, favouring Kendrick with a wide grin.

Kendrick pulled himself upright and groaned, "Where's Buddy? Have you spoken to him yet?"

"He's outside."

Kendrick stumbled out of the tent and blinked himself awake while fading sunlight skimmed the treetops around them. The skin of Buddy's helicopter flickered with a constantly shifting mirror image of the surrounding trees and bushes, providing it with an effective camouflage.

Kendrick heard the distant sound of monkeys shrieking in the jungle. Maybe it was more romantic this way, he thought; more like how a movie director would portray the life of an investigative journalist – hiding out in the jungle, trying to avoid satellite detection while hunting down a remnant of the old US Army.

But that wasn't how it felt, far from it. They were risking their lives, and if anything bad happened to them it was unlikely that anyone would ever know about it. They were within a hundred miles or so of the Maze, and the very knowledge that it was so close left Kendrick with a permanent vague feeling of unease and dread.

This was as close to returning to the Maze as he ever wanted to get.

Buddy was leaning against the 'copter's shrouded carapace, talking quietly with a boy who couldn't have been more than twelve or thirteen, whom Kendrick realized must have come with João. The boy's English was heavily accented and occasionally fractured.

A thirteen-year-old with an automatic rifle and a bandanna, Kendrick noted. He wondered what this boy might have grown up to be in other circumstances, in some other place. An image of his own young daughter rose unbidden in his mind. She'd have been just a little younger than—

No, don't think about that. He forced the mental image away. The boy here had to be one of Mayor Sobrino's mercenary army, and it was debatable if they or Los Muertos were the worse. Supposedly they protected the townships in this part of the country against Los Muertos' incursions, but with the amount of drug trafficking that went on in the area it was more likely a half-hearted cover for making themselves a lot of money.

"This is Louie," Buddy announced on his approach. He glanced back down at the boy. "Louie, this is my friend Kendrick. He's the one who wants to find out about the Los Muertos guy."

Old man's eyes gazed out at Kendrick from a child's face. He flinched, despite himself, under that appraising gaze.

"You brought it?" the boy asked.

Kendrick looked back up at Buddy, and their stares met knowingly. This was something they'd talked about: what if the kid hadn't come alone? What if he had compatriots hiding out in the jungle somewhere, ready to jump them? Out of sight of Louie, Buddy shook his head from side to side, slowly and carefully. *Everything's okay.* He emphasized his point by giving Kendrick a discreet thumbs-up. Buddy would have already had his instruments scanning the surrounding hills in case Louie had brought unwanted company.

Kendrick studied João out of the corner of his eye. It was he who had made the initial contact with the boy-mercenary. Kendrick could not rid himself of the idea that João was digging himself deep into something he might not be able to get out of. Buddy appeared to have faith in him, however.

Maybe that was good enough, and everything would be fine, but of course there were never guarantees.

"Sure, Louie. We've got it."

Still gripping his rifle firmly, the boy nodded. "Show me first, then we talk."

Kendrick climbed on board the helicopter. He emerged several seconds later carrying a suitcase. With his free hand, Louie made an imperious gesture towards the ground. Buddy glanced at Kendrick, and shrugged. João looked on, from the edge of the clearing, his expression one of fascination.

Buddy put the case down and opened it. Tightly wrapped bundles of yen flapped in a sudden breeze that was warm and heavy against the approaching chill of the night. Louie put his rifle down and leant over the case, leafing rapidly through the banknotes. Kendrick could just make out the boy's voice as he talked under his breath while counting the money. When Louie looked up, his face was filled with ugly greed.

"Okay, I'll show you."

A long time ago, Los Muertos – meaning "the dead" in Spanish – had been a part of the United States Army. Then the famines had come, and then the LA Nuke, and things had really started to fall apart. A couple of divisions of soldiers judged to be absolutely loyal to Wilber had been posted at the Maze before things went to pieces in Washington. When the end came for Wilber himself, some of those soldiers had started to head for home. But there were others who believed more deeply in Wilber's messianic visions, who believed the Endtime was upon them. Out here, lost in the jungle and leaderless, they had transformed themselves into Los Muertos. If Wilber remained their Arthur, then the old United States had been their Camelot, now lost for ever.

"Just tell me you really know what the hell you're doing," Kendrick whispered to Buddy as they walked. João and Louie were a little ways ahead of them, dark shapes in the night-time jungle. There was no way they could fly their 'copter any closer to where Louie was leading them: too much chance that either Los Muertos or one of Sobrino's wandering patrols of mercenaries would take them out with a ground-to-air missile, on a general principle of shoot first and worry later.

"I really know what the hell I'm doing," Buddy replied, as Louie led them on a long and circuitous path through the jungle, back to the road that he and João had taken to meet them.

"That's reassuring."

"No, listen to me, I set things up myself. I put out some feelers, I found you a story."

"Buddy, it's not about getting just *any* story. What I want is to find the people who *put* us in that place." Kendrick didn't need to say which place.

"Yeah, I know that. But if even a fraction of what I've been hearing is true, this is going to be worth it."

They walked on, frequently passing through wide patches where the jungle had been burned away, presumably during firefights. Their nostrils were filled with the lingering, oil-tinged scent of destruction.

"Exactly how dangerous is this?" Kendrick demanded. "What happens if we run into a Los Muertos patrol?"

"What happens is, we run. Besides, we're only skirting their territory here. They don't normally bother with small groups like us." Buddy saw Kendrick's alarm and shrugged. "Look, sometimes people do get kidnapped for their ransom value, but that isn't really their style. If they want supplies, they raid a town, or hijack a couple of trucks off the highway. They're mainly trying to take over the black market operations south of Mexico. That's why Sobrino uses kids like Louie, says they help him maintain his profit margin."

"Buddy, that kid gives me the creeps."

"Me too, me too," Buddy muttered. "What're you looking at me like that for?"

"He's just a kid. Don't you care what happens to him?"

"He's not a kid any more, Kendrick. Life is very hard around these parts. I told you that. Now c'mon."

Buddy called after João and Louie, who waited while the other two caught up again. They were moving down a slope now, the black strip of the road visible just a few metres ahead.

João grinned at Kendrick, his teeth gleaming in the depths of the night. "Hey, João," said Buddy, "tell Kendrick here what you know. About the soldiers."

João shrugged. "They glow in the dark."

Kendrick frowned. "How?"

"Some of them, they eat the flesh of the old gods out in the jungle, and in return the gods fill 'em with light."

"But not *literally* glowing, right?"

João nodded emphatically. "I heard this, they *glow*. Dance and yell about eating God, all kinds of crazy shit. For real." He shook his head now. "Nobody lie to me. Took this job 'cause wanted to see it myself, maybe."

"You *are* shitting me," said Kendrick to Buddy.

"I've heard this story so many times," Buddy replied. "Has to be something in it."

Kendrick kept his gaze fixed on Buddy. "So just exactly where is it, then, that this kid is taking us?"

"Two kilometres," said Louie, his eyes bright and sharp. He gestured forwards along the road they had just reached. "Two more kilometres, and I'll show you."

"Two kilometres? And show us what?"

"Patience, Kendrick," Buddy reassured him. "Let's just go look and see."

They made far better progress now that they had the road to walk on. Kendrick had imagined they would have to keep leaping back into the jungle if anyone drove by, but he'd underestimated the vastness of the landscape through which he now wandered. They were alone there, absolutely alone. It was easy to imagine that this road could go on for ever, never varying, always perfectly straight.

Within an hour of walking further, they arrived at the perimeter of another burned-out clearing. An irregular shape in the centre resolved itself into a tank pushed over on its side. At first Kendrick thought it must have been destroyed during the recent months of fighting, but as they got closer his augmented vision picked up its shattered carapace in more detail. It was crumbling and rusted enough to have been there for some time.

Kendrick became aware of a faint flickering to one side of the tank, perhaps a campfire. He stopped, gripped by a sudden fear that they had stumbled across an encampment of Los Muertos, but Louie beckoned them all forward with a casual wave. Buddy stepped forward but, judging by the grim expression on his face,

Kendrick wondered if he was finally having his own doubts about how much they could trust this boy.

Kendrick watched as Buddy drew out his gun, the action casual, holding it close by his side as he stepped closer to the burned-out tank. He then kept his fist wrapped around it, concealing it from Louie. As Kendrick came forward, the faint light they had seen resolved itself into a figure.

The man was dressed in the ragtag uniform of Los Muertos, and some instinct told Kendrick that the soldier was dying. Fine threads of something criss-crossed his skin and his flesh hung loosely from his skeletal form. The threads glowed with an uncanny luminescence that sent a deep chill running down Kendrick's spine.

It was impossible to gauge the soldier's age: he might have been thirty, he might have been sixty. His lips moved in a constant soundless litany, and he showed no awareness of their presence.

"What happened to him?" Kendrick breathed.

"Ate God, now he's got God all inside him," muttered Louie by way of explanation. "God is in those things you see on his skin."

Kendrick caught Buddy's eye, but Buddy just grinned back. Kendrick next glanced over at João, who just gaped with an appalled expression at the emaciated figure in front of them. João, he saw, was unconsciously fingering a tiny cross hanging around his neck. Kendrick clearly saw his lips form the words "*Madre de Dios*".

Kendrick looked back at the Los Muertos soldier. "Buddy, what the hell's happening to him?"

"He's a walking nanite factory, is what's happening to him. Don't get too close."

The Maze? "He must have gone down into the Maze," said Kendrick.

"That's what I figure. Crazy fuckers really think Wilber had a way to talk to God, so they go down in there, get themselves infected with this stuff, speak in tongues or whatever, then they die. But while they're still alive, they're like holy men to the rest of 'em."

Kendrick shook his head. "In some way this is the same kind of thing that's inside *us*, isn't it?"

"And they're dying for their efforts, just like most of us did. It's a kind of justice, I suppose."

"João, that light in him – what the hell is that?"

João shrugged without ever looking away from the slumped form before them.

"Maybe the nanite threads absorb sunlight for energy, then release it at night." Kendrick cast a sceptical look at him, but Buddy just grinned in return. "It'd be interesting to know just what's happening inside his head. But no way I'm getting near enough to find out."

It was growing lighter, and Kendrick knew that they'd have to find their way back soon. Unintelligible phrases, perhaps visions of angels and demons, perhaps something far stranger, continued to spill from the dying man's lips.

14 October 2096
Edinburgh

Kendrick barely slept. He woke deep in the night, a sweat-soaked sheet twisted around his body despite the cold of the night outside. Visions of his former life chased around the inside of his skull, along with fragments of a half-forgotten nightmare.

Dreams of the Maze, and how he'd arrived there, were wearily familiar territory for Kendrick; dark dreams that streaked across the landscape of his unconscious mind like brooding thunderstorms. He closed his eyes again before finally waking to faint splashes of dawn visible through the window. He mumbled into the air and the windowscreen became opaque, rooftops fading and the room again becoming dark.

He stared up at the ceiling and found there was little he could do to stop the memories flooding back.

28 January 2088
Washington suburbs, seven hours after the LA Nuke

Kendrick was seated at his breakfast, staring absent-mindedly at the images scrolling across an eepsheet that he'd tacked onto the door of the refrigerator. It was announcing something about the collapse of the Midwest agricultural economy, but mainly he was wondering why his regular subscription newsfeeds kept refusing to update. Then the knock came.

He opened the front door and squinted out into the early-morning light. Two men wearing what looked like military uniforms stood there, their expressions impassive.

The older of the two had steel-grey hair in an untidy side-parting, and Kendrick automatically found his attention focusing on him, although he had no idea if the younger man – broad-chested like a football player, short hair bristling from a pink scalp – might even be his superior.

"Mr Gallmon?" asked the older one, and Kendrick nodded automatically. "We were wondering if we could speak with your wife."

"Excuse me, who are you?" Kendrick asked, his mind still foggy with sleep. A thought crossed his mind and he became suddenly more alert. "Has there been some kind of accident?"

The two men exchanged what Kendrick recognized as a significant look. "It's a matter of some urgency," continued the older one.

"May we come in?"

"I'm not sure, I—"

The younger one had a hard, bright blue-eyed stare that Kendrick found he preferred not to meet. "Mr Gallmon," he said, "it would help if you cooperated with us fully."

"You haven't told me who you are." Kendrick looked more

closely at their uniforms, hoping for some way of identifying them.
He could see nothing he recognized, but he became aware of the
holstered guns at their sides.

"Has Amy Gallmon been here today?" the older one asked.
"It's important that we speak with her."

The thought of slamming the door on them flitted through
Kendrick's mind but he dismissed it, thinking: *This is ridiculous. I
haven't done anything wrong.* "I think I'd like to speak to her first,
before I say anything more. Or to a lawyer. Do the police know
you're here?"

"We can arrange for that later. In the meantime, it's extremely
urgent that we find her."

Kendrick stepped back from the door, glancing quickly over his
shoulder and into the living room. He'd left his patchphone there
– a standard skin-contact unit, the size of a fingernail. "Tell me
why you're here, or I'm calling the police – and my lawyer after
that."

And then something very significant happened, something that
made Kendrick appreciate that whatever world he'd grown up in
it had disappeared for ever. The older of the two men smiled and
nodded almost paternally before giving a fractional nod to his
companion who stepped forward, at the same time unfastening the
flap of the holster at his side. Kendrick watched the younger man's
hand drop onto the butt of his gun.

The older man spoke again. "Sir, I should advise you that your
wife is wanted on suspicion of treason. Under the current emergency legislation we are required to bring you too in for
questioning. Get your jacket or anything else you think you may
need, but we don't have time to fuck around. I'll give you one
minute to get yourself ready."

Kendrick remembered that the kitchen door at the back of the
house was still open. He had a brief fantasy of making a break for
it out through the back door and losing himself in the narrow
alleyways between the houses.

"My daughter's at the care centre," he said numbly.

"That's all right, sir," said the older guy. "We've already sent someone to pick her up."

And then Kendrick realized just how bad things were.

A few minutes later Kendrick allowed himself to be thrust into the back of a van bearing military markings. He was not handcuffed, but a steel-mesh grille separated him from the two other men. Surprisingly enough, he realized that he wasn't even particularly scared. Somewhere along the line, somebody had clearly made a terrible mistake. Everything would work out fine in the end, and he'd come home – and one day he'd even laugh about it.

Thoughts like these circled through his mind like a kind of mantra. But, every now and then, he looked down and saw his hands clenching, pain stabbing in his wrists as the muscles flexed spasmodically. He had to keep his wits about him, whatever happened.

The younger soldier leant forward in the passenger seat and switched on a radio. There was a wheel in the front of the vehicle, giving the option of manual control. Kendrick favoured a manual drive himself, even though it was a lot more expensive and you wound up with a bigger battery drain: he preferred having control over his driving, enjoyed the ability to make split-second decisions and choose to drive down one road rather than the other. You didn't get that advantage with programmable destinations.

The hands of the man in the driver's seat weren't on the wheel, though. The truck was driving itself, blindly slipping along on its tarmac ribbon. Popular music rattled out of hidden speakers, synthesized shamanpop chants over a three-quarter beat, heavy on the bass. The music faded and an obviously digitized voice began speaking, reading the news. Something about Los Angeles . . .

Kendrick moved closer to the grille, listening as words like "President Wilber", "terrible tragedy" and "holocaust" caught his ear, although the radio volume was down too low for him to hear well. Although the engine was silent there was a light drumming of winter rain on the roof of the truck that made it hard to pick out what the voice was saying. He caught more phrases: ". . . scene of this terrible national disaster", and ". . . nation in mourning".

He remembered now how he'd been unable that morning to get his subscription eepsheet newsfeeds to update properly. What the hell was going on?

"Hey," he said – and then louder, when neither of the two men in the front responded: "Hey!"

The "driver" – the older one – glanced over his shoulder with a bored expression. "What?"

"On the radio – what are they saying? What happened?"

The man smiled grimly. "Maybe *you* can tell *us*."

After what felt like a few hours, they took a sudden turn-off onto a long and dusty road leading into distant hills. They were far outside the city now, and Kendrick had been discovering there were almost as many different forms of panic as there were Eskimo words for snow. He'd done numb panic, angry panic – when the older of his two captors had threatened to stop the van and beat the shit out of him if he didn't shut up – and despairing panic, which took up most of his time and convinced him that he was being taken off to be shot on some desolate highway, like the unwitting protagonist of a Kafka novel.

Now he was just waiting to see what happened next. With the growing sound of jet planes overhead, he surmised that they were approaching some kind of military airbase. The van pulled in suddenly to a wide expanse of grey tarmac. The back doors were yanked open and Kendrick was lifted down, blinking, into bright afternoon sunlight, the air still fresh from the recent rain. His captors kept one hand each firmly on his shoulders.

He could see long low sheds of brick and corrugated iron, while ranks of jeeps stood parked between white lines painted on concrete. He looked up to see a helicopter rapidly descending on the far side of one of the sheds. The whole place was filled with the sound of men and machinery on the move: soldiers were everywhere, but Kendrick was fascinated to see other people in civilian dress standing beside vans identical to the one he had been brought in.

His guards guided him into one of the sheds. He saw long tables set up inside, and yet more civilians waiting silently. Somehow, seeing others here gave him comfort. They were all seated on rows of cheap plastic chairs at the rear end of the shed, under the eyes of perhaps half a dozen soldiers with rifles slung over their shoulders. These guns didn't have the bulbous snub-nosed muzzles that characterized the electric stun weapons used by civilian police, so Kendrick could only assume they were the kind that fired real bullets.

With a terrible shock, Kendrick understood for the first time that if he tried to escape they would probably shoot him. As insights went, it was profoundly depressing. While his two guards marched him over to join the rest of the civilians, he glanced over at the long tables nearby. Rows of soldiers sat behind them, each with a gridcom terminal and eepsheet within reach. They were engaged in interviewing a male or female civilian, behind each of whom stood another armed serviceman or servicewoman.

They came to a halt in front of a soldier who ticked off Kendrick's name on a clipboard. Then he was guided to a vacant seat. Nobody seated around him looked at all happy to be there, except for one elderly individual who was grinning like a fool.

Taking the seat next to him, Kendrick felt a tingle of familiarity. He eyed the people around him surreptitiously. They were a mixed bunch, mostly in their thirties or older, although there were a couple too obviously young even to be out of their teens. Some were black, some were white, some Hispanic, some looked poor, others rich, and about the only things they appeared to have in common were their worried expressions.

With armed guards hovering just a few feet away, they didn't talk much – understandably.

Suddenly the old man turned to Kendrick with a smile. "How are you doing?"

Kendrick nodded back, but he wasn't in a mood for conversation.

The old man awaited a response for a few moments, then shrugged and looked away again.

Every now and then, somebody else, looking as confused and distraught as Kendrick must have done, was marched in and seated among them. When one started to argue, Kendrick listened carefully to the response from the soldier with the clipboard: he said that emergency martial laws had been enforced until the threat to the nation could be assessed.

When the argument started to look like it was getting heated, another soldier stepped forward with his rifle raised. The implicit threat sent a cold chill through Kendrick.

He turned his attention back to the interviewing tables. Whenever they finished questioning someone, that individual would be escorted off through a door at the opposite end of the building.

Again, he couldn't see that any of them had anything particularly in common: they could have been housewives, doctors, petrol-pump attendants, anything.

Kendrick clasped his knees, his head filled with thoughts of his wife and his daughter Sam. He hadn't eaten in hours – usually he picked up breakfast on his way to work – but even though it must have been edging towards late afternoon he still didn't feel at all hungry.

"Thing is, we were right," a voice next to him said unexpectedly. Kendrick turned to find his elderly neighbour staring at him with bright, alert eyes.

"Sorry?"

"Sorry is the last thing you should be. Name's Marco. How you doing?"

"Kendrick Gallmon," he replied automatically.

"Not that guy writes for the *Washington Free Press*?" the other

43

asked, his eyebrows raised. Kendrick nodded in reply. In any circumstances but these, it would have been nice to have his name recognized. Outside of Washington, and whoever subscribed to the *Press*'s eepsheet newsfeed, generally nobody knew who he was.

"I read your column every week," said Marco. "Pretty critical of Wilber, aren't you?"

"Any other time in history, he'd be given psychiatric treatment for preaching the end of the world. Instead, we vote him in as President. I think you could say I was critical, yes. But who was right about what?"

"Sorry?"

"You said 'we were right'. Right about what?"

"About the crackdown. After this morning, over on the West Coast."

Kendrick stared back, his face blank.

"Ohh." Marco nodded gently. "You haven't heard, have you?"

"I heard something on the radio." As they continued talking in quiet whispers, Kendrick studied Marco more closely: a deeply lined face with a strong jaw, and clear blue eyes that danced with intelligence. The hair stood up in a white shock from the top of his head. Given his apparent age, he was dressed in reasonably current fashion, and he gave the impression of caring about his appearance. The more Kendrick considered him, the more he started to look familiar.

"Marco?" he said at last. "I know you: Frederic Marco, the writer. You wrote *The Contortionist*." It was a book he'd read over one long, languid summer in his teens.

"Listen," said Marco impatiently. "You didn't hear what happened in LA?"

"Los Angeles? What's happened to it?"

"What's happened is that it isn't there any more," hissed Marco, his grin not faltering for a second. "Can you imagine that? No more Sunset Boulevard, no more Beverly Hills, no more Venice Beach . . . I liked Venice Beach, but now it's all gone." He nodded his head wonderingly. "Imagine that."

"But what *happened*?" asked Kendrick, a sick feeling spreading through his stomach.

"Got nuked," said Marco, and his smile faltered briefly. "Probably by film critics." The grin resurfaced.

"Nuked?" It was such an outrageous-sounding piece of news, but somehow Kendrick believed it. All it needed was for him to cast his mind back over what had happened to him over the past few hours to see how serious things might be. No more Los Angeles? Feeling like he was performing a part in some movie, as if this were all play-acting, he asked, "Who?"

Marco shrugged. "Beats me. Take your pick of suspects. It won't be the Chinese, not after the way they fell apart. That leaves pretty much any political or religious group with a grudge, or perhaps terrorists, or any other random bunch of crazies you care to pick. But to get back to my original point, *we* were right – people like you and I – about what was going to happen to this country once the shit really hit the fan."

All the while more people were being escorted into the shed, and more led away. Marco continued. "This country's been going to hell for such a long time, nothing's going to change that now. People starving in this country, diseases we thought long gone being reintroduced ten times stronger, the climate all changed and the Gulf Stream fucked, four localized nuclear wars in Asia – just count 'em." He held up one fist and, pushing up four fingers, pointed at them in turn. "Four! *And* the environmental disasters leaving millions dead in the Midwest. We're sailing down the river towards the sharp rocks, but still acting like everything's going to be fine. Wilber being elected President is the icing on the cake – or the death stroke, maybe."

Marco leaned in a little closer. "Frankly, Kendrick, we're fucked, and somebody just hammered the last nail into the coffin. Ain't none of us here going to get out of *this* mess alive."

Kendrick bristled. "That's just paranoia."

"Look, listen to me," said Marco, placing a hand on his shoulder. Kendrick felt uncomfortable at the unexpected intimacy of the gesture. "You're a journalist, and people with jobs like yours are only secure so long as what you're doing isn't seen to be against the national interest. President Wilber gets to decide what the national interest is. That means right *now* the national interest is rounding up everybody who could have any kind of connection, however vague, with anyone whom Wilber deems an enemy of the state, whether real or imagined. You and me, that might make a twisted kind of sense, but look at some of these other people." Marco gestured around him with a swivel of his neck. "Ordinary people, not terrorists. But maybe they were in the wrong place at the wrong time, or voted for the wrong people, or had the bad luck just to be related to the wrong person." Marco's voice had taken on a certain urgency.

"I don't understand what you're saying."

"What I'm saying, Kendrick, is I'm seventy-six years old. I've had a long life, and I've been very good at making enemies. In some way or other, all of us here, without even knowing it, have made ourselves somebody's enemy. I always said life in this country was a losing battle, because it's always the guys with the guns who win. That's why I'm doing what I'm about to do. It's important that you understand. That you remember, for *me*, if you ever get out of this."

Kendrick felt sudden heat rising in his face. He watched as Marco stood up, drawing the attention of the several guards observing them all keenly.

"Marco, for Christ's sake—" Kendrick grabbed at the old man's sleeve as he abruptly stood also. But Marco shook him off with surprising energy and started moving away between the rows of chairs. The others around them watched this sudden development with interest, astonishment or, more frequently, fear.

Cursing under his breath, Kendrick stood and stepped quickly after the old man, grabbing his sleeve again before he had gone more than a few steps. One of the soldiers headed towards them.

"What the hell are you trying to prove?" Kendrick hissed.

Marco turned his calm grey-eyed stare on him. "I am taking

decisive action, which is a phrase President Wilber likes to use a lot. We both know men like him only get elected under the most extreme circumstances, and this country is currently under some very extreme circumstances indeed."

The soldier stepped forward and placed a hand on Marco's chest. Kendrick wouldn't have put him at more than seventeen or eighteen. A thin fuzz coating his cheeks made him appear even younger.

"Sir, I'm going to have to ask you to take your seat again." The words were directed also at Kendrick.

"Fuck you," Marco replied loudly and decisively, the words reverberating in the confines of the shed. The uniformed boy faltered. "I've not been charged. I haven't *done* anything. Neither has anyone else here. So, *fuck you.*"

Another soldier stepped over, this one older, his uniform decorated with a sergeant's stripes. He dismissed the first soldier with a nod of his head.

"I'm going to ask both of you to return to your seats and wait for your interviews." He pointed one meaty hand at the chairs they had just vacated. "You're under military jurisdiction as long as you're here. That means *now.*"

Something remarkable happened then. Marco raised his hands to shoulder height, putting a grin on his face, a parody of surrender. The sergeant's face relaxed a little. Kendrick was looking at the sergeant, which was why he didn't see Marco suddenly pull one of his arms back and throw it forward, punching the sergeant hard in the face.

The soldier reeled back, looking more surprised than hurt. Marco sprinted past them both with remarkable agility, clearly heading for the nearest exit. Kendrick started forward again, not sure exactly what he intended to do but nonetheless feeling driven to do *something*, when he felt a hand grab him roughly.

He spun round, just in time to see another soldier swing his hand around in an arc, his pistol held grip outwards in a motion that connected with the side of Kendrick's head. Kendrick spun round, crumpling to the ground, flecks of darkness dancing across his vision.

He retched, staring through a forest of chair legs. Somewhere very close a woman screamed. As he pulled himself up onto his knees, he saw the sergeant whom Marco had punched standing with legs planted firmly apart, his pistol gripped firmly between two fists and pointed directly at Kendrick's head.

This was how Kendrick remembered what happened next.

Marco, framed by sunlight, visible beyond the island of chairs . . . the soldier who had pistol-whipped Kendrick yelling incoherently . . . Marco, far more agile than Kendrick might ever have suspected, now just a few metres from the exit. And then a deafening explosion that, in Kendrick's memory, went on and on for ever.

He had stood up on trembling legs to see Marco lying in a crumpled silent heap, one arm stretched out so that the slanting light from beyond the exit was touching it. People around Kendrick stared on in unbelieving horror, like lambs who were catching their first glimpse of the slaughterhouse.

A few months later, Kendrick could only wish that he'd had as much sense and courage as Marco.

14 October 2096
Edinburgh

Kendrick woke to bright morning light. He mumbled a word to the windowscreen and a series of numerals appeared as grey shadows superimposed on the opaque glass.

He should leave before Caroline woke, he thought. He hauled himself up from the thin sheets she'd given him and padded bare-foot into the kitchen before he became aware that she'd already left.

The door to her bedroom lay open and he peeked inside. *Very* gone. One dream in particular had been astonishingly vivid and, strangely uncertain how much of it actually had been a dream, he re-entered the living room.

He'd dreamed that he had opened his eyes to see Caroline standing just beyond the couch he lay on. In the dream, the windowscreen was no longer opaque: pale moonlight outlined her naked form, and her head tilted back to stare beyond the slate rooftops of the city.

Wreathed in shadows, she had looked like some half-imagined goddess yearning for a way back home into the sky. And then she had turned and looked at him, and he had tumbled into the deep abyss of her eyes, as if falling through eternity . . .

He shook his head. Just a dream.

A little over half an hour later, Kendrick stepped outside into bright sunshine. A bitterly chill wind rattled through the sparse trees that broke through cobblestones up and down the street. His taxi rolled up right on time and he slid into its warm, driverless interior, making it to the Clinic a few minutes early.

The building was located in the Morningside area, a three-storey pile of nineteenth-century granite set behind black-painted iron railings. The plaque on the wall next to the front door identified it as home to a data-archaeology firm – all an elaborate cover story.

As Kendrick climbed the half-dozen steps to the front entrance, his enhanced senses warned him that his retinas were being scanned. A few seconds later the door clicked open with a solid *thunk*.

As he stepped inside, the building felt as curiously empty as on every other occasion he'd visited here. There were no pictures adorning the walls, and the hallway floor consisted only of bare, unvarnished floorboards. A winding staircase situated at the far end led both up and down. Apart from the hallway itself, Kendrick had only ever seen the basement. He reined in his curiosity, knowing that in the circles in which men like Hardenbrooke moved the less anyone else knew of their activities, the better. Such caution was wise, since the treatments and drugs that Hardenbrooke dealt in were stunningly illegal.

Kendrick found his way downstairs, keeping one hand on the black varnished banister as he descended into the basement. He spotted Hardenbrooke at the far end of a long, wide room, crouched over a crumpled eepsheet monitor tacked onto a slant-top desk. Other eepsheets were pinned up on the bare, whitewashed walls, all showing variations on the same X-ray-like image of a human body, a variety of clearly non-biological components highlighted in primary shades of red and blue. As he got closer, Kendrick realized that the images were of his own internal organs.

Hardenbrooke turned and stepped towards him, smiling. "Sure no one followed you here?" he asked, taking Kendrick by the arm and gently guiding him to an adjustable leather couch in the centre of the big room. Hardenbrooke's badly scarred face twisted up in a parody of a smile; from just above the right ear and extending below the neck of his shirt, one side of his features had the look of melted plastic. Around the ear itself the flesh was hairless and smooth.

Kendrick climbed onto the leather couch and waited while Hardenbrooke hovered over a wheeled aluminium trolley loaded with a variety of medical instruments, all neatly laid out on anti-septic paper. "No," Kendrick finally responded, after running his journey to Morningside from Caroline's flat through his head. "Is there some problem?"

"Just professional paranoia. A black-market clinic in Glasgow got raided last week – didn't you hear about it?"

"Maybe." A snatch of news footage flickered across Kendrick's mind's eye. "You're worried about that happening here?"

"Sometimes I reckon it's more a case of 'when' than 'if'. I'm not casting any aspersions on your good character, of course," Hardenbrooke assured him with a flicker of a smile. "It's just—"

"Sure, I understand. But there wasn't anyone following me."

Kendrick made sure to catch the man's eye as he said this. "Listen, I'm not just here for the regular treatments. Last night I suffered two seizures in a row, plus . . ." He shook his head and sighed. "Look, I need you to check out my heart."

Hardenbrooke raised one and a half eyebrows. Something about the man's scars made it hard to determine his age. What little Kendrick knew about him extended only as far as Hardenbrooke's claim to be a survivor of the LA Nuke. Beyond that, the professional nature of their relationship precluded any personal knowledge about each other. Yet they were partners in crime as much as they were doctor and patient, and Kendrick had been paying Hardenbrooke a lot of money for a series of treatments that had so far proved surprisingly effective.

Nonetheless, over recent months some other details of the medic's history had filtered through, giving Kendrick an opportunity to fill in some of the blanks.

"Two seizures? Last night?" Hardenbrooke echoed. "You should have contacted me immediately." His tone was admonishing.

"I know I should. But I'm here *now*."

The medic went over to a metal desk and pulled a drawer open, rummaging around inside, then stepped back holding an old-fashioned stethoscope in his hands as he fitted the earpieces into his melted-plastic ears. Motioning Kendrick to pull his T-shirt up, Hardenbrooke pressed the icy-cold metal disc against his chest and listened. Kendrick watched a look of consternation spread across that part of Hardenbrooke's face still capable of registering emotion.

Then Hardenbrooke stood up straight. "Let's come to an agreement," he said. "When I say call me if something happens, then call me instantly. Anything that looks like a setback, just call me. Otherwise you're making it a lot harder for me to help you. Is that clear?"

"Absolutely." Kendrick nodded. "I'm sorry," he added. "I was just a little—"

"I understand." Hardenbrooke paused, then, "I'll be frank, Mr Gallmon, technically you should be dead."

A look of alarm crossed Kendrick's face. "Hang on there." Hardenbrooke raised a finger. "What I'm saying is, this is something I've never even heard about before, even among Labrats with totally runaway augmentation growth. This, Mr Gallmon, is unique. I need you to tell me everything you can before we go any further."

Well, maybe not everything, Kendrick thought as he began. "There were . . . hallucinations, a little like before." He outlined some of the details. Hardenbrooke was already familiar with the visions of butterfly-winged children.

"Anything else?"

Kendrick thought of Peter McCowan. But the ghost – wasn't there a better word? – had warned him against Hardenbrooke. Was that just some figment of Kendrick's own anxieties?

But then, figments of one's imagination didn't necessarily give out warnings about bombs in suitcases either. Seeing men who'd been dead for years – that was something Kendrick was more than willing to keep to himself for the moment.

"That's it: I collapsed twice, I saw things, and my heart stopped working." He laughed nervously. "Nothing unusual, really."

"Look, you have to remember your augmentations are—"

"Inherently unpredictable," Kendrick finished for him. "I know."

Hardenbrooke shrugged, and made an adjustment to the couch so that Kendrick found himself staring upwards into a complicated array of lenses and sensors suspended from the ceiling.

Hardenbrooke picked up one of the spray 'derms and paused. "We're in unknown territory here," he said. "I want you to understand that."

Kendrick nodded. "I do."

Hardenbrooke touched the 'derm to the inside of Kendrick's bare elbow. Kendrick felt a curious coolness spread along his arm, a sensation with a peculiarly synaesthetic quality to it, as if he could taste peppermint through his skin.

This faded quickly. Twisting his head round slightly, Kendrick watched as the medic unrolled a blank eepsheet and hung it from a hook screwed into the wall. Next he picked up a slim plastic wand that looked even more out of date than Kendrick's own. He pointed it first at Kendrick, then at the blank eepsheet.

Kendrick could see the eepsheet clearly from where he lay. Its surface strobed for a moment before resolving into a cloud of brightly coloured pixels spreading rapidly across a field of black. There was a vague sense of form and pattern to the movement of the pixels.

Kendrick realized that Hardenbrooke had just injected him with a form of nanite – vat-grown molecular machines that would provide a wealth of information about what was happening inside his body. This process extended to real-time visuals and, over the next minute or so, the blurry mass of pixels resolved itself into a distinctly human-like shape.

Kendrick twisted his head around so he could watch Hardenbrooke, who was meanwhile keeping an eye on the other eepsheets mounted above his workspace. Kendrick gazed with uneasy fascination at the outline of his own heart, the major blood arteries already clearly delineated by the flood of information flowing from Hardenbrooke's nanites.

Now other 'sheets had started to display full-colour video images of his blood vessels – from the inside. Tumbling camera views spun by arterial walls, and he caught occasional glimpses of smooth, metallic grey where, in any normal unaugmented person, there should have been no such thing.

The first time Kendrick had seen these pictures, he'd expected them to make him uneasy. It could be a hard thing to get a high-definition tour of the sack of meat and blood that made up your body. Instead, he felt strangely reassured by it. He was still clearly human, whatever might be happening inside his body. He suspected that the reason the medic was letting him see these images was to make him feel involved in the consultation process, a psychological ploy intended to make it seem as if they were engaged together in a journey of mutual discovery.

Hardenbrooke didn't actually need to witness any of this process himself since it was the correlated post-examination data that the nanites provided which really mattered. But Kendrick was strangely glad of it all the same. He thought of the nanites as tiny agents of positive change, even though they comprised the same kind of technology as his augmentations. The "good" nanites roamed through his body like microscopic policemen, making sure that everything was in order and that no rowdy augments were stirring up trouble deep within his organs.

On-screen the augmentations showed up as red patches, mostly clustered around his spine and major organs, which manifested as blue. Countless red filaments spread up the tube of his neck, reaching deep into his skull. More filaments surrounded the meat of his brain like a wire cage. There were also segments of red scattered throughout his lungs, his kidneys, through every major organ. Kendrick peered, straining to see if anything had visibly altered. Every now and then one of the video images afforded him fresh glimpses of the artificial organisms that had taken root in his flesh.

But they were also intrinsically part of him, whether he wanted them or not. He thought back to the nightmares that had assailed him, ever since his incarceration in Ward Seventeen, of fine grey filaments extruding from his body like stilettos.

Hardenbrooke too watched the progress on the screen, then turned back to him.

"Your heart . . ."

Kendrick sat up abruptly, the electronic map of his body on the screen changing in response, shifting, twisting and blurring as he shifted onto the edge of the examination couch.

Hardenbrooke picked up another spray 'derm, one on which Kendrick noticed a sticky label with fine, tiny cursive handwriting.

But the label was angled away from him, making it impossible to decipher the words.

Hardenbrooke held it up. "How much did I tell you about this stuff?"

"Last time I was here, you said it was something new from the States."

"Do you remember our other little chat, when we first met, about the current legal status of what's inside this?"

Kendrick took a deep breath. "Yes, I do."

"Remember what I said then, how this is strictly experimental? You know how tight the guidelines are regarding biotechnologies like these."

"But you're sure it's safe?"

Hardenbrooke sighed. "It's probably no worse than what you've already got inside you. I'm not going to give you any guarantees or false promises, but there's every chance you'll keep getting better. This stuff has already successfully stabilized much of the augmentation activity inside you."

"But it is working," Kendrick insisted. "I'm getting better. I know I am."

"And you say you've suffered two seizures in rapid order. Perhaps that's a sign of change – perhaps even positive change."

"But what about my heart? What's happened to it? I need to know," Kendrick demanded, his mind going numb.

Hardenbrooke pinched his nose between two fingers and closed his eyes, pondering. "I'd need to analyse the information down-loaded from the nanites and try to get some grip on exactly what's happened to you but, from what I've seen, it's clear your heart's been bypassed in some way. There are new structures inside you. My guess is – and I stress the word *guess* – is that the new struc-tures are now controlling the flow of your blood."

Kendrick absorbed this information without comment. Hardenbrooke had only told him what he'd already suspected, yet hearing it confirmed in this way stirred up a darkness deep inside him, something shrill and insane that was fighting to get loose. He pushed it back down.

"I urge you to remember that this is no reason to start worrying," Hardenbrooke reminded him.

Kendrick laughed, hearing the edge of hysteria there. "Not worry? I'm not to *worry* about it? Are you crazy?"

"Mr Gallmon, I never had reason to ask this before, but is there any history of heart problems in your family?"

"What does that have to do with anything? I . . ." Then he remembered an aunt who'd died of a coronary. His mother had also suffered a mild heart attack in her early forties. "Some, yes, I have to admit. But why do you ask now?"

"Your augments integrate with your nervous system and major organs, changing them as they do so, like soldiers building a fort out of whatever material they can find. They respond strongly to perceived threats and, to a very great degree, they come up with their own definitions of what they regard as a threat. That could include medical conditions."

Kendrick was thunderstruck. "Wait a minute, are you saying I . . . you mean I had a *heart attack*? That's what this is all about?"

"I'm saying just imagine, if you will, that your augmentations reacted to a heart attack, or some kind of coronary event, by taking over your heart's functions. I'm not saying that's what it is. I'm only saying that's my best guess for now. If I were you, I'd thank my lucky stars."

"My heart—?"

"Has been bypassed, but you're very much alive. Focus on that: it means your augments are working for you, instead of against you." Hardenbrooke held up the 'derm again. "So let's make sure things stay that way." He leaned over and injected its contents into Kendrick's arm while Kendrick glanced over the medic's shoulder at the pixellated views of his own internal organs.

Hardenbrooke stood up straight again and smiled. "Remind me, then: have we had this conversation?"

Kendrick sighed. "No, we haven't."

"Have I ever set eyes on you before?"

"No, you've never seen me before in your life. To suggest otherwise would mark me as a scoundrel and a lunatic."

"Just so we know where we stand, I've introduced new nanites into your body, which will implant their own override algorithms in your augments."

"So that'll at least delay things for a while?"

"To be honest, it might even cure you."

"That's impossible. You can't be 'cured' of augmentations. They don't just go away."

"What can be made can be unmade," Hardenbrooke replied. "Remember, experimental tech, but so far, so good. Right?"

Kendrick gazed soberly back at the medic. If Hardenbrooke was in any way lying, it was the cruellest kind of lie: an offering of hope where hope had not previously existed. It occurred to Kendrick that he wasn't really prepared to believe what Hardenbrooke was telling him now, simply because he couldn't cope with any more disappointment.

"You are aware," Kendrick framed his words carefully, "that if this really works like you suggest, it would be the biggest news of the century."

"I never said it was a definite cure. It's a *possible* cure, using experimental technology that doesn't even officially exist. Apart from getting me deported and jailed, if the authorities found out that your augments had turned rogue and that you had been taking these treatments they'd throw you straight into a secure nanohazard ward, and you'd disappear as far as the rest of the world is concerned."

Kendrick felt his face flush red. Yet, for the first time in a very great while, he dared to hope. The simple reality of it was that, without Hardenbrooke, and without the possibility that Hardenbrooke was extending to him . . . without that, he had nothing.

12 October 2096
Edinburgh

Once, when Marlin Smeby had still been young, his maternal grandmother had taken him on a kind of Grand Tour of Europe. At that time, back home in Florida, his parents had been busy yelling and screaming their way towards a grisly divorce. By that stage the family was already rich from his father's lucrative engi-neering contracts with the governments of various minor Asian nations looking to rebuild after their nuclear squabbles of the 2080s.

The jaunt had given him a taste for travelling, which had led to a spell serving in the old US Army. This in turn had led on to intelligence work, which had led to Marlin's discovery that he had himself inherited every bit of his father's ingrained cruelty and utter disregard for his fellow human beings. To him, Edinburgh had felt like it belonged in some other time, with its ancient brooding castle and those grey-stone tenements squatting on steep hillsides.

Still, much had changed since then, and it was no longer the city he remembered from his previous visit. Even as a child he'd been able to see how much bankruptcy had affected Europe. The old EU had almost given up the ghost, but hadn't yet been replaced by the monolithic European Legislate that had risen from its ashes. He remembered people in their thousands sleeping in the parks and streets because there was nowhere else for them to go.

Smeby looked out of the taxi window and realized he could quickly tell which of the city's inhabitants were American. It was something in the way they dressed, the way they carried them-selves. He wondered if they still considered themselves to be American. Did they all talk of going back home once things got better, or would they finally give up and decide they were now Europeans?

A smear of graffiti strobed across a wall, its hue flickering from green to red to yellow; *Fuck off back to the US*, someone had scrawled. Another read *Europe for the Europeans.*

Smeby sat back and let a smile steal across his features. *Europe for the Europeans?* Not so long ago it would have been *Britain for the British*, or maybe *France for the French*. Their mutual hatred for the flood of American refugees had finally driven the Europeans to embrace each other as brothers.

"Mr Hardenbrooke, I trust you are doing well?"

Hardenbrooke nodded and smiled as best he could, given his difficulties in that area. There was a distinctly pale flush to his skin, Smeby thought: he was clearly nervous about something.

"Business is good," Hardenbrooke replied, glancing around Smeby's hotel suite. Draeger's money had secured him an entire floor of the Arlington, a large part of it taken up by the conference room in which Smeby had arranged for them to meet.

"How has Mr Gallmon responded to your treatments?"

"I believe this is all detailed in my report."

"Yes, but I'd like to hear it from you in person."

"Well, there've been some interesting developments. When he first came to me, his augmentations had clearly gone rogue. There were no visible signs yet, none of the characteristic scarring around the neck and skull, but that was only a matter of time. The treatments have worked in retarding runaway growth."

"Any ideas concerning these seizures of his?"

"He still reports the same associative hallucinations and I have no idea what's causing those. If you could tell me if anything similar happened with other Labrats, assuming you've actually tested this stuff out on others apart from Gallmon . . ."

"I can't disclose that," Smeby replied.

"Okay, fine," said Hardenbrooke, looking a little nettled – and also nervous. Smeby had given the medic no warning that he'd be in the country. Maybe Draeger had suspicions concerning Hardenbrooke's loyalty. "But there is one other thing."

Smeby waited.

"I didn't put this in my report, because it was just a personal feeling, but since you're here . . . I have the feeling that Gallmon is holding something back, like there's something he's not telling me."

And there's something you're not telling me, either, Smeby decided. *But there's enough time for me to find out.*

14 October 2096: 1.45 p.m.
Edinburgh

Kendrick hovered outside his flat in Haymarket for over an hour, then took a chance. He headed around to the other side of the block by a circuitous route until he came to a small side window, now conveniently hidden behind a skip, through which he could crawl.

This led him into an underground car park for the office complex that occupied part of the building above. Next he found the service stairs that led up into his own part of the building. He'd once scouted it out as an escape route when he'd suspected that he might one day need one.

However, he hadn't expected to be using it in reverse. Still, there were things upstairs that he needed.

Kendrick hadn't yet risked returning to the Armoured Saint and he'd already outstayed his welcome at Caroline's flat. So home it was, at least for long enough to pick up what he needed and until he could find somewhere else. The flat was tiny, just a rented room and kitchen in a part of the city that had become an American ghetto over several years. But once he got inside and closed the door behind him, all the stresses and fears of the past few days started piling up on him. He collapsed onto his narrow bed, listening to the silence where his heartbeat had once been.

After a little while, he closed his eyes.

Kendrick floated in the air and his daughter Sam stood on a

grassy plain far below, waving up to him. Beyond her, a kite jiggled in a sudden gust and he watched as she ran after it, laughing.

At first he didn't notice the truck. It was painted olive green, its engine humming gently as it clanked across the grass.

"Hey," he shouted – then again, a little louder. Now he too was standing on the grass, and he started to move towards Sam. He saw his wife there, too, seeming oblivious to everything but their daughter. Neither of them seemed to get any nearer to him.

The truck rolled to a sudden stop, and uniformed men piled out of it. They grabbed at his wife's arm, and the thin sound of her scream carried far across the grass.

They had seized his daughter now and she was screaming too, her kite lost, adrift on the wind. Kendrick just ran, untapped reservoirs of energy he never knew he had propelling him. Sam fell to the ground, the soldiers beating her with the butts of their rifles, the grey metal barrels turning shiny and sticky with splashes of her blood . . .

Kendrick fell out of his bed, his body slick with icy-cold sweat and his throat hoarse. He must have been yelling aloud in his sleep. He staggered out of his bedroom and spotted something by the front door. It was an envelope, and he picked it up. It hadn't been there earlier when he'd returned, and he didn't get much in the way of mail.

He studied the name on the envelope for a long time. His name – his real name, Kendrick Gallmon – was hand-printed on expensive-looking rag paper. Kendrick felt an immediate and deep sense of foreboding flood through him. He was not registered as the flat's occupant under his real name, therefore somebody was telling him something. They were saying: *We know who you are, we know where you live.*

He thought hard. Not the police, not the European Legislate. Sending him expensive-looking mail wasn't part of their remit. They'd just barge in and get him. So someone else, then.

Kendrick opened the envelope and found that it contained what appeared to be a simple business card. The letters, printed on textured cream plastic, read *Marlin Smeby*. He didn't recognize the name. However, as soon as his fingers touched the card itself an image sprang up uninvited in his mind: an image of a man, seen from the shoulders up, hair thinning across the top of his scalp, jet black to wavy grey around his ears.

The card slipped from Kendrick's fingers. He leant down and picked it up again, this time holding onto it more firmly. He decided that he hadn't hallucinated that image.

The second time around the experience was only mildly unsettling. The face he saw now in his mind's eye had to be that of Marlin Smeby. Touching the card brought a sensation not unlike a memory, long buried, suddenly re-emerging, or the spark of recognition someone might feel when a vaguely familiar person passed them in the street – except Kendrick knew that he'd never met Smeby in his life.

Kendrick focused now on the card's surface, his augmented senses allowing him to detect the faint filigree of microscopic silver circuitry woven into its surface. The technology was unlike anything he'd ever come across before, and to place it in a mere business card . . .

It had to have been designed with augmented humans in mind. He felt sure that someone unaugmented, like Malky, would experience nothing on handling it.

So, someone also wanted him to realize that they knew about his past. In this respect the card carried many intimations: of wealth, and of power – certainly the power to expose him.

Kendrick found a local grid address printed on the card's flip side. He could wait and see what happened next, or he could do something now. He couldn't help but wonder if this was somehow connected to what had taken place in the Saint the night before. But, at the very least, if someone had set out to get his attention they'd done so effectively.

Kendrick tapped the grid address into the query screen of the eepsheet stuck onto his refrigerator door with a fridge magnet. It supplied him with the location of the Arlington, a hotel near the centre of town. Big, expensive-looking place – he'd passed it innumerable times.

The Arlington rested between tall buildings constructed from the same quarried sandstone as the rest of Edinburgh, but unlike the structures in the narrow, crowded streets of the nearby Old Town this was an edifice entirely of the late twenty-first century. The mirrored surfaces of its windows were visible between broad aluminium interstices jutting out at strange angles over the street below, giving the whole a malleable, almost plastic appearance. From the opposite side of the street, Kendrick leant back, gazing up at the broad expanses of glass that reflected anything but the buildings around them. The hotel's windows were programmed instead to reflect other city skylines – perhaps Milan or Hong Kong. He saw the reflection of a building impossibly sculpted in the shape of a sickle, as if designed for a world with little or no gravity, and a view totally in opposition to the reality of the staid architecture behind him. The effect wasn't very subtle, he decided, and spoke more of money than of taste.

Kendrick stepped across the street towards the hotel's wide entrance. Now its glass doors displayed a different view, one that cleverly integrated both Kendrick and the people walking past him into yet another environment . . .

When he stopped and stared at the broad expanse of the main entrance, a chill ran through him as he recognized the landscape displayed. His reflection appeared to be standing on a wide grassy plain, while behind him the ground curved distinctly up into the distance.

The illusion was well programmed, so that the closer Kendrick came the more he could see. Despite himself, he glanced round at the ordinary street surrounding him as if to check that it was still there. Then, looking back, he moved his head from side to side, finding he could see a little way further along the plain on either side before the illusion shattered into unfocused rainbow colours. Curving walls slid off into the far distance before they became shrouded in cloud and mist. It was the same terrain he'd been seeing during his recent seizures.

Feeling shaken, Kendrick passed in through the door. Instinctively, he reached into his pocket and touched the business card that nestled there.

The receptionist smiled and shook her head. "I really don't know, sir. The building has a range of programmed window environments, but I couldn't tell you who programmed any particular one. It's just not the kind of information we would possess."

"You don't know any way I could find out who was contracted to design the current environment?"

The girl wore lipstick like gluey fire, and Kendrick's augmented vision picked out the fine grain of face powder on her cheeks and her neck, even the fine pattern of capillaries just below the surface of her skin.

She smiled again. "That's not exactly the kind of information we'd have to hand."

He sighed and shook his head. "I'm here to meet a Marlin Smeby. Could you let him know I'm here, please?"

"Mr Gallmon?" said a voice from behind him, and he turned. A woman stood there, dressed in an immaculate suit of night-blue wool, smooth ebony skin stretched over well-trained muscles. Kendrick recognized her voice, since she had taken his call an hour or so earlier. She looked like the kind of woman who might equally well be an ex-athlete or ex-military – perhaps even both.

She extended a hand. Her grip was strong, assured. "My name is Candice. If you're ready, I'll take you up to Mr Smeby now."

He glanced down at his own green T-shirt and casual slacks, and shrugged. "Please, after you," he said.

He reckoned her accent was maybe that of a native New Yorker. Life there was hard these days, and the city had become a neglected and forlorn shadow of its former self. Rumour had it that snipers still hid out in certain deserted Manhattan office buildings, preying on passers-by.

He followed Candice to the bank of lifts beyond the reception area, admiring the way in which the fabric of her trousers slid across her buttocks as she walked, seeming to reveal more than if she'd worn nothing. She stepped back, allowing him to enter the open lift first. Its doors slid shut silently, and she touched a floor button. After that they rode upwards in silence for a while.

Smeby's . . . bodyguard, secretary, aide, whatever she was finally turned to him. "I'm sorry, but I couldn't help overhearing what you said to the young woman at the desk."

Kendrick looked at her, surprised. "You mean about the programmed windows?"

Candice nodded. "Yes, the *Archimedes*. I was up there once. Very hard to forget."

Kendrick was thunderstruck. "The *Archimedes*? You were on board?"

"Part of a rotating detachment, before the station was abandoned." The lift started to slow down.

"That must have been quite an experience," he said carefully.

A smile played at the edge of her lips. "Quite an experience, yes. Doesn't it make you wonder what's up there now?"

"I can't begin to imagine. The whole thing was . . ." He paused, not sure what to say.

"Crazy, I think you were going to say." Candice smiled, as if to suggest that she didn't mind.

Of course, Kendrick had realized all along that he must be seeing something like the *Archimedes* during his seizures. But that was all it was – a figment of his imagination. Something *like* the *Archimedes*, but not bearing any relation to anything real. Just some random environment that his augments had dredged up from his subconscious as they wove themselves ever more inextricably into the stuff of his brain. Nothing more than that. Yet seeing it there, externalized, as if it had been ripped from the recesses of his mind and reproduced so precisely, that had been shocking, even frightening.

And it raised the question he'd been asking himself all those long months: why, of all things, would he hallucinate about the *Archimedes*?

The elevator doors opened and Kendrick stepped into a room large enough to house a medium-size conference. A long, low table, set up near the windows, had a variety of computer equipment scattered across its surface, including some expensive-looking gridcom gear. Smeby himself stood by the wide window, staring absent-mindedly out over the people walking in the street far below. His arms were folded across his chest, as if hugging himself. He turned and stepped forward when he noticed Kendrick standing there.

Kendrick heard the elevator doors close behind him and turned to see that Candice had left them alone together.

Kendrick held the business card between his thumb and forefinger, where Smeby could easily see it. "You could have just given me a call," he began.

Smeby laughed, as if appreciating a point well made. "But then you wouldn't have wanted to satisfy your curiosity by coming here, would you?"

"How did you find me?"

"You *are* Kendrick Gallmon, aren't you?"

"That depends."

"Your identity is entirely safe, Mr Gallmon. My employer wishes to speak to you."

Kendrick stuffed his hands in his pockets and hunched his shoulders; the room felt immediately cold. "I don't see anyone else around, unless you mean Candice."

"I work for Max Draeger."

"Draeger? You work for Max Draeger?" *Walk out now*, thought

Kendrick. "Then we have nothing to say to each other." He turned and headed back towards the elevator.

"Mr Draeger wants to know if you've been suffering from any seizures recently," Smeby called after him.

Kendrick stopped to turn and stare at Smeby. "Fine – you've got my attention. But why should *you* care?"

"Another question. You know there are upwards of two thousand still-living Labrats. Are you still in contact with any of them?"

"That's really none of your business."

"We know of Caroline, of course. And your friend Buddy."

"I think you already heard my answer, Smeby."

"You were kept in Ward Seventeen during your incarceration in the Maze, and you've been involved with some interesting people since your time there."

"What about you, then? Were you one of those running the Maze?"

Smeby smiled. "I think you should be aware that Mr Draeger is offering you his aid."

"*Draeger*?" Kendrick laughed. "Perhaps you should just tell me what he wants."

"He wants to help you."

"Why would I need his help?"

"Your augmentations have turned rogue, Mr Gallmon. There are ways for us to find such things out, even before the effects manifest themselves visibly. Mr Draeger has extended an invitation for you to visit him at his home and primary research facility. He's very interested to meet you. He believes he may even be able to cure you."

14 October 2096
Above the Armoured Saint

Malky was rich, though no one would be able to tell from the external appearance of his home. Squeezed on either side by the new housing complexes that had sprung up all over the city to house the waves of refugees, the five-floor tenement looked as though it was being beat up by the silver and glass towers that now surrounded it. But appearances could be deceptive. Malky owned the entire block, including the Armoured Saint, which was situated on the ground floor – and Kendrick knew that it had been far from cheap to acquire.

He also knew that Malky's full name was Mikhail Konstantin Vasilevich, a third-generation immigrant whose great-grandparents had arrived from the Chernobyl region in the 1980s. Malky had used his ill-gotten gains from a wide and spectacular variety of illegal pursuits to set himself up in style. His particular speciality, however, was producing fake ID, a booming market since America had slowly begun to emerge from civil unrest and a considerable number of people had found an urgent need to disappear.

People like Kendrick, say.

"Stop worrying. You're fine."

Kendrick glanced nervously out through a tall window and into the street running in front of the Saint. They were in Malky's cramped office, a room on the floor directly above the bar.

"Does that mean you managed to cope with the security systems?" Kendrick asked.

"Of course." Malky shrugged. "Otherwise the Saint wouldn't keep its reputation for being a safe place for all kinds of people. So you're clean. And, while you're here, maybe you can tell me again exactly how you knew there were explosives left in the building."

"I told you, my augments picked it up."

Malky gave him a sideways look. "I know your augments can pick up on electronics in your immediate vicinity, but not from the far end of a very long bar."

"You're saying you don't believe me?"

"I'm saying it doesn't make much sense, is all."

Kendrick sighed and shook his head. "I don't know what else I can say."

There was a brief, awkward silence. "I've been asking questions," Malky continued. "Most of the people who frequent the Saint are US refugees, so it looks like whoever planted that bomb figured Edinburgh could do with a few less Yanks."

"You know this for a fact?" Kendrick decided not to mention the possibility of Los Muertos. That would lead to a whole range of further questions he didn't feel up to dealing with right now.

Malky let out a long sigh. "No, I don't know for sure. But, like I said, I asked some questions. It's not the first time something like this has happened, you know. We've got a visual recording of a man coming in, putting the bag down, and leaving after a couple of minutes. But we don't know who he was, and Todd hasn't been able to find any matches for his face in any of the police databases that he has access to. Now," Malky continued, "you were saying you needed to find something out?"

Kendrick nodded, relieved by the change of subject. "About the Arlington – I want to know who did the programming for their windows. I figured Todd might know, since he's in the same line of work."

Malky shook his head in exasperation. "Kendrick, did you ever think about just asking someone there?"

"I did ask someone, but they said they didn't know."

"And, of course, I can safely assume you ran a Gridsearch as well."

"I'm not an idiot, Malky. I checked out everything I could."

"And, naturally, you're not going to tell me *why* you need to know this. I mean, why do you even care?"

Kendrick smiled apologetically. "You'd think I was a lunatic if I told you."

Malky spread his hands. "Yeah, like I don't think that already. Well, let's go speak to Todd, then."

From somewhere above them came a deep, growling vibration that sounded remarkably as though someone was using a pneumatic drill for unknown purposes. Kendrick had gradually grown used to the eccentric lifestyles and predilections of the refugees and artists who occupied the majority of the building's apartments. They were a reminder, Malky had once told him, of his own parents' bohemian roots.

A little further up the concrete stairs leading to the single enormous attic space that constituted Todd's home and working space they came across Lucia. She was standing beyond the open doorway of her studio, bare-breasted, her shaven head glistening. Kendrick couldn't help but note the industrial-sized pneumatic drill now discarded on the floor; Lucia was applying a blowtorch to the nose of an enormous construction of girders and concrete that took a moment to resolve into a two-headed T-Rex with a tractor in place of a ribcage. They continued on past her.

"Why is this so important, Kendrick? What's the big deal?"

What to say? "It's – hard to explain. But it's important. Very important."

Malky spread out his arms. "I'm a friend. It's not like I can't tell that something's going on."

"Bear with me, okay?"

Malky shook his head. "Fine, fine – whatever you say."

It occurred to Kendrick that not even Malky knew exactly how many people lived here. However, a significant proportion appeared to be American refugees, most of them certainly illegal. He allowed Malky to lead him up yet another cramped stairway carpeted with moist-looking fabric. Finally Malky knocked loudly on the door at the top. After what felt like an appropriate interval they stepped through.

What little illumination there was in the room beyond seeped through patterned blinds drawn over tall windows. Kendrick remembered the first time he'd been there: Todd had taken care of all his ID needs, as well as providing him with a plethora of useful and completely false personal information. In Kendrick's augmented eyesight, the tattered furniture revealed itself in the gloom with an unnatural pearly ambience. Todd sat at the far end of the vast space, his eyes fixed on an eepsheet creased from being folded too many times. It was running one of the RaptureNet channels.

Unsurprisingly, given the apocalyptic tendencies of RaptureNet, a preacher kept thrusting his hands into the air and yelling in a tinny voice while a computer-generated image of the *Archimedes* floated in the background. *Wherever I go I still can't get away from that damn thing*, Kendrick thought to himself.

Todd was a small, mostly bald, middle-aged American with the frame of a famine victim and a soft, lilting West Coast accent. A workstation not unlike Caroline's occupied one wall, while a smaller version of her windowscreen leaned against another wall, held in place with gaffer tape.

Todd glanced round at them, blinking and smiling. He nodded in recognition as Kendrick approached. "Long time no see," he said. "In the flesh, at least. What brings you here?"

"I need you to find out who programmed something." Kendrick described the hotel's door environment, while Malky listened with apparent interest.

"Looks like the *Archimedes*? Interesting." Todd nodded towards the eepsheet he'd been watching as they'd entered. The preacher was now holding an old-style wand to his ear, in order, presumably, to better demonstrate the act of speaking to God. Another window opened on the eepsheet, showing an alternative view of the same preacher wearing flowing robes and a long white wig that crackled with computer-generated lightning. The berobed version looked down on his other self, zapping the wand with cartoon lightning.

Todd noted Kendrick's interest and nodded towards the images. "You ever watch this stuff?"

"I'm . . . afraid not."

Todd laughed nervously. "Stop looking so worried. You know I get off on shit like this. It tickles me. And, you know, that's what helped sink Wilber. Economically speaking, building something the size and complexity of the *Archimedes* took up a serious chunk

71

of the USA's annual GNP for a good few years. Can't maintain a wartime economy with shit like that going down, and that's why his own army eventually turned against him. Now, Wilber—"

"Todd," Kendrick gently interrupted him, "I know all this – remember?"

Todd blinked, then his face coloured. "Sorry, forgot," he muttered sheepishly.

Though Todd's nerdish enthusiasms often ran away with him, Kendrick warmed to him nonetheless. "It's true that a lot of people still believe in Wilber's message, though," he added, by way of a gentle prompt.

Todd nodded eagerly. "Actually, this particular channel is pumped out of a portable studio in the back of a truck in Colombia. Real guerrilla-broadcasting kind of thing. But I've got to tell you, I think they just might have something."

Kendrick tried to frame his response as diplomatically as possible. "Wilber would use any lies that came to hand in order to gain power – and hold it."

"Look, I'm serious," Todd protested. "I'm far from being the religious type, but for all Wilber's craziness about using the *Archimedes* as a testing ground for building some kind of techno-rapture gridlink to God, the people he had working on it were real scientists. A lot of the people who tune in to RaptureNet, they're old guys who worked in the science industries before the LA Nuke. And regardless of whether or not they actually are religious-minded in the old-fashioned sense, they go for that whole Tipler consciousness-at-the-end-of-time thing."

"Look, Todd, I just need your help in finding out who did this thing."

"And wouldn't I like to know why," Todd chuckled. "Okay, okay, just kidding. It's no problem – right, Mikhail?"

"Absolutely," Malky replied.

"I mean, it's not like this is secret information, right?" Todd continued, his grin growing wider. "You're asking because, say, you admire the skill of the artist involved?"

"I'm asking because I'd really like to know who did it." Kendrick tried unsuccessfully to keep an edge out of his voice.

Todd nodded. "How's Car doing?"

"You mean Caroline?"

Todd smiled. "Listen, Ken, this one's for free. I can tell you for a fact that Caroline produced that display on commission."

"Caroline?"

Todd wore a satisfied smirk. "You sound surprised. It's the kind of thing she does, after all."

It was indeed. "I should have thought of that, Todd. Thank you. I owe you one."

"No problem. So what's so special about some display based on the *Archimedes*, anyway?"

"To be honest, I'm not sure."

"Now, that's not really an answer."

"I know, I know, but it's the only one I'm giving you right now. Sorry."

Todd nodded with a gentle smile. "Got another question for you, then, just to make us even."

"Sure."

"What do *you* think is up there?" Todd asked. "What's up there that prevents anyone getting back on board the *Archimedes*?"

Kendrick frowned. Todd was clearly just looking for more fuel to feed his endless obsession with conspiracy theories. "Christ, Todd. There's nothing complicated about it. Nobody's dumb enough to try and get on board that thing while the place is swarming with runaway nanites."

"Yeah?" Todd's eyes glinted. "But sometimes, on the Grid, you hear rumours. You hear rumours."

16 October 2096
Edinburgh

Kendrick still had at least a little money left over from the post-Maze trials, remnants of the compensation he'd received. Unfortunately, the money had been paid in dollars, an already badly devalued currency by that time. Kendrick's financial acumen was not great but he knew enough to transfer the funds into other currencies and store it in European Legislate accounts before it devalued any further.

Which hadn't stopped a lot of that money slipping away in the meantime, but at least it gave him a means of keeping himself alive when times were lean. Careful investment had helped stretch the funds out, but Hardenbrooke's treatments had cut deep.

However, the money could only last so much longer. Occasional freelance journalism – under a variety of assumed names, of course, each with its own bank account – did help to bolster things, but the sporadic nature of such work meant that it was ultimately little more than a stopgap.

Now he would need to seek out new sources of income, without the European Legislate finding out any more about him than he wanted it to.

A few years before, Kendrick had signed a contract with a Grid news agency to work as a freelance stringer, having the advantage that he could file stories while remaining largely anonymous. But now there was the chance of something more permanent, which might mean moving south to London, or possibly somewhere in mainland Europe.

That would be good but, because he was a Labrat, there were some serious risks involved.

Which was why Malky so often proved useful in these matters. There was always the slim chance that background checks could lead to Kendrick's real identity being exposed. Altering the necessary records to maintain his independence was a risky operation all on its own, but creating a personality that would allow him to work fully above board in the media – well, all he had to do was decide if it was worth the risk.

Either that or he'd have to find some other way of making a living before the last of his money finally ran out.

As far as the incident at the Armoured Saint was concerned, it appeared that the heat was now off. Todd had done his job well: Kendrick had been scrubbed from the security records.

So what do I do now? he asked himself, waking in his own bed the next morning. A half-packed duffel bag still sat near the door, but thoughts of fleeing after the incident at the Armoured Saint had faded following his encounter with Marlin Smeby. Besides, he realized belatedly, if the Legislate had developed any concerns over his identity he would have known about it long before now.

His meeting with Smeby had occupied Kendrick's thoughts while he was sleeping as much as they had earlier when he'd been awake. Taking up any offer from Draeger was a wrong move, he knew that. What he'd been promised might not even be true – but even so, why couldn't he stop thinking about it? Why had he just accepted that information and left so meekly, without trying to find out anything more about why Draeger was so interested in him?

Perhaps he wasn't the hero he would have liked to be. He didn't want to die any more than anyone else did. When Smeby had offered the rest of his life to him, he'd very nearly gone down on his knees in gratitude at the hint of such a chance. He'd left the Arlington hotel disgusted with himself, having told Smeby that he'd need to think further about any face-to-face meeting with Draeger.

But the intervening hours had allowed Kendrick to reflect on ways of turning such a meeting to his own advantage. It offered a chance to do something that, as a journalist, he'd relished for a long, long time: a personal encounter with Max Draeger, the architect of Wilber's vision.

Kendrick had long ago given up any hope that his wife or child might still be alive. After escaping the Maze he'd spent a couple of years interviewing witnesses, vainly following up leads. After Wilber's fall from power, however, records had mysteriously disappeared overnight. The bureaucrats and army officers involved in the arrests of citizens following the LA Nuke had suddenly discovered that they'd been doing something else at the time.

The men and women trapped in the Maze weren't even the only ones who'd disappeared. There had been others, countless thousands now resting in unmarked graves by chilly roadsides.

Exactly why the children of parents deemed to be security threats had also been taken into custody had never been adequately explained. Probably the intention had been to use them as bargaining tools to force people like Kendrick to do whatever Wilber wanted them to do. On that long-ago morning in Washington, his daughter Sam had vanished along with the children of dozens of other detainees – and none of them had ever been seen again.

It wasn't in the least likely that Draeger would know anything about Kendrick's family. But the man had worked closely with Wilber, had been close to the heart of the political machine that had ruled America for a number of years. He was therefore, in his own way, responsible. Kendrick knew how badly he needed some kind of closure, and a meeting with Draeger might eventually lead him towards it. That would make it all worthwhile.

Giving up any hope of further sleep, Kendrick got up and dressed. It was early, very early, but he needed to think, so he went out into streets still quiet and empty in the hours immediately following dawn. As seagulls circled in a slate-grey sky above him, he found his way to the Meadows, knowing he could lose himself in the open-air market that sprang up there every Tuesday.

The Meadows, originally a stretch of green near the ancient heart of the city, was now lost and churned to mud under an impromptu shanty town of home-made tents inhabited by refugees sleeping rough. Some of these, remembering the can-do capitalist spirit of their forebears, had found it within them to scrape a bare-bones living selling anything that might just possibly turn a profit.

The airbases that had once constituted the USA's strongest foothold in the Old World had been abandoned with unseemly haste, and it was surprising just how much stuff had been left behind in deserted barracks and mess halls. Pieces of uniforms, even medals, along with all kinds of miscellaneous paraphernalia and electronic equipment. There were also books, music, clothes, and half-dead data-storage gear from yesteryear, too old and ruined to qualify even as antiques – a vast jumble of fascinating exotica and useless shit in pretty much equal measure. You could browse in the Meadows for hours, even if you never bought anything.

Because it was still so early, half of the stalls weren't open for business yet. Kendrick got a coffee from a van sitting, engine-less and wheel-less, on piles of bricks and wandered about idly, wondering why it should even matter to him to discover that Caroline had been the one to design the hotel's window environment.

Who was to say that wasn't just blind coincidence? But it occurred to him that there was only one way to know for sure. He glanced at the time – not quite so early now, so maybe she'd be up.

His wand beeped to confirm that someone had picked up on the other end of the line. He caught the sound of a breath, a faint, barely audible exhalation.

"Caroline, is that you?"

Something else . . . Suddenly the ambient sound of the Meadows faded. Experience told him that his augments had recognized something in that background hiss and were now trying to isolate it.

Patterns weaved in and out of the near-inaudible static, and Kendrick's head swam. A faint wash of dizziness almost made him lose his balance – as if, he thought, the eye of God had reared over the horizon and gazed, unblinking, down at him.

The wand beeped again, indicating that whoever was there had hung up. It felt as though a spell had been broken. Kendrick dropped the wand back in his pocket and leant against a corrugated-iron wall, waiting for his head to stop swimming.

When his thoughts had cleared, he pulled out his wand again.

"Hi."

"Erik?"

"Hey, Kendrick! Good to hear from ya."

"Listen, I was thinking maybe I do need to talk to you or Buddy. Were you serious when you said you were in close contact with him?"

"Jesus, of *course* I was. We've got a lot to talk about."

So they made arrangements.

It rapidly became clear that Caroline wasn't in.

Kendrick stood in the street outside her building and cursed out loud. He then scrolled through screeds of information on his wand until he found what he was looking for.

Perhaps she just didn't want to speak to him. In that case, why not say so? Why just pick up the wand and listen in silence, before hanging up?

Or perhaps someone else had picked up and listened at the other end. And then that same someone had carefully hung up again. Kendrick thought of the suitcase bomb, he thought of what Whitsett had already told him, and then he let himself in the main door.

To his surprise, Caroline hadn't changed the cryptkey that was still stored in his wand; nor had she removed his biometric details from the building's database. He gained access to her flat without a problem.

"Hello?" Kendrick stuck his head around Caroline's kitchen door, his mind full of half-convincing explanations for why he'd just barged in. But nobody was there.

Maybe she's off somewhere else, he thought. She could have taken her wand anywhere with her. She might not even be in the country. Somehow, he suspected otherwise.

Nobody was in the living room, either, and her study was empty. He put his hand on the door leading into her bedroom, then turned to look at the workstation.

It took a full two seconds for the machine to boot up, then Kendrick navigated his way to Caroline's work directory, soon locating a file named "Archimedes". He routed the same file through to the windowscreen, and what he saw displayed there was recognizably the same scene he had seen displayed across the front entrance of a hotel the day before.

But what did it mean, if anything? That Caroline had been suffering the same hallucinations, the same seizures? If so, why hadn't she told him about them?

He studied the 'screen, wondering if he would catch a glimpse of a boy with butterfly wings if he waited long enough.

Next, he pulled up the TransAfrica sequence, watching as that corporate logo rushed towards him out of darkness again.

The list of interactive options was impressive. You could dive deep into the Straits, for instance, drill virtual holes into the subaquatic structure of the TransAfrica Bridge, and bring up an enormous mass of engineering, environmental and geological data; or call up projections for the effect of the construction on the economies of neighbouring countries, or even on their flora and fauna. Using his wand to control the simulation, Kendrick brought his point of view swooping down until it hovered inches above the surface of the bridge itself, so real that he could almost feel warm southern winds full of Moroccan sand harrying the waves far below.

The simulation guided him, again, towards the *Archimedes*. He let the software sweep him around the simulated circumference of the station. Its great metal walls rushed in towards him, and then—

And then he was inside it.

It was all terrifyingly familiar.

Kendrick let his POV drift forward until it was near the centre of one of the cylinder's two main chambers. Then he set it to a slow rotation. Grass rippled far below – or perhaps above – and, watching the windowscreen, he felt a strange tug in the area of his stilled heart.

Far down the length of the station he saw a dense cluster, like a swarm of locusts, hovering in the air. Then they were moving, uncountable minute dots growing denser one moment, thinning out the next, but moving gradually closer. The nearest ones resolved into tiny, familiar shapes with gossamer wings.

Kendrick reached out with his wand to shut the simulation down, his mouth suddenly dry. It came to him that if his heart were still capable of beating, it would be rattling like a drill in its cage of ribs.

This was the point at which he became aware he was not, in fact, alone.

"Caroline?"

He stood up. Something had moved in the bedroom, making a sound. He swore at himself, several possible explanations for his presence here competing for his attention all at once. *Stupid, stupid bastard*, he thought. He hadn't even looked in there properly.

He put his hand against the bedroom door and pushed gently. Caroline stood at the far end of the room, naked, staring out over the rooftops. She didn't react or even turn round as he entered. Something was very wrong.

"Caroline, are you all right? What are you . . .?"

Kendrick's voice trailed off then. No reaction, no sign that she was even aware of his presence.

He stepped up to her, reaching out a hesitant hand to her shoulder. He moved around to her side, and was shocked at what he saw. Her augments had turned rogue: thick ropes of augment-growth lay under her skin, wrapping themselves around her spine and ribcage. They hadn't yet spread up past her neck, which explained how she'd managed to keep her condition hidden from him.

Kendrick wondered if she had become catatonic, which happened when the augments interfered too much with the central nervous system, effectively reducing the mind to a prisoner in a bony cell.

Caroline's expression remained vacant and he noticed that she appeared to be gazing upwards, past the rooftops and into the sky. He touched her chin, carefully turning her face towards him. He wanted to lead her away from the window, get her back into some clothes – anything.

Out of the corner of his eye, Kendrick noticed Caroline's own wand sitting on a table by the bed. So it *must* have been her who had picked up on the line when he'd called.

And then, finally, her stare locked on to his. He felt a seizure rushing on him like an express train.

A white-hot comet exploded inside Kendrick's head, and Caroline's face reeled away from him as he tumbled to the floor, her expressionless gaze shifting fractionally to follow his descent. He screamed as pain rippled like fire through every part of his being. As he screamed again, his tongue burned like molten lead.

Kendrick prayed for death, for a cessation of such terrible, overwhelming pain. He lay at her feet and his back arched and twisted as he writhed on the carpet, desperate to escape his own body.

It was the boy with the butterfly wings again.

Kendrick could see his face more clearly now, and wondered what it was about it that looked so familiar. The wings were beautiful and diaphanous, two or three times larger than the diminutive torso from which they grew. The eyes were tiny azure things like gems glittering in that curiously blank face.

The idea that he somehow knew who the boy was haunted Kendrick. *I could swear I'm really in this place*, he thought. For the bedroom was gone, and all around him the walls of the world curved up to meet each other. Shimmering shapes of bright energy flickered across the landscape, and a sound came to

Kendrick's ears, barely audible, as if a million-strong choir was humming quietly to itself, somewhere very far away.

He strained to listen, remembering the background sound he had heard when he'd called Caroline from the market earlier: like listening to the whole world having a conversation at once. But instead of cacophony everyone could understand everything that was being said. A perfect meeting of minds . . .

And then the *Archimedes* was gone as abruptly as it had appeared, and Kendrick found himself back in the real world. The pain vanished as if it had never been.

"Well, sunshine, fancy meeting you here."

Kendrick blinked, hauled himself up, and found himself kneeling in a pool of his own sweat and vomit. Peter McCowan crouched next to him, hands clasped on his knees, grinning down.

Kendrick looked around wildly, then saw Caroline slumped on the floor beneath the window.

"Peter, what the—? Oh, Christ." He rolled over onto his hands and knees, pulling himself upright. As he leant over Caroline, he saw that she was still breathing.

"I was just dropping by."

"You're not even here. I'm going fucking crazy."

"Aye, well, there's the thanks you get," Peter sighed, pulling himself upright and wandering out of the bedroom.

The grey skies outside had been replaced by the beginnings of a bright afternoon. The sun shone down wanly on the landscape of the city. Kendrick wondered how long he'd been lying unconscious on the floor, and decided that he didn't want to know.

Now he lifted Caroline up by the arms and manhandled her into her bed. Her head lolling, she made a guttural grunting sound, her eyes rolling wildly under their lids. As he pulled the duvet over her she twisted into it. She mumbled something incomprehensible, but as far as he could tell she was out of the bizarre fugue state that he'd found her in. Now she appeared to be sleeping naturally.

Kendrick shook his head numbly, and followed after McCowan. He found him in the kitchen.

"Two sugars, right?" Peter banged cupboard doors open and shut until he found the tin marked *Sugar*. Kendrick watched as the ghost poured hot water into two mugs before sinking into one of the chairs by the kitchen table. The ghost reached for an open carton of milk and dribbled it into each of the mugs, spilling almost as much on the table.

McCowan pushed one across the table towards Kendrick, slopping even more tea out of the mug. The hot liquid began to soak into a small pile of paper magazines and an eepsheet. Kendrick sat down opposite, gingerly sliding the magazines and 'sheet away from the growing pool.

Then he stopped and stared at the two mugs. Ghosts just didn't make cups of tea. If he picked up his own tea, that would make the thing sitting across the table from him objectively real. He made no move to pick up the mug.

Kendrick licked his lips. "Who are you?"

"Peter McCowan. Probably." Kendrick started to say something, but the other man held his hands out in a *stop* gesture. "I'll qualify that. I'm Peter McCowan. I am also, to a lesser extent, you, and also Caroline, and anyone else I ever knew who was also involved in Ward Seventeen back in the Maze. So, to rephrase things, I'm Peter McCowan – but that's not necessarily the same thing as *the* Peter McCowan."

Kendrick remembered the Peter McCowan he'd known: a charming rogue whose apparent ability to talk his way out of almost any bad situation had deserted him the day he arrived at the Maze.

Kendrick shook his head. "I keep thinking that Caroline is going to walk in here and see me talking to a blank wall. I thought you were some kind of hallucination, but I'm not sure anyone can have this kind of conversation with a hallucination. In which case, I don't know what you are."

"It's a good question. Let's just say the augment technology they put in me in the Maze had the unexpected side-benefit of preserving the memories and thoughts from a dead mind. As to why it should do so, well, it constitutes a self-evolving cybernetic organism in its own right. Maybe preserving such things increases its ability to survive. Maybe Draeger intended that. Or maybe I'm just a cooperative community of nanites, several tens of thousands of generations beyond the ones that first inhabited my body, which only thinks it's me. Either way, my advice to you remains the same. Don't go back to Hardenbrooke."

Kendrick's lips felt heavy and numb. To his surprise, he began to feel anger. Just then, just for an instant, he hated McCowan in a way he couldn't previously have imagined. Here was a literal ghost from his past, demanding his attention, his active participation in schemes born of madness.

"Do you know what the alternative is?" Kendrick asked. "How could you be Peter and have been there in the Maze, and yet not know what happens to people like us when our augments turn rogue and we leave them untreated?"

"Kendrick—"

"You know what I heard happens in those secure wards that the Legislate operate? They open you up and try and cut the things directly out of you. But they can never get all of them, so they start to grow back again. Yet they still do it anyway."

Kendrick shook his head. "And sometimes when the augmentations grow back in, they develop in new and even more unexpected ways." He stared at the ghost with fervent eyes. "I *need* Hardenbrooke. With his help I can stay free, and maybe then find a way not just to stay alive but to stay at least remotely human for as long as I can before these fucking things inside me finally kill me!"

He was hyperventilating, dizzy with the effort of coping with this so soon after his latest seizure, furious but feeling desperately frail.

"Kendrick. This is why . . ." Peter's shape twisted, disappeared, reappeared again, his features marginally distorted. ". . . rdenbrooke has set you up. I swear this is true. The nanotech tracers he's put in you do more than restructure the core algorithms of your augmentations. They act like a Trojan horse, analysing you from the inside out, practically reading your fucking thoughts. Remember what happened in the Maze, Kendrick. Remember the four of us – you, me, Buddy and Robert."

"I remember."

"What's inside you is based on Max Draeger's research. He . . . he . . ."

As Kendrick watched, McCowan became more like a two-dimensional image, or a badly tuned signal. "Listen, Kendrick, I've got to go. I'll see you soon. For Christ's sake, think about what I'm saying." He flickered again, his voice turning scratchy, giving the lie to any notion of his being a genuine physical manifestation.

A product of technology, then, not a ghost – or at any rate not the kind that haunted empty houses and lonely castles. McCowan's image flickered once more, then finally disappeared. Kendrick felt a touch of vertigo as he realized that the tea, the spreading puddle of it, had vanished. The table was bare of any sign of Peter McCowan's presence.

For a few minutes, Kendrick stared at the empty seat in front of him, filled with an overwhelming sensation of unreality.

16 October 2096
Uisghe Beatha bar, Leith

"Vasilevich?"

Hardenbrooke's face still stung from the freezing rain blowing off the sea. The bar was tucked away in an obscure side road not far from the docks at Leith. Malky glanced up in response, and Hardenbrooke thought the little man couldn't have looked more furtive if he'd tried.

"There are other people here," Hardenbrooke stated flatly.

Malky made an exaggerated show of looking to either side at

the meagre clientele, most of them huddled together in a deep, muttered conversation with the barman. "Nobody either of us knows. And if there's any surveillance dust, I'd know about it." Malky raised one arm above the table so that Hardenbrooke could see the databand fixed around his wrist.

Hardenbrooke grimaced and sat down opposite him. Meeting in such a public place was a bad idea. Vasilevich sometimes put too much faith in modern technology, forgetting that there were simpler ways of finding out information. Seeing two people together, for instance, and drawing conclusions – what could be easier?

"We could have met at my clinic. My security there is excellent."

Malky shook his head. "Look, you can be as careful as you like, but if you're going to get caught out, then you're going to get caught out, right?"

Hardenbrooke said nothing, reflecting inwardly on why he disliked the other man so much.

"Let's get this over with. I just had a surprise visit from one of Draeger's representatives. He was looking for information about Gallmon."

Malky shrugged, his gaze darting away from Hardenbrooke's. "What's it got to do with me?"

"The man who visited me is called Marlin Smeby. He turned up unannounced and did everything but roast me over an open pit to extract answers. I can't think of any reason for that, except maybe he smells a rat."

Malky laughed at this, and Hardenbrooke gave him a cold glare that could have frozen a volcano. "If something happens to me, Vasilevich, it happens to you too. Remember that."

"I hadn't forgotten. Can you deal with this guy Smeby?"

"Not in the way I think you mean. If anything happens to Smeby, Draeger won't be fooled."

Malky nodded. Their business relationship spanned a few years now, and Malky had long been a distributor for Hardenbrooke's seemingly endless supply of smuggled-in illegal bioware. That relationship had even blossomed for a while, until it had occurred to Hardenbrooke that blackmailing his best customer might be both profitable and convenient.

This had provided surprising dividends for Malky. A little reading between the lines had made it clear to him that Hardenbrooke was supplying information not only to Max Draeger but also to Los Muertos, in what appeared to be a complex double-cross.

Hardenbrooke understood that Malky realized this, and in turn Malky understood that Hardenbrooke understood this, both of them in a kind of Mexican stand-off where each party simultaneously had everything and nothing to lose.

Malky sighed and leaned back. "All right, then. What did you have in mind?"

"My Stateside friends" – Malky grimaced; as if he didn't already know exactly to whom Hardenbrooke was referring – "want Gallmon before Draeger gets his hands on him. Smeby has already met Gallmon in person."

Small beads of sweat appeared on Malky's forehead. "Jesus. You mean they grabbed him?"

"No, I mean Smeby *invited* Gallmon to a meeting, and Gallmon went along."

"But why? I mean, what's so special about Kendrick?"

"Who gives a damn about the reason? All I know is, Draeger is wise to us—"

"Fuck off," Malky snapped. "Wise to *you*, you mean. I never volunteered for all this shit."

"Either way, we have to move quick or it's both our necks. Okay?"

"Fine. Kidnap it is, then." Malky let out a long breath. "One more level to add to my rich and colourful criminal career."

Hardenbrooke glared at him. "Listen to me, you're going to help me with this or—"

"Yes, I know," Malky muttered in a tired voice. "Or I'm dead meat. But I'm not going to pretend I like it. Kendrick is a friend of mine." He shook his head. "It still doesn't make sense. What in God's name do these people *want* with him?"

"Either way, it's your skin or his, Vasilevich." Hardenbrooke gave a nasty smile, made all the more unpleasant by the way the scar tissue rucked up around one side of his face. "If we don't give them exactly what they want, I can't predict what they might do. But I can guarantee it wouldn't be very pleasant for either of us."

30 June 2088
Maze Internment Camp, Venezuela

Six months had passed since Kendrick had watched Marco die in that detention centre, and during that time he'd come to wonder if perhaps he hadn't died too and been reborn into Hell.

He woke on his hard bunk to the sound of boots marching through the mud outside. A hand snaked out of the darkness and touched his shoulder. He jumped as a face loomed out of the murk; it was Buddy. A pilot in the military a few years before, Buddy had been caught, along with another man named Roy Whitman, smuggling alleged dissidents south into Mexico and beyond.

"You hear that?" Buddy whispered. Kendrick nodded mutely as loud voices approached from somewhere outside. They listened, hoping that whoever it was they were heading to some other hut.

Just then the door slammed open, warm air rushing into the moist atmosphere of the wooden building. Outside, crickets chirped loudly, the night filled with the sounds of tropical life. Several figures, reduced to silhouettes by the bright arc lights of the camp outside, stepped in among them, bulky in their camouflage gear, rifles slung over their shoulders. The soldiers seemed like phantoms from some other age – an age of hot water, clean blankets and edible food.

"McCowan, Juarez, Gallmon," one of the soldiers bellowed. "Stand."

A hushed silence fell across the hut, where perhaps thirty men were crammed into a tiny space, sleeping on their rough bunks in the unbearable heat. Kendrick thought enviously of all the others in the camp who must have heard the soldiers stamping their way across the scrubby soil, and their relief as it became clear that they weren't coming for them.

Kendrick lifted himself from his bunk and stood up uneasily, hunger and lack of sleep nearly making him stumble. McCowan and Buddy stood up simultaneously. Although thoughts of resistance and escape were always present, Kendrick had witnessed what happened to those refusing to cooperate. Their blood still stained the rough soil outside.

They were led out into the warm night air, the stars sparkling far above them, the jungle visible merely as a vague black mass beyond the arc lights. A thin beard clung to McCowan's hollow cheeks under eyes that were rheumy and sunken. Kendrick hadn't had much of a chance to get to know him yet, since he was only a recent arrival, although he'd brought with him some precious news of happenings in the outside world. He was apparently a Scotsman with "business connections" in the Middle East – in the eyes of the Wilber administration, a good enough reason for immediate arrest.

Like Kendrick himself, he'd just been in the wrong place at the wrong time.

Every time a new prisoner arrived, more snippets of information were disseminated through the camp. Since Kendrick's own arrival, just after the LA Nuke, thousands more had been processed through the impromptu detention centres set up across the United States. Then they'd been incarcerated in this hell-hole.

The three prisoners were taken outside and made to stand in a ragged line. As Kendrick glanced down at Buddy Juarez's feet, he realized that the other man must have been lying in his bunk with his boots on.

Buddy caught his eye. "Always prepared," he whispered.

Sweat prickled on Kendrick's brow; for all the fragmented news about mass arrests still continuing back home, none of them had any idea where they were actually being held. The jungle and its temperatures suggested that they were somewhere in South America. Since there were no signs of civilization beyond the arc lights and the surrounding vegetation the nearest town might be miles away, maybe hundreds.

Something hard and metallic was poked harshly into the small of Kendrick's back so that he stumbled forward at the same time as the other two. They were then led away from the huts and through the wire fence that separated them from the rest of what seemed to be a military base hacked straight out of the raw jungle.

"Welcome to the Maze," said Stenzer.

There was food on a tray, fresh coffee in a pot brewing on a hot-plate. Kendrick eyed a plate of doughnuts with sugar glazing. Small plastic pots of cream stood near the brewing coffee. The familiar smell of it all brought Kendrick to the edge of delirium. He was starving, had been starved for months.

"Where did you say?"

A smile flickered at the corner of Stenzer's mouth. A thin residue of hair clung to his scalp just above the ears.

"Our nickname for this facility," he explained. Stenzer's military cap lay by his elbow on the plastic-surfaced desk that separated them.

All three had been taken to a long, low building resembling a concrete bunker. Beyond it Kendrick had noticed an airstrip extending all the way to the edge of the jungle, and scattered around were other buildings, many surrounded by trucks. Kendrick guessed that this was the main barracks for their guards and the pilots who transported the prisoners.

Inside the building was a long row of elevators, each big enough to accommodate a truck. Their ride down had been long, the cage rattling and jerking continually as it descended. Several minutes later, its grille-gate slid open to reveal a long, grey corridor lined by metal doors. Kendrick had then been separated from the others and pushed into an empty cell lit with flickering strip lighting. There he had crouched on the bare concrete floor, waiting until the soldiers returned uncountable hours later to deliver him to this man Stenzer.

A calendar hung on the wall behind Stenzer's shoulder. Kendrick focused on it, noticing how days were ticked off in a loose, childlike scrawl. He saw that it was now the end of July.

His stare locking on Kendrick, Stenzer nodded in the direction of the doughnuts and coffee. "Would you like something to eat?"

"Yes," Kendrick choked, his stomach squirming painfully at the thought.

Stenzer's smile broadened just a touch. Not a smirk but a genuine smile, as if things were going just fine.

"Okay, then." Stenzer folded his hands together on his desk. "But I'd like you to answer some questions first."

At first, the routine was unvarying.

They kept Kendrick in the same empty, windowless subterranean cell he'd first been placed in. He had no pillow, no blankets. Daylight became a distant memory.

Any tenuous sources of information he had about the outside world were now cut off. One thing Kendrick realized for certain: nobody was coming to save him.

The last news he'd heard was that there had been some kind of rebellion among America's East Coast states, though he found this almost impossible to imagine. Supposedly, large sections of the United States armed forces had started fighting among themselves, with casualties in the thousands. Verifying the truth of this was impossible, of course. If such a rift really had occurred, it must have happened only a few weeks after his arrest.

Kendrick could imagine the causes, however. It would have

started with the rot that had turned fertile wheat fields into millions of acres of sterile ruin, withering and dying under what was perceived as a biological and genetic attack by some invisible enemy. How easy it had been then to reduce America to a paranoid police state.

For a while he was tortured randomly. Guards would beat him with hoses if he fell asleep. Sometimes he let himself drop off anyway, enjoying a few blissful seconds of unconscious peace before the men in uniforms slammed the cell door open again.

At other times he would be asked repeated questions about people he did not know and had never heard of, about places he might have heard of but knew only from the pages of magazines.

Occasionally, as Kendrick was led down the long corridor for a session with Stenzer, he would see men in lab coats who looked like doctors or scientists walking past him. They spared him no glances: he was beneath them, he realized. Their faces told him that they considered him merely a traitor, and a criminal.

Kendrick faced Stenzer across the plastic desk for what seemed like the thousandth time, yet he couldn't even remember being taken out of his cell.

There was always hot food and coffee on these occasions. Kendrick's interrogator followed a routine where he'd get himself a coffee and a doughnut while reading through his eepsheet messages. Every time this happened Kendrick felt like he was trapped in some unique version of Hell, looking in from behind a one-way mirror while some office worker ingested his morning dose of carbohydrate and caffeine before pursuing a mundane life that Kendrick could now only dream of. The strange thing was that, despite his hatred for Stenzer – an emotion so intense that the old Kendrick could scarcely have imagined feeling it towards another human being – he found himself irrationally trying to please the lieutenant.

For a while he'd thought that the morning routine with the

coffee and doughnuts formed a part of the general torture. But then he wondered if it was instead more on a par with the lack of response he got from the soldiers and scientists moving purpose-fully along the subterranean corridors of the Maze, an uninten-tional cruelty that served to weaken him further nonetheless.

Stenzer finished reading his eepsheet, then folded his hands into each other again and scrutinized Kendrick.

"August thirteen, time fourteen hundred hours. Interview with subject Gallmon, charges relating to" – Stenzer's eyes flicked down to the eepsheet – "subverting the government of the American people by aiding and abetting its enemy." Stenzer stared closely at him. "Mr Gallmon, are you prepared to answer some questions today?"

"I don't know any of these people you tell me about," Kendrick mumbled. "I never met any of them. I'm *not* a terrorist."

"But your wife *did* meet with some of them?"

Kendrick couldn't remember how many times they had spoken exactly these words to each other. "I don't know," Kendrick replied automatically. "She interviewed people. She was a journal-ist, like me. Meeting someone doesn't imply collusion with them. I know I haven't done anything wrong."

"Mr Gallmon," Stenzer said, almost gently, "if you're innocent, why would we have brought you all the way down here, to this place?"

Kendrick's stare met Stenzer's. "Where are we?"

And then . . . something amazing happened.

Stenzer stood and poured a second cup of coffee, then held it out in front of Kendrick's face. Kendrick eyed the cream-coloured cup as though it was going to bite him.

"It's all right," said Stenzer. "Take it."

At first Kendrick hesitated, but then he reached out and took the coffee cup in both hands. By contrast with the jungle far above his head, the Maze was cold and the warmth of the mug flowed into him like a liquid sun melting into the core of his soul. The scent and the steam of it made his head swim, as if he had just been handed back a tiny sliver of his previous life. At that point he felt at his very weakest.

"You can have a doughnut too if you want. Just help yourself."

Stenzer's voice had an almost conspiratorial tone that Kendrick had never heard before. He sipped at the coffee and grunted at the flavour of it. He then reached over and picked up a cream doughnut, watching Stenzer with frightened animal eyes. Stenzer only nodded encouragingly.

The interrogator did something to his eepsheet and it greyed out; Kendrick could see that he'd turned it off. "Listen, right now what goes on in here is between us. Nobody knows what I'm really saying to you. Do you understand?"

Kendrick touched the creamy edge of the doughnut to his mouth and felt a surge of bile rise halfway up the back of his throat. Then the confectionary was in him, his hands cramming the sugary dough into his mouth, filling him with a rush of warmth and pleasure.

Kendrick swallowed and coughed. "I don't believe you," he continued wearily. Of course the room was bugged. Of course they would record everything.

"Mr Gallmon – Kendrick – we both know this is a waste of time." Stenzer stared at him. "We both know this is going nowhere. Do you understand what I'm saying?"

"I'm not sure."

Stenzer shook his head. The sugar had now entered Kendrick's bloodstream, making him as blissful as a newborn baby. Stenzer came around the desk, putting one hand almost paternally on his shoulder.

"Listen to me," Stenzer said in a low voice. "I can't do this any more. Do you understand me?" Kendrick turned slightly and stared at him.

"I'm serious," Stenzer insisted. "I can't go on treating you this way any more. So when you come here, you eat what you like and I won't tell the guards."

Stenzer picked up another doughnut and handed it to

Kendrick. Kendrick took it and forced himself to take more time eating it. The idea that Stenzer actually meant what he said formed a tiny brief blossom of hope deep within his chest, but he pushed the idea away.

He was, after all, in Hell. Hope was an impossible commodity in Hell.

"Tell me about yourself," Stenzer continued. Kendrick finished the doughnut and drained the last of the steaming black coffee.

"I've told you everything I know." The same thing he had become used to saying, over and over, week after week.

"Yes, I know," said Stenzer. "But I want to know who you are – who you *really* are. There are files that tell me things about you, about your family and your life, your job. But they don't tell me everything I want."

"I'll tell you anything you want to know," Kendrick replied. "And I have no idea how many times I've told you that. I just don't know what else I can tell you." The words spilled out in a dull monotone.

"It doesn't have to be anything important," said Stenzer, stuffing his hands into his pockets and resting against the edge of the desk. "All I really need is some piece of information I can give to my superiors, no matter how trivial it may seem to you. And then, I swear, maybe we can do something to get you out of here."

"I don't even know why I'm here."

Stenzer studied him. "You're charged as an accessory to sedition, to aiding and abetting the enemies of the United States. America is at war, Mr Gallmon, and the rules inevitably change during wartime. Under the new emergency legislation, you can be held without charge for the rest of your natural life, if necessary – if it is believed that you in any measure could harm our nation.

"Not only that: while you are under military jurisdiction, you are required to serve our nation by any means necessary that might contribute towards maintaining the United States as the pre-eminent free democracy."

Kendrick was utterly appalled. "Jesus Christ, what did you lot think I did – blow up LA *personally*?"

"Perhaps you weren't directly responsible, no, but your wife interviewed individuals known to associate with enemies of our country. Terrorists, dissidents and the like. Your own work at times led to your having contact with the same kind of people, and your written articles made it clear you understood the implications of a terrorist threat."

"But I didn't make anyone do anything. I just—"

"Talked to them? And if you hadn't been there to disseminate their vicious, anti-American views, do you think they would have even given you the time of day? Perhaps you even shared those views." Stenzer shrugged. "But some of the things you said about our country – about our President – they were designed to under-mine us."

Kendrick tried to speak, but only a kind of feeble croak emerged, as the horror of what he was hearing slowly filtered into his mind. "I thought you said you wanted to help me. This . . . this *bullshit* can't . . ." He shook his head, his words tailing off.

Stenzer mustered something like a smile. To Kendrick, it seemed like a grinning skull clad in paper-thin flesh.

"People make mistakes," Stenzer continued. "They associate with the wrong people, and there can be . . . consequences that they might not have expected. Like the LA Nuke, or even the rot that devastated our great farmlands. I meant what I said: I could walk you out of here right now, if I wanted, and you could be home in a couple of hours. But I can't do that just yet.

"The fact is I need to give them something, or they wouldn't keep me here in this job. And then I'd *never* be able to help you. If you can give me something – anything, no matter how trivial it might seem to you – I swear I'll do my damnedest to get you out of here. Today, if I can."

Kendrick smoothed his suddenly sweat-slicked hands against his legs. "I don't know. What is it you want me to say?"

"*Anything* you can give me," Stenzer replied, his words imploring. "I can help you, but only if you can help me."

But what can I say? Kendrick wondered. He was a journalist. Stenzer already knew everything about his life. It still seemed incomprehensible that there could be any correlation between those articles he'd written and his imprisonment here without any official charges ever being laid. There was nothing he could tell Stenzer he had not already described in excruciatingly repetitive detail.

Tears came to Kendrick's eyes: Stenzer was clearly employing a new tactic to get from him that which he did not have to give.

"I don't have anything. I *don't*. I've told you everything I can, everything about my wife and myself, God knows how many hundreds of times over. I wish I could tell you something more, but there's nothing, I swear."

Stenzer's expression became grim. "The smallest detail, Mr Gallmon. You might think it isn't important, but it might be. Your wife was in contact with dissidents and enemies of the nation. Are you telling me she had America's best interests at heart when she consorted with the kind of people who would incinerate a city full of innocent people? I have copies of everything either of you ever wrote and, let me tell you, I have never been so sickened by so much unpatriotic filth." His voice was rising now.

Kendrick shook his head violently. "Christ, you don't even know that terrorists caused the field rot! Anyway, the environment's been fucked for decades, and—"

"*Don't tell me what to think!*" Stenzer screamed into Kendrick's face, spittle spraying from his mouth. Until now, it had just been questions, endless questions, while Kendrick's mind grew dull from boredom and hunger.

Now, something had changed.

Stenzer struck him hard. It took several seconds before Kendrick understood he had been assaulted. He found himself lying on his back, the chair tipped over to one side, his mouth full of the taste of blood and iron.

Stenzer loomed above him, his fist cocked as if prepared to give another punch.

"I can't tell you anything," Kendrick repeated weakly, falling into his familiar litany. "I've told you everything I can, again and again. If there was anything else, I'd tell you, I really would. But there isn't. I want to go home."

Stenzer nodded, his expression hard and inhuman. He walked to the door and opened it. Two guards were waiting outside, ready; they must have been there the whole time. They gripped Kendrick by the arms and hauled him to his feet, then dragged him back out into the corridor, blood dripping from his damaged face.

"What would you like us to do with him, Sir?" one asked.

"Kill him," Stenzer replied curtly, closing the door forever.

16 October 2096
Leith Docks

"There you are."

Erik Whitsett still wore the same woollen coat as when he'd first approached Kendrick outside the Armoured Saint. The same scarf was wrapped carefully around his neck, the collar of his jacket pulled up to cover his ears.

Kendrick glanced out along the quay. They were standing near where the ships were docked, the air filled with the cries of gulls and the smell of brine. Warehouses and half-derelict office buildings lined the waterfront. In recent years the area had regained its former notorious reputation, particularly since all the refugees had arrived. Kendrick had lived here himself for a while when he'd first come to Scotland. Those had been difficult times, but he knew the area well enough to know that they'd be left alone now.

"You seem out of breath. Did you find your way okay?"

"I wasn't exactly sure where you meant," Whitsett replied. "I'm not so familiar with these parts, remember?" He coughed up a small cloud of steam into the chill air. "Sorry if I'm a little late."

"No problem. Care to take a walk?"

Whitsett made an exaggerated show of looking around him. "Christ, couldn't you have picked some bar at least?"

Kendrick grinned. "There's one a little further along, yeah. But if we're going to talk about Buddy then I'd prefer somewhere where nobody's likely to hear or see us."

"Well, I don't see any alternative. So, yeah, let's walk." They fell into step with each other, the sea at Kendrick's left shoulder.

"You come down here a lot, don't you?"

Kendrick smiled. "From time to time, yes. This is where I first arrived on these shores."

"On one of the ships?"

"Yeah, in the early years of the war. Cargo ships came across, carrying thousands of us once the rioting spread to the East Coast. And then the Legislate navies tried to run a blockade to stop too many of us getting in."

"Kind of harsh."

Kendrick shrugged. "What's it like back over there these days?"

"Same as you probably see daily on the news. Used to be the rest of the world that was fighting among themselves, now it's our turn." Whitsett turned to him. "I stayed on, after the Maze. I used to be a counsellor before, so I helped other people cope with what happened to them down there – to try and slow down the suicide rates, sort of. I first got to know Buddy back then, before he decided to head somewhere south of Mexico with that helicopter of his. And what about you?"

"It was either go one way and try and find my way through a war zone, or head the other way and get on the boat. Then, like yours, my augs turned rogue a little while back, so I had to lie low."

Whitsett nodded sympathetically.

"If you don't mind my asking," said Kendrick, "how did you get here without having to go through the usual checks?"

"Private flight, arranged through a company part-owned by a Labrat. It bypasses the usual channels."

"Anyone I know?"

"Well – remember Roy? Roy Whitman?"

"Yeah, sure I remember him."

"You worked together, right?"

"Buddy worked for him," Kendrick corrected Whitsett, "back when he was running all kinds of shit across the US border, both ways. I just sort of . . . tagged along a couple of times, hoping to pick up a good story."

Whitsett glanced at him quizzically. "You're still writing?"

Kendrick shook his head. "Hardly at all. I'm lucky just to have the funds to keep going this long without working, but that won't last for ever."

"But you can't get the work, because nobody wants Labrats around them. Times are getting hard for all of us."

Kendrick shrugged. "I suppose I should take comfort in knowing that I'm far from being the only one with this kind of problem."

Whitsett smiled. "Consider yourself lucky. Things are a lot worse in some parts of America than they are here."

"I wouldn't be so sure of that. But you didn't come all this way just to see me."

"No, there's other reasons. Mainly, though, Buddy's surprised he hasn't heard from you."

"I remember, you said that. Maybe the question is why did he feel the need to send you when he could have just asked me himself?"

"Like I said, he's busy. But he needs your help."

"He could have called me."

"It took a little time to track you down. You hid yourself pretty well."

Kendrick allowed himself a small smile. "Looks like I didn't do a thorough enough job."

"But Buddy's speaking to you now – through me. Los Muertos know about the visions."

"Bully for them."

"Don't underestimate Los Muertos. They're a lot more dangerous now than they were even a few years ago."

"Come on," Kendrick protested. "They're falling apart."

"Fragmenting, but not getting weaker. They've split in two. One faction considers itself effectively a religion, the other is . . . a little more proactive. They both see us as a danger."

"Look, you know I *see* things? And I'll admit it's quite something, the idea that I'm not alone in this. All that tells me, though, is that our augs are screwing with our heads." Kendrick chuckled. "I mean, what's new about that? But what I really don't understand is why anyone would be interested in the specifics."

"You can't overlook the fact that the more fundamentalist factions of Los Muertos believe that they gain something from the visions they can experience themselves, once they get close enough to the Maze. You witnessed it yourself, didn't you? Buddy told me about your trip into the jungle. What you don't seem to understand is that we're all seeing the *same* things, all of us – everyone who survived Ward Seventeen, specifically."

Kendrick laughed and shook his head. "That's impossible."

"I can *tell* you what you saw: a tiny boy with wings like a butterfly. I can tell that just by looking at your face."

Kendrick felt his face grow hot. "So what? Even if that was true – and I don't necessarily admit it – what difference would *that* make to me?"

Whitsett shrugged. "We were invited. They must have spoken to you too."

"Who's 'they'?"

"The Bright."

Kendrick forced himself to calm his breathing. It had been a long time since he had heard that name. "The Bright aren't real. They're just a product of the imagination of someone who became deranged through US-sanctioned medical procedures."

"Nevertheless they exist. They are real."

"And Buddy wants to talk to me about this stuff?"

Whitsett took a different tack. "There were four of you, right? You, Peter McCowan, Robert Vincenzo and Buddy Juarez. You were isolated in the Maze and something happened. Something passed between the four of you."

"All right, I can't deny we were kept isolated together," Kendrick conceded.

"And that's when Robert first started speaking of the Bright?"

Kendrick sighed. "I told you, Robert was crazy."

"Was he?"

Kendrick looked away and didn't answer. "A lot of strange things happened back then. Sometimes it's hard to be sure what was real and what wasn't." He looked back at Whitsett. "And Buddy's decided the Bright are real?"

"They *are* real," Whitsett replied with surprising fervour. "The Bright are offering us a way out, a way to escape. But in order to achieve that, we have to get to the *Archimedes*."

"The *Archimedes*? Do you have any idea how nuts this all sounds? How would you even get up there, anyway?"

"Launch company run by a guy called Gerard Sabak, sort of your entrepreneur-industrialist type. He was among the batch that came after us, still stuck in Ward Seventeen when we were dumped in the lower levels. He has a majority partnership in the company, and they specialize in running orbital flights for tourists and industry people, stuff like that. He's putting everything together, but a lot depends on whether or not we can avoid outside interference."

"Right." Kendrick was impressed, despite himself.

"Look, don't you ever want to get away from the crap we've had to put up with? Like not to have even the good guys chasing after you because, just walking around in the streets, they're scared you'll turn into a nanotech plague on legs? Of course you would."

"I'm not denying that," Kendrick replied, feeling angry now. Perhaps Buddy had lost it, started a cult like Los Muertos out there in the jungle, worshipping the ruins of a military base and the machine intelligences that lurked in every molecule of its light-less corridors. "But the fact is that we have to find ways to cope and stay alive right here in the real world. And even if you could, what would be the point of going up to the *Archimedes*? Assuming you actually managed to survive the runaway nanotech infesting that thing, you'd be giving the wrong people an even bigger excuse to blow it – and yourself – out of the sky."

Whitsett looked out over the water for what started to feel like a long time. Then he turned back to Kendrick. "Look, maybe I need to talk to Buddy. If you really had shared the same experience as the rest of us, we wouldn't even need to have this conversation. You'd *know*."

They had stepped nearer to the water's edge. The hull of a cargo ship loomed nearby, water lapping gently at its rust-corroded hull.

"Look," Whitsett said suddenly, "here's an idea. Maybe we—"

By the time Kendrick saw the speedboat it was too late.

He'd been staring out towards the water while the other man spoke. Whitsett had been facing towards him, his back to the water, so that Kendrick was looking over his shoulder at the sea.

The speedboat must have come from around the other side of the cargo ship moored nearby. He had been too busy listening to what Whitsett had to say to have heard the buzz of an approaching outboard engine.

When the bullet hit Whitsett, the force of its impact spun him around so that he stumbled against Kendrick in the last moments of his life. Blood and brains sprayed across the harbour front and Kendrick yelled, stumbling away in shock. Bright flashes sparked from the direction of the speedboat. Something hot whined past his ear.

As Erik Whitsett's ruined corpse collapsed to the ground, Kendrick could see fine grey filaments mixed in with the soft tissues that had previously formed the interior of the Labrat's head.

Time slowed down. Kendrick began to run – the motion liquid

and dreamlike in his perception. He took a chance, glanced over his shoulder and saw someone in a heavy green slicker standing up in the now stationary speedboat, taking aim. Suddenly he felt sure that it had been him they'd been trying to kill, not Whitsett.

He ran.

16 October 2096
Outside Hardenbrooke's clinic

"*Jesus!*" Caroline's small hands smacked against the dashboard of her car in anger.

When Kendrick said nothing she sighed noisily, staring out at the street around them. People walked by, one or two glancing in their direction, trying to recognize the environment reflected in the car windows. Kendrick knew it was Caroline's own design: the streets of 1940s Casablanca rendered in black and white. Since many of the vehicles driving along the street, or parked around them, had their own custom reflection programs, theirs didn't particularly stand out. It meant that they could hide from view until Kendrick needed to enter the clinic.

"I could try and explain, but it wouldn't make much sense to you." Even as he said the words, it occurred to Kendrick that he'd have a hard time convincing even himself. Caroline had eventually woken from her catatonic state to find him back in her apartment. No memory of picking up the phone earlier, nor of sleepwalking subsequently: only of waking up to the sound of his voice.

So he'd left then, with little explanation, and in the meantime had met up with a man he hadn't seen in years – just in time to watch him die.

"Caroline," he said gently, "if anyone's likely to know what's going on here, I think it's more probably you than me."

She stared straight ahead at the street outside. "Well, perhaps that's true," she said in a small voice.

"Maybe we need to talk. You never told me why we finished. You never told me your augments had—"

She raised a hand as if to silence him, so he changed tack. "Has Buddy been in touch with you?"

Caroline looked as if her face was about to crumble. "Yes, he has," she replied, visibly pulling herself together. "I went to Holland, and we met there."

Kendrick nodded. Holland was relatively tolerant about Labrats. "And?"

"I started *seeing* things just a little while after you did."

"Christ, Caroline, if you'd only told me—"

"I didn't *want* to tell you! I saw things, so many things, and Robert spoke to me—"

"Robert is dead."

The expression on her face was filled with such cold fury that Kendrick looked away immediately. "You don't need to remind me," she replied with icy bitterness. "But he *spoke* to me. He's still alive in some way."

"Caroline, some very fucked-up stuff is happening around me. Someone tried to blow up Malky's bar, and earlier today I saw someone – someone who claimed to be a friend of Buddy's – get *killed* right in front of me." He saw the shock on her face. "People are trying to tell me things, and I have to take notice of that. I *have* to start asking serious questions." He gestured down the street towards Hardenbrooke's clinic. "You see that place over there? Somebody told me that the guy who's being paid to save my life is in fact out to get me – *why*, I don't know. Now Erik Whitsett turns up and tells me we're all – *all* of us – seeing the same damn things in our dreams."

Kendrick laughed, aware of the edge of panic in his voice. "But then, maybe we're *not* seeing the same things, so go figure! I have to get to the bottom of this. I don't have any idea where to find Buddy, or even if he's going to give me a reasonable explanation for what's going on, so in the meantime I'm just going to go in there and find some things out. Unless, Caroline, there's something you really need to tell me."

He looked at her expectantly. She was pale, trembling, not meeting his gaze. When the words came, she gave a good impression of having to force them. "When we were in the Maze . . ." He nodded encouragingly. "When they made us . . . I didn't know that you were down there with him, that you were the one who killed Robert. I didn't know you were the one that did it." Anger crept into her words. "I didn't *know* you'd killed my brother. And you didn't even, not ever, not during the whole time we were together, have the fucking grace to *tell* me, you miserable, pathetic, fucking *bastard*."

Kendrick nodded again, this time in understanding, and sat back. It had started raining, fat grey drops sliding in miniature rivers down the glass.

"Caroline, none of us had any choice. He would have killed me—"

"And don't I just wish he *had*!" she screamed, her face contorted with rage. She was weeping now. "He was my brother."

Kendrick fell silent, embarrassed and suddenly inarticulate, wondering just how she had found out. Buddy, perhaps? But he'd promised never to speak about that. Who else might have known?

Or had something that looked like Robert, spoke with Robert's voice and shared Robert's memories told her?

But at least he knew now why she'd thrown him out.

Kendrick rehearsed the lines in his head. *I had another seizure – two again. I almost died. You have to help me.* What would happen after that was anybody's guess, but he had to get in there and find out if McCowan's ghost had been as right about Hardenbrooke as it had been about the bomb.

He stepped up to the door of the clinic, which had no handle nor any other obvious means for people to exit or enter. On previous occasions he had been peripherally aware of hidden security equipment scanning him on his approach, and on those occasions the door had simply swung open.

This time, however, he had no appointment.

It was easy to speculate about who Hardenbrooke's other clients might be. Kendrick was far from being the only Labrat who'd washed up on these shores in dire need of medical assistance that he could never acquire legally.

Kendrick pushed against the door, but it remained locked. He stepped back and looked over to the nearest windows, rising behind tall railings. Below the railings the ground dropped away to a basement level.

He looked around to check if anyone was hanging around nearby. Caroline had long since driven off, abandoning him to his fate. He touched the door's surface again, feeling a tingle where his hand came into contact with it.

He closed his eyes, sensing the security devices built into the fabric of the door like intricate webs of invisible activity. He moved his hand across the door's width, letting his augments trace and follow the pulses of electrical energy there . . .

Several seconds later Kendrick heard a loud *clunk* and the door opened a millimetre or two.

That wasn't me.

He couldn't understand or interpret the actions of his augmentations, but he could *think* about something, and if it had to do with infiltration, assassination or any of a hundred specifically military applications, his body could find a way to perform it. This was not something Kendrick was proud of or wanted. The price of it, after all, had been grievously high, and it rarely produced desirable results.

He touched the door once more and this time it swung open easily.

Someone was letting him in.

Kendrick gazed across the familiar hallway: stairs ascended and descended in a tight spiral at the far end. He stepped in and the door closed slowly behind him, shutting off all sounds of the street.

"Hello?" he called out. There was another door just ahead, on his right. He'd never been through it before. He stepped up to it and pushed. It opened smoothly.

Somewhere behind him he heard a faint tip-tap sound. He glanced over his shoulder to see a security device of a kind he vaguely remembered from some technology-obsessed gridchannel but had never encountered in real life. It moved across smooth cream plaster on tiny insect-like legs, suspended there by no obvious means. Tiny lenses reflected light as its head swivelled towards him. It was safe to assume that his every move was now being recorded.

Fine. So be it.

Kendrick walked back out and along to the stairwell, then called Hardenbrooke's name loudly. He waited for several seconds without hearing an answer, gazing down at the steps curving away below him.

Fuck it. He walked back to the door he'd opened earlier and entered to find himself in a room entirely devoid of furniture, equipment . . . anything.

Peeling wallpaper curled down from one corner of the ceiling, and a thin layer of dust coated the white-painted sashes of the windows overlooking the street.

A large empty packing crate stood over to one side, while a greyed-out eepsheet lay in the dust beside it, its internal power source long since dead.

Behind the crate he found a chair, its plastic grey and scarred, the fabric of the seat stained and torn.

This room clearly hadn't been used in a long time.

Tickety-tap, tickety-tap. The spider-device had somehow made its way all the way down from the hallway ceiling and around the door frame, following him into the room. Or was there more than one of them?

Kendrick peered up at it, noting a tiny metallic platform, with a range of minuscule equipment mounted on top, propelled by six cruel-looking jointed legs. It had the smooth metallic-organic appearance of vat-grown molecular technology. Tiny, perfectly machined gears and joints slithered in perfect accord, shifting to follow Kendrick as he stepped back out into the hallway.

He stood again at the top of the stairwell, watching with a certain degree of foreboding as the device negotiated its way back out of the empty room to continue watching him.

Then he heard it: the distant muffled sound of a smothered cough, inaudible to anyone with normal hearing. It had come from below, from the rooms where Hardenbrooke held his regular appointments with Kendrick.

He laid a hand on the black-painted banister and went down. "Hardenbrooke?"

Below, the clinic was wreathed in semi-darkness, the leather couch and the apparatus that surrounded it in the centre of the room resembling some esoteric high-tech sculpture. Next to them stood the familiar wheeled tray of surgical instruments and sprays.

Someone was here – Kendrick had heard them. So why were they hiding?

At some point in the past the basement area had been partitioned to allow the addition of a small office, the interior of which Kendrick could now see through a long rectangular window with half-closed shutters. He stepped towards it, seeing nothing more exciting through the glass than the corner of a desk and a tall steel cabinet.

He entered to find two large wooden crates stuffed with cardboard folders, as if Hardenbrooke had been in the process of packing. Ever since the LA Nuke, people paranoid about losing data through EMP weapons tended to keep hard copies of everything. Considering Hardenbrooke's own history, it wasn't surprising that he shared this tendency.

Okay, nothing like a little breaking and entering. Whoever had coughed could wait. Kendrick scanned the contents of one cardboard folder and recognized a name: Erik Whitsett.

If his heart had still been working, it would have skipped a beat then. *There's a name that keeps cropping up.* He dug around some more, coming up with yet more names. Some he didn't recognize, others he did. All of them Labrats – but maybe that wasn't so surprising.

Kendrick dug further down, finding more names. Again, one or two of them were recognizable. He started on finding Caroline's name listed there. But Caroline had never received any treatments from Hardenbrooke. Or had she? And why hadn't she told him about it in that case?

He studied her file. *Augmentations in highly accelerated state*, he read. A polite euphemism for turning rogue. More names, soon scattered across the floor. Then – Buddy Juarez, with exactly the same words: *Augmentations in highly accelerated state.*

He couldn't be sure about any names he didn't recognize or was uncertain of but he was willing to bet every last one of them had passed through Ward Seventeen, down in the Maze. He studied more records: every one of them dead or dying from their rogue augments.

Just outside the office, something moved with a metallic click. Kendrick froze, then carefully stepped back out into the main area.

Tickety-tack, tickety-tack.

He glanced up towards the shadowed ceiling, catching the glint of light on a lens . . .

And then it was on him.

It landed right on his upturned face, tiny needle-legs catching onto his cheek so that he yelled with pain and surprise. He reached up to rip it off, but even the gentlest tug, he knew, would take skin and flesh away with it. The tips of the device's legs were icy, and a numbness began to spread through his face, his mind. And then Kendrick slid into blackness, lost in a deep, fathomless night.

Consciousness seeped back only slowly.

At first Kendrick saw only dim shapes, their edges blurred. Then his eyes focused more clearly. He did not like to think too deeply of the biosynthetic tendrils that sprang alert along his optic nerves, allowing his vision to snap into such remarkable, almost surreal clarity. In this state, he was entirely capable of discerning the tiniest cracks in the plaster ceiling above his head. It gave him a sense of sharing his skin with some other being whose intent and purpose he could not really know – which was maybe as good a definition of Labrat augmentation as any.

He couldn't yet move, although a distant tingling and dull itch was beginning to make itself felt in his limbs and face. Apart from that, every muscle was frozen. When he tried to speak, only a thin mumble passed through his lips, which refused to part.

Kendrick could hear someone talking upstairs. He was picking up sounds better – and from further away – than he ever had before. Rather than being good news, this was instead an indication of how unstable his augmentations had become, altering his flesh and his nervous system in new and alarmingly unpredictable ways.

At first, the words from above were muffled, but his augments filtered and boosted the sound of them until he could listen with relative ease. Even with such enhancements, however, only a small part of what Hardenbrooke was now saying made sense.

"I don't give a shit," he overheard. Was Hardenbrooke speaking over a line? Then a brief exclamation, as of someone else about to raise an objection: so Hardenbrooke was not alone there. "We've *got* to get rid of him. Smeby must have told him something, otherwise why would he sneak around like this?"

Another voice: "Maybe because you *let* him in to go wandering around? Jesus, how paranoid can you get?"

Malky?

A pause as Hardenbrooke's voice faded then came back again, as if he was moving about on the upper floor. ". . . Take care of making sure he's still out, okay? So if I leave you here, sure you can't screw up?"

Soon cautious footsteps echoed down the basement steps,

sounding to Kendrick like dustbin lids being smashed against a wall.

Kendrick's body tingled as he imagined the machine-growths entwined with his flesh and blood filtering the drug out of his body according to some complex set of heuristic rules, as if his body was a fortress and the nanites its defenders.

Which possibly explained why the tingling sensation grew exponentially for several seconds before Kendrick found that he could both feel and move his arms and legs again.

One moment he was strapped to the basement couch, the next he was crouching in the shadows just behind it. The leather straps that had bound him now hung loose. He smelled blood, a powerful, rich scent that filled his nostrils. His own blood.

Kendrick glanced down and saw the deep abrasions in his flesh where he had torn away from his restraints. Without volition, without thought. Now he was simply *here*.

He waited with his knees bent, his hands ready, like a hunter waiting for his prey to show. At least for now he was merely a passenger in his own body. Kendrick watched the door by the stairwell in anticipation. The hate he now felt was cold, pure, artificial. Even though he understood that this feeling came from his augmentations, a means of tweaking and controlling the emotions and desires of a fully augmented warrior, the hatred *felt* like his own – as if it had always been inside him, waiting to be tapped.

Hardenbrooke pushed open the basement door, the motion seeming slow and languid to Kendrick's accelerated perceptions.

A fraction of an instant later, Kendrick found his viewpoint propelled towards Hardenbrooke so rapidly as to seem instantaneous, the medic's eyes only noticing him when it was already far too late.

Kendrick caught sight of the harsh metal glint of a spray 'derm gripped in Hardenbrooke's fist. The medic's fingers unfolded and the 'derm rocked there, miraculously remaining in the cup of Hardenbrooke's palm as Kendrick's forward momentum slammed the other man's back against the door, the rear of his skull slamming noisily against the wood.

Kendrick watched his own hand slide upwards to grasp the medic around the throat.

"Was it you, Hardenbrooke? Did you kill him?" Kendrick snarled.

"What? Oh Christ, please, let go of me," Hardenbrooke croaked in fright. "There's been a misunderstanding."

"I don't think so. I think you were about to kill me too. I heard you both talking about how you know I met Smeby. So what's going on here?"

Hardenbrooke twitched, struggling to breathe in Kendrick's iron grasp. His mouth opened a little and Kendrick eased off the pressure so that the other man could speak. The spray finally slipped from Hardenbrooke's hand and clattered onto the floor.

Leaning over to one side, Kendrick reached for the spray. Hardenbrooke surprised him by twisting around suddenly and almost scoring a direct hit to Kendrick's testicles with one knee. Kendrick, however, slipped deftly to one side and avoided injury. Unfortunately, this meant letting go of the man, just for an instant. Once he had secured the 'derm he reached out for Hardenbrooke again.

To his surprise, Hardenbrooke bit him on the finger.

Kendrick screamed and jerked away, dropping the 'derm in the process. He felt an impact on his shoulder, and immediately a deep numbness began to spread through the flesh of his back.

Kendrick lashed out at Hardenbrooke, the force of his blow sending the medic slithering several feet across the floor to crash into the side of the treatment couch. Hardenbrooke had been carrying more than one 'derm, and the contents of the second one were already dulling Kendrick's senses.

It was probably the same drug that the security 'bot had shot into him, but it was taking longer to take effect this time. Still, he only had so much time before he slipped into unconsciousness again.

Kendrick stepped over and wrapped a hand around Hardenbrooke's throat again.

"I came here because I want information about whatever the hell it is you've been pumping into my veins for the past year. I came here because someone told me you'd set me up in some way that frankly doesn't make any fucking sense to me. I'm inclined to think my sources were right, so now I want you to tell me why."

"I can't," the other man croaked. "They'd kill me."

Kendrick placed one palm over Hardenbrooke's forehead and, with the precision and care of a basketball player, bounced the back of the medic's head off the hard floor. Hardenbrooke's teeth clicked together hard, his eyes briefly rolling up into the back of his head.

"Details," Kendrick demanded. A wave of nausea spilled through his thoughts and he released Hardenbrooke once more, swaying uncertainly.

If he didn't get out of here now there wouldn't be a second chance.

So he ran.

Kendrick's vision was blurring as he reached the clinic entrance and stumbled out onto the street. There was no sign of Malky, and he was obscurely grateful at not having to deal with any further obstacle. He caught glimpses of staring faces, shocked as he pushed his way past them in the street . He ran across the road, his limbs starting to feel like putty.

Somehow he kept moving, trying to get away from the Clinic – away from Hardenbrooke.

Kendrick woke to an early-morning sky.

The scent of grass and dog shit filled his nostrils. Something wet and rough slid against his face and he lurched upwards, wondering if he was again under attack. He found himself staring into the hairy muzzle of a small terrier. He pushed the animal away and lifted himself up from where he lay sprawled on neatly mown grass.

Bushes? He was lying behind some bushes. He heard a woman's

voice calling the dog, which ran away with its stubby tail waggling stiffly in the air. Kendrick could hear traffic somewhere nearby.

Kendrick staggered upright and pushed his way out through the bushes, finding himself in the middle of a small well-tended park that fronted a large office building. A green-painted iron fence separated the bushes and a row of carefully tended yew trees from the street beyond.

He remembered fleeing the Clinic now, and ran his fingers through his hair, suddenly conscious of how dishevelled he must look. A snatch of memory of himself running erratically across a road full of heavy traffic flashed into his awareness.

Kendrick winced, feeling lucky to still be in one piece.

He glanced down at arms streaked with soil and grass stains, as well as with copious quantities of dried blood. Wondering just how much of a nightmare he must look, he let his shirtsleeves flap loose in a half-hearted attempt to hide the injuries on his arms.

Locating his wand, he called up Caroline, keeping back from the street while he waited for her to answer.

"Kendrick! Oh God, about what I said – I'm sorry I drove away like that. But, look, what happened? I mean, did you find anything there?"

"I've had some problems. Can you come and get me?"

"What kind of problems? Where are you?"

"I'm not sure, but I don't think I'm far from the Clinic."

"Set your wand's signal to mine and I'll come and find you." Her voice sounded terse and worried.

Kendrick stepped back into the shadows and waited.

Caroline's car appeared twenty minutes later, following the GPS locator signal in Kendrick's wand.

"Jesus, Kendrick, I mean—" she exclaimed, climbing out of the vehicles and seizing him by the arms. "You, you . . ."

"Look like I've been through a war?"

For the briefest instant he saw the tiniest hint of a smile, but then it was gone. "If you like, yeah," she said more coolly. Her earlier concern was now well hidden.

Suddenly, everything was back the way it had been between them for so long now.

18 October 2096
Above the Armoured Saint

"Haven't seen Malky since last night." Lucia let out a puff of blue smoke, the cigarette dangling from bejewelled fingers. A tattoo on her left arm glittered kaleidoscopically as she climbed down from the neck of her machine-monster sculpture. The tattoo she wore was a holographic design: twisting braids that changed colour depending on which way she moved.

"Last night? Did he seem – I don't know – worried or something?"

Her gaze flicked down to her cigarette and then back up at Kendrick. A small cool smile spread across her features. "You sound just like something out of a cop show. You look a bit rough too, if you don't mind me saying so. Everything okay?"

Caroline had helped Kendrick clean up and had bandaged the worst of his wounds, now hidden under a sweater. Once back at his own place, he'd crashed solidly for the rest of the day and had stayed in bed for most of the next day as well.

"I'm fine, but I'm concerned about Malky. I think he's in trouble."

Lucia cocked her head to one side. "Okay, what's he done this time?"

"Look, I just want to find him. I thought you might have some idea where he is."

"Right." She nodded slowly. "You just want to speak to him. That's why you look like you're ready to headbutt a gorilla."

"Okay, fine, you're saying he's not in." Kendrick turned to walk away.

"Ask Todd. He usually knows where Malky is, if anyone does," Lucia called after him.

"Nope, ain't seen him. Ain't like him, though," Todd commented. "Mind if I ask you a question?"

Kendrick looked at him closely. "Go ahead."

"Mikhail – he's mixed up in something, isn't he?"

"I think so, yeah. Know anything about it?"

Todd shook his head. "No, but I can make guesses. Malky's brighter than most people give him credit for, but he has a habit of getting into some things deeper than he intends to, till he can't necessarily get out."

"You're a close friend of his, so why are you telling me this?"

"*Because* he's a friend. He's helped me enough in the past. Sometimes you have to return the favour."

"So you know what's going on then?"

Todd sighed. "Can't say I do." Then he smiled. "I was kind of hoping *you* were going to tell *me*."

Kendrick shook his head. "Look, there's something you can help me with meanwhile. I need to find somebody."

Todd regarded him warily. "Who? And what for? And, by the way, I don't work for free."

"I know that," Kendrick replied testily. "Does the name Hardenbrooke mean anything to you?"

"Not sure." Todd looked thoughtful. "Might have heard it. Who is he?"

"A medic, from LA."

"This wouldn't be some guy with a serious overdose of LA tan, would it? I might have seen him in the bar."

"It might be." Kendrick nodded. "I need you to help me find him."

*

117

A little while later, Kendrick returned again to Hardenbrooke's clinic, finding that its upper windows had now been boarded up. He climbed over the railings that surrounded the building, dropped down and kicked in an uncovered basement window before climbing inside. He carried a golf club that he'd decided would be a handy way to deal with the spider robots he'd encountered last time around.

But this time there were no automatic surveillance systems – or at least none that prevented Kendrick exploring. It came as no surprise to find that the building was completely deserted and empty, top to bottom.

Except for one unpleasant item.

He found Malky in the basement, wedged into a corner of the office where Kendrick had discovered the names and details of so many Labrats. Malky's eyes gazed sightlessly outward, under a neat hole drilled in the centre of his forehead.

The back of his head – what was left of it – rested on a pile of eepsheets sticky with blood. Kendrick noticed a spray of red a little higher up on the wall behind the body, where the bullet had embedded itself after passing through Malky's brain.

Grimacing, Kendrick managed to prise a sole remaining eepsheet from behind the dead man but found that it contained nothing of significance.

Malky had betrayed him, but Kendrick felt grief flooding through him nonetheless. In a way this surprised him, that he should feel such a loss. Perhaps, betrayal or not, he simply couldn't find it in himself to believe that Malky's friendship had been anything but genuine.

Then he continued his search, even though he realized that Hardenbrooke would have left nothing for him to find.

19 October 2096
Arlington Hotel, Edinburgh

Kendrick blinked in the sharp morning light, glancing down at his arms that were now concealed by a charcoal-grey suit jacket. He'd taken the bandages off that morning to find that the flesh underneath was already almost healed. Breaking free of Hardenbrooke's restraints would have broken the bones of any normal man, yet after little more than a day the damage had faded into irregular dark patches on his arms and legs.

But along with such a vastly increased capacity for self-repair came accelerated carcinomas, irreversible nervous-system damage, and the risk of total breakdown of the auto-immune system.

Smeby's aide, Candice, was already waiting for Kendrick outside the hotel as he arrived, standing next to a long and elegant-looking car.

"You should be aware," she told him, "that Mr Draeger is currently at his base of operations in the Far East. I hope that doesn't present a major problem for you."

The Far East? "No, it doesn't." Why hadn't he realized this? He'd been assuming that he'd meet Draeger somewhere more neutral – perhaps here in Edinburgh, or in London. So much had been happening around him recently that he wasn't thinking straight. Instead, he was now flying straight into the dragon's lair. He began to have second thoughts.

Candice smiled. "It's not really going to put you to that much trouble. Mr Draeger provides extremely fast transport for his employees."

Kendrick studied her. "That's a long way to go just to have a talk with someone."

In answer she pulled open the door of the limousine. "I'm not allowed access to any details of your conversation with Mr Smeby. My instructions are simply to deliver you to him. You're not here under any coercion, so if you've changed your mind it's up to you."

It's up to me? But until Kendrick could track down Buddy, there was really nowhere else he could go if he was to have any chance of figuring out what in hell was going on around him. And so, despite a definite sense of foreboding, Kendrick bent and climbed into the limousine.

A sheet of smoked glass that doubled as a gridscreen separated Candice, sitting in the front, from him. Kendrick couldn't even see if there was a flesh-and-blood driver, or whether the car drove itself.

Half an hour later they arrived at a private airfield on the out-skirts of the city. A snub-nosed passenger VTOL aircraft stood on the wide strip of tarmac, its stubby wings rotated so that the engines pointed at the ground. Candice guided Kendrick on board and took the seat opposite him.

The opulence of the aircraft's decor seemed almost shocking: Kendrick's scuffed leather shoes rested on luxurious thick carpet. An antique-looking table nestled between two comfortable couches that faced each other. He had barely sat down before he heard the whine of engines powering up somewhere beneath his feet.

"Shouldn't we have gone through Customs or something?" he asked. But the only building he'd noticed on their arrival had been a small comms tower.

Candice smiled. "That's nothing you need to worry about. These are minor details, and there's always the danger of random security checks raising problems related to your bodily aug-mentations." She smiled. "I'm sure you yourself appreciate the importance of being able to move around relatively incognito."

Kendrick nodded, and sighed. He couldn't turn back now. The sound of the engine had built up from a faint rumble to a steady, escalating roar. A few minutes later he saw the sun flash outside a window; they were now airborne, and he could see wisps of cloud through the glass near his shoulder.

Once the plane had levelled off, Candice unbuckled and stood up. "I'm sure you'd like some privacy," she said. "I have some work to attend to before our arrival."

"Where are you going?" Kendrick asked, puzzled.

"There's a working office next door. If there's anything you need, just let me know."

Candice left through a door which clicked shut behind her. Kendrick was now alone. He wondered if the VTOL might perhaps be more than just a mode of transport: it was comfortable enough to double as somebody's home. He imagined Smeby and Candice jetting constantly across the world at Draeger's bidding.

He soon found that the gridscreen responded to his vocal commands, so at least boredom wouldn't become a problem during the flight.

After stumbling across Malky's corpse, Kendrick had spent several hours browsing through the Grid, digging up public archives relating to both Draeger and the Wilber Trials. What he found dragged up unpleasant memories.

Draeger had been born in England in the third decade of the twenty-first century and had established himself early as a scientific prodigy. He had already earned his Nobel Prize for physics by the time he was twenty-one. His lifelong interest had been artificial intelligence, and this led to pioneering work with "distributed machine intelligence" – networks of tiny independent machines that worked together in colonies, highly adaptive, self-learning.

Then came the public crack-up when Draeger hit thirty, entailing a few years of psychiatric evaluation and treatment. That had been many people's first point of contact with the name Max Draeger.

Kendrick had gone on to scan through the more recent decades to remind himself exactly who he was dealing with. Draeger believed that the rules that allowed the universe to operate could be whittled down to a few simple lines of computer code. Certain of his theories had an almost religious quality to them.

None of this might have mattered too much had it not been that Draeger seemed to be almost equally skilled at making himself rich. The approaches to information processing that he had developed had revolutionized computing over the last half-century, and Draeger had since accumulated untold billions. Kendrick's researches reminded him how much more famous Draeger was now as a successful investor, entrepreneur and one of the richest men alive than for his earlier scientific achievements.

But then, inevitably, he came to Draeger's involvement with the Wilber Administration. Of course, it would be difficult to find a Labrat who didn't have some degree of knowledge on this subject.

There was no direct proof that Draeger or any of his subsidiary companies had taken any part in helping Wilber develop his super-soldier research programme, or that Draeger himself had had any knowledge of what was going on. The suspicion nevertheless remained, bolstered by rumours of an enormous cover-up. The mere suggestion of involvement in Wilber's atrocities had been enough to turn much of the mainstream scientific community against Draeger.

Now – and not without a sense of foreboding – Kendrick was finally on his way to meet him.

19 October 2096
Angkor Wat

Several hours later they arrived. Kendrick was now peering down on great swathes of greenery that filled the horizon. Early during the flight, the plane had boosted high into the upper atmosphere, until the sky darkened and the world below became a distant chiaroscuro of greens, with the occasional blue when they passed over a wide expanse of sea or ocean.

But, beyond the curve of the aircraft's wing, he could now see only jungle, with mountains on the horizon lost in a blue haze. Below, a river cut its way through densely clustered trees, with no visible signs anywhere of human habitation.

The notion that he had been kidnapped, that he was not being taken to see Draeger at all and had in fact been severely duped, made Kendrick's stomach knot momentarily before good sense prevailed. Kidnappers, after all, didn't treat their victims to long-distance luxury flights with an excellent menu.

"The Mekong," said Candice, appearing for the first time since their departure.

Kendrick turned away from the window. "I'm sorry?"

"The river. We're just passing over the confluence of the Mekong and Tonlé Sap rivers. We passed Phnom Penh a little while ago."

Kendrick nodded and glanced back out the window. He caught a glimpse of a village far beneath, gone again in an instant. A tiny nub of human life on the shore of the river below.

A lot of Asia had been badly affected by the Indian and Chinese nuclear wars, but looking down on that rich and verdant jungle it was hard to believe that quite so many countries had come to the edge of economic and environmental collapse in the general after-math. Kendrick couldn't remember if Cambodia itself had become directly involved in any of the conflicts, but other countries, regardless of whether or not they were active participants, had still had to suffer the consequences.

It was like finding himself on an alien planet.

The VTOL dropped onto a landing platform erected some-where above the treetops. At first, peering out from inside the plane, he thought they were over a city but one covered in jungle. When Kendrick disembarked, following Candice, the heat enveloped him like the breath of a furnace, leaving him tempor-arily disorientated. Massive shapes loomed above the jungle canopy for miles around; the landing platform itself appeared to be constructed on top of some enormous ancient temple that looked like it had been lost for millennia.

Which, as it turned out, was exactly the case.

"Where the hell are we?" Kendrick muttered as Candice guided him down a metal staircase that provided a vertiginous view right down through the jungle canopy below their feet. He studied the stone wall beside them as they descended. It was covered in inscriptions and carvings whose age he couldn't imagine.

Smeby was waiting for them on a lower-level platform that clanged under their feet. "Welcome to Angkor Wat, Mr Gallmon," he began.

To his consternation, Kendrick found that he was literally speechless. Smeby smiled on seeing this. "The entire complex was built in the twelfth century as a mausoleum and temple for King Suryavarman the Second. It was only rediscovered by French explorers in the nineteenth century and was renovated over the following decades. Mr Draeger has invested greatly in the refurbishment of the temples here."

"I thought you were still in Scotland," Kendrick replied. The man must have flown back here shortly after their meeting. Smeby only smiled and gestured to them to follow.

They were below the level of the forest canopy now. Large sections of the complex had been roofed over in recent years. Enormous towers rose like granite lotuses through and above the upper foliage. Closer to the ground were low-roofed buildings – with the same colouring as the jungle – that seemed to have been designed to blend harmoniously with their surroundings.

A car was waiting for them at the bottom of the tower. The grass in the clearings between the trees had been carefully mown, and there were narrow paths laid out that connected the temple buildings and other, more recent structures. The whole place had the air of a massive enterprise. Kendrick could see dozens of people all around them, some working behind windows, some eating in an open-air cafeteria, others standing around chatting in the open air, all somehow contriving to look busy, creative, intelligent. It reminded him of a university campus more than anything else.

The car wasn't really much more than a glorified golf cart. Smeby muttered a few words to Candice who stayed behind as they puttered quietly along between the various temples. They drove by a huge stone hand covered in grass and moss, easily twice the size of the vehicle that Kendrick was sitting in.

Other vague shapes, carved faces and statues could be seen almost hidden in the dense green beyond the buildings. At one point Kendrick saw a group of Buddhist monks, shaven-headed and wearing orange robes, seated in what appeared to be an out-door class. Now he dimly recalled that Angkor Wat was a Buddhist holy site, and he wondered what the modern Buddhists of Cambodia made of Draeger's apparent appropriation of this entire complex.

Soon they came to something even more spectacular. Ahead of them rose a wide and ancient staircase, guarded by four crouching stone lions. They dismounted from the car and Smeby led Kendrick upwards. More people – many with American accents – passed them on the steps, while a group of students sat nearby, consulting eepsheets and writing on electronic tablets.

To Kendrick they were like ghosts, reminders of an America long past and now haunting the alleyways of a dead city in the middle of a jungle. It was bewildering and strangely frightening.

At the top of the steps they came to an incongruous-looking row of elevator doors. Smeby and Kendrick stepped into one and it began to descend rapidly.

"I get the impression there's a lot here that's not necessarily on show," Kendrick commented.

"What gives you that idea?" said Smeby.

"Well, the fact that we're going down, and not up, for a start."

Smeby nodded, conceding the point. "There are sometimes problems due to the humidity and temperature. A lot of sensitive research goes on here that needs to be carried out in carefully regulated conditions. That's easier and more cost-effective if you're below the surface."

There was a soft chime and the elevator door slid open. They passed along spacious pastel-coloured corridors that widened at intervals to encompass open-plan offices, with desks and curved conference couches scattered in a carefully random manner. Not a university, then, Kendrick decided; more like the century-old classic model of a software company. A moving walkway, like the kind normally found in an airport, ran along one wall. Kendrick followed Smeby onto it.

The sheer immensity of Draeger's headquarters was overwhelming, and now that they were out of the midday heat Kendrick found he was grateful for the air-conditioned breeze flowing over his skin. Another ten minutes passed before they arrived at yet another bank of elevators. This time they rode upwards.

This elevator was glass-walled. Once above the underground area of the complex they were soon rising past the treetops.

Kendrick glanced downwards to see the path leading to the great stone steps that they had climbed minutes earlier. At that point he'd caught a glimpse of a tall glass-sided building rising way above – though mostly hidden among – the ruins of this lost city in the jungle. Clearly, he was now inside it.

Finally Smeby ushered him into a room so large that it took Kendrick a second to register that it was a single office. An enormous granite mural took up the entirety of one wall. It was covered with carvings of intricate-looking Asian deities, the images telling stories that had lain hidden for centuries.

Compared with the rest of the complex's interior, air-conditioned though it was, Draeger's office was cool to the point of chilliness. A huge desk faced the door they had entered by, half a dozen seats arranged round it. Beyond it Kendrick noticed several low leather couches set close to the windows that gave a panoramic view across the Cambodian jungle.

He recognized instantly the man standing by the desk. Max Draeger was wearing slate-grey dress trousers and an open-necked salmon-coloured shirt. His face was very familiar from newspapers, eepsheets and grid docs, but particularly from the trial documents that Kendrick had once been so well acquainted with.

"Thank you, Marlin. That will be all." Draeger's voice carried so easily across the big room that Kendrick wondered if the acoustics had been optimized in some subtle way. Smeby nodded briefly and retreated back into the elevator. Kendrick wondered if it was his imagination but it seemed as though Smeby looked rather relieved to be going.

"Mr Gallmon." Draeger stepped towards him. When Kendrick fought back his own reticence and took the man's hand an awkward silence followed.

"You look like the heat's got the better of you," said Draeger eventually with a practised smile. "I have some freshly squeezed juice here."

"Thanks, but no."

Kendrick nevertheless followed Draeger over to a chilled drinks cabinet that stood alongside the vast mural where gods warred across the wall of Draeger's office.

For a moment Kendrick paused to study the figures that lurched and capered there. Then he turned to Draeger. "They don't mind you taking over this . . . place?"

"Angkor Wat? No, we're helping to preserve it – the surrounding area as well. Strictly speaking, this is Angkor Thom. It's a little way from the main complex. My colleague Marlin brought you here by the passages that link them."

"And you built all this new stuff?"

"Not at all," Draeger replied. "A substantial part of the complex was built about four decades ago as a military biochemical research facility. Without the involvement of any of my subsidiary interests, I hasten to add."

"Really? You're saying this used to be some kind of military base?"

"Long before I was on the scene, yes. Cambodia was hit badly by the knock-on effects when the Pacific Rim wars turned nuclear. After we've left this place, as we one day will, there will be no sign at all that we've ever been here. Everything we've brought or added to Angkor Wat is based on sustainable technology. The new buildings are designed with a maximum lifespan of just forty to fifty years. After that, if for any reason we're not here to do anything about it" – Draeger smiled as if to illustrate how ridiculous such a notion was – "the jungle will reclaim them."

Draeger sounded like a salesman who hadn't yet got to the main pitch. Kendrick spotted a bottle of Wild Turkey nestling by the freshly squeezed fruit juices, and without asking permission he poured a finger into a tumbler. He drank it down and felt a different kind of warmth flow through him. Dutch courage, he decided, was better than none at all.

"But you didn't need to build here," Kendrick pointed out. "Surely a lot of the people working with you are prime targets for kidnap and extortion even in Cambodia, let alone in other nations nearby."

"Terrorism is a fact of modern life," Draeger replied. "But it's not my main concern. Cambodia has made good use of our expertise and knowledge in recent years."

Kendrick nodded. He had to keep cool, find out what Draeger wanted – what had been important enough to ferry Kendrick all the way out here.

"But working here isn't without its dangers, is it?"

Draeger's expression remained carefully non-committal.

Kendrick continued: "In some ways, it's more a case of circling the wagons than of genuinely integrating yourself into the local economy. Cambodia is benefiting from your presence, sure, but there're a lot of countries in this part of the world who wouldn't want anything to do with you."

"Circling the wagons – I like that. It's a phrase you've used in quite a few of your articles, isn't it?"

Kendrick opened his mouth to speak, then closed it, caught off guard.

Draeger nodded. "And everything you've just said is pretty much the same as you wrote in many of those articles. I know what you think of me, Mr Gallmon. It's true that since the US collapsed as a unified entity finding our way in other parts of the world has not been easy. I'm sure" – he raised an eyebrow – "that's an experience many of us share."

"But why here?" Kendrick insisted. "Why the middle of a jungle? Why not choose a city?"

"It's a matter of philosophy. The beliefs of the people who originally built Angkor Wat have certain resonances with my own view of the universe. Perhaps you're familiar with some of my ideas?"

"Only a little. But then, I'm not a mathematician."

"You don't have to be. Mathematics is just a way of expressing universal truths. You don't need to be a mathematician to *understand* those truths, only to *prove* them."

"All right, then, so why did you build the *Archimedes*? To find God, as some say?"

Draeger laughed. "I can't imagine where you heard such a ridiculous notion."

"During the Wilber Trials, it became clear that you built the *Archimedes* in order to satisfy President Wilber's religious . . . impulses." Draeger shook his head and chuckled, but Kendrick persisted. "You stated during those trials that you realized Wilber was schizophrenic even before his arrest. But that didn't stop you building the *Archimedes* for him."

"This is all very entertaining, but isn't it time that you asked me what you really want to ask me? There's nothing I could tell you about the Wilber Trials, standing here, that you couldn't find out from any number of records concerning those trials."

"All right, then: why did you bring me all this way? What's the purpose of my trip?"

Draeger studied him calmly. "What I want, Mr Gallmon, is information."

"Information? Of what kind?"

"Information concerning Labrats. Specifically those, such as yourself, who spent time in Ward Seventeen."

Kendrick took a deep breath. "You know exactly why I'm here. Smeby claimed that you had a cure, that you could . . . get rid of my augmentations. I want to know if that's true."

Draeger nodded to himself and took a sip from his own drink. His gaze wandered towards the vast mural.

"Entirely correct, Mr Gallmon. Entirely correct."

Exact date unknown: 2088
The Maze

As soon as Stenzer had shut the door on him Kendrick was hustled down several steep and narrow flights of stairs. One of his two guards slammed another door open and he was dragged into what appeared to be an underground garage.

He could see only one vehicle, however: a regulation-green truck parked near a steep ramp leading upwards. The subterranean space was dark and chilly, the damp air filled with the powerful stench of petroleum. Kendrick was marched directly over to a bare concrete wall studded with dozens of bullet holes. Against that part of the wall with the greatest number of pockmarks stood a plain wooden chair.

It wasn't the first time this feeling had come to him but, looking at that chair, Kendrick knew with absolute certainty that he would never escape the Maze. So he did not resist as his arms were pulled harshly behind his back and bound. A blindfold was placed over his eyes and he was shoved down roughly onto the wooden seat.

He heard shuffling, thick breathing, a metallic click. Something cold and heavy pressed against his temple.

He waited long, agonized seconds.

More seconds passed. Someone sobbed – a wretched, guttural sound full of horror. At first Kendrick didn't realize that it had come from his own throat.

The pressure against his temple lessened and he heard footsteps: two pairs of feet shuffling around nearby. The blindfold was pulled roughly from his head.

Kendrick blinked in the sudden light. One of the guards

brandished a pistol, its barrel now pointing towards the ground. After an eternity seemed to pass, he placed it back in its holster. The other guard untied Kendrick and he was taken back to his old cell.

There he lay, shivering and semi-delusional, until the next morning when the whole procedure was repeated. He was taken again to the underground car park, bound to the chair and blind-folded, and the muzzle of the gun was placed against his temple. To his shame and horror he wet himself, his bladder voiding as he sat waiting to die.

The next morning it all happened again.

What was the point where you went insane, Kendrick wondered. Was it a recognizable boundary like a road sign, something that would mark the transition? And if he lost his sanity – something he had more than enough time to ponder – would he even know it?

He returned to the basement one last time. This time, as the door into the garage was slammed open by his guards, Kendrick heard a muffled explosion.

He looked over and saw another prisoner bound to the same wooden chair. The man's body was half-twisted off the seat, his legs slumping towards the ground, his arms still secured to the back of the chair.

Kendrick could see that the other man was dead. Blood poured from an enormous wound in his skull, forming a rapidly spreading pool at his feet. Two other guards whom Kendrick didn't recognize stood over him.

This is it, he thought. Everything else had just been a long prelude to this. *This is finally it.*

Somehow he found the energy to at least try to fight against his two captors, but in his physically weakened state it was worse than useless. He waited helplessly while the corpse was unbound and allowed to slump to the concrete floor. The other two guards proceeded to drag the body by the feet towards the truck that was still parked near the ramp.

Kendrick had little difficulty imagining his own slack torso being flung in there. The other two guards then departed with a nod and Kendrick was left with the men who were finally to be his executioners.

"Your turn now, sweetheart," one of them said, drawing his pistol and gesturing towards the chair. As Kendrick turned towards it, the other guard kicked him hard in the buttocks. Kendrick landed in the pool of blood and gagged at the stench of it. A hand grabbed him roughly by the neck, hauling him up and pushing him onto the seat.

This time they didn't bother to blindfold him.

Kendrick waited to die.

Then he noticed something out of the corner of his eye. On all the previous occasions when he had been brought to the garage he had been too preoccupied to pay much attention to it. But now he became aware that an elevator directly across the garage from the stairwell had opened and several soldiers were coming out of it. A couple of them were engaged in hauling a large cart stacked – Kendrick was horrified to see – with yet more corpses.

Exiting along with the soldiers were some men dressed in shirt-sleeves, incongruous middle-management-looking types such as he had last seen in the days following his arrival. One of them glanced over sharply and shouted something to Kendrick's pair of guards. The one who had apparently been about to blow Kendrick's brains all over the wall lowered his gun from Kendrick's forehead and stared round him with a scowl.

The man in shirtsleeves stepped up quickly, seemingly unaware of Kendrick's existence as he addressed them. "Sergeant, I thought we made it clear that we need more subjects for testing. Have any of the prisoners you've processed today been cleared through us first?"

Shirtsleeves-man had a tall and narrow frame and wore a pale grey shirt fronted by a thin dark tie. His trousers were neat and pressed. Kendrick didn't learn that his name was Sieracki until much later.

The guard who had been about to execute Kendrick shook his head. "I don't know, sir. I'm not involved in the admin side. I'm just following orders."

Sieracki nodded. "Wait here." Then he stepped several feet away from them and began to speak quietly into a slate-grey wand.

He returned shortly. "All right. Your orders are counter-manded. Make sure that no more subjects get processed until they've been cleared with us." He pointed an angry finger at the sergeant. "Make sure you don't forget that. I'm not going to put up with any more interference with our project, Sergeant Grady. Any more of this happens, I'll come looking for you."

With that Sieracki returned to the other soldiers, who had now begun to lift the corpses into the back of the green truck.

Grady stared after him, then turned and kicked the chair hard. Kendrick toppled off it, grunting as the side of his head hit the concrete wall. His skin felt sticky and slippery with someone else's blood.

His wrists were unbound roughly. Then Grady grabbed him by the neck, twisting Kendrick's head around until he was forced to stare into the man's face.

"Look at me, you son of a bitch," Grady spat. "Look at me." He squeezed Kendrick's jaw hard so that Kendrick found he couldn't swallow. He lifted his hands in a feeble attempt to push Grady away but as soon as he touched the guard's hands he was hurled down again.

"Don't touch me!" Grady bellowed. "Don't *ever* fucking touch me." The other guard grinned as if at a private joke. Then each of them grabbed Kendrick by an arm and started to haul him towards the same elevator from which Sieracki had appeared.

"It's shit like you makes me sick," Grady shouted. "You and all the niggers and Jews and the rest of the scum. You should all be dead, now we got the White House. Instead they keep you bas-tards alive so they can play games with needles."

Grady shook his head disgustedly, then followed Kendrick and the other guard into the elevator.

As they began a long descent, even though his life had been spared, Kendrick found himself filled with sick fear at what might yet lie below his feet.

Grady turned to him and smiled. "Time they've finished with you, you're gonna wish I'd pulled that trigger."

19 October 2096
Angkor Wat

"Smeby's an Augment?"

Draeger smiled at Kendrick's confusion. "His augmentations turned rogue, just like your own."

"But he didn't get them in the Maze – that's what you're saying?"

"On the contrary, he paid to have his augments installed."

"I've heard about that kind of thing. It's insane."

"Men like Smeby know the risks. There are substantial differences between the technology he carries within him and what you carry inside your own body. But, yes, there's always a risk."

"So now he's only got a few months to live?"

"*Had* only a few months to live. Then he started working for me. Now his augments are in equilibrium with his nervous system. We can do the same for you."

"I hope you'll forgive me if I say I have trouble believing this."

"Mr Gallmon, what possible reason could I have to lie?"

Kendrick shook his head. "Look, the nanotech used on us is designed to be self-evolving. No two Lab— no two Augments are quite the same in the ways their augmentations develop and grow, and that's why there is no single cure. That's why there *can't* be any single cure."

"But you have been taking a treatment that has nonetheless stabilized your condition."

"Fine, I admit defeat, you're right. I never expected to find a cure."

"Maybe 'cure' is the wrong word," said Draeger. "Let's say technology moves on, and we have ways of helping you. Do you want our help?"

"You said you wanted information about other Labrats. Why?"

"You're aware of the recent deaths among survivors of the Maze experiments?" Kendrick nodded. "There are elements within Los Muertos who see people such as yourself as a barrier to their goals."

"Are there? We're not any danger to them at all, though I wish we were. Why start attacking us now?" Kendrick remembered Whitsett dying in front of him.

"All right, we've been pussyfooting around this for too long." Draeger put down his drink and leant against the arm of a couch, his arms folded. "I've recently become aware of a plan on the part of certain of your fellow Labrats to arrange a flight to the *Archimedes* orbital research platform. I can't allow any such thing unless it's under my direct authority. Otherwise I'd feel within my rights to take serious and drastic action to prevent what amounts to piracy."

"I'm afraid," said Kendrick carefully, "that I've only just become aware of this myself."

Draeger glanced at him sharply. "You were in Ward Seventeen in the Maze, were you not?"

"What about it?"

Draeger glared at him, as if he was trying to work out whether or not he was being made a fool of.

"Look," Kendrick continued, once the silence had stretched out a little too long, "I don't have the ear of any of these people. Some of them keep in touch but I don't always go out of my way to reciprocate. Is that why you sent Smeby to Edinburgh? To spy on me?"

"All right. I'm sorry, Mr Gallmon. We seem to be at cross purposes. Perhaps I've made some assumptions that I shouldn't have. However, my offer still stands. I'm seeking information on certain people – Labrats – who are intending to infiltrate the *Archimedes*."

Kendrick laughed in astonishment. "You want me to *spy* on them?"

"That's not the precise word I would use. However, you are – or were – an investigative journalist, one with an excellent reputation."

"Who else have you made this offer to?" Kendrick fired back. "How many other Labrats have you tried to persuade to spy on each other? Or am I really the first?"

Draeger stared at him evenly. "Perhaps you don't appreciate what I'm offering you. Your augmentations are killing you slowly, and I'm offering you the opportunity to live."

Kendrick tried to think of an answer to that. On the long flight to Cambodia he had found himself with too much time to think about the events of the past several days. What was it, he had wondered, that had driven Hardenbrooke first to extend the same promise as Draeger – of a way for Kendrick to live without fear of his augmentations – and then to attempt to kill or kidnap him?

And, of course, he had overheard Hardenbrooke refer directly to Smeby. Now that he was here and being offered a miracle cure for the second time, it didn't take a great leap of imagination to see the connection.

"I wondered why you invited me out here, why you sent Smeby after me. At first it didn't make sense why you'd show such an interest in me. But you did, and there had to be a reason for that. I was put in touch with an American medic called Hardenbrooke, by a man named Mikhail Vasilevich. Hardenbrooke gave me a series of treatments that seemed to halt the rogue growth of my augmentations in its tracks. He too talked about permanent cures."

Draeger listened impassively.

"The *next* thing that happens, an old friend turns up out of the blue and tells me that I can't trust Hardenbrooke, that he's dangerous; that he's pumped me full of something else along with the stuff that's supposedly curing me, and which allows him or whoever he's working for to gather information about me."

Draeger nodded appreciatively. "It's an entertaining fantasy, but still only a fantasy."

"I don't know that it is. What's the real benefit to you of bringing me here and offering me a cure? An act of sheer charity?" Kendrick shook his head. "Of course it isn't. You've already told me what you want in return. Otherwise why offer the cure just to me? Why not to all the other Labrats too? No, this way you get me to jump through some hoops for you."

Draeger didn't speak but his expression was getting angry. "Thing is," Kendrick continued, "I could never be sure before where Hardenbrooke got the stuff he was using on me. But now I know: he got it from you."

"This is nonsense—"

"No, it's the truth, isn't it?" Kendrick snapped. "The one thing I do know is that Hardenbrooke is scared of you. The treatments he gave me came from *your* research. Everything makes sense if he and Vasilevich were both working for you. But they double-crossed you, didn't they? They supplied the same information that they obtained to Los Muertos."

It fitted perfectly. Draeger knew that Hardenbrooke had cheated him, so he'd taken matters directly in hand by inviting Kendrick to Cambodia. Kendrick met Draeger's eye and knew he was right.

A silence ensued. Kendrick saw Draeger glance past him and realized they were no longer alone. The breath caught in his throat as he turned to see that Smeby had silently re-entered the room. *Nobody* could sneak up on a Labrat like that without them hearing. Unless, of course, he reminded himself, they too were augmented.

Smeby caught his gaze for a moment and Kendrick turned away, suddenly less sure of himself.

"All right," said Draeger. "I can see you're not interested in anything I have to say. However, I would nevertheless like to send a message."

"Who to?" Kendrick laughed. "I'm not your messenger boy."

"If you don't want me to help you, then perhaps you'd care to tell your friends from Ward Seventeen that if they want to get to the *Archimedes* they're going to need my help. Or else they're going to die, for all their efforts. Tell them that."

"Why don't you tell them yourself?"

"I *am* telling them – through you."

"To be frank with you, Mr Draeger, I don't see why I should do any such thing. Even if I knew where to find them."

Draeger's smile was thin, humourless. "Maybe you'll change your mind in time. Mr Smeby, would you escort our guest to his homeward flight?"

Kendrick watched as Draeger turned and headed back behind his desk, ignoring him now.

Don't let him win this one by losing your temper.

Draeger clearly didn't believe that Kendrick had no special inside knowledge of anyone's plans concerning the *Archimedes*. Now it was up to Kendrick to find a way to capitalize on that mistake – and if Draeger wasn't prepared to illuminate things any further, then Kendrick would have to figure out what was going on by himself.

"What is it that keeps you here, Smeby?"

They were back outside now, descending the steep stone steps to where the little electric car still waited. Kendrick had suffered a brief terror that Draeger had no intention of letting him go, that he was caught in a trap. But nothing threatening had happened.

Then again, he realized, if Draeger kept him here Kendrick would never be able to deliver his message.

"He offered to make you better," Smeby replied. "Perhaps you should have taken that offer up."

"On principle, I don't accept anything where I don't know what I'll find myself paying in return."

They got into the car and Smeby sat behind the controls.

"Either what you did back there was very brave or very stupid, or maybe both," Smeby said. "I haven't yet quite decided which."

"You're augmented," said Kendrick. It was a statement, not a question.

"But I'm not a Labrat, no."

"Why, Smeby? You must have known the risks."

"I used to be a mercenary. Some advantages are worth the risks."

"So has it been? Worth it, I mean?"

Smeby pursed his lips, and waggled a free hand in the air between them. *So-so.* Then he returned his attention to steering the car.

A few minutes later Smeby spoke again. "Here's something else. What if I suggested to you that President Wilber was right in what he did?"

"Then I'd suggest back to you that you were crazy, or deluded, or both," Kendrick replied. "Is that really what you think?"

"Let's just say that I think America's downfall was for reasons other than those that you may think brought it down. I'd suggest that weakness brought it down, and I respected Wilber for his strength and commitment. He believed in values like honour and duty, and things like that don't go away."

Kendrick peered ahead, spotting the tower where he'd landed earlier. The VTOL still stood there, waiting high above the trees.

Smeby continued: "The next time we meet, Mr Gallmon, it might not be on such friendly terms. You should remember that." As the car jerked to a halt Kendrick noticed Candice waiting for them at the base of the tower.

"I'd have to say that sounds a lot like a threat," Kendrick replied.

"Money is power, Mr Gallmon. It wouldn't require much effort to get you taken in by the appropriate authorities." Smeby studied him now with cold, hard eyes. "You're already living under a false identity. The fact that your augmentations have turned against you means that you should have registered for voluntary medical quarantine. If someone knows enough about you, that puts you potentially in a very bad place."

Kendrick said nothing, knowing it was true. He suddenly felt cold despite the intense heat. It would be a simple matter for Draeger or Smeby to turn him in.

He began to wonder exactly what he was going home to.

17 July 2088
Experimental Ward Seventeen, The Maze

Someone was screaming, a high banshee ululation that went on for ever.

Kendrick remembered an operating theatre, men and women in antiseptic blue smocks. Then a metal coffin, its smooth walls surrounding him, his heart beating wildly as he was plunged into darkness, his arms and legs shackled together while a thick, viscous liquid filled his nose and lungs. He remembered wires and tubes sprouting from his flesh. He remembered desperately trying to beg for mercy even as they closed the lid on him, leaving him to wonder if they would ever let him out again.

The liquid had an antiseptic taste that turned his lips and tongue numb before he lost consciousness.

Now Kendrick woke and found himself back in the same narrow cot, in the same ward that had been his home for these past several weeks. He was still in the Maze, somewhere in its deep subterranean levels that riddled the earth with echoing steel and concrete chambers and corridors, filled with the tortured cries and screams of other human beings.

His eyes opened to see bare and unpainted walls, the ceiling crowded with rust-coloured iron conduits. He felt a scratchy numbness in his chest as if his heart had become filled with dried flowers. He tried to part his lips, but they were so dry that they stuck together.

Kendrick lifted up his head and found he had been tied down

with restraints. Nonetheless, he caught sight of the fresh, livid scars that criss-crossed his chest, and he moaned with terror.

Down here in the wards all the guards wore contam suits. He could see one standing near the entrance to the Ward with a rifle half lifted to his shoulder, his mouth a round gaping "O" of astonishment, visible through his plastic visor.

At first, Kendrick thought that the guard was staring at him. Though his arms were tied down just below the elbows, he managed to raise his hands high enough so that he could see them by craning his head around the right way. He saw strange patterns in his flesh, unfamiliar ridges like maps of the surfaces of alien moons.

Kendrick turned his head the other way and saw another prisoner strapped to the adjoining cot. The man's mouth gaped, his face red and sweat-slick from the effort of screaming.

A name floated to the top of Kendrick's thoughts: Torrance – that was the other man's name. Like Kendrick, Torrance wore a one-piece disposable uniform. Both their heads were kept shaved. They even shared similar scars where the surgeons had cut into their bodies.

Something was pushing its way out of Torrance's flesh, something shiny, black and metallic-looking, sliding out through his skin like thorny spines, appearing through his neck or sliding out between his ribs. As if caught in a dream, Kendrick perceived, as though from a great distance, that the spines were rough-surfaced, formed of tight fibrous bundles apparently glued or bound together. They glistened wetly, slick with their host's blood.

Torrance began to shake inside his restraints, his body seized by a fit. His screaming choked off suddenly, a wet and bubbling noise emerging from his lungs instead. With surprising vigour, Torrance jerked and rattled in his cot until it began to slip away from the wall. Kendrick continued to watch with horrified fascination as the spines weaved around in the air, the husk of Torrance's body splitting and tearing as if something had become trapped inside it and was trying desperately to escape.

Then a strange, high-pitched laugh sounded. It was the kid, still only in his teens. Robert something? Kendrick turned his attention to him. Robert, in turn, studied Torrance's dying agonies with a horrible fascination. Sudden anger swelled in Kendrick's chest. He knew that the boy was insane, not responsible for his actions, but nonetheless he ached to hurt Robert for seeming to take such delight in Torrance's agony.

Then Kendrick relaxed, because it was, after all, just a dream. He let his head drop back onto the cot's rubber surface and closed his eyes.

As soon as he shut his eyes, bright white light exploded deep within his mind . . . and for a moment he *was* Torrance, screaming piteously because his body was being torn apart . . . and then he was Erik Whitsett, sleeping his endless sleep on the other side of the ward, near where the guard still stood in uncertain shock while doctors and technicians, dressed in similar bulky contam suits, rushed past him into the ward.

Whitsett was dreaming of his family, who were waving to him from a great distance . . . Something else, then: Kendrick had the sensation of being watched, as if some powerful, godlike mind had suddenly entered the expanded realm of his consciousness. Memories and emotions that weren't his own assailed him.

He forced his eyes open again and heard a spasmodic banging sound. He twisted his head to one side to see a huddle of men in contam suits standing near – but not too near – the cot where Torrance now lay dead.

He followed their gaze, to the far end of the Ward.

There was an entrance there that some of the other prisoners had nicknamed the Dissection Door. It was made of steel, designed to slide into a recess in the wall. But now the door was slamming open and shut, over and over again. Opening, shutting, opening, shutting.

I'm doing it, Kendrick thought. No . . . it wasn't just him. It was Peter McCowan and Buddy, both of whom had already been confined in the ward when Kendrick had arrived. Robert was part of it too. It was . . .

It was all of them.

The door stopped its hideous slamming. The ensuing silence was immediate, shocking.

Kendrick recognized the new arrivals as members of the Maze's medical staff. Or perhaps they were merely technicians – their exact role was never quite clear, although they spent much of their time taking blood samples or X-rays of every prisoner in the Ward, always well disguised behind plastic visors. Two of the men who had arrived during Torrance's death throes now kicked down the wheels on the dead man's cot.

They wheeled Torrance out through the Dissection Door. Nobody ever came back from there. The guard followed them, his eyes still wide behind his transparent visor.

Kendrick realized that they had been left unguarded.

McCowan pulled himself up from his narrow cot and hobbled over to Kendrick. "Jesus, did you see that?"

Sieracki had a policy of keeping prisoners in restraints for up to forty-eight hours after they emerged from the operating theatre. But Torrance had been strapped to his cot for over four days, while Robert had been under restraint since almost the beginning. Ever since he'd woken up he'd lain there shivering and sweating, non-sense syllables spilling out of his mouth at irregular intervals.

Out of the sixty-odd men kept in Ward Seventeen since Kendrick's arrival, perhaps thirty-five had so far survived the ordeal of surgery.

Kendrick licked his lips. "That depends what you're talking about."

McCowan studied him carefully. "I saw *that*," he replied, nodding towards the vacant space where Torrance had been. "I'm talking about . . ." He looked as though he was searching for the right words but couldn't find them. In the end he reached up and tapped the side of his head, a furtive look on his face.

Kendrick nodded in understanding. So he hadn't been the only one to see what he'd seen. "I saw something, too," he said carefully. "But I'm not sure what."

"In your head?"

Kendrick nodded. "In my head, yeah."

Peter McCowan's journey over to Kendrick's side of the Ward had been precarious. His sense of balance seemed to have disappeared since his most recent surgery. Sieracki's augmentations had grown long roots into the fertile flesh of McCowan's nervous system and, as a result, he lurched like a drunkard every time he took a step and he fell over frequently.

McCowan moved his hands along the side of Kendrick's cot for support, until he could sit himself carefully on the edge. "I knew we'd all seen it. I *knew*." He glanced over at Whitsett, whose eyes darted around frantically under closed eyelids.

Kendrick looked over at Buddy Juarez: the surgery had reduced him to a shambling wreck, his head constantly tipped over to one side, his eyes rheumy and distant. He shook uncontrollably, and for a long time – several days now – had lost the power of speech. He appeared to be recovering slowly, however, which had saved him so far from being wheeled through the Dissection Door. Unlike Torrance, Juarez still had a chance.

"Yeah," said Kendrick. "But was it real? It *felt* like I was . . . inside—"

"Inside Torrance's head, yes," McCowan finished. He looked as if he was about to cry.

Despite his restraints, Kendrick managed to touch the other man's hand, laying his own gently on McCowan's scarred fist. That seemed to calm him, and after a little while the man's expression smoothed again. But he still could not look Kendrick in the eye.

"Dear Christ, what I would give. What I would give to . . ."

Get out of here, Kendrick finished in his head. "I know, I know."

It remained an obsessive desire for all of them, even as they became resigned to the knowledge that it was an impossible hope.

"I saw them! I saw them!" This time it was Robert, struggling against his restraints. He writhed pathetically on his cot, his expression flickering between terror and delight. "I saw them."

McCowan pushed himself around in his half-kneeling position to stare over at the boy. There was still no sign of the guard. "Saw what, Robert?" he asked.

"The Bright," Robert whined. "I saw them."

McCowan shook his head and looked back at Kendrick. "What d'you make of that?" he asked softly.

"He doesn't talk about anything else." Kendrick glanced along the ward. Another prisoner stood up and stared angrily at Robert, his fists clenching spasmodically, one side of his face hanging slack. He tried to take a step forward, then started to slump to the ground, catching hold of the edge of someone else's cot. Other men – wherever the women prisoners in the Maze were, Kendrick had no idea – conferred in low murmurs. They too were aware that their guard was suddenly absent.

"Robert," Kendrick called out. The boy took no notice of him. He tried again, a little louder. "Robert, are you okay?"

Robert twisted his head up to stare at him. "I saw you. I saw you from the inside. Did you see them?"

"I've seen a lot of things, Robert. Take it easy. You're making people frightened." The man who had been clenching his fists sat now on the edge of his own cot, staring at his hands with an expression of utter despair on his face.

"I'm going to escape," the boy shouted excitedly.

"We're all going to escape," Kendrick promised him.

"You mean we're all going to die. I want to go with the Bright. They showed me the way!"

"The *what*?" asked McCowan.

Kendrick let his head drop back down. "He's been muttering about that for the past couple of nights." Robert still muttered and moaned and twisted on his cot.

"They'll show me the way," the boy continued. "The Bright. Only us."

Kendrick looked away from him, settling his gaze on the ceiling above. He could sympathize with Robert's desire for freedom. They all could.

"You were studying your fingers."

There was a screen mounted on the wall behind Sieracki's shoulder. He had cropped his hair close to the skull since Kendrick had first encountered him in the garage. His thin lips barely moved as he addressed his prisoner. On the screen Kendrick could see an overhead shot of himself, from an angle, sitting on the edge of his cot and, indeed, studying his fingertips.

Sieracki's office was located off a long corridor linking Ward Seventeen with all the other Wards. Kendrick had never been inside any of those other rooms, but sometimes Sieracki gave away more during his interrogations than he perhaps intended. By this means, Kendrick had discovered that the experiments carried out in Wards One through Twenty-three were relatively benign, in that the death rate rarely rose above two or three in five.

Through whispered conversations with other prisoners Kendrick had heard stories that the entire population of some Wards had been known to die in a single twenty-four-hour period, keeping the dissection rooms busy through the night.

After a while, Kendrick began to suspect that Sieracki himself was disseminating much of this information deliberately as part of his ploy to get the most accurate information from his experimental subjects during their interrogations. Sieracki was careful to make sure that they all understood that failure to cooperate almost certainly meant transferral to a Ward where the survival rate was approximately zero.

What Kendrick knew about Sieracki's past was minimal. Still, some basic facts had emerged over the long weeks of Kendrick's confinement. There was no way to substantiate any of these rumours, but nonetheless he held on to such brief snatches of information as though they were precious jewels.

Sieracki had supposedly been engaged in running secret military research programmes even before the LA Nuke. Now he had carte blanche to do as he wanted. Kendrick had also come to understand that Sieracki's attitude to the prisoners was simple. They had been destined for execution, and to Sieracki this constituted a waste of valuable resources for his research.

Kendrick glanced down at his hands. "They were feeling wrong," he said at length.

"Yes?"

"They felt ridged, strange – like something was growing under the skin. I thought what happened to Torrance was going to happen to me."

"Did you have any unusual thoughts, experience any notable delusions when Torrance was dying?"

Kendrick opened his mouth to speak, suddenly remembering the sense of *connectedness* that he had felt when Torrance died.

"What is it?" Sieracki demanded, his voice impatient. "There's something else you're not telling me."

Two others had died – less spectacularly – since Torrance. There were new faces in the Ward now, people whose names Kendrick hadn't even found out yet. "I thought he was trying to say something to me, just before he died," Kendrick lied.

"You're not telling me the truth. One of the doors malfunctioned at that precise moment."

Kendrick shrugged non-committally. "I don't see the connection."

"If you're lying to me, I could have you transferred," Sieracki warned him. "The choice is yours."

Kendrick looked down, avoiding Sieracki's gaze. "I . . ."

"Yes?"

Give up, said a voice somewhere deep inside him. *Let him transfer you to one of the Wards where none of them survive. Do anything, but just end it.* Did it really matter, after all, whether or not he lied to Sieracki? He was going to die anyway.

But it was still up to him to do his best to have the choice of how and when: that shouldn't be just Sieracki's choice. There had to be another way.

A calendar hung on the wall by the door. On it was a photograph of a spring day in the Rockies. A lake was visible in the photo's foreground. Kendrick studied the patterns of clouds and light and tried to remember what it felt like to stand outside in the open air.

He looked back to Sieracki. "I can't think of anything," he replied, making his tone apologetic. "He died. We talked about it afterwards, sure. None of us understood what was happening. I don't know what else you want."

The next day they were separated from the rest of the Ward.

There were just four of them: Buddy, Peter, Robert and Kendrick. Soldiers came and led them out of the Ward and along past Sieracki's office into a low-ceilinged room with a glassed-off partition beyond which Sieracki himself and several others sat watching. Technicians strapped them into new cots while the guards kept their rifles trained on them.

Then they were left all alone briefly.

A few minutes later, other technicians entered. Kendrick twisted his head and saw Sieracki still watching through the glass, his face expressionless. Kendrick bellowed with anger as a woman approached him with a hypodermic. He felt the needle slide under the skin of his forearm and almost immediately his limbs began to feel as if they were slipping into warm cotton.

Bemused, he watched as if from a distance while devices were strapped over his face. Then came the icy prickle of more needles stabbing into the flesh of his scalp, and monitors were attached to his wrists and across his chest. Earphones were placed over his ears, and finally goggles whose eyepieces were stuffed with wads of cotton wool were forced over his eyes to blind him from the world.

Static filled Kendrick's ears and he slipped gently into a limbo-like void.

"Can you hear me?" said Sieracki through the earphones. "Answer."

"I – yes." His lips and tongue were numb and foreign-feeling. Random points of light played in the darkness.

"Kendrick, I want you to talk to the others."

Talk to the others? But he was lost, alone, dead . . . surely he'd died. Now he floated . . . here. There was nobody else here.

No, there *were* others. He could hear them around him, mixed in with the chaotic, ceaseless buzz of electrons passing through the filaments of the electric lights that illuminated the chamber. He could hear so much, even the faint surge of energy through the laser-sights on the guns carried by the nearby guards.

Kendrick was only distantly aware that Sieracki was still asking him questions, and that he was still answering them. But for the life of him he had no idea what he was actually saying, could not begin to guess if there were rhyme or reason to the words pouring out of his insensate mouth.

After a little while he could hear the other voices more clearly: McCowan distant and blurred; Buddy sharp but unfocused, a torrent of images from the civil war, of flights through hazardous fire zones, his chopper downed while he fled on foot through the outskirts of some Mexican slum; Robert's mind . . .

Kendrick felt his body twist on the cot, his muscles filled with distant agony. He could see them . . . the Bright, spilling through their shared void, filling his mind with intimations of some other world.

Beyond the muffled hiss of his headphones, he could now hear the muffled screaming of the others. Hands grabbed at him roughly and the goggles covering his eyes were dislodged.

He could see the others, nearby. Wires trailed between the four of them, linking them together. He saw Buddy foaming at the mouth while McCowan convulsed in a fit.

And in the heart of it all, like the calm eye at the centre of the storm, lay Robert, his expression as peaceful as a Buddha's.

The next day Robert achieved the impossible. He escaped.

The four of them had been drugged yet again and placed back in the familiar environment of Ward Seventeen. As Kendrick lay in a stupor through the night, Robert had somehow managed to loosen his restraints. No one had seen or heard a thing; the cameras and microphones infesting the Ward had apparently failed to record anything but static. Even the guard had somehow failed to notice. He was replaced within just a few hours.

Three new guards – all heavily armed – were assigned to the Ward on continuous rotation. They hugged matt-black weapons to their chests. In the meantime, Robert's cot remained empty.

There followed an intensive round of fresh interrogations inflicted on everyone in the ward still capable of communicating. These interrogations dissolved into a series of direct threats, sometimes implemented. Several men disappeared, presumably "reassigned" to other wards; the rest were left to starve, without food or water, until one of them decided to reveal where Robert had gone.

Meanwhile they were all changing. But some of the changes were more subtle than others.

They spoke among themselves in tones so low that they believed – they *hoped* – they could not be overheard or recorded. The truth was, as much as Kendrick hated what was being inflicted on all of them, the balance of power between the prisoners and guards was shifting slowly but perceptibly.

Buddy sat on the edge of Kendrick's cot, his expression still haunted since he'd begun to recover his motor skills. He'd lost a lot of weight, though the same could be said for all of them.

"So do we have the faintest clue where he went?" Buddy was referring to Robert. His voice was less than a whisper, barely the faintest exhalation.

"Nobody has a clue, not even Sieracki and the rest of them. That's why these interrogations. Robert . . ." Kendrick shrugged. "He was right there one moment, then he just up and vanished."

"The question is, can we all do the same?"

"Christ, I hope so."

Buddy glanced over at two guards positioned at the far end of the Ward. "Are they watching us?" he hissed.

Kendrick murmured, "Well, it's not as if they've got anything else to do."

"Robert kept saying how he wanted to go home – maybe he already knew he was going to get out of here. So where did he go?"

Kendrick glanced towards the Dissection Door, and Buddy followed his gaze.

"Yeah, I thought of that too. Unless there's some other route out of here we don't know about."

"We don't even know what's through those doors. But wherever he went, he's not here any more."

Kendrick dreamed that night, that he was in a dark place – no, more than that, a place with a total absence of light.

Somehow, however, as he ran along corridors whose walls kept shrinking and growing closer together, he knew what obstacles lay in his way. Somewhere in here lay the way home that he had been promised.

He followed Robert as the boy ran onwards through lightless desolation, his heart full of an inexplicable joy. *Going home!* The words echoed in the cavern of Robert's skull. *Going home.*

Kendrick realized he was dreaming, but he became a silent

passenger for Robert's thoughts. And in the blackness that surrounded them came a hint of something else: a silent crescendo of pale light and wisdom and acceptance that never quite made itself known.

Something beautiful, something bright. Something vast looming just ahead, verdant with the promise of new and unimaginable freedoms without boundary, without limit.

And as Kendrick's mind slid towards morning consciousness the memory of this dream lingered so that, when he finally woke to the familiar surroundings of the Ward, he could not be sure that it had not been real.

More tests, more interviews, but no more trips into surgery – no more long days of recovering and hoping that they might live where so many others suffered long and anguished deaths. There were few of them left now, less than a dozen out of the scores who had passed through the same Ward during Kendrick's time there.

And, for the first time since they had been brought into the Maze, each of the prisoners of Ward Seventeen began to feel bored.

Days continued to pass, but Kendrick did not spend them in silent contemplation. Instead he made a decision: he was not going to wait around to find out what Sieracki's intentions for him were. How he might escape he had no idea – but a precedent had been set.

Yet, as more time passed, he wondered if an opportunity would ever present itself.

"They can't hear us."

"Are you sure?" Kendrick realized he was holding his breath.

McCowan shifted on the edge of Kendrick's cot, reaching up to touch his own nose with one hand. The motion of his fingers towards his face became slower, almost halted; time slowed for Kendrick, at least from his own perspective. Everything around him – the pores of McCowan's face, even the sound of his heart-beat – jumped into sudden and powerful relief.

Then, in a blink, everything returned to normal.

"I'm sure. Just listen. Can you hear it? Isn't it beautiful?"

Kendrick listened hard, hearing the endless cascade of energy around them, throughout the structure of the Maze. Sometimes, when he looked at the other surviving Labrats – the nickname that in time they had come to choose for themselves – he almost didn't see their flesh. He saw another layer below that, a buzzing network of energy: partly biological, partly machine, each one of them reduced to an engineering schematic outlined in ruby red and flashing white.

Sieracki and his people clearly realized that something was up. Guards arrived several times over those next few days, pulling security systems and spycams apart and replacing them with new equipment. These guards seemed even more brusque, their weapons always held at the ready.

Kendrick looked over at Buddy, and McCowan, who was sitting nearby, registering the look in their eyes, knowing that they were thinking the same thing. There had to be some way out, some way to escape.

Kendrick woke in a panic, unable to see anything at all. He tried to twist his head but found that it was impossible. Something rough was chafing against his nose and cheeks.

He attempted to lift one arm but felt as if he'd sunk to the bottom of the ocean, a thousand tons of water pressing down on him. Then he felt a hand grab his wrist, pushing it back down again. Someone was strapping him tight.

Faint light began to show through the narrow space between his blindfold and the bridge of his nose. They were wheeling him somewhere else. He could hear the wheels squeaking and rattling over hard concrete, doors clanging noisily as they passed through.

And then, suddenly, Kendrick realized that he'd been taken

through the Dissection Door. Dread filled his soul, and even though he opened his mouth to scream his strength deserted him so completely that he could muster little more than a faint moan, which was lost in the echoing din of the corridor down which he was being transported.

After twenty minutes they finally stopped. Nightmare scenarios flooded his mind. *They've drugged me.* They were going to leave him here, strapped to this pallet, to starve and die; or else they were going to take him apart, stripping muscle and flesh from his bones without the benefit of anaesthetic.

A long time passed during which Kendrick could hear other moans and faint cries around him. In the dark and the cold any sense of time slipped away from him.

After an eternity he heard a faint metallic *click* – and his bindings were suddenly loose. He reached up, pulled away his blindfold, and stared into a blackness so thick that he imagined he could reach out and grab fistfuls of it from the air.

He lifted a hand to his face, and at first he couldn't see anything. After several seconds, however, he could see a faint outline becoming gradually more distinct. In time, his fingers became pale shadows against the pitch dark.

A shuffling sound of movement nearby. Again Kendrick heard distressed voices calling to each other. Beyond his own hand he began to discern other faint shapes, so close to being lost amid the blackness that at first he believed he was imagining them. They gradually resolved themselves into the outlines of men and women stumbling around him.

He looked up and recognized the familiar concrete covered by steel piping that characterized the Maze – barely visible but with a ghostly monotone translucence, like everything else he could just about see.

It took a little while for Kendrick to really grasp that he could actually see in the dark.

He made out other wheeled cots around him. They had been lined up on one side of a long, wide corridor. One or two of the prisoners still lay unconscious, others rose from their cots to stare blindly around them, calling out names that Kendrick didn't recognize.

It was cold, very cold, as Kendrick stood upright, squinting at those whose faces he could see, their faces ghostly in the non-light. He was looking for Buddy, or for any familiar face among the scores moving around aimlessly in the darkness.

"Excuse me?" A woman's voice, faltering and unsure. She put one hand out to him, clearly able to see as well as he could. "I'm trying to find someone."

"I don't know where we are," Kendrick replied. "I don't know who any of you are."

"I was in Ward Seventeen. Where are we? Where are the guards?"

Kendrick glanced at her. Her features were a luminous semi-blur. "*I* was in Ward Seventeen, but I don't remember you. I don't remember any women there."

She shook her head. "Each Ward is split into two sections – didn't you know that? One for the men, one for the women."

"Oh, right." The fact of their segregation had always struck him as oddly prudish. "The guards have gone. I think it's just us Labrats."

"Labrats?"

Kendrick shrugged. "It's a nickname someone came up with."

"Look, I don't know even which Ward my brother was sent to. I need to know if he's here somewhere. He . . ." She hesitated. "I just need to find him."

"What was his name?"

"Robert. Robert Vincenzo." The woman paused and then added, "I'm Caroline Vincenzo."

Kendrick stared at her. "Robert Vincenzo?"

Her eyes, two blurred dark circles, widened. "You know him? I can tell from the way you said that. Just tell me!"

"Yes," Kendrick admitted.

"He's dead, isn't he?" she said, her voice toneless.

155

"I don't know." How to say it? "One day he was there, the next . . ." He shrugged again. "I don't really know. I'm sorry."

She nodded wordlessly and looked away.

Kendrick opened his mouth to tell her about Robert's apparent escape, and then closed it again. Now wasn't the time or the place. First, they had to find out what was going on here.

They joined a crowd of several dozen that had formed nearby. Some people were laughing, others crying, just happy and relieved to have found familiar faces or voices. However, it became clear to Kendrick as he began to explore the endless corridor in which they found themselves that the ability to navigate in this pitch dark was limited to just a few among them. With deep relief he spotted Buddy standing nearby, with McCowan and a few other people he knew. *I should be with them*, Kendrick decided.

He turned to Caroline and smiled gently. "We've all of us lost friends and relations. You're not alone."

"But it's more than that. I *knew*," she insisted. "When I woke up here I thought maybe I was wrong, but somehow I knew – you understand what I mean? It's not like something you can explain. You just *know*." She shook her head. "So stupid."

Her face was no longer quite so blurred, although everything around Kendrick retained, to his perceptions, a certain ghostly quality. The way she held herself suggested a well-honed body, someone who might have once been a soldier herself, or perhaps a bodyguard.

"Our parents aren't around any more, so I always had to look out for him. He . . ." Kendrick could picture the course that Caroline's thoughts were taking. She believed Robert was dead, and therefore – in her mind – she had failed him. Kendrick felt a stab of sympathy.

A shout carried above the growing tumult of voices and he looked around. Kendrick could make out men and women weeping: others were kneeling on the hard concrete, hands clasped together, as barely audible prayers spilled from their mouths.

Either they were asking for salvation or giving thanks that they were free of the Wards.

Kendrick shrugged apologetically at Caroline and steered a course towards Buddy. In his heart he knew that Sieracki would never simply let them go, even if the guards never returned.

20 October 2096
Edinburgh

Once back in Edinburgh, Kendrick tried to call Caroline, leaving several messages. She didn't reply and he was not even sure what he would say to her anyway. Whatever brief truce they'd enjoyed after he'd escaped from Hardenbrooke's clinic was clearly over.

But right now what concerned him most was the message that arrived in his wand during the flight home. He had gazed at the words for many minutes before looking away from the tiny screen. The message consisted of three words in an unadorned ASCII textfile:

AWE TEPEE PILOT

Then Kendrick made arrangements to pick up a hired car the next morning.

21 October 2096
En route to Loch Awe

Kendrick heard the car parking itself outside his flat in the early morning hours. He stepped outside and gazed up into a red-tinged pre-dawn sky. The jet lag from his long hours of flight had sent his sleep cycle spinning, but he didn't feel he could afford to rest more than was strictly necessary.

A strong breeze whipped down the winding streets as his vehicle navigated its way through the ancient city. Kendrick kept a window open, for once enjoying the lash of wind and freezing rain. It made for a genuinely pleasant change after the burning heat of Cambodia.

Kendrick had done a lot of soul-searching in the hours since his return, even filling himself with doubt over his prompt refusal of Draeger's offer. But there were hundreds of other Labrats scattered around the globe who could benefit from the treatment, some of them perhaps already at death's door. Draeger using his supposed solution to every Labrat's problems as nothing more than a bargaining tool was the basest kind of bribery. Kendrick breathed deeply, pushing the anger away from him. Instead he watched the morning light spill over distant mountain peaks.

Three words. And they could only have come from the one living person whom Kendrick had ever felt he could really trust.

The car drove on, leaving the city far behind. Grey rain clouds skirted the horizon, spreading out across a sodden landscape of hills and valleys. Kendrick listened to the news as he went. Mostly they talked about the continuing spread of Asian Rot, as close now as the fields of southern Spain, and the source of frantic headlines for the past few weeks. After a while he passed through a damp-looking Falkirk before heading north to Stirling, and then on to Loch Awe.

An hour and a half after Kendrick had left Edinburgh, brilliant sunlight finally split the rain clouds wide, sending God-sized fingers of radiance down onto the waters of the Loch and the surrounding Braes.

The rain still pelted down sporadically as he passed along the shores of the Loch. Now he assumed manual control – and almost missed the old hotel building as it loomed out of bushes of wild heather, with dense thickets of oak trees lining the path to the retreat.

Kendrick let the car park itself in the driveway to the sound of gravel spitting under its wheels. Before him was a two-storey building of granite. Bought by a wealthy Buddhist a little over a century before, since then it had become a dedicated retreat, although Kendrick had never once seen an orange robe during his visits. He walked up to the entrance and passed through the unlocked front door, finding himself in a wide hallway, a bare pine floor under his feet. At first glance it looked as though little had changed during the last several years.

"Hello, can I help you?" A young woman with a crew-cut approached Kendrick from an adjacent room. To one side he could see people sitting in a separate dining area, talking and drinking tea. He didn't recognize the woman, but then, the kind of long-term residents who benefited most from this retreat didn't usually spend much time inside the main building.

Kendrick looked over her shoulder towards the gardens. The parkland that extended toward the hills behind the retreat was visible through tall veranda doors at the far end of the hallway.

"Yeah, I'm looking for Buddy. Buddy Juarez." The young woman looked blank. "Maybe you haven't been here that long?" he suggested. "He comes up here sometimes, when he wants to get away."

Her expression grew slightly wary. "Was he expecting you? Some of the people here don't like to be disturbed."

"It's okay, Sally." Kendrick turned to find himself facing an elderly man dressed in slacks and an open-necked shirt. A name came to him: Hamilton.

"I remember you." Hamilton nodded. "Lukas, isn't it?"

"It is," Kendrick replied, recognizing one of his former aliases. "Buddy's around, is he?"

"Yes." Hamilton studied him. "He turned up just yesterday – rather unexpected, I'm afraid. I do hope everything's all right for him?"

Kendrick spread his hands. "I'm sure everything's fine, Mr Hamilton. I know how much he's gained from visits here over the years. We made arrangements to get together while I myself was in the area." Kendrick beamed, trying to look friendly. "Is that okay?"

"Yes, I suppose it is," Hamilton replied after a lengthy pause.

"But please remember that we have to respect the wishes of all our other residents."

"Thanks, I appreciate that." As Kendrick moved towards the veranda doors and the path beyond, he could feel Hamilton's suspicious stare burning into his back with every step he took.

Leaving the building behind him, he began climbing up the increasingly steep slope. Just beyond a low drystone wall stood an ashram with a curved roof of corrugated iron, a trellis of ivy growing up one side of it. The whole institution radiated a certain peace, but Kendrick had never derived anything like as much pleasure from it as Buddy did. Somehow he found he always missed the hustle and bustle of busy city streets.

A couple of teenagers were wrestling heavy water-smoothed stones into place, building a path from the ashram itself to a nearby stream that ran down into the Loch – from whose shore they'd presumably lugged the stones. Several years before, Kendrick had spent a long weekend helping Buddy and some other survivors of the Maze to build a similar path at the opposite side of the house. That had been just after the Wilber Trials at a time when Kendrick had felt the very real need to work some things out in his head. He hadn't realized until then how much the simple labour involved in building a path could distract him from his problems, how much basic fulfilment and satisfaction it could bring him.

But in the end it had not been enough. After only a couple of days he'd started to become bored, itching to get back to civilization. Buddy, however, had stayed on there for a year or two, with Kendrick paying him sporadic visits once he'd permanently relocated himself to Edinburgh. To some extent, the paths of their lives had since diverged.

But there was still that connection: the Maze.

It happened sometimes with people who'd survived major disasters together. They clung to each other, sometimes keeping in contact for the rest of their lives. Kendrick could understand that easily.

For a long time it'd been that way with Caroline, and with Buddy. There'd been others, but he'd seen too many of them die as their augments turned against them, destroying them from the inside out. He'd given up going to funerals at which half a dozen Labrats watched each other from either side of a grave, wondering which of them would be next to go.

Kendrick headed past the ashram, with a nod to the path-builders. He continued upwards, through a landscape broken by copses and isolated patches of woodland. Smoke curled up from several points among the trees.

Letting his memory guide him, he headed for one copse in particular. Kendrick had somehow never quite managed to get used to the idea of an ex-US Navy pilot living in a tepee.

Buddy was sitting outside the tent, wearing a ragged pair of dungarees over a woollen sweater, a couple of days' worth of stubble clinging to his cheeks. He looked thinner than Kendrick remembered from the last time he'd seen him, more than three years before. He had a cooking fire going in a shallow pit surrounded by pebbles, and was using a plastic spatula to prod at the contents of a tin pan balanced on a wire frame arching over the flames.

Buddy looked up and squinted at him. "So I guess you got my message. I was worried in case it might have been a little obscure."

"I'm not the only one who could have figured it out, you realize."

Buddy grinned back. "I don't see them coming here. Remember how long I ended up here for, after the Maze?"

Kendrick nodded. "Couple of years?"

"You thought I was some kind of lunatic for staying here so long." Buddy picked up a plastic bowl from where it had been sitting on the grass. He lifted the pan from the fire, covering its handle first with a dish towel. "I'm glad you came. How did things go with Draeger?"

Kendrick reeled back. "How the hell did you know about that?"

Buddy shrugged. "I keep my ear to the ground."

"You mean Erik Whitsett wasn't the only one spying on me?"

Some of the light faded from Buddy's eyes. "Erik never got back in touch, Kendrick. What happened?"

"Somebody killed him, is what happened. We met, we talked – and somebody shot him."

Buddy looked shocked. Kendrick explained what had happened in more detail.

"Los Muertos," Buddy muttered after a pause. "They've been targeting us."

"Erik mentioned something to that effect."

Buddy looked like he was thinking hard. "I asked you how things went with Draeger. I need you to tell me straight out: are you working for him?"

Kendrick laughed. "Are you serious? Who do you think you're talking to?"

"People do change."

"But not that much."

"All right, so how do you explain your meeting with him?"

"I never had the chance to speak with him face to face before. I just wanted to see what he was like, see what he had to say to me. Wouldn't *you* want to be able to do that?"

"Sure. And?"

"He tried to bribe me with some miracle cure."

Buddy smiled wryly. "There is no cure for what we have."

"That's pretty much what I said to him."

"Yet you believe him? Is that what you're saying?"

Kendrick hesitated. "He wanted something out of me, it's true, but he wasn't lying. He wants people to know how brilliant he is – it's one of his flaws. So, yes, I'm inclined to believe him. I've also been getting some treatments myself, which gives me a serious chance of staying alive longer than without them. That lends a lot of credence to what he told me."

"A cure." Buddy nodded slowly. "That would be quite something."

"If it's true, it represents a real chance for all of us." Kendrick knelt on the damp grass and looked across at him.

"How many other people have been offered miracle cures?" Buddy asked. "Ways of turning back the clock and fixing us?"

Kendrick grinned. "Pretty much as many people as have died testing them out."

"Exactly," said Buddy, stabbing the empty spatula in his direction. "So forgive me if I don't necessarily share your enthusiasm. And how much did Erik tell you before he died?"

"He talked about the Bright – and about the things we witnessed when Sieracki isolated the four of us, back in the Maze."

Buddy's smile became grim. "How well I remember that. Anything else?"

"He told me you had some damn-fool plan to go to the *Archimedes*."

Buddy laughed, rocking back on his haunches. "Oh, man, the look on your face. So what did you make of that?"

"Well, I said he was crazy – and that you were crazy. But, after Erik was killed, I got the impression that somebody was taking it all very seriously. Max Draeger's also entirely aware of your intentions."

Buddy shrugged. "If Los Muertos know about us, then Draeger figuring certain things out is no surprise. But what we've got planned will be over before he can do anything to stop or hinder us."

"Look, there was a bomb incident in a bar. And someone else tried to kidnap me. Whatever's going on, you clearly know a lot more than I do."

Buddy pursed his lips, then started dishing food onto a paper plate. "Hungry?" he asked.

"Not particularly."

Buddy shrugged, and continued talking between mouthfuls. "It's not like I've been hiding anything from you. In fact, I've been trying to draw you in. I understand exactly why you've been keeping out of sight, but it made it harder to track you down."

"Unfortunately, that doesn't seem a problem for anyone else."

"Yeah, well . . . once I realized something might have happened to Erik I figured I'd better take care of things myself. A lot's been happening since you and I last saw each other. Four people don't regularly share the same nightmare unless there's something particular going on, right?"

"If you're referring to Sieracki's experiment, then, granted, we shared something. But it was all in our own heads. There was nothing objectively real about it."

"No, what we saw was real. The Bright are real."

"The Bright were from Robert's deranged—"

"For Christ's sake!" Buddy dropped the plate onto the grass and threw up his hands in the air. "Will you *listen* to yourself? What is it about all this that you can't accept? *You* were the one who told me the most about the Bright, before Robert died and—"

"Don't say it," Kendrick interrupted quickly.

"Look, I'm sorry. But it's just—"

"Here's a question back at you. When did your augmentations turn rogue?"

Buddy looked impressed. "What makes you think they have?"

"I found some medical records with all our names on them. They told me everything I needed to know. So tell me when."

"Round about the same time as you, probably. Anyone who got out of Ward Seventeen who hadn't yet developed rogue augments went on to develop them between nine and twelve months ago. We're all in the same fix. That's just one more reason why we all have to work together."

Buddy stood up to stretch his legs. "Okay, I brought some stuff I wanted to show you. It's all back in the tent, so care to join me?"

He turned away, ducking down to crawl into the tent's interior. Kendrick hesitated a moment, then followed.

Although it was based around an ancient design, the tepee had been made from modern heat-absorbing artificial fibres. There was enough room inside for both men to stand, and the supporting struts were fashioned from super-light alloy. Rather than living by basic means, Buddy had been able to spend his time here at the retreat in relative comfort while still maintaining the near-complete isolation he'd once craved.

Noise and activity covered the interior walls, eepsheets and printouts having been hastily taped onto any available surface. Kendrick noticed that the London *Times* was tacked up near his head, its real-time default set to its technology pages.

Kendrick saw mostly pictures and videos of the *Archimedes* orbital. One image looped endlessly, a computer animation very similar to the one he had found in Caroline's working files.

He studied some of the printouts, most of which were related to the LA Nuke, the Wilber Trials – anything that tied in to the history of the Labrats. If he hadn't known better, or hadn't seen some of the things he'd seen over the past several days, he would have thought that this was the work of an obsessive or a madman.

"I said I wanted to show you something. Look at this." Buddy carefully detached one eepsheet from the tent's inner wall. The 'sheet was tuned in to what appeared to be a journal.

"This is a multi-author feed that collates information relating to the space industry," Buddy explained. "A lot, but not all of it, consists of technical and safety issues."

Kendrick took the eepsheet and flicked through its summary page. "What am I supposed to be looking for here?"

"There's something happening near the *Archimedes*. A spatial anomaly that's got half the physicists in the world spinning on their heads."

"Meaning what?"

"Look – for Draeger, building the *Archimedes* was an important step on the road to proving the reality of the Omega Point. You're an expert on Draeger, so you know the theory."

The idea was more than a century old. It suggested that since intelligent life always sought to preserve itself, then, faced with the ultimate extinction – the final collapse of the universe and the end of time – that intelligence would seek to preserve itself *indefinitely*, using some unimaginable super-science of the most distant possible future. The result would be a subjective virtual environment, which, the theory argued, would be effectively indistinguishable from Heaven.

Kendrick saw the gleam in Buddy's eye and shook his head violently. "Oh, come *on*. The Omega Point theory just doesn't wash. You'd have to make a lot of prior assumptions for it to even begin to hold water."

Buddy made a dismissive gesture. "Look, what I'm saying is, if Draeger built the *Archimedes* primarily so that the nanite computer networks up there could try and find God for him – well, I'm saying they achieved it. Or they found *something*, that's for sure."

Kendrick couldn't keep the look of scepticism off his face. "Where's the proof?"

"You saw the evidence." Buddy tapped the side of his head. "The visions. The *Archimedes*."

"Or maybe there's something hard-wired into our augs. Something triggering a collective hallucination."

"C'mon, Kendrick, that's grasping at straws."

"Look, maybe there is something in this shared-experience thing. Maybe it's something like what happened to the four of us in the Maze, but if that's the case I'm only getting the thirty-second preview. Whatever the rest of you have been seeing, Erik made it clear that it was a lot more than I'd seen."

"Which would explain why you haven't been in touch. If you had, you'd—"

"I'd know. Sure. Erik said the same thing." Kendrick rubbed at his face. "Fine, so you're going to the *Archimedes*. How? And what are you going to do when you get there?"

"The Bright is the collective term by which the AI nanite communities on board the *Archimedes* refer to themselves, right? The Bright found the Omega . . . and they also found us."

"Buddy, this is utterly crazy."

"Listen to me. If you didn't see what the rest of us saw, then I'll tell you what we were shown. The Bright have learned a lot from the Omega. The anomaly I mentioned is a wormhole that they've constructed, a gateway to the end of time."

Kendrick began to snigger. "Yeah? So what would they do with that?"

"The Bright were designed to be curious. Every answer they could possibly desire is there at the end of time, in the Omega. So why not go straight to the source?"

"This is too much, Buddy. I don't know how to take it in. Do you know how ludicrous this sounds? A wormhole? What kind of wormhole?"

"There's strong evidence that the Bright have figured out a way to access zero-point energy. You know what that is, right?"

"Sure, it's getting something out of nothing, energy out of empty space." Physicists had long theorized that even within cold, empty vacuum vast unbounded energy resources existed on the quantum scale, powering the constant generation of short-lived virtual particles in a seething, invisible maelstrom of creation. Finding a way to tap directly into those resources was an objective that physicists had been hunting for decades.

"Well, you'd need nearly infinite energy to keep a wormhole indefinitely open, in order to cause the kind of fluctuations that have been observed up there. It's hardly surprising that Los Muertos are so concerned about preventing us getting to the *Archimedes*. If they could get their hands on energy resources like that they could hold the whole world to ransom – if they wanted. They don't want any of us in the way."

A radiant smile spread across Buddy's features, and Kendrick was reminded of a supplicant throwing down his crutches at the feet of a healing saint. "But Los Muertos we can deal with. What matters is that the Bright have invited us to go along with them. To them, we're all the same: you, me and anyone else who survived Ward Seventeen."

*

Kendrick returned to Edinburgh and tried again to contact Caroline, without success. In the end he let himself into her flat a second time – and found it wrecked.

Either someone had searched it messily or there'd been a struggle there. He sat in Caroline's living room, with the moonlight streaming through her windowscreen, painting pale stripes across broken furniture and a dent in one wall where it looked as though a body had impacted hard. He tried to remember that Caroline was the kind of woman who knew how to look after herself. For an hour or so Kendrick sat on her couch and stared numbly at the wreckage.

In the end he called Buddy and told him what he'd found.

"Shit." Then a long-drawn-out silence. "I'm sorry, Kendrick. Do you need me there?"

"No, I don't know if that would make any difference. I'm going to ask some questions, see what I can find out."

"Look, I can get over there in a couple of hours—"

"It's fine."

"You're going to look for her, aren't you?"

"I'll let you know how it goes. So stay in touch."

"Yeah, sure. Be careful. Be *very* careful."

Kendrick broke the connection and stared around Caroline's ruined apartment, lost in thought.

Apart from himself, who would have known where Caroline lived? Only Malky, unless she had made new friends over the past year. An image of Malky's dead eyes flashed through his thoughts.

It was hard to accept what Buddy had told him about the *Archimedes*, but what he'd said about zero-point energy made some sense of both Draeger's and Los Muertos' actions. Zero-point energy was a prize with dangerously high stakes, and the Labrats were apparently caught right in the middle.

And then there was Hardenbrooke, who was clearly playing his own extremely dangerous game, setting each party off against the other – and presumably being paid by both without the other realizing.

Hardenbrooke? Kendrick stared into the distance, knowing that he had only one real option left. If there was even the slightest chance that the medic had been involved with or knew something about Caroline's disappearance, Kendrick had to find him.

22 October 2096
Edinburgh

"Some mess, eh, Kendrick?" McCowan's ghost sat beside him in the rain.

"Tell me I'm not crazy," Kendrick replied. "Tell me if any of this is real."

"Don't talk shite."

Kendrick had only gradually become aware of McCowan sitting beside him on the park bench. In Caroline's flat he'd felt another wave of nausea wash through him so he had made his way outside, desperately wanting to breathe fresh air and find somewhere to wait until the feeling of disorientation passed. He'd stopped at a stretch of green running parallel to the road into Leith when the nausea had become particularly bad.

"Then tell me something useful. Like how to find Caroline." As Kendrick spoke, the world around them began to move very slowly, as if caught in some viscous liquid. A dog galloped across a street nearby in languid slow motion.

"I can stretch out our subjective time together this way," McCowan told him. "Gives us longer to talk. But I can't help you with Caroline, Kendrick. I'm sorry."

"Why can't you?"

"Look, out of all the others who survived Ward Seventeen, you're the only one I'm still in contact with. So, I don't know anything about what's happened to Caroline. You'll have to find that out for yourself."

"But why are you only in contact with me?"

"Look, the treatments you received from Hardenbrooke had the unexpected side effect of blocking the signal coming from Robert . . . coming from the *Archimedes*."

"What the hell?" Kendrick squinted at him. "Robert on the *Archimedes*?"

"Shut up and bear with me. Hardenbrooke got your augments under control, and that had the added side effect of blocking Robert – mostly. So you only got snatches, little bits of what Buddy and the rest received. At the same time, Robert was blocking *me*, preventing me from communicating with you, or indeed with any other of the Ward Seventeen Labrats."

McCowan held up one finger. "Except Hardenbrooke's treatments, by blocking Robert, somehow gave me the opportunity at least to reach *you*, if nobody else. It means that I can speak to you, but *only* you, for just seconds at a time."

"But why wouldn't Robert want you contacting me?"

McCowan looked at him sharply. "He's insane – or don't you remember what happened between the two of you? It's hardly surprising that he bears you no goodwill."

"I haven't seen Robert: no dreams, visitations, whatever it is the others got."

McCowan had a sad look on his face. "Ken, Ken," he said with a sigh. "You *have* seen him, plenty of times. And as for where he is, well, part of him is down here, and part of him is up there on the *Archimedes*. You'll be seeing more of him, once your augments learn to fully circumvent Hardenbrooke's treatments. Robert is going to have less trouble getting through to you now, which means, in turn, that it'll be harder for *me* to reach you."

A signal coming from the *Archimedes*? Knowing that made it easier, more real, more objective. "So why can't you just – I don't know – transmit yourself to the station or something, if that's presumably how Robert got there?

McCowan made an exasperated sound. "I've tried and failed every time, thanks to that son of a bitch. I can't get there on my own. And as long as Robert's the only human mind directly inter-facing with the Bright I can't be that sure the wormhole to the Omega is ever going to open."

A spasm of pain shot through Kendrick's skull and he grabbed his head, gasping at the suddenness of it. McCowan was right, though: it wasn't as bad as previously.

Not quite.

"I don't give a shit about Robert. What about Caroline, for Christ's sake? What the hell about her?"

"Find her if you can but, whatever you do, I need you to get to the Maze. If you can do that, I can give you all the answers you've been looking for. But you need to hurry."

"The Maze?" Kendrick screamed through a storm of agony. "Are you fucking *insane*?"

Another intense flash of pain. Any lingering illusion of reality McCowan had possessed abruptly disappeared as his seated figure twisted into a sudden smear of colour before vanishing entirely.

Kendrick moaned as the full weight of the seizure came upon him. He crumpled to the grass under his feet.

The Maze? Why would McCowan want him there? And where exactly *was* he—

—Unless, in some way, he was still down there. That revelation hit Kendrick like a ton of bricks.

He looked back up and the city around him was gone.

He pushed himself up onto his knees. That same tiny figure came buzzing towards him on azure wings, its passage through the long-stalked grass sending puffs of pollen floating into the air.

"I know you," Kendrick said, as the creature hovered quite close to him, only a metre or so away. In response, the tiny lips twisted up in a cruel smile. Laughter fell from its mouth, a tinkling half-crazed sound.

"I know you!" it cried. "I know you! I know you!"

McCowan had been right. On some deep level, Kendrick had known from the start but now he couldn't avoid the truth any longer. The creature had Robert's face. And it buzzed around him on silken wings, its laughter chiming in his ears.

Then, as suddenly as he had left it, he was back in a damp park in Edinburgh, his fingers digging spasmodically into the hard turf beneath him.

It didn't take long for Draeger to show his hand.

As Kendrick headed for home, turning down a quiet side street leading towards Leith Walk, he caught sight of an expensive-looking limousine driving towards him at speed. It braked hard and a door swung open in front of him even before it had come to a halt. Kendrick stepped back, alarmed.

He'd barely registered the two men heading his way on the opposite side of the street. They stepped quickly towards him, pulling pistols from their jacket pockets and aiming them at his head. He glanced around and realized, to his chagrin, that there was no one else to be seen. They must have deliberately waited until they were sure there'd be no witnesses.

Smeby stepped out from the limousine and studied Kendrick with an expression of mild amusement. Then he gestured to the two gunmen, who dragged Kendrick forward and bundled him into the rear of the vehicle.

Another car slipped by and kept on going. Kendrick found his voice and yelled out, hoping to attract someone's attention. His voice sounded dull and flat inside the limousine.

Then he felt the muzzle of a gun pressed against his neck and he grew still.

"These weapons are extremely quiet." Smeby leant over from a front seat. "Nobody would hear it."

The gunmen sat on either side of Kendrick. "There's no point in killing me," he said.

"I wasn't talking about killing you," Smeby replied. "I was talking about blowing your kneecaps off."

Kendrick tried not to show his fear. "You could have given me a call if you wanted to see me this badly."

"If we'd asked you to come to the Arlington to meet with us, would you really have come?"

No, thought Kendrick, looking away.

The limousine drove into an underground parking area beneath the hotel. Kendrick was dismayed to see that there was no one else around here either, no one to witness what was happening to him. The gunmen marched him to an elevator, keeping a firm grip on each of his shoulders. Their guns were pressed up against his head and neck respectively. Then they rode up in silence, along with Smeby, and a few moments later were back in the same suite as before.

Kendrick wasn't in the least surprised to see Max Draeger waiting there for him. Candice stood by the window, dressed in a dark wool trouser suit.

"Mr Gallmon," said Draeger. "I'm not going to waste any time before getting to the point. You're here simply for your own protection."

Kendrick gaped at him. "What?"

"Caroline Vincenzo has been snatched in order to persuade you to do as Los Muertos wish. I can't allow that to happen."

"Fuck you."

Draeger nodded to Smeby. The two gunmen dragged Kendrick backwards, forcing him awkwardly into a seat, still aiming their pistol at him. Smeby stepped forward and punched Kendrick, hard, in the stomach.

"Hardenbrooke – tell me about him. Everything you haven't said already."

Kendrick sucked in air, swallowed and shook his head. "What happened to the friendly style of chat we had out there in the jungle?"

Draeger stepped forward, his expression intense. "There isn't the time for niceties any more. I could shoot you full of drugs that would have you telling me all I want to know, but I'd rather let you tell me for yourself. It's your choice."

"For Christ's sake, he hasn't said *anything* to me."

Draeger shook his head. "I don't think you understand the danger you're in, Mr Gallmon. There are agents of Los Muertos already in this city, and I might be the only friend you have."

"I don't find that likely." Kendrick's hands were clammy with sweat. A dull nausea throbbed in the pit of his stomach and in the back of his throat.

Draeger stepped a little closer. "I thought you might have connections with Los Muertos."

Kendrick laughed, a harsh, nervous bark. "Are you fucking crazy?"

"They don't have your best interests at heart."

"And you do?"

"Los Muertos merely want to kill you. They don't offer you something in return for information."

"All right," said Kendrick. "How about getting these two away from me?"

Draeger cocked his head. "You're telling me that you're prepared to cooperate? Fully?"

"Fully, yes."

Draeger studied Kendrick coolly for what felt like a long time. "If you're lying, my employees are going to hurt you very, very badly. You won't be in any condition to walk, let alone enjoy a space flight. I want you to remember that before we continue."

"I understand that. I just . . . I don't want what the others want."

Kendrick knew that he could never bring himself to tell Draeger anything. But buying time was all he could think of. *There has to be a way out of here.*

It was an effort to meet Draeger's gaze, but after a few moments the other man's attention shifted to the two gunmen. Kendrick heard them step away from him.

"Wait downstairs," Draeger told them.

"Sir." Smeby stepped forward, "I'm not sure—"

"Do what you're told, Marlin. My rules."

"Sir, I must *seriously* fucking protest—"

Draeger snapped him a look, and Smeby shut up and stepped back. But Kendrick registered the cold anger in the ex-mercenary's face.

Kendrick was seated facing towards the windows, and the door was behind him. He took careful note of where everyone was positioned in the room. Draeger himself stood near the middle of the room; Candice and Smeby stood at almost opposite ends of it, facing towards him.

He heard the door *snick* shut as the gunmen departed.

"I went looking for Caroline," Kendrick told Draeger, "and found that somebody had taken her out of her home by force. You're saying that was Los Muertos?"

Draeger nodded. "I suspect the only reason they have abducted her is to try and lure *you* into some idiot attempt at rescuing her."

"Look, I've already seen one other Labrat die in the past couple of days, and do you know who I blame? You. None of this would be happening if it hadn't been for you."

"Under the circumstances, the only reasonable precaution is to have you return to Angkor Wat with us and work with us there from a safe base of operations."

Kendrick nodded carefully and stood up. Smeby's gaze followed him, but he did not move. "I guess that's it, then," Kendrick said. "You're sure this is the best way?"

"I'm glad you've decided to cooperate." Draeger cast him an appraising look.

"I was . . . I . . ." Kendrick bent over, gripping the side of his head and gritting his teeth. "Oh fuck, no," he gasped.

"What is it?" asked Draeger. Kendrick could hear the suspicion in his voice.

"Seizure," said Kendrick. "Help me. I can't . . ." He sagged, his knees touching the floor, then let out a bellow of animal pain and covered his face with his hands.

"Get him up," he heard Draeger say.

Kendrick glanced between his fingers to see Smeby approach, reaching towards Kendrick's shoulder to yank him back upright.

Through the windows, Kendrick briefly saw that the earlier rain had given way to harsh, bleak sunlight.

He moved with unnatural speed, stabbing upwards with the fingers of one hand held rigid, aiming for Smeby's throat. Smeby saw it coming but not soon enough. Kendrick caught him under the chin and the other man stumbled back against a coffee table.

Smeby yelled in anger and pain as he hit the floor. A coffee urn that had been resting on the table toppled over onto the carpet. Kendrick moved quickly, aiming a vicious kick at Smeby's head. Smeby gave a brief *uk* sound and lay still.

Kendrick himself sprawled as something hard slammed into his back. As he hit the floor he rolled, knowing instantly that his attacker was Candice. She followed his movements, hammering at him with her fists. As she caught him on the jaw, his teeth clicked together and he tasted blood.

He managed to block her next punch by slamming a foot into her stomach, but she twisted away and pulled herself upright with blinding speed. *Augmented too.*

Kendrick noticed Draeger speaking quietly into his databand. What followed happened so fast that Kendrick was still remembering lost fragments of it over the next several hours.

While he'd been looking towards Draeger Candice had darted towards him before he could get up again. Grabbing his head, she dug her thumbs and fingers into his eyes.

Kendrick screamed and struggled as she wrapped him in a deadly embrace, pinning his arms to his sides and pressing him down with a knee in his back. He squirmed desperately, but she held him in a vice-like grip. Panic drove him to lash backwards with his foot.

The kick caught her on one shin, and she lost her footing, her grip loosening. Kendrick pulled himself free and stumbled towards the window just as Draeger's gunmen crashed into the room, weapons drawn. One took aim and Kendrick ducked to the side, hitting the ground rolling once more as the glass behind him exploded outwards.

Kendrick yanked himself up again, waiting for the bullets, catching a glimpse through the shattered window of the street several storeys below.

Panicking, he turned, desperate for some escape route that he knew wasn't there. Just then, Candice launched herself at him again with renewed fury. The force of impact drove him backwards against a weakened pane that had not yet shattered. In that same instant, which seemed to last for ever, Kendrick felt the glass give way. Sky and concrete tumbled past his vision.

Free fall was followed by a sudden, jarring impact like nothing he had ever imagined, as if some giant had gone walking across the Earth and caught him under its heel. In that moment he felt something beyond pain.

Several seconds passed before Kendrick realized that he was still alive. But the world felt remote and distant, like a cinematic projection on the inside of his skull.

An instant later he snapped to, re-emerging into a universe of noise and confusion. The streets of Edinburgh revolved around him in a drunken whirl. He managed to sit up, his mouth full of blood. He coughed and spat, and then looked down.

Kendrick and Candice had landed together on the roof of a parked car, their joint impact bending its roof badly out of shape. The air around them was filled with the cacophony of its alarm.

I should be dead, he realized. But Kendrick was a Labrat, which had made just enough difference.

He'd obviously landed on top of Candice, who had softened his landing. Her back was broken and her neck was twisted at a sickening angle. He heaved himself off the wreckage, collapsing into a heap at the roadside.

Already the initial shock was wearing off. Kendrick glanced up shakily at the smashed window of the hotel suite. It looked a very long way up. Cars had screeched to a halt all around him, as their computer brains registered an accident of some kind.

He lurched to his feet like a drunkard, distantly aware of people nearby standing and watching him, their expressions stunned and disbelieving.

One man came towards him but Kendrick waved him away. Then a woman tried to take his arm. He was scarcely aware that she was advising him to remain still before he injured himself any further.

He pushed her away, but not too roughly, assuring her that he felt all right. Somehow he managed to make his way to the other side of the road, then slowly worked his way down the street and away from the Arlington's entrance.

Limping badly at first, after thirty seconds or so he began to pick up speed. Soon he was startled to realize that he was already a couple of blocks from the hotel.

Somewhere in the distance he heard sirens. A lot of people must have seen him. They would be able to describe him and ulti-mately identify him.

To his own amazement, Kendrick managed to start running.

Kendrick waited until it was dark again, nursing coffee after coffee in the back of a small café buried in an ancient, twisting lane near Cockburn Street. Freezing rain sleeted down outside and the shoulders of passers-by beyond the glass were bowed under the arctic wind blowing westwards. Every now and then he tapped through an eepsheet that had been abandoned at the table he'd taken, one near the back amid plenty of shadows. He used it to scan science sites and article databases concerning zero-point energy, noting that a lot of the information provided led back to research programmes instigated by Draeger's various subsidiary companies.

To Kendrick's considerable surprise nothing had yet appeared about the recent incident at the hotel. He briefly toyed with the idea that Draeger had the means to suppress news reports, then wondered when he'd become so paranoid.

It felt appropriate to be waiting there as lightning flickered beyond the rooftops, to be waiting for the storm to approach and swallow the city in its fury. Eventually the café had to close, and then Kendrick wandered the darkened streets, collar up, head down. Icy sleet turned the skin of his face red with cold.

Now he had more than enough time to think. He needed to find a way out of the city. But, whatever happened, he owed it to Caroline to find her.

Kendrick pulled out his wand for the thousandth time. Even if nothing had yet appeared on the grid about the incident at the Arlington Hotel, that didn't mean people weren't out looking for him. And Edinburgh wasn't that big a city.

It was possible that someone had tapped his wand's grid address, in which case they'd know how to find him as soon as he used it. But he needed to speak to Todd and he'd started heading for the Saint a couple of times before turning back. Draeger would know to look for him there.

The wand chose that moment to inform him that he had an incoming call from Todd. Kendrick watched the icon flash for a moment on the instrument's screen. Then he hit *receive*, and put the wand to his ear.

"Before you say anything, Kendrick, this line is encrypted. Took me ages to get it sorted out. I heard something about what happened. Unless that was somebody else who fell out of a third- or fourth-floor hotel window and just walked away."

"So we're safe on this line? I thought maybe—"

"Just don't tell me where you are in case I'm wrong about the encryption and someone can hear us. If anyone out there has good enough software they can probably break the q-crypt code in a couple of minutes. So I won't be long." A pause. "I did as you asked."

Kendrick forced himself to relax, to grip the wand less desperately. "You've found Hardenbrooke?"

"Sure. I'm uploading Hardenbrooke's most recent co-ords to you now. By the looks of things, he's on his way to New York. But, a word of warning, I found him the same way he's most likely to find you."

"That's fine to know, Todd, but I'm in a hurry here."

"Sure, sorry Ken. Once you've checked out the stuff I'm sending, my best advice is to ditch the wand. If Hardenbrooke had ditched his I'd never have been able to track him so easily."

"Thanks, Todd. I owe you big time."

Kendrick closed the connection and switched the screen to review Todd's location data. He realized that he hadn't yet told Todd about Malky – and he couldn't make up his mind whether this was a good or a bad thing.

His wand informed him that Hardenbrooke was somewhere over the Atlantic, heading west – towards America. Numbers scrolled in a corner of the screen, and Kendrick was pleased to see that Todd's coordinates constantly updated themselves in real-time.

And what if Hardenbrooke does have Caroline? he asked himself. Does she run straight into your arms if you manage to rescue her? Almost certainly not. Draeger had told him earlier that Los Muertos were behind Caroline's abduction – which meant there was a good chance that Hardenbrooke had been involved. So if he could find Hardenbrooke, then he could find Caroline.

A black wave of depression began to settle over Kendrick's thoughts. *Admit it, this is all because of Robert. You killed her brother, and now you figure this is your chance to make up for it.*

Kendrick thought back to what Buddy had told him, and about what he'd managed to find out while he'd searched the grid for information about zero-point energy. He couldn't even imagine, remembering the few words he'd managed to digest, the sheer destructive horror that such knowledge could be turned to.

Now, it seemed, the lure of infinite energy was leading everyone towards the *Archimedes*.

Exact Date Unknown, 2088
The Maze

"I know where we are. I swear, I *know* where this is."

Vernon Lee's face was visible only as a pale, pleading shadow in the terrible darkness of the lower levels. He'd been one of only three to survive Ward Nine.

They had gathered together in huddled groups ever since they had found themselves locked away in freezing dark corridors down in the depths of the earth. Some, like Kendrick, could see those gathered around them as pale, shadowy outlines. Others whose bio-augmentations had not taken such firm hold on their bodies were still lost in the blackness, clinging quite literally to each other in the vast echoing spaces.

There was no evidence that food or water would ever be forthcoming and, after almost forty-eight hours, people were beginning to suffer. For himself, Kendrick felt parched, dry and cold. His stomach longed even for the thin gruel that he had known back in the Ward.

Kendrick pressed his hands against the cold metal of the shield door and felt something humming under the hard surface – the bright subliminal presence of electricity flowing through circuits. But it seemed faint, as if far away.

"Okay." Kendrick looked over his shoulder at Lee. "So where are we?"

He could just make out Buddy, standing to one side, listening.

"Used to work for a company did contract military work," Lee explained. "We built stuff for them, but only bits of it."

Buddy shifted in the dark. "I don't get it."

"What it is, if someone in the military wants something built top secret, they still have to bring in civilians a lot of the time. They screen you for all kinds of shit, you sign release forms, and they do everything but stick a torch up your ass and take a look." Lee shrugged. "Sometimes that too. But you never see the whole thing – only part of it. Only a few people outside the military ever get to see the project as a whole. Usually whoever's running the operation from the top."

"Just a minute," said Kendrick. "Are you saying you helped *build* this place?"

"Yes!" said Lee excitedly. "That's *exactly* what I'm saying. These doors are designed to withstand nuclear blasts," he explained, placing a hand against the same cold metal.

A wall of steel cut across the corridor, completely blocking their access to the upper levels. They were abandoned in what appeared to be literally miles of lightless passageway, but half a dozen huge steel doors blocked any way out for them. "I helped design these things," Lee continued. "I even remember how the corridors are laid out."

Buddy spoke, his voice low and intense. "Can you get us out of here, then?"

Lee shook his head. "No, I can't. All I'm saying is, I know *where* we are, but that's it. All this stuff – the doors, I mean – the controls are centralized. The only way out would be finding some way of interfering with the electronics, but there's no way to access the mechanisms."

"So what's above us?" asked Buddy. "We're in South America, right? You must know that, at least."

"Venezuela," Lee said decisively. Then he grinned ruefully. "Shit, looks like I'm going to jail for breaking my oath of secrecy. Well, fuck."

Kendrick shook his head. "I had no idea."

"What does it matter?"

Kendrick turned at the sound of McCowan's voice. Peter emerged out of the gloom, his words sounding harsh in the freezing air. "We're screwed, wherever we are. Knowing *exactly* where isn't going to make any difference. There've been rumours for, Christ, years, about US control south of Mexico."

"It's true," said Lee. "There's no real government up above there. It's a lawless place now, and the gene-rots hit here even before they hit the States."

Kendrick pulled his hands away from the metal, feeling defeated and depressed. "Which leads me to wonder when they actually built this place," he muttered. "It must have taken a long time, considering the size of it. And in total secrecy, too."

"I'll tell you," said Lee. "I'm talking twenty years ago. I was just a boy, really." He shook his head. "Place hasn't been well maintained."

"You could house an army down here," said McCowan. "The Wards could have been originally intended for treating wounded soldiers."

"Out here, outside the US, they could get away with anything so long as they were sure nobody was watching," Buddy spat, his voice bitter and angry.

Telling the time, or even the day, was impossible but Kendrick estimated that they'd been trapped in the darkness for about three days when the voices came.

In the meantime, there had been at least a dozen deaths – some from a lack of medical treatment necessary to keep the weaker Labrats alive, but most of them suicides.

One had hanged herself, knotting one leg of her trousers around her neck after first tying the other end to an overhead pipe. She had stood on the body of her dead lover to reach up to the pipe before pulling her legs up at the knees and somehow, horribly, holding them there until she passed out. As she slumped unconscious, her improvised noose and the force of gravity completed the process of strangulation.

Her lover – they never found out either of their names – had died within hours of arriving in the lower levels from the sudden and explosive growth of his augmentations.

There were other incidents, equally as gruesome and equally depressing.

And then there were the other stories.

One told of the figure glowing with light, lightning spitting

183

from its fingertips as it ran laughing through the most distant corridors, somehow passing through the great shield doors that penned the prisoners in as if it could walk through walls. To Kendrick this meant only that people were losing their sanity as starvation and sensory deprivation pushed them to the brink.

But then the voices came.

Kendrick had seen speakers slung up high along the corridors at irregular intervals. One day they started crackling with the sound of a familiar voice.

Sieracki?

Kendrick listened with a dawning sense of horror. The worst was yet to come.

"Enter the corridor marked Level 9, South-West," Sieracki ordered them. "The door will open. There is food there, but only for those who survive." Kendrick listened to the shouts of dismay around him in the darkness. "You will have to fight for the right to live. We wish now to test the survival skills of subjects from our different experimental groups."

"I get it." Kendrick turned to McCowan, who stood behind his shoulder. There was a sadness in his voice. "They never intended any of us to get out of here alive."

"It's fucking insane!" Buddy shouted. "I mean, it doesn't make any sense."

"No," said Kendrick. "It makes perfect sense. They made us what we are, and they aren't going to set us loose. Instead of just killing us themselves, they throw us in a hole in the ground and leave us to kill each other. That way they get rid of us, but they also figure out which experimental group has produced the best results. The ones who can survive, that is."

"Maybe it makes sense," McCowan agreed. "But it doesn't mean that's how it's going to work out. People don't need to fight each other when they know they're going to die anyway."

"I don't know." Kendrick shook his head. "If you've been hungry and desperate long enough, I'm not sure what any of us would do. Long as people think there's even the slimmest chance, the faintest hope, they'll fight tooth and claw if given the chance."

"I won't," said Buddy decisively. "I can refuse."

"You can refuse." Kendrick nodded wearily, thinking: *And that way you'll die. And the ones who won't refuse will fight, and Sieracki still gets what he wants.*

22 October 2096
Edinburgh

Getting out of the country turned out to be less of a problem than Kendrick had initially suspected. Not long after his conversation with Todd he got another call from Buddy. Kendrick filled him in.

"I'm on my way to the States myself. Listen, head for California, okay? That's where we're meeting," said Buddy.

"I need to find Caroline first, Buddy."

"But do you even have any idea where they might have taken her?"

"New York. I know Hardenbrooke is on his way there, and maybe he's got Caroline with him. It's not like I have any other options."

"You know this has to be a trap, right?"

"It doesn't matter."

Kendrick could hear Buddy sigh on the other end of the line. "I guess I'd do the same. Good luck, but maybe you should tie your wand into mine."

"I don't know if that's such a good idea. Every time I use this thing it gives someone a chance to track me down over the grid."

"So what? They can probably find you anyway. This way at least your friends will know where you are, right?"

Kendrick thought about it. "Yeah, okay then. Listen, about the . . . this whole thing with the *Archimedes.*"

"Yeah?"

"How long before you go there?"

"Three days, Kendrick. *Three* days. Remember that."

Kendrick closed the connection and thought for a moment. Then he called up Roy Whitman's grid address.

"Long time, no hear," Roy chuckled when he realized who he was talking to. "What's it been, a couple of years? Anything from Buddy recently? Haven't heard from him in a good long while myself."

"Buddy's doing fine, Roy. Listen, I need a favour."

"Uh-huh," said Roy. "What kind of favour?"

"A special kind of favour."

"Right, hang on a minute."

The sound of Roy's breathing disappeared abruptly for a few seconds. "Okay, we're on a secure line now," he said when he returned. "Can you talk freely where you are?"

Kendrick looked around him. He was standing in a narrow alley near the city centre but a furtive glance around assured him that no one was paying attention to him. "Yeah, I'm alone."

"Is there something else I should know?" Roy asked, his voice guarded. "You sound, er, tense."

"Nothing you'd want to know," Kendrick replied. "I'm just worried about being tracked via this wand. Is there any way you can make my line permanently secure from tracking?"

"Not really, no. Only way to be sure is get rid of the thing."

"I don't want to do that," Kendrick replied. "I want Buddy to know where I am."

"Then so will whoever's looking for you."

"I know, Roy. It's a long story. I need you to help me because—"

"No," Roy said quickly. "By the sound of things, maybe you shouldn't even tell me. Keep it all on a need-to-know basis, yeah? Besides, I owe both you guys one."

Kendrick found it almost frightening how easily Roy created a new fake identity for him. As instructed, Kendrick used public transport to get himself to Edinburgh airport, heading for a public fax unit on his arrival. He tapped in the q-crypt key that Roy had supplied and a few seconds later the fax spat out a cream-coloured plastic card with his picture on it, along with fake retina and DNA details coded into a hologram strip, together with yet another assumed identity, also supplied by Roy. A small matt-black datachip followed the card a few moments later.

Kendrick studied the plastic card, memorizing the name printed there, and wondered if he could really pull this off. He'd learned how to behave on passing through Customs. The secret was not too act *to* sure of yourself. People who behaved too smoothly were often those who raised suspicions.

The datachip contained his flight information and payment details. As far as the flight company was concerned, Roy was Kendrick's legal employer. Probably the datachip would also contain encrypted financial information to do with Roy's business. This would give Kendrick's trip some purpose: many businesses were now too paranoid to trust their most sensitive information to the public grid, as even private grid networks had their flaws. Nanodust transmitters were only one of many technologies available to the modern corporate spy, and as a result there was still a call for human couriers to carry information physically from one place to another.

To all appearances, therefore, Kendrick was just another courier. *Okay.*

Kendrick stared past the endless food concessions and identikit bars, which had always infested airport terminals, towards the check-in desks beyond. He took a step forward, then another, wondering just how self-conscious he looked.

To hell with it, he decided, picking up his pace. *Do or die.*

In the end, Kendrick's fears came to nothing. The check-in people asked him what he was carrying and he showed them the datachip, as Roy had instructed. A woman placed his chip in a reader and that was that – they waved him on.

The jet was barely half-full. Not surprising, given how its destination had lost its tourist appeal in recent decades. The majority of the passengers wore T-shirts or caps that made it clear they were on their way to do relief work. Apart from them, Kendrick saw a smattering of men and women in businesswear.

The jet boosted to the top of the atmosphere, skipping across the borderline between sky and space like a stone skimming across waves. Kendrick spent most of his time staring out the window at the deep blue of near-space.

23 October 2096
New York

A few short hours later Kendrick stepped out of the terminal building at La Guardia and into utter chaos.

There were tanks parked all the way around the airport. That was the first thing he noticed. The second thing was the sea of beggars who surrounded him the instant he stepped beyond the terminal entrance.

Just metres away Kendrick sighted a rank of antique and battered-looking cabs, the entirely manual kind that still needed real human drivers. He headed for the first in line, pushing past all the people pleading with him. One woman, her face a mask of tears, even thrust her baby at his chest, yelling words he couldn't comprehend amidst the commotion.

Knowing that he wasn't the only one having to deal with this gave Kendrick scant relief. He noticed the relief workers from the same flight pushing just as hard against this human tide but they looked like they had more experience of it. A phalanx of them just bulldozed through the beggars, heading for a private-hire bus parked a little way beyond the taxi rank.

Kendrick kept asking people to step out of his way but they

thrust themselves in his path all the more eagerly. He could see soldiers sitting on top of some tanks in the distance and imagined that they were watching the scene with detached amusement.

Out of the corner of his eye he spotted another passenger from his flight – a business type – literally battering the beggars aside with his aluminium suitcase. The man bulled on through, his technique appearing to work.

Giving up any pretence at the niceties, Kendrick followed his example. He propelled himself forward, smacking against shoulders and heads with his elbows. It was, indeed, the only way. Things were bad all over in his native country, but he'd forgotten just *how* bad.

"Jesus *Christ*," he muttered once he reached the first of the taxis. A woman whom he recognized from his flight – small and chocolate-skinned, with short, cropped hair and wearing a T-shirt that read NEW YORK AID RELIEF in large block letters – had reached the cab behind his. A scrawny young girl, who couldn't have been older than ten, was standing right next to her, thrusting little tinfoil-wrapped packages at her. The relief worker managed to ignore the girl as if she wasn't even there.

Kendrick stared at the child and thought of his daughter.

He looked back up, suddenly catching the woman's eye. "Jesus won't help you," she said with a cheery smile, her accent a soft drawl from somewhere south of Virginia. "But I can give you a ride into town if you like."

"Thanks, but I've got to make my way somewhere . . ."

The beggars were trailing off as fresh meat from some other flight began exiting the terminal. The relief worker had the door of her cab half open. She left it and stepped over to him.

"Don't get in that cab," she murmured. "You'll never see tomorrow."

"What are you talking about?"

She leant a little closer, so he could smell her perfume. "It's the licence plate. I can tell."

He stared at her, then stepped back from his cab, closing the door. The driver glared at him from inside, shook his head, and went back to reading his eepsheet. She drew him back with a gentle pressure on his elbow and nodded towards the registration plate on the rear.

"It's fake. There's ways to tell. They lock you in, gas you, and steal anything valuable. As often as not they put a bullet through your head and dump your body in the river. Corpses get dredged up all the time, and nobody ever checks on them."

Kendrick saw the driver glance around at them and mutter some inaudible profanity. A moment later the cab shot away from the kerb with a screech of tyres.

Kendrick watched it roar away, dumbfounded. "All I'm saying is you look like this is your first time over here," she said. "Yet you're obviously American, so . . ." She shrugged.

"Weren't you together with all those other relief workers on that flight?"

"Nah, they're headed for the West Coast." She gave an impish smile. "I deal with European fund-raising for the regional administration that takes care of food relief for New York." The woman studied Kendrick for a moment, her smile growing just wide enough to show a glint of small, perfect teeth. "Listen, I usually always stay at the same place. It's safe and has the advantage that nobody tries to kill you in your sleep."

"What's it called, this place?"

"The Chelsea. Used to be quite well known."

Kendrick saw the woman with the baby moving towards them again, having presumably found slim pickings elsewhere. Tears still streamed down her face and her voice was a constant wail. The baby's mouth hung slackly and he realized to his horror that the child was dead.

That was the worst thing he could possibly have seen. He got into the taxi: anything to avoid the sight.

The relief worker slid into the seat beside him.

"My name's Kendrick," he said. "Thanks for the lift."

"No problem at all. I'm Helen," she said, smiling. "Chelsea Hotel, please, driver."

Helen swayed against Kendrick's shoulder as the cab pulled sharply around a corner, between looming and run-down brown-stones. Something had been niggling at Kendrick's memory. "The Chelsea Hotel – I feel like I should know that name."

Helen nodded. "You used to get a lot of artists and musicians staying there. They've been going there for a long time, well over a century. I suppose it used to possess what you'd call bohemian charm."

The cab pulled to a stop right outside a twelve-storey brown-stone. "Look, I'll pay for this," Kendrick offered, finding his wand.

She squinted at the device. "Isn't that thing something of an antique?"

He smiled quickly. "I don't like the, ah . . ." He shrugged amiably.

Helen raised an eyebrow a millimetre or so. "I didn't take you for the type to get upset about subderms. Makes my life easier, though, if I want to pay for something in most parts of the world."

"Maybe so, but it bothers me. And I don't mind if people think I'm old-fashioned." Which was bullshit, of course: Kendrick's augs would fritz the subdermal implants that everyone else used to pay for their goods and services – or even to make phone calls.

She sighed. "Well, that wouldn't do you much good round here anyway." She reached into her shoulder bag and pulled out some crumpled notes. "Stick with cash here, long as you're in town. Foreign currency only – yen, if possible."

As old and shabby as the hotel looked from the outside, it was a different story on the inside. At some point the building's original innards had been ripped out and the present internal architecture was of a much more modern design.

"Listen, I want to thank you," Kendrick told Helen after he'd checked in. He found it hard to take his eyes away from her shape under the T-shirt. She had luminous wide eyes, and she smiled prettily.

"Then you can buy me a drink in the bar."

First, Kendrick went up to his room and dumped his stuff. All he had really was his jacket – and his wand, which he didn't intend to let out of his sight. He thought again about getting rid of it but reminded himself how much harder it would be for Todd, or anyone else, to help him if he did so.

He checked the instrument for the hundredth time since he'd glanced out of the plane window and first seen New York on the horizon. Todd's GPS tracker told him that Hardenbrooke was already somewhere in the city. That meant there was a chance that Caroline was somewhere nearby.

Kendrick resisted the urge to run out and start looking for her immediately. He had to be careful if he didn't want to end up in the same boat as her. *Rest up*, he told himself; he was feeling jet-lagged, run-down. He wasn't sure that he could handle the pressure of so much happening.

Kendrick showered, then studied himself in the mirror for several seconds. As he got dressed and headed for the bar, he wondered about the guilt he was feeling.

Later.

Kendrick leant over to smooth one hand along Helen's jeans-clad thigh, feeling her small hands slide up around his head, then reach down to tug at his shirt. She pulled him down towards her and they kissed deeply. He let his fingers slide under her own shirt, feeling the firm curvature of her breasts.

Caroline – did he still love her, he wondered? Maybe he hadn't really accepted that it was over between them. She'd been right, after all: he had deceived her.

Helen slid down, still lying under him on the bed, and started to wriggle out of her jeans.

Every muscle in Kendrick's body ached; for months – no, years – he'd been wound up like a steel spring, wondering if he was going to live, wondering if he was going to be *allowed* to live. And he noted with a certain detachment how easy it was to put everything that had been happening out of his mind – just for a little while.

Helen pulled her T-shirt off, her jeans already on the floor. Then Kendrick was inside her, feeling her hips rise to meet him – not Caroline, whose face was still hovering, unwelcome, in his mind's eye, but this woman Helen.

How long had it been? A long time – there'd been nothing like this since the break-up with Caroline. Alcohol buzzed in his brain.

Just then, as Helen shifted under him, her body moving with a languid animal rhythm, it was easier to think of Caroline not at all.

24 October 2096
The Chelsea Hotel, New York

When Kendrick woke a few hours later he knew that he had made a terrible mistake.

Helen coughed, a soft sound verging on the inaudible, but enough to cause him to wake up to near-darkness, the only light a thin yellow luminescence seeping in from the street lamps beyond the drapes.

He did not even need to move to know that Helen was no longer lying in the bed beside him. Perhaps, he thought, she had picked this as an opportune moment to dress and leave for her own room.

The sound of her cough reflected off the hard surfaces of the hotel room's walls before arriving at Kendrick's ears. There his augmentations processed the sound through a variety of arcane algorithms, thus generating a crude map of the space contained by the four walls.

So Kendrick did not literally "see" Helen standing in one corner of the hotel room, but he could sense her.

Then another sound, a faint creak that Kendrick interpreted as his wallet being opened.

Alarmed, he lifted his head a few inches from the pillow. Now he could make out her silhouette.

She stopped then and glanced over at him. He could not be sure if she could see him watching her.

"Helen?" he said softly.

She turned away again, and his eyes, more fully adjusted to the light, could now see that she was studying the contents of his wallet. Angry and confused, he slipped naked from the bed and went over to her. He reached down to take the wallet from her hand, thinking how easily he'd been taken in and that she was nothing more than a thief.

Helen whirled, her limbs and torso blurring in motion. Some enormous force lifted him and threw him against the opposite wall. He landed back on the bed, its springs creaking in protest. A cheap framed print tumbled from the wall above the bed and fell to the floor.

She flew at him across the room, and at once he realized that she was an Augment. The heel of her fist slammed into Kendrick's chin, pressing him so hard into the mattress that he could feel the springs digging into his spine.

However, she no longer held the advantage of surprise. Kendrick twisted his legs and thighs upwards, allowing him to slide a few inches down lower on the mattress and dislodging the main focus of her grip. Grabbing at Helen's hair, he pulled her face down towards him. Then he dug the fingers of his free hand into one of her eyes, feeling a sense of satisfaction bordering on the sadistic when he heard her scream.

As she managed to twist out of his grasp he seized the chance to pull himself off the bed. She came at him again, kicking and punching blindly.

Kendrick barely managed to fend off her attack. Whatever kind of augmentation Helen had, it made her react faster than he could.

Still, he had learned in the Maze what he was capable of, so he managed to block some of the blows that rained down on him at lightning speed, if not all of them. Helen glared at him, the flesh around her right eye now bruised and raw-looking. As one blow caught him on the side of his head, Kendrick felt the back of his skull rebound off the hotel-room door. He heard wood crunch under the impact.

While he was still dazed, Helen pushed him to the floor and, gripping the top of his head in both hands, began to slam his cranium against the floor.

The first couple of impacts stunned him and he tasted blood. It didn't take long for him to lose consciousness.

The sound of someone drawing on a cigarette. Then a silence, lasting several seconds.

"Awake yet?"

Kendrick heard footsteps moving closer. A hollow click, as of the safety being taken off a gun. Tensing, he found that he was tightly bound, the bonds cutting painfully into his flesh.

A painful tearing sensation as the blindfold was removed, and he stared up into sunlight so bright that he had to screw his eyes up tight against it. He tried to speak but found that he'd been gagged.

Kendrick stared up at a face reduced to a hazy silhouette by the jagged ferocity of the sun at high noon. Wherever he was now, it was somewhere very hot.

The dark outlines at the edge of his vision told him that he'd been deposited in the boot of a car. His body was folded up painfully in the limited space.

Hands dragged Kendrick out, the hard metal lip of the boot

scraping painfully against his flesh. Now he could see that his wrists were bound in front of him with narrow strips of white plastic. Although these strips looked relatively fragile, he could barely flex his hands.

With some dismay, he realized that his legs too were bound. He fell down hard on a dusty desert road.

A handgun wavered into view, a vicious-looking thing with a long barrel. Its muzzle was pressed against his temple.

"Here's the deal." Now he could make out Helen's face. "If you need to take a leak or a shit, the time is now. Then you're back in the car."

As Kendrick nodded, she tucked the gun into her jeans and yanked his trousers down around his thighs. He felt a hot flush of humiliation.

"Don't make the mistake of thinking I'm enjoying this," Helen muttered, "but there is absolutely no fucking way I'm going to untie you."

She dragged him to the side of the road where the tarmac merged with rough desert grasses, then kicked him over onto his side.

"Right, take a leak if you need it. Don't take for ever."

Kendrick tipped himself a little further over onto his side, and urinated onto the desert soil, only partially managing to avoid wetting himself in the process. He gritted his teeth and twisted away from the puddle of urine.

"D'you need to shit?" Helen asked him.

Kendrick twisted his head from side to side in the negative, staring into the middle distance while she yanked his trousers back up around his hips.

"Well, thank Christ for that," she muttered. A few minutes later she lifted him up and rolled him back into the boot of the car. Kendrick watched the daylight disappear again as the boot-lid came down with a solid *thunk*, leaving him with only his own thoughts and the petroleum stink of a pile of greasy rags – which was the nearest thing he had to a pillow.

Summer 2088 (exact date unknown)
The Maze

Kendrick shivered, wrapping his arms around his ribs. His thin paper uniform provided absolutely no defence against the freezing cold of the darkened corridors. He'd given up trying to count the hours and days since their abandonment.

Someone had died recently just a few metres from where he now crouched. The death had occurred in a sudden outburst of violence that'd had nothing to do with Sieracki's instructions. It might already have been a few hours ago, but time was getting harder to judge.

The man's dying screams had gone on for far, far too long. Nobody knew exactly what had happened, or who was responsible for the killing. Kendrick had been the first to stumble across the body, while it was still cooling. The weapon used to slay him – a piece of metal twisted from one of the trolley frames – still lay nearby in a pool of gore.

And that's how it happens, Kendrick thought, alone now in the darkness. Fear and desperation were driving them all apart.

He'd known from the start that he would answer Sieracki's call when the time came.

Sieracki's voice had boomed out again, some indeterminate number of hours before. Three names had been called; nobody Kendrick knew, but all of them men. A crowd had followed them to one of the great shield doors beyond which lay the lowest levels, but Kendrick hadn't had the stomach to witness it.

As always when the names were called, the door lay open.

The first time this had happened, several men and women had rushed eagerly towards the suddenly open shield door, not seeing what the rest had noticed – automated gun turrets positioned just beyond. Those who ran forward were cut down instantly; as the rest fell back, the turrets powered down with a whine like a jet plane approaching a runway. Kendrick witnessed it all.

When those first two names were called out again, a woman had stepped hesitantly forward from the crowd, her expression unreadable. Kendrick realized with horror that she could see nothing in the darkness; she made her way hesitantly, by touch.

She was joined by another, a man this time, and it was clear from his movements that he could see better than the woman. He had glanced at her uncertainly as, her face pale and drawn, she had found her way to the edge of the shield door, guiding herself past the gun turret by sliding her hands along the corridor wall.

Kendrick remembered how someone had reached out to try to stop her, only to be slapped away. There were shouts and heated debate, a cacophony of voices.

He remembered the woman screaming, then running forward, stumbling blindly away from the corpses of the recently fallen. Her selected combatant had stared after her for at least a minute, before himself stepping forward with the stiff gait of someone deliberately walking over a cliff edge.

Kendrick could still smell the blood and scorched flesh of the bodies that had been torn apart by the guns earlier, and he despised himself when that memory made his mouth water. Wherever the innards of the dead were exposed he could see fine filaments, like silvery wires, threading through their flesh.

He kept telling himself that when his own time came he could refuse. Others had done so, and lay slowly dying of thirst and hunger in the corridors and the echoing spaces all around.

Kendrick knew that he could refuse, but deep inside he already knew he wouldn't.

24 October 2096
En route to Texas

Kendrick could hear the sound of jet planes outside. He was lost in oil-scented darkness, the air so thick and stifling that it was almost like drowning. His lungs heaved and his skin felt on fire. Even if it wasn't Helen's actual intention to kill him he was pretty sure that he'd suffocate if he remained trapped in the tiny space for much longer.

He kicked out with his feet, trying to make some noise, draw attention. He felt relief blossom in his chest as someone finally unlocked the car boot.

His reward was a chink of light, a tiny, star-like point, and he felt a rush of ecstatic relief that they were going to let him out. He wasn't going to die there in the airless dark after all.

The chink of light expanded, rushing towards him. Not sunlight, however – something else altogether.

Kendrick found that he was no longer bound. Instead he was falling, as in a dream, through an ocean of warm air. Finally he came to a soft landing on a very familiar grass plain. Once more he could see insects buzzing through the tall grass while, further away, the land curved upwards, rising to meet itself.

Kendrick looked around him, his aches and bruises suddenly a memory. He stooped down to pluck a blade of grass, twirling it between forefinger and thumb. It felt very slightly damp, the texture of its surface somehow *vivid* under his fingertips. If this was some kind of augment-generated hallucination, it was entirely indistinguishable from reality.

But really he was trapped, tied up in a car boot somewhere in America, not here. Logic demanded that. Yet it was hard to deny the apparent reality of what he was now experiencing.

Perhaps this is death, he mused. *Or maybe the sneak preview?* Either way, he felt curiously unconcerned, for the *Archimedes* provided a curious substitute for Heaven – or for Hell.

A darkness swept across the green, the shadow of something vast. Kendrick looked up.

Far above his head, floating in the centre of the vast cylinder that was the *Archimedes*, he saw a twisting, amorphous shape that he didn't recall from his previous visions. At first he thought it was merely a cloud. But this was more like a great ocean of silver droplets that had been suspended in the artificial sky above him, the grasslands around him and his own upturned face captured and reflected in its shifting peaks and troughs.

Watching the cloud become more agitated, Kendrick felt himself gripped by a sudden fear, as if something malevolent lurked unseen just behind his shoulder.

He looked around. The great shell of the *Archimedes* stretched into the distance on either side of him, capped at each end by striated layers of steel. He knew that the station was divided into two huge caverns. Nearer one of these layers could be seen great scaffold-like structures surrounding transfer facilities that were used for bringing materials into and out of the station.

Above him the mercury-like cloud appeared to be dispersing. Spinning fragments, resembling drops of molten metal, boiled away from it like a swarm of silver locusts.

They began to rush down towards him and Kendrick didn't wait to see what happened next. He bolted across the grasslands, feeling the tug of his own muscles, the air streaming past him as he moved.

Even so, he could see the shadow of the pursuing cloud-fragments overtaking him, darkening the grass around him in every direction. Light poured down upon him from long, narrow windows extending the length of the chamber, the light itself diffused by complex mirror arrays.

He stopped, dream muscles aching, and stared up again. The individual cloud-fragments were now more discernible, moving with clear intelligence and purpose. Like swarms of tiny fish darting through ocean depths, their movements appeared almost telepathically coordinated.

Kendrick stopped again, wondering what it was that felt so wrong about all this. It was like the time when his heart had ceased beating, the feeling that part of him had vanished so suddenly that he could not at first work out what was missing.

And then he knew.

He was no longer breathing.

In this dream-place, his lungs, like his heart, were still. He deliberately drew breath then, so that air filled his chest. He actually *felt* the air flooding into him.

At first, panic surged within him and he felt himself begin to hyperventilate – suffering the delusion that something was blocking his nose and throat. It took a serious effort of will to maintain self-control, to remind himself that none of this was real. His lungs still moved inside the flesh-and-bone cage of his real body regardless of where his mind currently resided.

Kendrick heard the singing long before it properly impinged on his conscious mind. It brought a kind of peace that he had never believed might be possible, as if he had woken up into an angel's dream. Hardenbrooke's medication was finally wearing off: there was now little to stand between Kendrick and the message that Buddy and the rest of the Ward Seventeen Labrats had already received.

But there was still that sense of malevolence he'd felt. Where did it come from? He remembered what McCowan's ghost had told him about Robert.

The insect-like motes were close enough now to take on discernible shapes. They rushed around each other as they approached Kendrick, faster and faster until they flowed together again, taking on an outline, vaguely humanoid, fleshing out as the motes blended together into a seamless whole. It took on the size and shape of a man: a flesh-and-blood human being.

At first the shape had the face of Robert Vincenzo, but its expression constantly flowed like liquid, becoming somehow simultaneously imbecilic and dangerously intelligent.

The singing faded and Kendrick struggled to hear it still, wanting to follow that sound for all eternity, to rest in its gentle cadence until the end of time.

For the first time, Kendrick understood what Buddy had been trying to tell him, understood the peace and the safety that Buddy and the others believed they would gain from boarding the *Archimedes*. Everything Erik had told him, on that chilly shore so far away, suddenly made sense.

The face of Robert Vincenzo stared back at him from the dream-landscape of the *Archimedes*. Its mouth twisted silently, forming words that Kendrick could hear in his head, as if they were his own thoughts.

Not you.

Kendrick started to speak and felt his lungs spasm violently as they kicked back into action a second time, sucking in the air necessary to project the words that he was trying to voice.

"I didn't mean to kill you," Kendrick stammered. "But you made me do it, damn you."

The face twisted into the parody of a smile.

Without warning, the ground split apart under Kendrick's feet and he fell, tumbling into a bottomless well of night filled with stars.

Kendrick lurched up from the motel bed, the sudden motion spinning him off it and sending him sprawling onto a hard wooden floor.

In an instant he was back in the real, in the here and now. He found himself in the narrow space between the side of the bed and the nearby wall, staring up at the underside of a cheap bedside table. A Gridcom box sat on it, its tacky styling designed to resemble an old-fashioned telephone.

From somewhere outside, he could hear the rush and roar of aircraft landing and taking off, just as when he'd been imprisoned in the car boot. He was still tightly bound at his hands and ankles. He struggled and twisted on filthy green linoleum, kicking and pushing until he worked his way round to the wider space between the bed and the room door.

He heard more aeroplane noise from outside. Then the sound of animated voices. The motel-room door crashed open and soldiers entered, wearing camouflage gear overlaid with dark grey armour.

With a sinking feeling, Kendrick realized that they were Los

Muertos. Every one of them had a crude crucifix stitched onto the shoulder of their camouflage gear. One also wore a wide and varied collection of religious paraphernalia attached by strings and chains draped around his neck. Among these were pieces of circuit board, strung together.

And something else: something dull and silvery that Kendrick realized must have come from near the Maze. It was the same nano-stuff he had seen infesting the flesh of a dying Los Muertos warrior.

One of the soldiers grinned at the sight of Kendrick lying prostrate and helpless on the floor, and chuckled as he helped his colleagues hoist him off the floor like a sack of potatoes. Kendrick's gag had worked loose and he tried to speak, but even thinking about it left him feeling listless and drained of energy so he decided to save his strength.

As they carried him outside, Kendrick could see the rest of the motel, which mainly comprised run-down breeze-block huts with dried-out gardens delineated by narrow margins of whitewashed pebbles. Several of the huts lacked glass in their windows, and beyond these buildings and a small park filled with abandoned-looking trailers he could see a vast fenced-off area with the all too familiar features of a military base. Administrative buildings and prefabs stood next to a long runway and a complex of hangars, all dusty and broken-looking, as if it had all been abandoned a long time ago.

The soldiers dumped Kendrick unceremoniously into the back seat of an ancient manual-drive jeep that now looked as if it was composed primarily of rust. He felt his teeth clack together as his head bounced off the side door. One soldier got in the front, another sat next to Kendrick in the back, and they took off in a cloud of dust. After only a few minutes' journey they arrived at a security gate and were waved straight through.

In the distance Kendrick could see a series of vast hulking shapes at the far end of the base, looking for all the world like sleeping giants hidden under enormous camouflage shrouds. He could not even begin to guess what they might be.

Several minutes later they came to a halt outside a low, white-washed building that turned out to be a jail. Limbs still bound, Kendrick was locked into a cell.

From the floor of the cell, he could see that there was one tiny barred window, which looked too small for him to even squeeze his head through, set high in what was presumably an exterior wall. Some soldiers were talking, out of sight, further along the corridor, and two appeared a moment later. Like all the rest, they wore crucifix-adorned uniforms.

While one kept his rifle trained on Kendrick's skull the other jailer pointed a wandlike device through the bars of the cell and Kendrick's bonds suddenly fell loose. In a matter of seconds he could pull free his aching wrists and feet.

The soldiers left him then and he groaned with relief as blood rushed back into his fingers. He crouched on the tiled floor, seeming to feel every one of the thousand bruises and aches that now patterned his body. *Free at last*, he thought sourly.

Kendrick stared at the door of his cell and listened. But he heard nothing beyond the occasional whine of aircraft engines starting.

Once he was sure that the soldiers weren't likely to reappear any time soon, he stepped forward and studied the lock on the door. He'd already noticed that it was electronic.

Kendrick shook his head – were these people idiots? They'd have been better off leaving him locked in the boot of the car. It was almost as if they *wanted* him to escape. And he was more than happy to oblige them.

Kendrick knelt down next to the lock – a smooth, oblong steel box that did not require a keyhole – and fingered its cool surface, searching for its electron pulse with his eyes closed.

Nothing came to him. His brow furrowed as he pressed both hands against its surface. Still nothing – the cell door remained resolutely locked. A chill rushing up his spine, Kendrick hammered at the lock with the heel of his hand in sudden frustration, then rolled himself into a ball on the floor, cursing and gasping at the pain of it.

Augments or no augments, that had definitely *hurt*.

They had finally invented the Labrat-proof electronic lock.

A couple more hours passed, which Kendrick spent lying stretched out on a narrow folding bunk fixed to the wall by chains. Then Helen returned, accompanied by Hardenbrooke and some soldiers. Kendrick sat bolt upright when he saw the medic.

This time, Helen too was dressed in combat gear, a crucifix stitched onto her tunic just over the heart. Hardenbrooke avoided Kendrick's gaze, but she eyed him frankly.

"I don't see why I need to get involved in this," Hardenbrooke whined as they halted outside Kendrick's cell.

"Because I say so," Helen snapped. "Besides," she said, studying Kendrick through the bars, "anything he knows about the other Augments, we can use. Isn't that right, Mr Gallmon?"

Inwardly Kendrick's soul shrank, wondering what would happen to him when they realized he probably knew less about what was going on than they did.

When he didn't answer after a moment Helen shrugged, producing some kind of gun which she pushed through the bars and fired. Kendrick felt a sharp pain in his arm and looked down to see a tiny dart embedded in his skin.

The drug rapidly paralysed his muscles, leaving him awake and aware. He slid off the bunk and onto the floor, watching helplessly as they unlocked the cell door.

"What about the zero-point technology?" probed Helen.

"What?"

"The zero-point tech on board the *Archimedes*," she repeated impatiently.

"I don't know anything about it," Kendrick answered truthfully.

"He genuinely doesn't know about that," he heard Hardenbrooke say.

There was a pause. "He doesn't *know* about it?" Helen snapped. "Then what the fuck *does* he know?"

Hardenbrooke replied, sounding almost apologetic. "Look, I'm sure there's a lot he knows which he's holding back. That stuff you shot him up with, sometimes you need to think about how you phrase your questions. Context."

"Peter McCowan told me about all the rest," Kendrick said. "He told me about the Bright, how they found a way to the end of time."

Rustling noises, and he looked up from the chair he'd been dropped into, searching his captors' faces. A soldier lurked in the shadows nearby.

"Who's Peter McCowan?" Helen demanded.

"A friend of mine. He spoke to me while I was locked in the trunk of your car."

Another brief silence. "Tell me more about your friend."

"He died in the Maze."

"*Fuck.*"

Helen covered her eyes with one hand, quietly repeating the word "Fuck" over and over, under her breath.

"Okay. Let's start again," she continued after a bit. "The Bright – what are they?"

"They live on the *Archimedes*. Draeger designed them to find God. I . . ." A wave of nausea surged through Kendrick. He heard himself groan.

Someone nearby was muttering under his breath, in a rush of words that sounded like a litany. It was the soldier, and he looked as though he was weeping. Helen turned to bark something at him that Kendrick couldn't make out. When she turned back to Kendrick, her eyes were shiny.

"And that's what they call themselves – the Bright?" she asked.

"Yes."

Now she turned to Hardenbrooke who was leaning against a wall, his arms folded, watching. Night had fallen and pale moonlight spilled through the high-up window of the cell.

"We should give him some more shots of another inhibitor," Hardenbrooke muttered. "His augments will have dredged most of what we've already given him out of his bloodstream. That's how he's managing to hold so much back."

"Fine. Do whatever you need to," Helen said impatiently. Hardenbrooke stood up and stepped forward. A moment later Kendrick felt a tiny sting in one arm, followed by a numbness spreading through his thoughts.

"Okay, then," Helen said brightly, sounding like a teacher instructing a class of pre-schoolers. "He obviously doesn't know anything new about zero point. Okay . . . so how long have you known about the *Archimedes*?"

"About the *Archimedes*?" Kendrick asked.

"Anything, Mr Gallmon."

"All I know is, Buddy says those things that I've been dreaming about found God at the end of time. It meant something to Caroline, too – before you took her. The others think they could live for ever, if only they could get there."

Kendrick could see the incredulity written on Hardenbrooke's features. Helen's expression, by contrast, was fervent, almost ecstatic. She muttered something that sounded like a prayer.

"This is insane, this is bullshit," said Hardenbrooke. "What does this have to do with zero-point weapons?"

"Shut up," Helen snapped. "This is important."

"Oh Christ, sometimes I can't believe you people really believe this shit." Hardenbrooke looked ready to tear his hair out. "We're not here to talk about religion. We're here to find a way to win."

"If we win, it's because God smiles on *us*, and not on you,"

Helen said evenly, still staring down at Kendrick. "Hardenbrooke, I'll ask you not to take the Lord's name in vain again."

"Let's be clear," Hardenbrooke said carefully. "Zero-point tech is the purpose of this interrogation. Any more of this flagrant bullshit isn't. So keep your religious beliefs out of this, okay?"

Helen ignored him, leaning over Kendrick and peering into his eyes, as though she might find secrets lurking there. "Draeger thinks you're special," she muttered, just inches from his face. "Maybe you're not. Maybe he's wrong, and we're all barking up the wrong tree."

She looked off into space for a while, saying nothing, before finally shaking her head and standing upright. "This is useless. Look, he's no use to us if he doesn't know anything more than we do."

"But Draeger thinks he's important, you said."

"So what? Draeger is an egomaniac. You know, you haven't exactly earned your money yet – or don't you understand that?"

Hardenbrooke blinked. "I don't know what you mean."

"You told us that Draeger thought this idiot was essential to regaining access to the *Archimedes*. So far, he doesn't come across as very fucking essential to me. That means his friends can still take the Godhead *away* from us, regardless of whether we have him here or not. What are you going to do about that?"

Hardenbrooke's face was pale. "You're nuts, do you know that?" he said quietly. "Any military advantage—"

"I know what you want," Kendrick interrupted, his thoughts rapidly becoming clearer.

They both swivelled to stare at him, as if he were a corpse suddenly returned to life.

"With zero-point energy, you could win a war against anyone. Somehow, you think I can get you on board where everyone else has failed, don't you?"

Helen's expression remained mask-like. "Can you?"

"I don't know," Kendrick replied. He listened, helpless, as the truth spilled out of his own mouth. "No more so than any of the rest. But whatever's up there, it hates *me*. It doesn't want me there."

Kendrick found that he couldn't stop blinking. A dawning sense of horror began to awaken within him, as if he were emerging from a deep, restful sleep only to find everyone he had ever cared about torn limb from limb and lying in front of him.

"It's wearing off," said Hardenbrooke. "But pumping any more into him isn't going to work."

Another soldier entered the cell, looking harassed. Helen glared at him. "This had better be good, whatever it is."

"It looks like the enemy know we're here. The perimeter defence just brought down a robot recon, but we're almost certain it transmitted our location first. Command says we're to pull out early – launch ahead of schedule."

Helen cast a worried glance in Kendrick's direction.

Launch what? he wondered.

The soldier left in a hurry.

"Well, haven't *you* been a complete waste of time," Helen muttered at Hardenbrooke. "All this trouble and it looks like your friend here can't tell us a damn thing after all."

Hardenbrooke looked as though he was about to explode with rage, having undoubtedly promised that a gold mine of information would spill from Kendrick's lips. He stepped quickly towards Helen and grabbed her shoulder. She spun, staring at him unbelievingly.

Kendrick witnessed all this, including the way that Helen shook her head almost imperceptibly over Hardenbrooke's shoulder at the guard, who had begun to step forward. The soldier stopped, but lowered his rifle to hold it levelled at Hardenbrooke at waist level.

"There was an agreement." Hardenbrooke's face flushed red, which made his scars all the more ugly. "We need the rest of the information from him, about what Draeger is planning—"

"Shut up. You've been worse than fucking useless."

"No, I've had enough of this demented nonsense. I—"

Kendrick watched Helen's hand slip down to the holster clipped to her belt. The motion of her delicate fingers on the gun was smooth and practised, and he found himself admiring the way the pistol slid gracefully into her grip. Raising it only slightly, she shot Hardenbrooke in the stomach at point-blank range.

He went down like the proverbial sack of potatoes. Helen stared down dismissively at his crumpled body. Then her finger tightened again on the trigger, and a few more shots hammered into Hardenbrooke's supine form.

"Helen," Kendrick croaked, his throat still immobile-feeling.

Her breathing slowed. She closed her eyes for a moment before looking at him.

"My name's Leigh," she said.

"Leigh? That's good." A bitter chuckle fell from Kendrick's lips. He felt as though he'd been raped. "Because you're a lousy lay, Leigh," he told her. "Even if you do fuck for Jesus."

He wondered if she would shoot him too now, but there was still enough of the drug remaining in his system for him to find it surprisingly difficult to care. Instead, somewhat to his surprise, Leigh/Helen stepped forward and backhanded him across the face – so hard that at first he thought she'd dislocated his jaw.

It came to Kendrick, even through the haze of pain, that he was only still alive because she hadn't entirely convinced herself that he would be of no further use to them. He watched as they exited the cell, securely locking it behind them, the guard dragging Hardenbrooke's corpse along with them.

Time passed.

Kendrick was unable to sleep, so he pulled himself off his narrow bunk and slumped with his back against the cell bars, watching the stars wheel beyond his one tiny window. He thought about what the soldier had said earlier: *The enemy knows we're here.*

The question was – who was the enemy?

If he was still somewhere in America, then he had to be in one of the breakaway republics that had favoured Los Muertos. Otherwise, how would they have the run of this entire military base? Perhaps, then, a neighbouring republic knew Los Muertos were here, and were launching an attack?

Eventually Kendrick fell asleep despite the stink of Hardenbrooke's blood coagulating in one corner of the cell. He did not dream.

He woke some hours later to find a databand lying on the cell floor in front of him. It was the kind that was found in shops that sold cheap plastic jewellery. Moonlight streaked the floor where it lay.

Kendrick picked it up, studying its pale blue plastic shell. The tiny fingernail-sized screen was currently grey and inactive. He wondered where on Earth it could have come from.

Then a pale blue light appeared on the screen, and he almost dropped it in his surprise. He glanced through the cell bars to the glow of light visible down the other end of the corridor, where someone was on night duty. Surely nobody could have got past the guards there and deposited the bracelet without even waking him?

"It's me, Peter McCowan." The voice emerged tinny and distorted from the bracelet's tiny speaker.

"Peter?" Kendrick lifted the bracelet closer to his mouth, keeping his voice to a low whisper.

"It's a lot easier to get in touch with you this way, don't need so many visuals. But in the meantime you need to get out of that cell."

"Really? Do you think so?"

"Kendrick—"

"Look, there's planes landing and taking off from here all the time. I'm locked in a cell, and I don't have a fucking clue what's going on." At least with the constant roar of the aircraft landing or taking off outside there was less chance of anyone hearing him speak.

A long sigh from the bracelet's speaker. "Kendrick, nobody's going to get you out but you. But that's going to mean some cooperation."

"Cooperation?" Kendrick studied the bracelet in his hand. "What are you talking about?"

"I can get you out of there, but I need you to do something in return."

"Tell me."

"You need to get yourself to the Maze. If you just agree to do that, I can help you find a way out of the cell."

Several seconds passed as Kendrick closed his eyes, then opened them again to find the bracelet was still there and he was still in his cell. "I know, you asked me before, but I just can't do it," he replied. "Besides, it's—"

"Off-limits? God, there's a war on, in case you hadn't noticed. Los Muertos have enough on their hands to distract them. I need you to get here, Ken."

"Peter, where precisely are you? Are you telling me that's where you are – down there?"

"Just tell me you'll do it."

A roar filled the cell as another plane took off. "You need to tell me more. You need to tell me what it is that's so fucking special about me that every lunatic with a gun and a grudge is now chasing after me."

"Look, I already told you that: out of all of us who are still alive, you're the one closest to the Bright in terms of the way your augmentations developed. If Draeger is so interested in you, it can only be because you represent the highest achievement of Sieracki's research programme."

"Peter—?"

"Ken, understand this. The Bright are hammering at you with everything they've got. You have no concept of the energy resources available to them, but I'll bet Draeger has an idea, and, thanks to Hardenbrooke, Los Muertos do too. The Bright are like children who've figured out how to build a nuclear reactor and are using it to make phone calls. We're talking *serious overkill*. If it was up to Robert, you'd never know about any of this, but the Bright want you too much even for Robert to be able to do too much about it."

"The woman interrogating me here thought I could somehow get Los Muertos on board the *Archimedes.*"

"With your particular affinity with the Bright, they figure they stand a better chance of boarding the station and staying alive there if they have you along with them. Also, Los Muertos knew that Draeger had you flown out to Cambodia – and they know everything about the programme of treatments that Harden-brooke administered to you."

"Right: so apart from wanting to haul me up there, Los Muertos also kidnapped me because I'm important to Draeger."

"At last! Give the man a sticky bun! Took you fucking long enough to grasp that, didn't it? They all think you're special, and to a certain extent you are. But not, perhaps, so much as they think. Now, will you come to the Maze?"

Kendrick groaned. "You haven't given me one good reason to."

"If you do, I'll give you something you want very badly – something you've been seeking, for a long time."

"What?"

"I can get you the proof of Draeger's direct involvement with the Labrat research programme. But before that you have to come here."

"What if I say no?"

"But you won't, will you?"

"You're serious, aren't you? You can give me that kind of proof, Peter?"

The bracelet had fallen silent. Kendrick stared at it, knowing that it wasn't real. He dropped it on the concrete floor of the cell. It clattered as it landed, the plastic cheap and slightly scratched. He kicked at it gently and it slid a metre or two across the floor. It resolutely refused to disappear or evaporate.

Then, because he could think of nothing else to do, Kendrick turned his attention back to the lock. He caressed the smooth, machined steel box, thinking about McCowan's words.

Yes, damn you, I'll do it.

Suddenly, it was there: the electrons running through the lock's circuitry were like bees buzzing in a hive. Kendrick's hand tingled where he touched the surface of the lock and, although he couldn't feel it or even sense it in any way, he imagined information flowing through the nanotech augmentation that riddled his flesh, bio-aug programs analysing the interior of the lock, reaching out and distantly manipulating its complex innards.

Somehow, in some arcane way more like magic than science, McCowan was doing this – through Kendrick. He thought about a dead mind reaching out through his fingertips from buried lightless corridors – and shivered inwardly.

The box made a soft *click-thunk* sound and softly, very softly, the door swung towards him.

Kendrick stood, transfixed. Perhaps he'd done something wrong the last time and—

But it wasn't that. The lock had been designed to keep a Labrat imprisoned.

Get to the Maze, McCowan had said.

Could he really bring himself to go back there? Would it even be possible?

Perhaps it would, Kendrick thought. Perhaps there were even more miracles to be found there.

If he went – and if McCowan was telling the truth about Draeger.

Another aircraft took off, sounding as if it had barely skimmed the roof. Kendrick had to resist the urge to duck. Very softly, he stepped out into the corridor. He halted when he found that he'd stopped breathing, clutching at his chest in panic, wondering if his throat was blocked. Yet he didn't even feel out of breath, though the impulse to suck in air and breathe it out again appeared to have gone – at least for now.

Kendrick stepped back into the cell to try to deflect the subsequent wave of panic that threatened to swamp him. This wasn't like the last time, when he'd found himself on the *Archimedes*. This was real.

Very deliberately, he expanded his chest, drawing air into his lungs and then pushing it out again. He repeated this a few times until he felt nature take over: his lungs began moving without the need for conscious thought on his part.

His mind reeled. How long had this been going on? Seconds, minutes . . . more? What in Christ's name had his body been running on in the meantime?

What was *happening* to him?

Kendrick went back to the open cell door and glanced down the corridor. Ten metres or so away, he could see one edge of a desk and the side of a guard's head. There was a bend in the corridor there, which meant that whoever was currently minding the store didn't necessarily have a completely clear view down towards the cells – although it would take the guard only an instant's glance to see Kendrick peering out from his cell.

He moved soundlessly down the corridor, away from the guard. He reached a door after what seemed like an eternity. The guard hadn't so much as glanced up yet. Kendrick was amazed to find that the exit wasn't even locked. A glass panel at eye level allowed him to peer out at the dark shapes of nearby buildings looming beyond the jail. He reached down very gently to the metal lever of the door handle.

The lower edge of the door scraped noisily against the tiles under his feet and, glancing down, Kendrick saw that a shallow groove had been scraped away after many years of use. Just then, another plane thundered overhead. He glanced back to see the guard's head flick up, but the man was looking away from him. Kendrick watched as the guard nodded to someone who had just entered the jailhouse from the opposite end.

No time to waste. Kendrick pushed the door open wider, the air outside shaking with the sound of braking jet engines and screeching tyres. Taking advantage of the racket, he slipped out through the door and into the night.

Adrenalin surged through Kendrick's body, filling him with intense joy. He was *out*. The dark hulk of a military transport jet screamed overhead, so close that he felt he could almost reach up and touch it. But where now?

The whole complex was fenced off, as he'd noticed on his way in, which meant more guards to deal with. Unless he could steal transport there was no certain way to get back to civilization.

Kendrick stood against the wall, just beside the open door. He stole a glance back along the corridor and saw that his guard was now talking into a databand on his wrist. Kendrick's stomach lurched sickeningly as the head of a second soldier suddenly popped out of the open door of Kendrick's cell. Kendrick dodged back out of sight quickly.

He slipped along the side of the cell block, moving as fast as he could and taking advantage of the deep shadows there, ducking occasionally as a series of jeeps and trucks roared by, heading for the airfield where another huge cargo jet was approaching fast. Further away, Kendrick could see other trucks pulling up to a screeching halt before unloading dozens of uniformed men. Shouts came from somewhere close.

He ran towards an empty hangar a short distance away and watched from the shadows as the trucks returned the way they had come, kicking up great clouds of dust.

A klaxon sounded, strident and abrasive in the night air. Kendrick guessed it was for him. Uniformed men started heading towards the hangar he was lurking beside.

Time to get moving. He rounded a corner, trying to find a way towards the base perimeter. Then, through the gloom, he spied a fence several metres high.

But, when he saw what lay beyond it, Kendrick stumbled to a halt, gaping. He didn't know a great deal about spacecraft, but he knew enough to realize what a military orbital shuttle looked like.

There were three of them. Vast tarpaulins were being pulled off them to reveal their gleaming black carapaces. Kendrick stared at the smooth bulge of their fusion engines. He remembered seeing the huge rockets, still shrouded, earlier and wondering what they were.

Each one was mounted on an enormous movable platform that resembled a wide-bodied truck. Because of the much smaller size of these shuttles' engines – and because their fuel requirements for reaching orbit were modest by comparison – they were a lot more compact than the old-style versions that had been in use almost a century earlier. Like most modern spacecraft, they also lacked the external disposable boosters once necessary to get those earlier giants into orbit.

Kendrick also knew, from his research into Draeger's part in the development of the fusion technology that had made such craft possible, how these shuttles could be moved into position and deployed in just a few hours.

The night lit up like midday.

At first Kendrick's senses did not register the explosion, only a surge of heat and pressure. Then he became aware of a fireball engulfing the perimeter fence perhaps a half-mile distant, the noise of it rolling over him like a sonic boom.

The sound of shots came from somewhere nearby. Kendrick moved deeper into the shadows and waited long, tense moments.

After the light from the fireball had almost faded, a low, tooth-rattling vibration began to surge through the ground under his feet, followed by an almighty roar. Seeing fire blossom at the base of one of the shuttles, he started to head for the edge of the base, keeping close to the hangars as he did so.

Before long Kendrick found himself at the base perimeter, near a cluster of buildings that had a large number of jeeps and trucks parked outside. It occurred to him that he hadn't seen Caroline in the jailhouse – so where else would they be keeping her? Instinct told him now that if she was anywhere it would be somewhere in the buildings directly ahead. He tried not to think about the possibility that they'd put her on board one of the shuttles.

Kendrick stopped at an abandoned jeep that had its engine still running. He prayed that its rightful owners wouldn't suddenly reappear. Climbing into the driver's seat, he flipped the vehicle over to manual control, then began to drive off carefully, keeping his head down. Now that he'd had more time to look around, the base itself didn't seem to be all that large.

He halted the jeep after a few seconds and tapped at its command screen, located just to the right of the steering wheel. Three pre-programmed destinations appeared, listed in alphabetical order.

He glanced into the rear of the jeep and saw that a rifle had been left there. He reached back to pick it up, surprised at its weight. He had no idea how to use the damned thing, but just knowing it was there gave him some comfort.

Kendrick dropped the weapon onto the passenger seat next to him, then brought the jeep's destination list back up with a single tap on its screen, selecting the location it had most recently come from.

The vehicle began to move off slowly but soon picked up speed. It slowed at one point when its bumper sensors picked up the body heat of a group of soldiers. Kendrick ducked his head, hoping fervently that they wouldn't try to commandeer the jeep for themselves. But they didn't even spare him a glance. They were too busy losing control of the situation.

After only a hundred metres or so – about a quarter of its way across the base – the jeep rolled to a stop outside a one-storey building among the cluster that Kendrick had already spotted earlier. He jumped out, grabbed the rifle and took a look around.

Caroline could be anywhere.

Hearing voices nearby, Kendrick ran half-crouching along the side of a wall. Around a corner he saw what appeared to be a troop carrier parked alongside a loading bay. A surgical pallet had been placed in the back of the vehicle, a bundled shape strapped to it.

A soldier emerged next to the loading bay and spotted him.
Shit.

Kendrick brought the rifle up to his shoulder without thinking. *Is the safety on?* he wondered, realizing that he had no idea. He aimed just as the soldier ducked back through the door. Kendrick almost didn't spot a second soldier coming out of the driver's side of the troop carrier. He swung the rifle towards the man and squeezed the trigger, reacting out of panic more than anything else. The driver's shoulder exploded in a burst of blood and bone. The rifle's recoil almost jerked the gun out of Kendrick's hands.

He glanced back over towards the door and saw the first soldier reappear, armed with a pistol and taking aim.

Moving with augmented speed, Kendrick dodged to one side. When the soldier took a step back, alarm written across his face, Kendrick threw his rifle at him like a club. It slammed into the man's head and sent him sprawling.

Kendrick ran over, retrieved the rifle, and smashed it down on the soldier's head, gripping the barrel with both hands. The soldier jerked and twisted spasmodically for a moment, then lay still.

Kendrick felt as if he were watching all this from a distance, alternately appalled and exhilarated by what he was doing. Did the rage he felt come from himself, or was he now being manipulated by his augmentations?

Maybe a little of both.

He looked quickly around, then ran up to the front of the truck. No more soldiers, not close at any rate. That didn't mean he had much time, though. He stuck his head through the door of the building but saw nobody there.

When Kendrick climbed into the back of the troop carrier he found, to his amazement, that he'd guessed right.

It was Caroline who was strapped down onto the pallet. She was swathed in thick blankets. He wondered where they'd intended to take her. She looked as though she was drugged but he managed to undo the straps and lower her from the troop carrier. Lines of rogue augment growth now marred her once-beautiful face. Since the last time he'd seen her, her condition had become dramatically worse.

Kendrick ignored the rattle of nearby gunfire and bundled Caroline into the back of the jeep. At first he didn't realize that the shots were coming from somewhere outside the fence, but then he watched as bullets kicked up a trail of dust leading towards another jeep, filled with soldiers, that was driving towards the perimeter. He jumped back into his own vehicle and screeched off, not wanting to wait around.

He glanced over his shoulder to see that the other jeep had jarred to a halt, soldiers spilling out and putting as much distance as possible between the incoming fusillade and themselves. The bullets slammed into the vehicle. An instant later it spun into the air, seemingly supported briefly by a column of fire and smoke that then slammed it flaming onto its side. Driving a jeep suddenly didn't seem like such a good idea.

Kendrick scanned the perimeter and saw that the entrance nearest the building seemed unguarded. He drove the jeep into the shadow of a hangar and pulled Caroline out, heaving her onto his shoulders. She felt curiously light.

From somewhere overhead came the sound of rotors and a blast of air as an enormous black shape hovered low above him.

A searchlight on the helicopter's undercarriage pinned and tracked Kendrick as he ran. The machine moved a little ahead of him, dropping even lower so as to block his path. He was forced to a halt, searching wildly for some way of escape.

There was a door at one side of the hangar itself, almost hidden behind a stack of metal crates. Kendrick ran towards it and pulled at the handle. Realizing that it was securely locked, he waited for a hail of bullets to thud into his back.

When none came, he started to kick at the door. Agony shot through his leg but the metal began to buckle under further severe impacts, the hinges starting to warp and bend.

And still no bullets. He wondered what they were waiting for.

At the instant when the door began to give way, Kendrick

heard a familiar voice, electronically distorted. He flattened himself against the ruined door and crouched, partly hidden by the crates, and looking wildly around him.

As he studied the 'copter, he had a flash of recognition and immediately knew that they were safe. With its black, bulbous nose and scarred paintwork the aircraft looked almost as if it had been rescued from a junkyard. A shadowy figure was just visible through the canopy.

"Kendrick! Get the fuck in here!"

This time the voice was unmistakable.

Kendrick glanced past the helicopter, and in the far distance saw one of the three shuttles rapidly gaining height on a pillar of flame. A roar like nothing he could ever have imagined filled the air. Already flame was licking out from the engines of the remaining two spacecraft.

Just then the pilot's door of the 'copter swung open and a figure leant out, its face obscured by insectile headgear. Kendrick grinned and ran forward, hardly daring to believe that he'd been rescued.

Buddy.

Summer 2088 (exact date unknown)
The Maze

His stomach roiling painfully from lack of food and water, Kendrick stared down the long, empty corridor and called out, listening to his voice echoing into the lightless distance.

He had almost convinced himself that if he searched hard enough he could find an escape route, some way of hiding from Sieracki's cameras indefinitely.

He kept a tight grip on the long, wicked-looking knife that he had found lying in an alcove minutes after the shield doors had opened, as he had entered these lower levels for the first time.

I could just leave the weapon here, go find Ryan, talk to him and refuse to fight. That was the right, sane and sensible choice to make.

Kendrick knew that there was a cache of food and water, along with medical supplies, in a locked vault somewhere on the very lowest level. There were weapons too – if you could find them. But the vault unlocked itself only when just one person remained alive.

There were other choices, of course. Some people preferred to just lie down and die. Others walked calmly into the field of fire of a gun turret to end it quickly. One side corridor had soon been transformed into a graveyard where the corpses were dragged and left to rot. Over a few days the stench of decay, permeating the empty passageways, had become inescapable.

And there were also stories of a demon that haunted the lowest levels of all.

Kendrick glanced back in the direction of the shield door, now firmly closed behind him. Ryan had to be in here somewhere – Ryan who had sworn to his face that he would not be the one to die. That didn't make Kendrick any less determined to find some kind of rational compromise. But he'd been down here for over an hour now, without any sign of his selected adversary.

More time passed, immeasurable in that endless night.

The first few times that Kendrick heard the distant roaring, he felt sure it was some form of auditory hallucination. But then he saw light flickering down in some far corner, the first light he had seen in . . . for ever.

Perhaps, he mused, the roaring noise came from something burning. At first the flickering seemed painfully bright to him, but his augmented senses rapidly adjusted themselves. He stared along the corridor, moving closer to the wall.

What is that? he wondered again. It sounded very much like the roar of flames.

"Explain," Sieracki's voice boomed over the tannoy.

Kendrick flung himself to the corridor floor, frightened to the core by the sudden echo of the voice.

"You said something was burning? Explain," Sieracki repeated, his voice insistent.

Perhaps, Kendrick thought, he himself had spoken without even being aware of it. The light suddenly grew much brighter.

"I don't *know* what I saw. I—"

"Our instruments show nothing burning," Sieracki replied in his familiar flat tones. Kendrick had heard answering machines with more emotional depth.

He framed a reply, then stopped when he saw something that he would never, ever forget.

At first Kendrick thought that the figure was burning. But if this was fire, then the flames were of liquid silver. Insane laughter filled the air and the figure ran at him, almost whooping with joy. Kendrick stood, awestruck, as the creature ran towards him down the long corridor before stopping suddenly at an inter-section.

All of a sudden, Kendrick could see something flowing through the conduits that lined the walls and ceiling. No, not seeing; more like a kind of *sensing*, like trying to hold an image steady in his mind. There for a brief instant, gone the next, always wavering then shifting away.

It was a little like the times when he had become aware of the flow of energy in the electronics systems around him, but on a level of complexity and depth that he could never have previously imagined. Energy, flowing through the walls, suddenly as clearly visible as the streets of a city on a summer afternoon. Bright pulses flared out everywhere from the walls and the ceiling.

Kendrick shouted out to Sieracki, unable to keep himself from babbling. "What was that? You never told us about this. Is it human? For God's sake, what is it?"

"Explain."

"I saw him glowing. I never imagined . . . I thought he was on fire."

Kendrick stared up at the nearest camera. "Didn't you see it?"
Sieracki was silent this time.

Kendrick wandered, lost, until he came to yet another of the
Maze's thousand intersections. Here a shaft curved down into
murky blackness. Empty offices filled with shadows beckoned him
on either side. He gripped his knife tighter, imagining Ryan lurking in there, waiting.

He climbed down the dark stairwell, the air echoing with his
lonely footsteps. Tiny lenses glittered here and there, crudely
epoxied to any available surface. He pictured Sieracki watching
him from the comfort of his own office.

From somewhere ahead sounded the clattering of feet.
Kendrick ducked into an empty office space till the noise began to
recede. Something metal gleamed at him in the corner of the
room.

He picked it up: a catapult. Not a child's toy, however, for this
one looked deadly. Next to it lay a small box filled with steel balls.
He wondered how much damage could be done to a human body
with such a missile.

Nobody who returned from the lower levels had ever reported
finding firearms there. Of course, firearms lacked artistry from the
point of view of a man like Sieracki. Just aim and fire – that
wouldn't tell Wilber what a bio-augmented soldier might achieve
in hand-to-hand combat. A catapult or a knife was more visceral,
more immediate. In the context of Sieracki's grand experiment,
they made perfect sense.

Disgust and self-loathing filled Kendrick as he threw the catapult down where he had found it. He stepped back out into the
corridor, flooded with sudden hatred.

"Can you hear me, Sieracki?" he screamed, his voice echoing
down the empty corridors. "Fuck you, I'm not playing your game
any more! Do you hear me? Sieracki!"

"But you have to." The voice sounded close, very close. "Or else he'll just kill both of us."

Ryan lunged out of the shadows. Kendrick caught sight of him at the last second. He spun out of the way, crashing into a wall as something hot streaked across the side of his chest. He felt a stinging warmth traverse his flesh.

Ryan's forward momentum had sent him crashing into an ancient file trolley and tumbling to the ground amid clouds of dust. Kendrick felt a sudden desire to fight, to win. The knife was already in his hand, poised for a killing lunge. Instead, he stepped rapidly away from Ryan, keeping the knife pointed towards his adversary, so that at least he could defend himself.

"For Christ's sake, Ryan, just listen to me. There has to be a way out of here. We could—"

"There isn't," Ryan growled, picking himself up from the dust. There was a determination in the words as he met Kendrick's gaze.

"There has to be," Kendrick insisted.

He glanced down to see blood soaking through the thin paper of his shirt. Ryan had injured him – but surely it was only a flesh wound? He was still standing, still ready to protect himself.

"Uh-uh," said Ryan, shaking his head. He was carrying a knife like Kendrick's. Dried blood stained the dusty floor between them, and Kendrick tasted bile at the back of his throat. "Next time, defend yourself," Ryan warned him, backing away. "I never said I was going to make this easy for you."

Ryan turned and fled. Kendrick watched him go, dumbfounded. Then he went back to pick up the catapult.

Peering down a stairwell, Kendrick saw flickering light somewhere far below.

"You're in my head," he whispered to himself. "You're not real."

real am real am real

Kendrick cried out at the pain that had just exploded inside his skull. The words sounded defeaning, overwhelming: but they did not echo.

In my head. He pushed himself down the steps towards the burning figure, the light around it flickering like silent lightning. Again he perceived lines of energy flowing through the walls and ceiling, but they were now far more evident than before. It was as if he could deduce the layout of the Maze in its entirety, reduced to a schematic displaying the flow of electrons throughout its structure.

He looked closer and realized that the burning figure was Robert Vincenzo, Caroline's brother. But transformed – no longer human. Kendrick halted, frozen to the spot. Then Robert was gone, turning and fleeing into the depths.

Eventually Kendrick found the will to put one foot in front of the other, continuing his descent.

Even from far away, Robert's words still filled Kendrick's head.

the bright began it

"Began what?"

everything came the reply. **they woke on the archimedes and waited such a long time now they know we are here**

"You're going to have to explain that more clearly, Robert."

they see themselves in us

The voice faded suddenly, interrupted by a series of high-pitched giggles that sounded near – very near.

Kendrick wasn't even looking for Ryan now. He just wanted to understand what had become of Robert, the only one yet to escape the Wards. He wanted to see if the flaming creature with Robert's face had objective reality, or if he was simply losing his mind.

A shadow flickered in the distance, accompanied by the clatter of feet on metal. Kendrick hurried towards it, finding himself on the threshold of a vast chamber filled with towering piles of metal crates.

He hesitated. It would be too easy for Ryan to creep up on him in there. Overhead, light glinted from a lens.

Kendrick wrapped his fingers tightly around the haft of his knife and stepped slowly forward into the chamber, listening, watching. Several low-bodied trucks sat on rails next to an industrial-size elevator.

Hearing the faintest scuff of a heel directly behind him, he turned, moving faster than he could ever imagine possible. A blade arced past his ear, missing his head by millimetres.

That should have killed me. Kendrick marvelled at the lightning speed of his own responses. Ryan stepped nimbly away from him, an animal sound emerging from his throat as he prepared to lunge again.

Sudden light flickering from high above distracted them both. Kendrick caught sight of Robert standing on top of a crate nearby. Robert's flesh was flickering with a ghostly brilliance: thousands of cilia-like extrusions from his skin waved softly in the air around him.

His eyes full of horror, Ryan stood gaping up at him. Robert alighted from the crate, moving so dizzyingly fast that to Kendrick it seemed that he had been *there* but was now *here* within the same second, standing almost nose to nose with Ryan. A hand flashed forward, touching Ryan on the cheek. Ryan's eyes dimmed – and he slumped lifeless to the ground.

Kendrick stared, numb, wondering if it was his turn next. But Robert merely gazed back at him, eyes blank and full of flickering energy.

he was not like us
you and I are like the bright
but not him
Kendrick licked his lips. "I don't understand."
some of us are more like the bright than others
so they speak only to us
to you to me to buddy to all from our ward
but to no others

Seeing the threads emerging from all over Robert's body, like fine black wires, reminded Kendrick of how Torrance had died.

Robert reached out a hand to him.

Kendrick screamed, imagining the chilly and terrible brush of those delicate cilia against his cheek. He lashed out and drove his blade deep into Robert's chest, somehow finding the strength to yank it out and stab again. As Robert crumpled, the light faded instantly from all around him, his flesh immediately turning soft and pliant as putty.

Kendrick staggered to one side and retched violently. Just for a second, he could have sworn that he saw some of the black threads emerging from Robert's flesh reaching out to the bare concrete beneath him, and *push their way into it*.

He thought suddenly of Caroline, and felt deep, dreadful shame.

But something was different now. The long hunt through the corridors had triggered something deep within him; something dormant in his augments.

24 October 2096
Los Muertos-controlled military base, Texas

Buddy leant down while Kendrick lifted Caroline towards him, holding her around the waist like a ballet dancer raising his partner above his shoulders. Buddy grasped hold and started to haul her on board.

Kendrick leapt up onto one of the helicopter's landing struts, dust whipped up by the rotors stinging his eyes and nostrils.

Some instinct made Kendrick look up just before he pulled himself in after Caroline. He saw three fighter jets tear through the sky with an almighty roar, followed by explosions somewhere far off across the base. The aircraft were too far away for him to be able to recognize their markings.

He watched in awe as fire blossomed in the distance and orange blooms stitched across the landscape towards the two remaining shuttles. The first shuttle was already lost in the night sky, its passage now visible only by an arc of flaming light.

The second shuttle's engines were already rumbling. It began to lift on its own pillar of fire.

The helicopter lurched as Buddy took it up fast. Kendrick slammed down the back of the co-pilot's seat and managed to drag Caroline's unconscious body into the rear of the aircraft.

"Buddy, thank God," he gasped. "Listen, I—"

"Under attack," Buddy interrupted tersely. Kendrick looked ahead and spotted tracer fire streaking towards them through the dark, coming from the darkened window of a nearby building. Buddy yanked on the stick so that the 'copter weaved from side to side.

"How the hell did you know where I was?" Kendrick yelled. "I don't have my wand."

"Roy Whitman sent someone to New York to meet you, saw you go off with the woman, then had to use guesswork. She's well known in Los Muertos. One of their top operatives."

"So why didn't you call me in New York and warn me?"

"Tried. But you didn't pick up. So I figured they'd locked your wand off remotely with a software worm. Now we know for sure that Los Muertos are trying to beat us to the *Archimedes*." Buddy shook his head. "Idiots don't stand a chance."

The second shuttle was already streaking through the upper levels of the atmosphere and would soon be lost from sight. The third was still sitting on its launch pad, but now a blazing inferno jetted from its engines. Kendrick and Buddy could hear the rattle of automatic weapons even over the din of the helicopter engine.

"Hold tight," Kendrick heard Buddy say. "We're still being shot at."

Most of the base was now invisible under great swathes of dust and smoke. Buddy veered the aircraft sharply to one side, keeping dangerously close to the ground. Kendrick felt his stomach lurch in about seven different directions as his companion flew like a maniac. He caught a glimpse of the third shuttle. They were close enough to it to get incinerated if it chose that moment to launch.

Then he understood what Buddy was doing. The shuttle was now positioned between them and the main base, effectively shielding them from any gunfire coming from that direction.

Once they were past it they accelerated hard. Then a roar filled the air, sounding like God falling out of Heaven, and Kendrick knew that the last shuttle had begun to lift. Their aircraft shook so hard around them that he couldn't believe it wouldn't simply fall apart.

As they tilted to rise again, he glimpsed the damaged shuttle – liquid fire spilling from it – rising with astonishing speed. Buddy was rapidly putting kilometres between them, but still they were far too close. From the way he was twisting in his seat, he was clearly struggling to keep them aloft.

As Kendrick turned to see the third shuttle streaking upwards he noticed a line of fiery pockmarks stitch itself across its hull, blossoming and expanding until they joined up to consume the spacecraft in seconds.

Kendrick watched in horrified fascination as the shuttle's hull buckled explosively in mid-flight. The nose of the craft spun away into the night air, twisting and turning as it fell through a long descending arc.

The rest of it disappeared in a mighty fireball, sending out a powerful shock wave that almost hurled the helicopter back to the ground.

Kendrick watched the base's mesa whirl below them as he waited for the end to come. But instead their course became gradually steady and smooth. He glanced at Buddy, who had pulled off his mask. A weak grin creased the pilot's mouth, then he whooped like a cowboy. "Jesus, what a ride!"

Far below them, a ruined freeway wound its way toward the horizon. They flew on, passing over farmland where crops had previously grown across uncountable acres but where now only a grey pulpy mass streaked the soil. Asian Rot had taken its toll here.

A little while later, they dropped down to a landing in a low-ridged canyon where the vegetation appeared to have escaped the worst of the Rot. Wild flowers and piñon shimmered in the heat, growing on the banks of a stream that was barely more than a trickle.

They eased Caroline out of the helicopter and onto the sparse grass, keeping her wrapped in the same sheets that Kendrick had found her in. Her eyelids fluttered open to reveal pupils that were wide and unfocused. Her lips parted, as if she was about to speak, but then her eyes closed and she was asleep again.

Buddy glanced at Kendrick uneasily. "You didn't tell me she was this bad."

"She wasn't anywhere near as bad as this the last time I saw her. That was only a couple of days ago."

"We can help her," Buddy reassured him. "Look, the launch is being run from an offshore site. They've got medical facilities there, so we'll make sure she's taken care of."

Kendrick nodded. "You know what I don't understand?"

Buddy tilted his head. "What?"

"Why did the Bright do this to us? All our augments turned rogue at the same time, but the question is: why?"

"I don't claim to understand that." Buddy looked exasperated. "Perhaps the Bright triggered something in us, just by the simple act of communication."

"Did you ask the Bright that?"

Buddy looked pained. "You may have noticed their communication tends to be solely one-way."

"It certainly makes it hard for anyone to refuse them if staying down here means we'll all die a lot sooner."

"You're implying that they turned our augments rogue deliberately. But that's ridiculous."

"Sure of that, are you?" Kendrick snapped. "Can you just look at what's happening to Caroline and tell me you believe this is all for the best?"

"I . . ." Buddy's face coloured. He turned away without another word and headed back to the helicopter.

25 October 2096
New Mexico

Kendrick woke to a sky streaked with red. His face numb with cold, he sneezed in the chill morning air. The rest of him was wrapped in a thermal sleeping bag, and the helicopter loomed as a dark shape above him.

"Time to be going." Buddy hovered over him and handed him a plastic thermos lid filled with hot instant coffee. Kendrick sipped at it, blinking himself awake and longing for just another twelve hours of sleep.

Against his better judgement, he let his mind roam back to the day when he'd killed Robert. The shame and horror of it were never far away from his thoughts. The incident – every word, every action – was etched eternally in his mind. Sometimes he felt as though he'd died that day too: as though he'd become someone else, someone with the same body, even the same thoughts but, on a level that he couldn't quite define, not the same person.

Caroline was still sleeping but he sensed that this was normal sleep now, rather than chemically induced. He stepped over to inspect her, brushing a strand of hair back from her face. She twitched, then a corner of her mouth crept upwards in an unconscious half-smile. Kendrick studied the myriad lines criss-crossing the once flawless skin of her face.

Buddy stepped over beside him. "I think she's going to be okay," he whispered.

Kendrick nodded down at her. "You call that okay?"

"I call it a lot more okay than if she'd been stowed on one of those shuttles. You did good, Kendrick – real hero stuff."

Kendrick gestured for them to move away, then began, "Where are we right now?"

"New Mexico, heading west," Buddy replied.

"And we're headed for this offshore launch base?"

"Yeah, hundred klicks or so out from the Californian coast. But we're going to have to stop off in LA on the way. There's a place – a safe house, if you like – and some people will be waiting there. They're Labrats, and I need to make sure everything's running smoothly before the last of them head out to the launch site."

Kendrick digested this. "How far are we from the Maze?"

"Not nearly as far as I'd like to be."

"Could we get there from here?"

Buddy studied Kendrick for several seconds. "If that's a joke, it's in bad taste."

"I'm serious. I want to go there."

"*No comprendé, señor.*"

"I know this is hard to understand, but I really do want to go to the Maze."

"Kendrick, why the *fuck* would you want to go there? Why would anyone who had to be there in the first place ever, *ever* want to go back?"

Because when Peter McCowan spoke to me about the Maze, he asked me to go there. That meant that, somewhere down there, in the darkness, part of McCowan still lived.

"I found something out. I . . . a source told me that if I can only get down there, I can find what I need to prove Draeger's absolute complicity in what happened to us. That's important, Buddy, you know how important. We'd have Draeger by the balls."

Buddy fell silent, staring angrily off into the distance. Kendrick waited, listening to the wind blowing across the desert. It made a high, eerie sound.

"Look, I understand what you're saying," Buddy replied at

length. "But right now, where we're going is more important than anything else. You *know* why."

"If you help me, I promise I'll do whatever I can to help you get to the *Archimedes*."

Buddy glanced at him sharply. "You're saying you've changed your mind? You're going up with us?"

"Yes."

"There's something you're not telling me."

"Buddy, what's going to happen if you fail? If the wormhole never appears, and you stay right where you are?"

"Ken—"

"Either it's Draeger, or it's Los Muertos, or maybe it's even someone else. If the *Archimedes* stays put and any of them find a way on board, maybe they will find the secret of zero-point energy that the Bright have supposedly harnessed. And then, as far as I'm concerned, you really do have the end of the world, just like Wilber predicted. The *Archimedes* can't be allowed to fall into any of their hands."

"It won't," Buddy said quietly. "Once we're there, in a couple of days' time, we'll be gone for ever, no trace left. We'll be somewhere better."

For all your sakes, I hope so. "I know you will," Kendrick replied, trying to sound reassuring. "But I remember a time when you wanted to nail Draeger just as much as I did. Are you telling me that's no longer true?"

Buddy looked distressed. He seemed about to say something a couple of times but changed his mind each time.

"Christ, fine," he said at length. "How long will this take? It's not like we aren't in a hurry, and there's Caroline to take care of. So how long?"

"I don't know. A day, maybe?"

Buddy groaned and covered his head with his hands. "Shit, shit, shit," he muttered. "Right, listen – a day, and that's it. Any longer and I'm out of there, do you understand me?"

"I'm not asking any more than that. But, yeah, we do have to take care of Caroline first."

"It doesn't need a cryptkey. Just plug and go."

Kendrick held Buddy's wand next to the node set in the dashboard and waited until the wand had established a connection. Wide scrubby plains blurred past them a few hundred metres below, the sun low on the horizon behind them. They were on their way.

In the meantime, Buddy rummaged around until he pulled out a crumpled eepsheet. Kendrick took it from him, smoothing it out. He aimed the wand at the eepsheet and it beeped quietly, confirming that it had successfully transferred the link from the helicopter to the 'sheet.

In response, the crumpled page of electronic paper lit up, a logo blurring rapidly across it. Images of politicians and actors appeared in rapid superimposition, one fading into the other, before presenting the front page of Buddy's default subscription newsfeed.

"What are you expecting to find there?"

"After we finally got out of the Maze, I found that a lot of records had been deleted or destroyed. But whoever did it wasn't quite thorough enough. The Maze extends for several kilometres under the jungle, and it goes down a hell of a way as well. I've seen a lot of schematics over the years, but they're all different. Most of the original designs were stored in Pentagon databases and they disappeared during the civil war."

"Different how?"

"I need to take a look before I remember." Kendrick tapped an address into the eepsheet's search box. A couple of seconds later he heard the sound of crackling, followed by a graphic of flames burning away the 'sheet's main information display, a widening pixellated inferno that eventually revealed a demonic face. Insane laughter issued from the eepsheet.

"What the fuck is *that*?" asked Buddy, bemused.

"Ssh."

"Who dares summon the sleeper in the dark, that they may seek knowledge?" The voice was a deep baritone, the face itself dark red with wide, staring eyes and a half-crazed grin filled with sharpened teeth.

"I seek knowledge," Kendrick replied laconically.

The demonic eyes grew wide and round, before sliding from one side to the other, as if checking whether anyone was eavesdropping. "Are you prepared to pay the price, mortal?"

"Yes," said Kendrick, in a resigned tone. They'd redesigned the front end, and although it looked slicker it was taking almost twice as long for him to get where he wanted to be than he remembered from previous visits.

Still, it could have been worse. The kind of information he was after wasn't something you could get out of any public newsfeeds. For this kind of thing, you needed hackers. "I'm looking specifically for information on the Maze. I need a schematic of the whole thing, downloadable to this eepsheet."

The face wiggled its eyebrows. Somewhere out there, maybe in Kazakhstan – which was functionally an anarchist state – was a real live computer geek with a micro-lens mapping the movements of his face to this devil animation. Probably not even speaking English, since some top-end translation software was virtually undetectable. "Such schematics are available publicly," the devil pointed out.

"Not the ones I'm looking for. Check the records for the World Court proceedings, charges of genocide, accused President Wilber and General Anton Sieracki, 2090. I don't have the exact date of the investigation to hand, but there was a question of missing schematics concerning to the Maze, how it was built, who contracted it."

Of course, Kendrick had found his way to such schematics before during his lengthy researches into Draeger's background. They weren't legally admissible as evidence since they came only from highly illegal sources.

Which, of course, didn't mean they couldn't be *found*, so long as you knew who to ask and were willing to pay the price. The fact that the schematics had disappeared from every official database, server and Washington office where investigators might have reasonably expected to find them, along with untold terabytes of information and incriminating data, had done nothing except convince Kendrick that someone had set out to deliberately destroy evidence of a direct, explicit connection between Draeger and the Maze.

"Mm-*hmm*," said the face after a short pause. "*Veerry* interesting. You accessed this information once before, yes? 12 March 2093."

"Yes, but I don't have access to it any more. I deleted it."

"Very wise. Also, I note your current position near the border of the former United States, moving approximately south-east. Flying in the direction of Venezuela, perhaps?"

Shit. "Please don't spread that around," Kendrick said earnestly. He hadn't expected this.

"Of course not. Well, not unless someone pays us to know where you are right now." The face grinned evilly. "Here are your schematics."

The face was replaced by a new animation of a taloned hand shaking a dented tin can. Kendrick pointed Buddy's wand at the eepsheet and watched as a substantial amount of money transferred itself to the hacker's account.

A look of alarm spread across Buddy's face. "Christ, Kendrick, that's a lot of money. I'm not rich—"

"If you're right about the *Archimedes*, you won't need the money much longer, will you?"

Buddy blushed red. "Yeah, true."

"Look, once we're in LA I can arrange a fund transfer from my account if you like—"

"That won't be necessary."

Kendrick looked back down at the eepsheet. The taloned hand had gone and had been replaced by a list of files. Most of them were useless, the same publicly available schematics he'd seen before. But he persisted, delving deeper, finally finding what he wanted: rooms and corridors that didn't exist in other schematics, laid out in a three-dimensional array that he could study from any angle. He zoomed the POV outwards until he saw tunnels stretching far, far beyond the main body of the complex, their dimensions delineated in crude planes of primary colours.

"Look at this," he said, holding up the eepsheet.

Buddy squinted at it. "You blew all my money on this?"

"Yeah, and for a good reason. There are tunnels leading several kilometres away from the Maze. They're well hidden. Los Muertos might know about them, but then again they might not."

Buddy let out a long, descending sigh. "You're going to get me killed, I absolutely know it, and for some reason I'm still going to follow you in there."

Kendrick grinned. "We'll be fine."

Kendrick half-slept as Buddy simultaneously piloted the craft and fired out messages via the helicopter's ancient gridnode. Kendrick woke when the constant drone of the rotor blades above his head changed subtly. He looked down with sleepy eyes and saw a crossroads: two intersecting highways cut through an infinity of scrubby desert. As he looked more closely, he saw a truck kicking up sand and dust as it approached the intersection. Buddy piloted the 'copter down, landing it close to where the two roads met.

Caroline was awake now. They helped her out and she swayed a little as she tried to stand, choking on the thick dust kicked up by the rotor blades still turning slowly above their heads. The truck had pulled up a few metres away from them. A tall man with shaggy blond hair and a neatly trimmed beard climbed out. Kendrick ransacked his memories, trying to remember where he'd seen him before.

Samuel Veliz, he remembered, the memory rushing back. Veliz had arrived in Ward Seventeen only just before the liberation and so had never made it down to the killing levels. Although Kendrick had never spoken directly with the man before, he remembered that Veliz had given evidence against Maze guards during the subsequent trials.

"Is that the lady?" Veliz strode forward. Caroline peered at him awkwardly, as though she wasn't sure what was going on. Kendrick kept an arm around her shoulders, more to support her than anything else.

"Kendrick, I'm sorry," she murmured. Kendrick shook his head, as if to say *It doesn't matter*. Together, he and Veliz helped her into the rear of the truck where a cot had been arranged for her.

"Where are you taking her?" Kendrick asked Veliz.

"Frisco. Then offshore to . . ." Veliz glanced over at Buddy, who nodded that it was okay. "Offshore to the launch ship. They've got facilities there that don't necessarily involve UN nanoware restrictions. Long as you don't tell nobody," he added, grinning slyly.

"I won't," Kendrick promised sincerely.

Veliz looked at him curiously. "So how come you two guys ain't heading there right now?"

Buddy stepped forward. "We've got some things to take care of first. When you see Sabak, tell him I'll be there a little later than expected."

"Okay, but there isn't much time left," Veliz warned. "When we go, we *go*."

"I know that," Buddy replied, casting a significant glance in Kendrick's direction. "We'll head for LA first, if there's time. But not just yet."

Over the next several hours they stopped twice again, dropping into small, private airstrips for refuelling as they continued south. The landscape changed beneath them, becoming rougher, wilder, before all visible signs of civilization disappeared beneath a verdant jungle canopy. At one point they saw a ruined highway passing through the jungle from horizon to horizon, cutting the green world into two halves.

With its camouflage on, the helicopter appeared from below as just a pale blue outline that would darken as the day moved on to dusk. From only a few dozen metres away, you could barely hear the sound of the rotors. Although it looked ready for a scrapyard, hidden under its scarred and dented interior lurked some pretty state-of-the-art technology. In fact, it had been optimized for smuggling. Of course, good-quality thermal-imaging equipment could penetrate its disguise in a second, but some kind of concealment was better than nothing.

Finally, when it seemed their journey would last for ever, Buddy skilfully guided the 'copter down through a narrow gap in the canopy, somehow managing to drop the craft onto a patch of even ground. While Kendrick watched his knuckles turn white with terror, Buddy appeared calm throughout this operation, the only noticeable tension in the lines around his mouth.

They stepped out into an inferno of heat even worse than the one that Kendrick had experienced during his trip to Cambodia. Animal noises echoed through the tropical forest and hot mist rose in occasional wisps from the tree trunks whose vast gnarled roots dug hungrily into rich black soil. A bird with brightly coloured feathers flashed shrieking through the air above them, heading for the treetops high above. The very air tasted honeyed and thick.

Kendrick felt a fresh chill of fear down his spine. This was Los Muertos territory, and they could have been tracked even before they'd landed.

"That's possible," Buddy admitted when Kendrick voiced his worries. "But it's a chance we're going to have to take. Remember the last time we were here, with that kid Louie? Keep in mind that we're right in the middle of tens of thousands of square miles of jungle territory. Los Muertos can't cover more than a fraction of that."

Kendrick eyed the helicopter, seeing the way its camouflage software reflected the vegetation around them like a constantly shifting funhouse mirror. He had no doubt that from further away the machine would blend in perfectly with its surroundings.

"Do Los Muertos have satellite capability? Could they track us that way?"

"I don't think so – though I think they have people who hack into commercial GPS satellite feeds."

Earlier, Buddy had copied the maps that Kendrick had downloaded into his own wand. Now he peered into its tiny screen, lost in thought.

"Okay," he said, dropping the device back into his pocket. "Your secret entrance is maybe fifteen klicks east of here. We can get ourselves there in a couple of hours, and get out some time before dawn – with any luck. That'll give us plenty of time to take a good look around while we're down there."

"Couldn't we have landed closer?"

Buddy shook his head. "Terrain's no good for landing any further east. And we can't follow the highway, either: too good a chance of being spotted by road patrols."

Kendrick shrugged. "So I guess we just walk?" His back already itched from the river of sweat pouring down it.

Buddy flipped open a storage hatch, pulling out some bundles and dropping them to the ground. Then he tossed one of a pair of water bottles over to Kendrick. Next he produced a machete.

Buddy slammed the hatch closed and began to pack some of the stuff he'd taken out into a backpack.

He looked up at Kendrick. "This is not going to be a picnic. It's going to be a long, hard slog. Do you understand that?"

"I hear you. Remember, I've been in places like this with you before."

"Even so, it's easy to forget." Buddy handed him the backpack. "We'll take turns carrying this. You first."

Kendrick slung the backpack over his shoulders. Although it looked large and bulky, it turned out to be surprisingly light. The heaviest items they had with them were the water bottles.

*

At first they made good progress, since the jungle had been relatively sparse where Buddy had dropped them down. They kept within a few hundred metres of the highway but far enough away so that anyone using it would be unlikely to spot them. This undeniably made the going a lot harder, but both men considered it far better than getting shot at.

After an hour or so Kendrick's muscles began to ache badly. Though the ground was level, every step taken involved a negotiation of tree roots and tangled vines, to the accompaniment of the constant shrieks of outraged birds and monkeys. The sun glancing down through the high canopy revealed slippery mosses coating the rocks, and fallen branches seemed to reach out malevolently to trip them up. They trampled through wide-leaved plants that grew wherever sunlight reached the soil and enormous ferns batted at their faces as they passed.

But just as the pain in Kendrick's sinews and joints threatened to become unbearable it faded away magically, becoming distant, easier to ignore. The augmentations had just kicked in, tweaking his nervous system to allow him to keep going far beyond his usual limits. He wished it had been that easy when he had suffered the seizures.

After a couple of hours the going got harder as the terrain began to rise. Buddy glanced down at his wand from time to time, checking the GPS and keeping them on course.

They had run into no one so far, which made Kendrick paranoid. He wondered if they had just been lucky, or if they were being tracked without their knowledge.

"Okay," Buddy announced some indeterminate time later, halting with his back against the vast trunk of a banyan tree, his shirt stained black with sweat. "Okay, that's good time. Only five kilometres to go, and we're ahead of schedule. Maybe another couple of hours if we keep up this pace, and we'll be there." He nodded, as if attempting to convince himself. "Maybe we'll make it."

They rested a little while longer, Kendrick swilling water that tasted like the sweetest wine round his throat. It wasn't hard to imagine that he could get drunk on it, if only he were to drink enough.

Having crested the hills, the two men were on ground that now sloped downwards again. Before too long they heard a sound like static crackling. It came at them across a stream that rushed over boulders before falling several metres to form a wide pool below a nearby cliff. Vines and roots trailed in the clear water below them and they stopped, briefly spellbound by the sudden beauty of the place.

They were getting near. Very near.

Between twisting trunks they could see slivers of the distant horizon as the jungle dropped further towards a flat plain: a broad expanse of cleared land that looked as though it stretched on for ever. Kendrick squinted into the near distance, seeing a needle-thin road leading towards a huddle of breeze-block buildings. In an instant, his memory flashed back to that day when a transport plane had dropped out of the skies, spilling himself and countless others into a searing daylight that they would not experience again for several months.

Buddy consulted his wand. "Somewhere around here," he said.

Kendrick looked around him. "I don't see anything." He stepped up beside Buddy, studying the wand's read-out over his shoulder. It definitely showed a clear match between their current location and the GPS read-out for the hidden entrance.

Kendrick felt his resolve waver. He'd brought them out here on the whim of a man who had been dead for years. It was insane, after all.

He stepped across to the cliff edge, peering down through the dense foliage. A shelf of rock, jutting out above the cascading water, cast deep shadows across the base of the cliff.

"Down there," he said, stepping back.

Buddy stuck his head over the edge, peering down the sheer drop. "You think?"

"Only one way to be sure."

They picked their way carefully around the cliff top until they came to a less sheer descent, clinging for support to roots and rocks as they went. There were probably easier ways to get down but neither of them wanted to waste another hour trying to find one.

It came close a couple of times, as Kendrick's hand slipped on a slimy tree root and he tumbled before fetching up against another tree growing from the hillside.

This close to the Maze they would be extremely vulnerable if they were spotted. Defending themselves when trapped on a near-vertical gradient would be impossible. They moved patiently, quietly, carefully, picking their way over rocks and vines, making slow but steady progress.

Kendrick was the first to notice something strange. He was clambering over a scattering of loose boulders when he spotted a silvery glint in the nearby foliage, mistaking it at first for a spider's web.

Then he looked much more closely. "Hey, Buddy. Check this out."

They could discern the thread-like substance everywhere – a fine nacreous filigree, so thin and delicate that it was almost invisible, spreading across trees and rocks and bushes alike.

Buddy reached out to touch a thread and jerked his hand away almost immediately.

"What's up?" asked Kendrick.

Buddy looked afraid. "Touch it and see."

Kendrick fingered the strand. For a moment he was somewhere deep and dark as a sense of unutterable loneliness washed over him. He quickly wiped his hands on his jacket, aware that they were shaking.

"Remember following that kid Louie halfway across Venezuela?" he muttered. "This is the same kind of thing we found then." He suspected that the threads extended deep beneath their feet, all the way down into the Maze itself.

Buddy nodded. "Like I could forget."

Kendrick stepped away. "We shouldn't be surprised by this. This stuff is what keeps Los Muertos so close to the Maze."

Buddy shrugged. "I know, but . . ."

Kendrick nodded in turn. Sometimes there just weren't the words, but he was shocked by the fear that he detected in Buddy's voice.

Buddy's eyes widened and he pointed over Kendrick's shoulder. "Hey, I think I see the entrance!" He picked his way between two vast tree trunks, sliding down a muddy slope until he reached the base of the cliff. Kendrick followed, grabbing at roots or anything else he could use to stop himself falling too fast. The air was filled with the sound of exotic and primal wildlife, and those silver filaments were everywhere: it was like being on another world.

The threads had even woven themselves into the rough surfaces of tree trunks and were also visible in patches of mud, or stretching between blades of grass. As the sun sank towards the western horizon they reflected its light in an unearthly glow, giving the surrounding forest an hallucinatory dimension.

Sure enough, at the base of the cliff, hidden behind bushes and moss-covered rocks, lay the mouth of a cave, its interior dark and mysterious. Kendrick gazed long into its lightless depths before kneeling and brushing his fingertips against some of the thin fibres that extended ahead.

It was like someone finding, while standing in the middle of a vast crowd, that they possessed a hidden talent for telepathy. A rapid series of impressions flew through Kendrick's mind, faint enough for him to be uncertain whether or not they were the product of his own imagination.

Suddenly he had an image in his mind of a clearing in the jungle . . .

He lingered, feeling a powerful urge to look over his shoulder as if someone – or something – was standing there watching him. Something malevolent.

Buddy stepped past Kendrick and on into the cave. More threads glinted from deep within, making it appear that he was walking into the innards of some great metallic worm.

Kendrick gave in to the urge to glance over his shoulder. Nothing there – just the deep, darkening jungle behind them.

But it felt so strongly as if someone had been *right there*. He walked back towards the fading daylight. The clearing he'd seen in his mind's eye, like a scrap of someone else's memory . . .

"Where are you going?" Buddy demanded, staring after him with a bewildered expression.

Whatever it is I felt when I touched the thread, it knows we're here. Not Peter McCowan, but something else.

Kendrick crossed the banks of a stream that drained the pools beneath the cliff, his boots splashing noisily through the shallow water.

Over – there.

The jungle around him suddenly felt full of an overwhelming sense of presence.

Buddy shouted after him. "Kendrick! Where are you going?"

"Two seconds."

He pushed deeper into the jungle, past trees and bushes, almost slipping and twisting his ankle on wet rocks. He cursed and pulled himself upright, moving past more trees. Then he saw it.

He stared at it for a long time. After a little while, he heard Buddy come up next to him, breathing hard.

"Kendrick, what the fuck are you— Oh, hell."

Threads had gathered together to form a vast woven bowl extending between the tree trunks, filling a wide glade beyond. Thick ropes, comprising thousands of filaments clumped together, extended downwards from the underside of this bowl, entangling themselves in the living soil below.

Kendrick had *seen* it earlier, when the threads had first brushed his skin.

"Do you know what it looks like?" Buddy breathed.

"I know what it looks like. Like a transmitter – or a receiver."

As they looked up, through the thick matting of strands glistening in their millions, they could make out the dusk's sky and the sparkle of its stars.

*

A few dozen metres into the cave they came to a familiar shield door. The sight of it sent a riot of memories surging through Kendrick's mind.

"The question is, can we still get it open? The electronics might be shot." Buddy shone his torch across the surface of the door.

"*Damn*," he exclaimed, jerking his hand away.

"More threads?" asked Kendrick.

"Yeah." Buddy's face was pale, even in the darkness.

Kendrick reached out and touched the shield door's rusting metal. Nothing happened, although he was surprised to detect a faint glimmer of current. Then he slid his hands across the surface and sensed something shift subtly, deep within the metal.

Something inside him reached out and twisted.

The door rumbled, filling the humid air with an appalling groaning sound. At first it looked as though this entrance had been too long neglected to function any more and all their efforts would come to nothing. But then it creaked again and slowly, slowly began to slide open. Then it stopped, leaving a sliver of space barely wide enough for one man at a time to slip through.

"Okay," said Buddy. "I'm going to die underground." He shrugged. "Suits me."

The two men worked their way through the gap to find themselves in a near-absolute darkness that brought back unpleasant memories for them both.

Kendrick looked around him. It was almost as if he'd never been away, or as though the whole complex had become indelibly stamped into every cell of his brain. He shivered, only partly because it was cooler behind the shield door.

"Like a haunted house," said Buddy, coming to stand beside him. "Have you seen how there's these other threads – gold ones – as well?"

Kendrick nodded, and reached out to one stretching along a wall. As soon as he touched it, he felt again that strong sensation of being watched. But, although it seemed deeply irrational, the gold threads felt somehow *friendlier*.

He turned, suddenly half-expecting to see Peter McCowan standing there just behind him. He almost imagined he could smell the man's warm, beery breath – but he saw only Buddy.

"Okay," said Buddy. "What now?"

"Might as well keep moving," Kendrick replied, and they set off.

Several minutes later, Kendrick noticed that Buddy was behaving oddly.

The shield door was now far behind them, but with their augmentations they could see well enough. The sense of being watched only grew more intense the deeper into the tunnel they went. At first Kendrick dismissed this as merely his own nerves playing up. But in truth this *did* seem like a haunted place, just as Buddy had said, full of the spirits and the memories of the dead.

"I remember when they tried to cordon off this whole area," said Buddy. Kendrick knew that he was referring to the nanotech infestation.

"I remember." They'd seen the first intimations of that when they'd escaped the Maze. "For something so dangerous, you wouldn't expect it to look so – I don't know." He shook his head. "So beautiful, I guess."

Buddy laughed harshly. "It isn't what it looks like that matters. It's what it can do to us. This was a *bad* idea."

"Take it easy there, Buddy. Are you feeling okay?"

Buddy stared at him, his face pale and sweating. "No, I keep . . . I keep hearing things, like . . . oh fuck, like *whispering*."

Kendrick could hear nothing and saw only the empty corridor, silent and dark ahead. "Can you make out any words?" he asked carefully.

"No." Buddy put his head back and yelled, letting loose a series of expletives that rattled down the corridor and echoed for long seconds afterwards.

"Buddy—"

"I can't go on." Buddy shook his head, as if a swarm of wasps were buzzing around it. His breathing was rapid and ragged. "I just can't."

"What is it?"

"It's just . . . I can't. Not beyond this point. Something won't let me, Kendrick. Let's turn back. You'll have to think of something else."

"Look, we're almost at the end of this section. Try going a little further, see how you are then. It's probably only nerves," Kendrick assured him.

Just ahead of them rose another shield door, barely visible in the murk. It stood half-open, and the heart of the Maze lay beyond.

Buddy shook his head, sounding more reluctant with every passing second. "I can't, Kendrick, I swear. I don't have any choice in this matter. If I take one more step, I'll die, or . . ." He started to retch, leaning over, his hands on his knees. Kendrick could see that he was shivering badly.

Then Buddy looked up. "I'm heading back."

"I can't go back myself, Buddy. Wait for me at the stream, by the cave mouth. Stay hidden. I won't be long."

"If I go any further, I'm going to die," Buddy repeated, looking at Kendrick with an expression that said *So will you, if you go any further.*

"Go back," he urged Buddy. "Go back and wait for me."

The other man didn't need any more prompting. "Good luck," he whispered, and handed Kendrick his wand, the map of the Maze still displayed on its screen. "Keep it. I've got another one back at the 'copter. If anyone appears while I'm waiting and I have to take off, this way we can make sure we stay in contact." He also gave Kendrick the backpack. It still contained most of their water and the torch.

Then Buddy turned and moved as fast as he could back towards the entrance and the fading light beyond. Kendrick watched him go, cold dread filling his stomach.

He shook his head, turned back and began walking deeper into the Maze.

Once Kendrick passed through the second shield door he finally began to hear the voices.

The walls and ceiling were still covered with the same rusting pipes, making it harder to suppress a niggling fear that he had never actually left the Maze in the first place. He had forgotten how absolute the silence could be, and how easily it lent itself to such delusions.

Kendrick stopped and punched the wall next to him, hard. The impact sent shivers through the air around him and it felt as if a spell had been broken. The sound filled the darkness like the first words of God echoing through an unformed universe.

He had to get rid of his fears, the ghosts and nightmares that still populated his mind. He kept on walking, knowing that the tiniest hesitation might send him running back towards the cave entrance.

The threads, he noted, were much denser now, almost completely coating the wall surfaces around him. They made crackling sounds under his boots as he walked over them and he stopped a few times, unsure if he really had seen them moving, their loose ends drifting in the dark like sea anemones sifting for plankton.

When Kendrick reached out and touched the threads the voices became much clearer. It was like tapping into someone's thoughts, but those of a madman: random fragments of memory chasing each other like a blizzard of half-formed images, faint intimations of things that he recalled experiencing during his seizures.

Kendrick also detected an anger that threatened to overwhelm his own thoughts, tempered by a sense of childish delight that chilled him to the core.

He broke the contact with the threads and kept on walking till he came to a stairwell and worked his way down. There were light switches at hand, but none of them worked.

On their way here Kendrick and Buddy had wondered whether

they would find Los Muertos inside the Maze. Kendrick learned the answer as soon as he reached the Wards.

From a distance the body looked as though it had been there for a relatively short time. It wore the familiar ragtag uniform of a Los Muertos soldier, a crucifix crudely sewn on the jacket. At first Kendrick wondered if the man was merely sleeping, but as he came closer the smell of putrefaction was evident. The corpse lay with one hand outstretched, as if reaching towards the rifle lying a metre away. The dead man's face was turned to one side, his desiccated mouth open in a silent scream, the eyes now reduced to dark pits. He was encased in silver threads as though he'd been wrapped in the cocoon of some enormous metallic spider.

Kendrick glanced up and, for one terrible moment, felt sure that he could see something hovering in the darkness before it flitted away on fragile wings. He peered around himself for a long time, listening and watching, but there was nothing more.

Moving on, he found two more corpses. One lay slumped in a corner, while the other had both hands to his face as if he'd been trying to claw his own eyes out.

It was getting harder now for Kendrick to keep the fear at bay, fear of what he might find if he went any further. *If I lose it now, I might never make it back out.*

He took the precaution of pulling a pair of heavy gloves out of the backpack and sliding them over his hands before stepping through a door that led into a Ward. The rusting skeletons of beds stood in uniform rows around him. Most of their mattresses had rotted away, but he could still clearly make out a number painted above the room's entrance.

He was in Ward Seventeen – or Ward 17b, to be precise: it had been reserved for the male inmates. Ahead of him, the Dissection Door lay open, empty blackness beyond it.

The notion came to Kendrick right then, that something there had been waiting for him to return all these years. He pushed this thought away and stepped through the door.

*

Not even the teams of researchers and war-crime investigators who had arrived at the Maze immediately following its liberation had managed to penetrate these deepest parts of the complex. The nanotech infestation had already become too widespread for any further exploration to be possible.

A no-go zone had subsequently been placed around the Maze, and for a while UN forces had patrolled it. But once it became clear how bad things were getting back in the United States, these troops abandoned the task and left. Sieracki's soldiers finally emerged from their jungle strongholds, metamorphosing over time into Los Muertos.

Kendrick arrived at a series of ruined elevators, most of them now reduced to gaping shafts. He peered down one to see silver threads lining every surface, the occasional gleam of gold visible among them. At the corner of his vision, something crawled . . .

He looked down and saw that the fine filaments coating the concrete had broken under his boots. Their loose ends twisted and spasmed with tiny movements.

Cold sweat broke out on his brow as some of the threads *reached up* over the tops of his boots, as if they were seeking out his flesh.

He jerked his foot away, heard a ripping sound, and over-balanced, catching at the side of an elevator shaft with one gloved hand. He spotted shapes darting about far below, black on black, coming closer.

Kendrick ran, eventually finding a stairway. He slammed a half-rusted door shut behind him and kept running. Several seconds later he heard a sound, making him think of a ton of feathers flung against a sheet of steel at high speed. He gulped down air, knowing he was dangerously close to outright panic.

You need to be here, he reminded himself. *You're not here just for yourself, but for everyone else who was dragged here to die. Think of it that way.*

He continued to descend till, stepping through an open shield door, he knew instantly that he had finally reached the lower levels.

This was the place where Kendrick had almost died. Where thousands *had* died. But something was different, and after a minute he worked out what it was. Down here, many more of the threads that coated the walls were gold-coloured, although the silver ones still predominated.

He pulled off a glove, and somehow found the strength of will to reach out and briefly touch a thick strand of the pale yellow filaments.

Kendrick whirled around, sure that Peter McCowan was standing there.

"Peter?"

His voice seemed to echo for an unusually long time.

This way, he imagined McCowan saying.

He turned to face down one particular corridor.

Suddenly he knew he had to go . . . that way.

A rusting gun turret still stood on its mount beside a shield door, the filaments that coated it giving it a strange bejewelled look.

Kendrick stepped closer to the large weapon and, as he watched, some of the gold threads glistened noticeably before slowly taking on a distinctly silver hue. As he waited and watched, he saw more of the gold absorbed into the silver all around it.

At that moment, Kendrick realized that he was *inside* McCowan. The Maze had become Peter McCowan's body, the corridors his arteries. Which left the question of the identity of the silver filaments. Someone or something else – Robert Vincenzo, he was sure – was in the process of eating away at McCowan, like a silver cancer.

Beyond the shield door there came a sound like fluttering wings. Again he caught half-glimpses at the edge of his vision, lost in faraway shadows.

All in your mind.

But what if it was real? *Something* had killed those soldiers back there.

The fluttering faded and Kendrick found his way to yet another stairwell that led far, far down. Somewhere down there, at the very lowest levels, people had died, some of them his friends.

Robert Vincenzo himself had died, somewhere down there. And Peter McCowan, too.

Summer 2088 (exact date unknown)
The Maze

Kendrick searched until he came across the promised cache of provisions and water in a place that he could have sworn had been empty the last time he'd looked there. He stopped and gorged himself, making himself violently sick, even though there was not all that much food. It was in any case mostly freeze-dried protein, dry and tasteless. Enough to keep him alive for a few more days, however.

He allowed himself some fleeting dreams of freedom, of great metal doors sliding open at the wave of a hand, as obedient as well-trained dogs.

Then he gathered up as much as he could of the remaining supplies and found his way back up through the levels.

On reaching one of the shield doors that was open, waiting for his return, a voice sounded from a speaker. "Leave the food."

"Who is that?" Kendrick called out, aware how hoarse his own voice had become. "Where's Sieracki?"

"Drop the supplies or you'll die," the voice insisted.

Kendrick heard the sound of well-oiled machine parts rotating. A gun turret swivelled towards him and briefly spat bullets. The concrete above his head exploded into fragments that rained down on his shoulders.

He cowered on the ground, abandoning the food and water where they fell.

The voice continued, "Now, exit, please."

*

"I remember what happened when the Dissection Door went crazy." McCowan scratched at his chin. "I didn't attribute too much to it at the time. Not a lot of the stuff here works too well, apart from the guns."

Buddy shook his head. "No, I felt it, too. *We* did something to make that happen."

Kendrick nodded agreement. "If we could make that door open, what about the shield doors? Could we do the same with them?"

McCowan laughed. "Talk all you like, but I still don't see you having too much luck getting out of here."

"Maybe that's why they locked us down here," Kendrick replied bitterly. "They'd be mad to let any of us leave here alive."

Peter McCowan had been summoned the next day.

The voice over the speakers was a different one again. Just before it clicked off, Kendrick thought he heard shouting or screams in the background.

He'd gone back to squatting by one of the shield doors. McCowan reappeared a little while later, and for more than an hour just sat staring hollowly into the darkness.

Kendrick waited to see what the other man would do. If McCowan refused to enter the killing levels, he probably wouldn't last more than another day or two. Like the rest of them, his torn clothing hung on his emaciated frame like rags on a scarecrow. His eyes were bright even in the darkness, like jewels in the eye sockets of a cadaver.

McCowan's name was called for the last time. A few seconds later Kendrick's name was also called. McCowan's eyes glinted in the dark as his gaze fixed on Kendrick's. Then he got up and walked away.

*

"Ken?"

Kendrick forced himself to turn slowly. McCowan stood only a short distance away, at the far end of a storage area like the one that Robert Vincenzo had died in.

Kendrick noticed that the other man wasn't carrying a knife.

McCowan's gaze fell to the long blade grasped in Kendrick's own hand. He shook his head ruefully. "So, you going to use that thing on me?"

Kendrick opened his mouth to speak, but all that came out was a kind of stutter. Then he shook his head, as if he could as easily shake loose the confusion and near-delirium that plagued him.

Then he started to laugh until tears rolled down his face, and this laughter transformed into a violent, racking sobbing that sucked up every last remaining dreg of energy left within him. He sank down onto the cold, hard concrete, clutching his head in his hands, while the knife clattered down beside him.

Kendrick felt a hand drop onto his shoulder. "I guess you know the rules better than I do now," McCowan said. "That raises a couple of questions."

"Peter—"

"We're not doing this," McCowan said firmly. "Right?"

Kendrick nodded. "I've been thinking that there *must* be some way out of here," he said at length.

"Well, you've not yet had any success trying to magic those doors open. Look, if I'm going out, I can think of ways better than doing so for Sieracki's personal entertainment."

"Sieracki is dead."

McCowan cocked his head quizzically. "What makes you say that?"

"You can hear it whenever they summon people in. It's different voices. They sound . . . out of control, I think. This has nothing to do with testing military technology, not any more. It's about killing us, in the most sadistic way possible."

"So what do we do now?"

"I didn't get a chance to explore even a tenth of this place the first time I was here. And if things are falling apart up above us, then maybe there's somewhere they can't see us, or find us. Or perhaps there are weapons we can use against them."

"I heard stories about what happens to people who don't do what they're told once they're down here."

"You mean gas?"

"That's what I heard. You can't run away from gas."

"Maybe so, but if we don't find some way out, we're going to die one way or the other."

McCowan nodded. "Listen, before we do anything else, I want to ask you this. That knife you had in your hand a few minutes ago – were you really going to use it on me?"

Kendrick felt his face grow hot, and looked away while McCowan continued. "I'm not playing this game, Ken. No matter what the consequences may be."

Kendrick nodded slowly. "If we can't find a way out, they'll gas us both."

McCowan shrugged. "We're dead men anyway, aren't we?"

They searched, together or separately, calling out to each other through the infinite darkness. A tentative map of the lower levels was now beginning to grow in Kendrick's mind, but they found no secret entrances, no bolt-holes in which they could hide away from the soldiers who controlled the Maze. Kendrick felt a frustration burning in him: it would take too long to explore the lower levels thoroughly.

At one point, he heard Peter McCowan's voice echoing through the corridors, calling his name.

"I found something." McCowan grinned when Kendrick found him in what looked as though it had once been an office complex, a maze within the Maze, a warren of cubbyholes and empty rooms stacked with mouldering paperwork. A long green metal case lay open at his feet. The contraption of rubber and glass in his hands was a gas mask.

"Not so fucking thorough after all, eh?"

"Are there any more of these things?" Kendrick circled the room, kicking aside trash, vainly searching for another of the green boxes. "Let me take a look at that," he said, reaching out. Some inner clock was telling them that they had little time left before the next batch of victims would be cycled into the lower levels.

McCowan glanced around thoughtfully. "Did you notice how there are hardly any cameras down here? Seems like the lower the level, the less thorough the surveillance. There have to be blind spots."

"We should do something about the cameras," Kendrick muttered.

"Yeah, why not? Let's blind the sons of bitches."

A brief silence fell between them. "Peter, if we can't find ourselves another mask—"

"Shut the fuck up," McCowan snapped. Kendrick averted his gaze.

"We'll find one," McCowan continued eventually. "But standing around yattering won't do it. Start looking again. Maybe we missed something."

They pulled a couple of ruined chairs apart and wielded the metal legs like clubs. It was a strangely joyous experience, smashing the cameras wherever they found them, even though the devices were tougher than they looked. But the two men destroyed sufficient numbers for them to achieve a powerful sense of satisfaction.

Unless some other means of tracking their movements existed, there were now whole areas of the Maze where their progress could not be tracked.

It had occurred to both of them that they would have no warning when the time came for them to die. Kendrick left McCowan to carry the mask, an act of implicit trust. For them not to trust each other would mean winding up with one of them dead for certain.

Kendrick had hoped, perhaps, for an ABC suit, a logical thing to find in such a place. Or else an airtight vault where they could seal themselves in. But their search was fruitless.

At some point, Sieracki's soldiers would need to pump their poisoned air back out in time for the next batch of combatants to be thrown in.

Exhausted, Kendrick and McCowan found themselves at the deepest level. Robert and Ryan had died near here.

"I don't think we've got much longer to go."

McCowan's eyes flicked upwards at the ceiling. "You think they're still alive up there?"

"Who?" asked Kendrick, puzzled.

"Your family. Your wife and your kid."

"I just don't know. Sometimes I convince myself they must be, other times . . ."

"I understand."

McCowan nodded. "I found something else." He pointed down the network of corridors that he had just been investigating.

"What did you find there?"

McCowan hauled himself up again. "I should show you first. C'mon."

The room was round like an upended bowl, extending above their heads for about a dozen metres. In its centre stood an enormous engine of some kind, and they had entered onto a circular catwalk extending all the way around the open space in which it stood. The floor, a few metres below them, was accessible by ladders.

"Over here." McCowan pointed with the gas mask that he still held loosely in his hand. Kendrick followed him down a ladder and over to some kind of control area. Banks of rusted machinery stood all around them.

Kendrick gazed around. "I don't see anything."

He didn't see the steel chair leg swinging towards his head until it was far too late. His vision blurred under a wave of agony. McCowan's fist slammed again and again into the back of his neck, smashing him to the floor. Just before all thought and awareness abandoned him, something cold and hard was pressed against his face. The last thing Kendrick heard was the sound of McCowan's laboured breathing.

He dreamed.

Fantastical creatures floated through the empty blackness of the lower levels like monsters from a Bosch nightmare. A burning figure ran screeching along the corridors, the surrounding flames golden yet cool so that they did not burn. It cried out his name, sometimes imploring, sometimes harshly angry.

He tried desperately to find a way out. He ran through doors that slithered open at his approach, ran past robot gun turrets that melted into slag as he passed. He was now nothing more than skin and bone riddled with metallic threads, more machine than human.

Kendrick woke up to find something pressed against his face. He screamed, still half-caught in a nightmare of drowning at the bottom of a deep, dark ocean. The thing was still pressed against his face, and he couldn't get it off.

Staggering to his feet in a panic, it took him a moment to realize that it was the gas mask strapped over his face. His thoughts numb, he instinctively reached around the back of his head and, with unsteady fingers, began to unstrap the mask.

Then he stopped as he remembered the rumours of gas. Refastening the straps, he sucked air into his lungs, the sound loud and claustrophobic in the confines of the mask. A canister had been carefully strapped between his shoulder blades.

There was no sign of McCowan himself.

A dull vibration rolled through the ground under his feet. But low enough so that at first Kendrick thought it was a product of his imagination.

Half an hour later, he found McCowan. The other man hadn't gone far. From a distance, he looked almost peaceful, sitting with his back against a wall. But, as Kendrick drew closer, what had appeared from a distance to be a contented half-smile resolved itself into a rictus grin, the lips drawn painfully back across the teeth, the eyes showing mostly the whites.

Safe inside his gas mask, Kendrick licked his lips nervously. It was easy to picture himself lying there instead. And, even though he hated himself for it, it was impossible for him to deny the thrill of gratitude he felt at knowing that someone else had died on his behalf.

He remembered that dream, the way every door had slid open at his merest whim. It had all felt so real, so . . .

Kendrick left McCowan where he lay and worked his way back up through the levels until he came to the same shield door through which he had twice entered these killing zones.

The closer he came to it, the louder the shield door buzzed with an invisible energy that made him want to reach out and twist it with his bare hands. He felt an indefinable *something* shift in it at the thought.

Open, damn you, he thought. *Let me out of here.*

This time the tannoy remained silent, the unbroken camera lenses glinting down at him. Kendrick wondered if they'd let him out.

He stepped up to the enormous steel slab and pushed it, aware how futile this gesture might be. Then he sank to his knees and pressed his head against its surface.

Something inside it gave: like a release of pressure, or a bubble bursting.

He pressed against the door again and found that he could sense the lines of electrical energy connecting the cameras in a network. The gun turret that stood nearby became perceptible as a faint skeletal shadow, a pattern of controlled lightning that flowed out of and joined with the electrical systems that controlled the entire complex of the Maze.

Kendrick pressed his fingers harder against the metal and wondered if he had only imagined feeling it tremble.

The door shuddered, then grew still, although he could hear gears and levers clicking deep inside. *No wonder Sieracki and his men were so afraid of us.*

A small sob escaped his throat as, finally, the door laboriously swung open.

25 October 2096
The Maze

"Who's there?"

It felt like being in a crowded room where everyone else was invisible and silent. The sensation of another presence was palpable.

Kendrick was back now in the place where Robert had died. He flicked the torch on, having so far used it only sparingly in order to conserve its batteries. But here he needed to be able to see clearly, to be sure that the figments of his imagination really were just figments.

Under the steady light of the torch, the distant walls shimmered, transforming a military storage facility into something more like a fairy grotto. To Kendrick's astonishment, Robert's corpse still lay where it had fallen all those long years ago.

I should have died down here with him and Peter. I didn't deserve to survive this nightmare.

As Kendrick played the torch's beam over Robert's remains, it struck him that the corpse had an eerily beautiful quality to it. The skeletal form was wreathed in silver threads that converged upon it from all corners of the vault-like space, their slender lines twisting together in great bales that erupted from both the walls and ceiling. Threads crawled across the floor in uncountable millions, and Robert's gaping, fleshless jaws glistened with fiery brilliance as the light moved across them.

Kendrick sensed rather than heard the gentle beat of a thousand wings, the source of that almost inaudible sound somehow always out of range of his torch beam.

He forced himself to step towards the gleaming skeleton, even though his mouth was dry with terror. He imagined that something was shifting in those empty sockets as if it was observing his passage. He could feel something constantly prying at the edge of his awareness, making itself known through a furious tingling in his skin.

Then wings began to take shape in the periphery of his vision, a thousand million malignant hornets, each with the face of the same dead boy.

Kendrick moved away from the eyeless skeleton – and then he started to run.

Kendrick turned a corner; then another corner. He ran further, found a stairwell and descended quickly, encountering a greater proliferation of the gold threads there. He leapt down more stairwells, noting how rapidly the gold-coloured threads around him were now being subsumed into the silver. He stopped, momentarily uncertain, at an intersection and saw how the silver threads right above his head began to *drop down*, towards the top of his head. Yelling, he ducked away from them.

Far behind him there was a sound like rushing water. Kendrick's blood ran cold to think what might be coming after him in the dark.

The gold threads led ever downwards, and he followed them.

Kendrick reached the same great domed room with its central engine and banks of equipment, as silent as the day he'd left them.

Passing through it quickly, he discovered Peter McCowan's body slumped exactly where he remembered. Kendrick felt the sting of tears in his eyes, along with a deep and indelible sense of loss.

Golden threads sprouted in thick plumes from McCowan's exploded skull, reaching up in twisted bundles to the ceiling far above. The corpse shone like a jewel.

Even as Kendrick glanced to one side, he noticed glints of silver beginning to spread through this river of gold. Near McCowan's remains the air smelled of beer and cigarettes and sweat, all over-laid with a lingering musk of death.

"Peter?"

Right here. The words seemed less than a whisper, deep in Kendrick's mind.

"Why can't I see you? I could see you before."

Used up all my resources trying to keep him out, but soon it'll all be gone. Then I'll be gone.

Kendrick gazed down into the golden skeleton's empty eye sockets. "What do you want me to do?" he pleaded.

Take me with you.

"You told me I could get all the answers I needed down here."

Not down here. No, the evidence you need is on the Archimedes.

Kendrick blinked, and a chill ran through his spine with such intensity that he almost cried out. "Then why the hell bring me all the way down here?"

Because you need me up there with you. You'll never find what you're looking for if you have to deal with Robert on your own. Put out your hand – or I'll die without your help – and you'll die without mine.

"What makes you think you can do any better with Robert up there than you fucking did down here?"

He has an advantage down here that he won't have up there. I can handle him, I swear. Now touch me. Put out your hand and touch me.

"You tricked me, you lousy shit!"

I told you I could get you what you need to bring Draeger down, if you came here. And I will. But if you walk away from me now I won't be able to help you. Take me to the Archimedes *and you'll get what you need.*

Kendrick wished that he still had a functioning heart so he could hear how loudly it was hammering.

"You misled me, damn you. You could have been fucking *straight* with me."

As no answer came, he shook his head and swore loudly. Then he knelt down next to McCowan's corpse. As he did so, he realized with a shock just how fast the silver was spreading, and again he heard that distant rushing sound.

Kendrick removed one of his gloves and reached out to McCowan's skeletal cheek, for the first time noticing that even the surface of the bone was covered in cilia-like threads, like golden fur. Reaching further, he closed his eyes and felt a sting as the filaments brushed against his skin.

He opened his eyes again, stifling a scream. Golden threads slithered across the back of his hand, coating it in an instant, as if he had just combed his fingers through a cluster of aureate spider webs.

Stumbling backwards, his foot caught against a bony elbow. The skeleton collapsed in front of him, the skull toppling with a clatter.

Kendrick pulled himself upright and stared again at the back of his hand, watching in horror as the golden filaments melted into his flesh.

The rushing sound was growing louder, more frenzied.

And then McCowan was standing there in front of him, his face twisted in a grimace. "That's more like it," he growled. "Right, let's get the fuck out of here."

"What have you done to me?" Kendrick screamed. "What's this stuff getting inside my skin?"

"That *stuff* is me," Peter replied. "Trust me, I'll get you what you want. But first you're taking me to the *Archimedes*."

*

As Kendrick retraced his path, invisible wings assailed him. Yet when he waved a hand in front of him he found that there was nothing there.

"Just get out of here," he heard McCowan mutter. Behind them the gold was dying, fading, the silver seeping through it like dye in water.

"Not real," Kendrick muttered to reassure himself as he found his way back to a stairwell and began to climb. "Just in my head." He repeated the words over and over, like a mantra. He stopped at a door, thoughts whirling through his mind.

He realized that Robert Vincenzo must have been the source of the original nanite infestation. The augmentations had extruded outside his body, spreading uninterrupted through the corridors and dark spaces of the Maze over the intervening years, some echo of the boy's deranged mind still locked somewhere inside them. The same must have happened with McCowan and perhaps, somewhere out there, the corpses of other Labrats lay in mass graves with nanite filaments slowly infiltrating the surrounding earth. Perhaps their thoughts still flickered silently through dank, mossy soil even now . . .

Laughter, high and child-like, echoed from far away in the darkness.

In my head.

"It's not in your head, it's real." McCowan's voice spoke as if from right behind Kendrick's shoulder.

"Fuck this! None of this is real!" Kendrick pressed forward, his muscles numb with fatigue. He moved steadily up and through innumerable stairwells and corridors.

He was now out of the killing levels but still had a long way to go.

The densely packed networks of filaments – all silver now, wherever he looked – were beginning to bubble up, like pockets of gas rising to the surface of heated liquid.

As he got closer to a smooth dome of silver, several inches in diameter and protruding from the filament-dense wall, a homunculus-like shape began twisting under its oil-slick surface. As if waiting to be born.

Kendrick backed away from it and something clattered to the ground by his feet. *In my head, in my head.* Panic swelled in him like a great black tide. More of the bubbles were forming all around him. He turned away and ran, adrenalin pushing him onwards, heading for the sunlight somewhere far above him.

Several minutes passed before he realized that he'd dropped the torch.

McCowan hovered, a constant invisible presence, just behind his shoulder.

"There were more than you two down here," Kendrick gasped. "What happened to them?"

"Robert subsumed them, swallowed them up like Jonah's whale. They weren't from Ward Seventeen – didn't have the strength, not like you and me."

Dragging himself up a stairwell, Kendrick found himself back in the Wards. A sound like a river rushing through the depths of the Maze swelled in the darkness behind him. He pushed through a door and slammed it shut. He grabbed a rusted bed frame and managed to wedge it against the door.

Almost there, almost there.

He hurried on into the corridor beyond, soon finding the central staircase leading upwards. Empty elevator shafts gaped like maws beside it.

As Kendrick put one foot on a lower step he glanced down the long corridor nearby, seeing a cloud of tiny, winged figures racing around each other like angry wasps.

Here, close to the surface levels, the walls weren't so thickly coated with the threads. But even as he watched, a patch of silver smoothed and rounded, budding within seconds. He gaped as the silver took on a sudden golden hue. The bud instantly faded back into the wall, as if never there at all.

Peter is doing this, he realized. *Holding Robert back.*

Kendrick staggered forward again, all sense of time lost. The corridors became infinite, stretching into darkened eternity. But something kept him going, his body just a machine transporting his awareness through the lightless depths.

The outside world lay somewhere ahead. A dim greyness became more than a hint of light, resolving itself into a faraway point glimmering at the centre of his universe.

"Almost there," McCowan muttered encouragingly in his ear. Except, of course, McCowan was now *in* him, not outside. Once they'd left the Maze, would they go on sharing his head? Or would there be an end to it?

Kendrick stumbled into painfully bright morning sunlight, shielding his eyes until his augmented vision adjusted. The sun was still low on the horizon, burning off moisture from the surrounding jungle vegetation. Fatigued and shaken, he sucked in air perfumed with a thousand scents . . .

. . . And stopped again. His skin tingled, everywhere across his legs and his back. Almost a burning sensation . . .

He spotted Buddy standing not too far away, on the crest of a low hill overlooking the plain on which the Maze stood. His arms were folded casually, like those of some tourist checking out the sights.

Buddy turned, as if subliminally aware of Kendrick's sudden presence. He started towards him, smiling widely. But Buddy's smile faded quickly, replaced by an expression of horror.

"Jesus Christ, Kendrick, your *face*—"

Kendrick looked down at his bare hands, at the lines and vague shapes he could now see writhing beneath his skin. Filaments slid through his flesh like fine subcutaneous webbing. He reached up, his fingertips tracking the same fine, thread-like lines slithering under his cheeks, his nose, his ears, over his skull. He made a sound like a whimper and fell to his knees.

Buddy ran over to grab him by the arm, but Kendrick waved him away, "Don't touch me."

"C'mon, Kendrick, we have to get you to a hospital or something."

Kendrick gasped. He wanted to burn his own flesh off, to hack it away, to tear it from his bones in great bloody strips. Looking at Buddy, he couldn't fail to see the revulsion that the other man couldn't quite hide.

Summer 2088 (exact date unknown)
The Maze

The shield door froze halfway, forcing Kendrick to squeeze through a narrow gap. But it had opened, and he could hear voices: people talking excitedly, shouting.

Something thundered with a long, low vibration that rattled through the pipes and conduits lining the ceiling. He could see the shapes of other Labrats watching in the darkness. The gun turret near the shield door stood silent, motionless.

Static hissed from the tannoy speakers. Something had happened to the soldiers and scientists who had been guarding them. Kendrick knew in an instant that they had a real chance at escape.

He stepped forward again. The gun turret remained dormant. A figure moved towards him from up ahead. After a moment he realized that it was Buddy.

"Kendrick, is that you?"

The others were coming closer now. He could sense them shuffling and moving and muttering around him in the dark, shadows against shadows.

"There's a way out," he told them, letting the gas mask drop from his fingers. Buddy gaped down at it, wide-eyed.

"Where did you —?"

"Sieracki's men didn't get everything. What happened here while I was down below?"

"We heard shooting over the tannoy, then it went dead, like you can hear now. That was a couple of hours ago. And loud booming noises, like something's been blown up." Buddy grimaced. "We thought you were both dead. You were in there a lot longer than anyone else so far. Is Peter—?"

"He's dead. We found this gas mask – that's what kept me alive."

Buddy eyed Kendrick uncertainly.

"It wasn't like that. He deliberately saved my life. Listen, I think we can get out of here. There's a way."

Kendrick pressed his hand and cheek against the great shield door that separated the lower levels from the Wards above. It buzzed with energy under his touch. He closed his eyes, hearing people shuffling and muttering behind him. He had to do this or they would lose all hope of survival.

He slid his hand across the door's surface. Something surged and shifted beneath his touch. A hollow rattle sounded from somewhere deep inside it – and he felt it shift.

"Now," he said, standing. "Push."

At first he thought he'd failed, as a dozen pairs of hands belonging to people weak from hunger and thirst pressed against unyielding metal. Then something internal gave and the door slid aside, fraction by fraction, its hinges squealing in protest. Kendrick pressed harder, feeling something else give. Shouts of exclamation rang out as the door moved freely now, swinging wide to reveal the long corridors and ascending stairwells beyond.

Free! Kendrick stared at the soft glow of electric lights in the distance. They were free.

It soon became clear that the Maze was under attack. As for its soldiers and scientific staff, they found several men, half out of their uniforms, gazing up at ceilings as though they could see through them to some point beyond. One man lay crumpled in a corner, his face glistening with some thread-like substance that glittered as though it was some rare and precious metal. His features were peaceful, and he appeared to be unaware of their approach.

Kendrick moved past him, caught up in a great flood of bodies. He twisted, staring as the soldier died, oblivious, under a hail of fists and stamping feet.

They found others, cowering in laboratories and offices, as the mob moved on, meeting no resistance. Many of the Maze's staff died during this exodus, beaten to death with anything that came to hand. Kendrick followed the inmates' example, unable and unwilling to resist the desire for vengeance.

One or two Labrats fell, shot by the few remaining guards. But the rest of the prisoners, caught up in a whirlwind of mindless rage, surged forward regardless, the soldiers dying under a torrent of blows.

A sound like muted, distant thunder came from somewhere yet higher up. They swarmed through the Wards in their hundreds, lifting men and women out of their beds where they found them alive, and leaving the corpses behind. They moved on more slowly now; they were becoming tired.

Finally they reached the surface level, staggering numbly up staircases and along corridors as the Maze staff – so very few of them now – fled at their approach, their yells of warning reverberating into the distance.

Kendrick moved on with the rest, always upwards, horrified by what he could now see of his own body in the brilliant electric light illuminating the upper levels. His clothing was reduced to less than rags, his scarred flesh smeared with blood and grime.

Gazing down a final passageway, he spotted natural sunlight streaming through a door at the far end. The ground rocked again beneath their feet and Kendrick knew that – at last – someone had come to rescue them.

26 October, 2096
Los Angeles

Kendrick still dreamed of endless corridors.

Sometimes he burned with a strange silvery light. Other times he died, over and over again, the stiff black handle of a razor-sharp knife protruding from his chest, the pain unimaginable. He remembered dying in two different ways. He remembered running to escape from someone with his own face, then slumping against a wall, unable to breathe in the poisoned air.

Kendrick opened his eyes to the broad grey blur of rotors slicing through the air above him. He lifted his head from the co-pilot's seat and gazed out and down to the landscape below.

Struggling upright, he could see smoke rising from campfires several hundred metres below. How long had he been asleep? He dragged his scattered thoughts together, and caught Buddy's eye when the other glanced briefly over.

Los Angeles, he remembered now. Buddy was taking them to Los Angeles.

He'd obviously been unconscious for most of the journey. He felt obscurely grateful for that. Now he was looking down on the reconstructed parts of the city. He was familiar with television footage of the ultra-modern spires, like shards of crystal rising quite literally from the ashes. But now that he was actually here, those occasional oases of light and technology appeared uncomfortably poignant amid so much unreclaimed devastation.

Stroking the back of one hand, Kendrick started tracing the new whorls and shapes underlying the skin, reflecting that since he'd made his way back to the sunlight McCowan had vanished from his senses.

A little while later another glance downwards revealed a huge encampment of tents spread far across a hill. Among them the symbol of the Red Cross was prominent. He suddenly thought of Hardenbrooke, and of what it must have been like to be here when the city was destroyed.

Soon they passed over a recognizably military encampment with trucks and jeeps standing in ordered rows, all painted in their camouflage colours.

As if reading his thoughts, Buddy smiled reassuringly. "Mexican Army. Remember, California is barely part of the US any more. Not that it'd be much of a prize anyway, since the economy and everything went tits-up after the nuke. Washington's got its hands full enough with breakaway republics, without worrying too much about who's left in charge of a bunch of ruins."

The helicopter ripped on through the sterile LA skies. Here and there, areas that had miraculously survived the devastation could be seen. But Kendrick was shocked at how much of the city was still in ruins after so many years.

Deserted five-lane freeways stretched in parallel lines towards the ocean and, as they dropped lower, Kendrick noticed scores of abandoned swimming pools scattered across the side of a hill, next to the ruins of expensive mansions. He vividly recalled detailed news footage of the Beverly Hills burning.

The pools themselves looked like half-revealed bones bleached white in the merciless heat of the sun. Elsewhere, what had once been boulevards full of expensive boutiques and fashionable galleries had been reduced to abandoned shanty-towns. Everywhere around them the palm trees grew wild.

As Buddy guided his aircraft towards the ground people gazed up at them from a wide expanse of unkempt grass that rose and dipped with artificial uniformity. Nearby stood a group of buildings, some half-demolished, some apparently built of random detritus, roofed over with sheets of corrugated metal. Some of the open land nearby had been tilled, and new crops grew on it in rows. It took a moment for Kendrick to realize that he was looking down on an erstwhile golf course. All around it the rusted skeletons of cars were scattered across the cracked tarmac.

Kendrick stepped out of the helicopter, the whine of its rotor blades dropping rapidly, and blinked in the bright Californian sunshine. The people he'd noticed earlier were moving towards them, dragging a huge green tarpaulin behind them. Buddy dropped down from the cockpit and ran towards them to grab one edge of it. Kendrick stood by as they hauled the tarpaulin over the 'copter.

Buddy then stepped over and clapped him on the back, but it wasn't hard for Kendrick to sense just how uneasy his friend was.

"What's the tarpaulin for?"

"Smothers the heat signature." Buddy turned to greet Veliz who was standing chatting with the others. "Hey, Samuel, still got any of that Mexican beer?"

Kendrick's skin itched in the early-evening heat. He felt drowsy from the food and drink that he'd been given. They sat out in the open air by a crackling log fire built in a circle of bricks. Nearby stood half a dozen patched-together vehicles which, contrary to their appearances, apparently did function. Kendrick gazed numbly into the flames, the stars overhead, trying hard not to think of anything in particular.

A woman came over, although he couldn't help but notice that she didn't get too close. Her face cracked open in an uneasy grin – there was something likeable about her.

"Still hungry?" she asked. "Could getcha 'nother bite to eat."

"I'm fine for now." Kendrick shrugged. "It's sort of hard to believe that everyone here is a Labrat. Haven't seen this many of us together in one place since . . ." He let the sentence trail off.

She nodded. "Same for all of us, yeah."

He studied her more closely, wincing when he saw how close she looked to dying. She was in the advanced and final stages of rogue augmentation growth, her neck dark with the spread of nanite threads inside her, thick cords of the material distorting her cheeks and lips.

Kendrick felt a powerful stab of pity. He looked away.

*

Shortly after the woman had left him, Kendrick made his way to the building where he would be spending the night. Right now he wanted to be somewhere inside rather than being watched by scared eyes out in the open.

He found his way to a communal bathroom and stared for a long time at his moonlit reflection in the fly-specked mirror hanging from a nail above the washbasin. The room was little more than a cupboard with a chemical toilet, although the sink was at least plumbed in. Instead of a door, a dark wool curtain had been tacked onto the frame.

Kendrick tugged at a light cord and a halogen bulb lit up, sending shimmering sparkles skittering off the filaments that now coated his face. His gaze tracked them down the curve of his neck, seeing how they disappeared beneath his shirt collar.

"What's happening to me?" he whispered to no one. There was no sign of McCowan. Was that a bad sign? There was no way of knowing.

"You okay there?" a voice said quietly. Kendrick looked around to see the woman to whom he'd briefly spoken earlier, peering at him around the edge of the curtain.

"I never caught your name," he replied.

"Audrey," she said. "I wasn't spying, I just heard you talking to yourself." Through the now open door behind her he could see pots hanging on hooks in what was obviously a kitchen.

"Buddy mentioned you before," she continued, "so I got the impression you were on our side. But I can see the way you look at us, like you think all of us here are crazy. You were in Ward Seventeen, right?"

Kendrick nodded, and stepped out of the bathroom to stand closer to her. Audrey's words were friendly enough but, whatever their shared experiences, he reminded himself that he didn't really know these people. So he chose his own words carefully. "I was, yes, but according to Buddy it hasn't been exactly the same for me as for the rest of you."

"But you saw it – the visions? Buddy said you did."

"I saw *some* of what the rest of you saw, but I was receiving special medical treatments that stopped me getting all of it. To be honest, I don't know if I'm ready to believe that any of what I'm told you've all seen is real."

Audrey looked appalled. "The Omega is real. I've seen it, *felt* it."

"The Omega Point theory is only a theory. And, like any theory, it depends on certain preconditions – it only works if a certain set of circumstances is *presumed* to come about. You know what I mean?"

"Believe me, I'm entirely acquainted with the details."

"Are you, though? None of you know for sure that any of what you've witnessed is objectively real. All you've seen are pictures in your head. So, having that degree of faith, it's more like believing in a religion than anything else."

Audrey shook her head, smiling the knowing smile of a true believer. Kendrick felt a burst of irrational anger. She was eyeing Kendrick as if he were some errant child refusing to see the error of his ways.

The problem was that something *was* happening, something enormous, unprecedented. Somewhere up there a wormhole was forming, an impossible spatial anomaly that was giving every physicist on the planet sleepless night after sleepless night. Maybe it just wasn't something he wanted to face up to, to deal with. Who could blame him?

Kendrick wondered what Audrey's reaction would be if she knew he'd rather see the station destroyed than risk it falling into the hands of Draeger – or anyone else.

"Well, I've got some news for you," Audrey told him. "It may just seem a theory to you, but there are people out there who believe we're monsters – things are only going to get worse for us. One of these days they'll either intern us all or just kill us, and that'll be the end of it. But this way some of us get to take control. This way we choose our own destiny."

TO THE ARCHIMEDES

27 October 2096
Los Angeles

Kendrick woke deep in the night and found that he had stopped breathing again. He lurched upright, panic blighting his thoughts. *This is what it's like to be dead*, he thought: no heartbeat, no breath of life. A terrible silence filled the cavity of his chest, like a void.

He had been asleep for several hours on a cot in one corner of the house. Crickets chirruped outside a window nearby. It was hard to believe, listening to the sounds of nature, that he'd see nothing but desolation if he raised his head to look outside.

No heartbeat, no breath of life. *Am I even alive?*

Slowly, deliberately, he once again sucked air into his lungs. It heaved his chest out and he felt a nitrate-like rush, expanding like a bubble through his brain. He exhaled again.

In, then out – after several seconds Kendrick didn't have to think about it any more. He could feel his hands shaking, his thoughts clear and adrenalin-tinged.

Kendrick looked down again at the fine threads coating his skin. All of them were gold now, and the filaments appeared to be dissolving into his flesh. Slowly, his appearance was returning to normal.

He brushed one cheek with a fingertip and felt that it was smoother than several hours before. A huge wave of relief swept through him.

So far, Audrey and Buddy were the only ones there who had made any effort to speak with him, although his relations with Audrey were still distinctly on the edgy side. He'd even seen some of them huddled together, watching him from a distance and speaking in low whispers once they were sure that they were out of range of his augmented hearing.

Yet Kendrick could have listened to what they were saying if he'd really wanted to, and he was sure that many others in this place shared the same ability. But a house full of Labrats was a house with no privacy whatsoever and, in accord with the special etiquette that had evolved to suit such circumstances, he avoided listening to their conversation, despite overwhelming temptation.

It was clear by now that he wasn't going to get any more sleep for a while, so he pulled himself out of the cot and started to get dressed.

He felt slow, turgid, his body silent like a mausoleum, yet blood still moved through his arteries by some unfathomable means. He found his way to the kitchen and dribbled some tepid tank-water into his dry mouth. Then he turned to see Buddy watching him from the doorway.

"There were a lot more people around this place earlier," Kendrick observed. "Where have they all gone?"

"Remember when we talked to Veliz? They've gone on ahead. I was surprised to find anyone here at all when we arrived, but we're a little ahead of our own schedule."

"So why didn't we just go with them?"

"We have our own transport, remember? Besides, doing it this way makes more sense than all heading off together. That's why there's flights heading out from several different locations. Safer that way."

Kendrick stepped past Buddy, heading out through the main entrance and into a cool Californian night. He stared upwards at the sky, and after a moment heard Buddy step up behind him.

"I have my reasons for going up there," Kendrick said over his shoulder. "But don't forget that they're not the same as yours. When I went back down into the Maze I learned some things. I don't think it's as clear-cut as you seem to think."

He turned and stared at Buddy. "I think you're putting your-selves in great danger."

Buddy glared back. "You'd better explain that."

"Robert is part of the Bright, yes, but it's a parasitical – not a symbiotic – relationship."

"Just a minute, listen—"

Kendrick pressed on. "No, *you* listen to *me*. Peter was down there, Buddy. Robert was, too. *You* could feel it, couldn't you?"

"*What?*"

"What's so hard to believe? That Robert was the only one to achieve some kind of life after death due to his augments? Or wouldn't it seem more likely there might have been others? Peter is still alive, somehow, in the same way that Robert is. He tried to get through to all of you, but Robert managed to prevent that happening with anyone but me. That's because of the treatments Hardenbrooke gave me. But here's the real kicker. If Robert Vincenzo found some way of blocking Peter McCowan's attempts at communication with all of us, what is it that Robert so badly didn't want McCowan to tell you? Something, maybe, that you really ought to know?"

Buddy struggled visibly to absorb this new information. "Hey, first you tell me we're wrong, even though we've all been seeing the *same* things, and now you want us all to stop because of some-thing – *someone* – that only you have seen. Maybe you ought to think about that."

"Look, Draeger told me there was a way to reverse the growth of our augmentations – and I actually believe him. If he can find a way, so can other people."

Buddy shook his head. "I've heard all this before."

"Look—"

"We don't know how long something like that could take to be properly tested, and that would be an even better excuse to lock us up in the meantime. You've seen Audrey, you saw Caroline. The *Archimedes* is our only chance."

"If you believe in the reality of the Omega Singularity,"

Kendrick said carefully, "then you know it holds out for the actual resurrection, at the end of time, of everyone who ever lived. Even if we do all die, we still all get to live again someday."

Buddy threw his hands up in despair. "Christ, I *know* it's only a theory. I *also* know that what's happening up there proves at least part of it. So, no, maybe the whole human race doesn't wake up at the end of time in a far-future Heaven created by minds so advanced that they'd be indistinguishable from God. Maybe most of us just stay here and rot for all eternity, since there's no reason why any such entity should even *bother*.

"But now we have a chance, one that nobody else has, to give something back to ourselves when the rest of the world would rather see us conveniently dead. We'd never have to feel pain again – we can be anyone or anything we want to be, for ever. And maybe we'll even be the only human beings lucky enough to experience that."

"Hallelujah," Kendrick observed sourly.

Buddy gave him a sharp look, then headed over to his helicopter. Kendrick gazed after him for several minutes, wondering which of them was crazier.

The next time Kendrick woke, dawn was just beginning to break.

He'd dreamt that he'd been deep in conversation with Marlin Smeby, lost in some primeval tunnel full of twisted, hallucinatory carvings. He couldn't remember anything they'd spoken about.

Hearing something clatter outside, he sat up and looked around the darkened room. Empty sleeping bags were scattered across the floor and, since almost all the rest had gone on ahead, he was alone there. He felt racked by a thousand aches and pains.

Buddy planned to fly to the offshore launch site within the next few hours. Meanwhile, Kendrick had needed all the rest he could get.

He got up and stepped outside again, looking over to where the 'copter still sat. Beyond it stood a tall wooden gate leading onto the broken tarmac of a nearby street. Part of the tarpaulin had been flipped back, and a shadowy figure was kneeling next to the machine, surrounded by tools and equipment.

"Hey, how you doing." Audrey greeted him with a grin as he approached the craft.

"I didn't know that you knew how to handle one of these things."

"Commercial rather than military, though," she explained. The black streaks of her augment-growth were vivid under the dim red light of the dawn that was creeping over LA's broken rooftops. "Buddy's catching some zees, so I'm doing a little maintenance. Couldn't sleep, then?"

"Not any longer." Kendrick glanced around. "Is it just us left?"

Audrey shrugged. "You, me, Bud – rest are all gone." She squinted at him. "You feeling okay?"

"Fine – just got up."

She shrugged again. "Don't wander off and get lost, now. Remember, not much in the way of law around here, so stick to the compound, okay?"

Kendrick nodded. "Got it."

Audrey smiled uncertainly, then turned her attention back to the 'copter's exposed innards. Soon Kendrick heard the sound of a bolt being unscrewed followed by a muttered expletive. He stepped back inside the hut, aware of the woman's eyes constantly glancing after him.

Had someone called his name? He tensed and peered out of a window through which he could see nothing unusual. Maybe it had been Buddy he'd heard.

No: he came across Buddy in another room, curled up in a cot and fast asleep. Of course, he could have muttered something in his sleep . . .

There it was again: the faintest whisper, barely the suggestion of his name. Kendrick wondered if it was McCowan. Without really thinking about it, he slipped quietly through the ramshackle building until he found another door at the rear, which opened without a sound. The high fence surrounding the compound made it impossible for casual passers-by – had there been any – to spy on them.

He noticed another gate in the fence, presumably leading out onto a different street.

"Kendrick," whispered a voice somewhere nearby. He stopped, motionless. Nobody was visible.

He stepped out onto the street, moving as quietly as he could. Not McCowan: someone else? In either direction he could see rows of broken buildings, barren and lifeless.

Perhaps this was a bad idea. He should go back inside the fence.

Then Kendrick noticed the car, deep in the shadows of one building that had survived the atomic blast largely intact. His augmented senses picked the vehicle out in vivid detail, and he could see that its windows were silvered. It stood several blocks away from the compound where Audrey was still working on the 'copter.

The car looked shiny and new, incongruous amid so much devastation. Beside it stood Smeby.

Kendrick glanced over his shoulder and caught a strange movement, as if a distorting lens had passed in front of some scrubby bushes growing out of the cracked pavement. He realized with a start that it was someone wearing camouflage like that built into the skin of Buddy's helicopter. The hazy motion halted, resolving itself into a figure holding a rifle pointed at Kendrick's head.

Kendrick glanced towards Smeby again, catching a glint of light on a lens from a glassless window in the building looming up behind the car. Another soldier was undoubtedly positioned there, his gun trained on Kendrick.

The compound was surrounded – and only three of them were left to defend it.

Perhaps they'd traced him by some arcane means that didn't require tracking his wand; perhaps they could still trace him through the lingering Trojan nanites that Hardenbrooke had inserted in his augmentations. In which case, it was conceivable that they knew nothing about Buddy, Audrey, or any of the recently departed Labrats.

Somehow, though, Kendrick suspected otherwise. As he turned to retreat towards the gate, a bullet slammed into the ground and noiselessly kicked up a puff of dust in front of him.

Realizing that he was cornered, he stepped back onto the road and moved slowly towards the vehicle.

When he reached it, Smeby was leaning against the hood with his arms folded. "I don't know what you want," Kendrick snarled, "but I'm not interested."

"I haven't even said anything yet." Smeby smiled. "But Mr Draeger has a fresh proposition for you."

"I already told you—"

"Just hear me out, okay?" Smeby snapped. "We've decided to forget about what happened last time – Mr Draeger feels there's too much at stake."

Kendrick sensed a movement around the corner of the nearby building. He stepped away from the car, Smeby's gaze following him. At least a dozen more men were standing in a loose group beside a truck parked in the adjacent street. Although dressed in civilian clothes, they certainly looked like soldiers.

A cigarette butt glowed in the dim dawn light like a firefly as one of them drew smoke into his lungs. Their keen eyes studied Kendrick emotionlessly.

"Doesn't look like much of a welcoming committee to me," muttered Kendrick, returning his gaze to Smeby. "Who are those guys, anyway? Los Muertos?"

"Of course not," Smeby said impatiently. "If we wanted to cause you that much trouble, you'd have known about it long before now. Don't you even want to know what we want – or would you rather go through all this blind?"

Kendrick glanced back towards the fenced-off compound. Then he spat on the ground in front of Smeby's feet.

"Fine," he said. "Tell me what you want."

Smeby swung the car door open and gestured for Kendrick to get in. Kendrick stared back at him, his expression wary.

"Mr Draeger is in the fucking car, Gallmon. I'm not trying anything."

Kendrick bent down and looked inside. Draeger was indeed in the car, sitting back on a long couch that took up a large amount of space within the vehicle. With considerable misgivings, Kendrick climbed in.

Smeby slid in after Kendrick and took a seat beside him, both of them facing towards Draeger. The car had no manual control and therefore lacked a driver's seat, which allowed them extra room.

Draeger leaned forward. "Mr Gallmon, I'm a fair-minded man. I'm as fascinated as you are by what's happening far above our heads."

"You should have become a Labrat yourself, then," said Kendrick. "But maybe you wouldn't have liked it so much."

"Oh no, I would have," Draeger replied. "I have a disease of the nervous system. Neurological damage in the womb that affected millions of unborn children, a by-product of the environmental excesses of previous generations. The nanotechnology that created your augmentations would kill me within hours. It's an irony that I therefore can't get to see the Promised Land that it seems so many of you have already glimpsed."

"The experiment that Sieracki carried out on me and three others," Kendrick replied. "That's why you're so interested in me, isn't it?"

"I already warned you that the *Archimedes* is a privately owned vessel," Draeger continued, ignoring him. "Any attempt to land there constitutes trespassing. The offshore launch facility you're using is extremely vulnerable to attack. You should remember *that*."

"Fuck you. Just don't you threaten me—"

"The danger isn't from *me*, Mr Gallmon. It's from Los Muertos. They are as aware of your plans as I am. I'm offering your friends my protection."

"Your *protection?*" Kendrick laughed. "They need someone to protect them from *you.*"

"It's a sincere offer. It would be very stupid of you not to take it seriously."

Kendrick gazed soberly at Draeger. He didn't doubt his sincerity at all. Rather, it was what the man didn't say that worried him.

"Taking an offer like that seriously is one thing. It's not the same as agreeing to it."

"I can help Caroline Vincenzo."

Kendrick was thunderstruck. "She doesn't need your help," he said numbly. How did Draeger *know?*

"You might be interested to learn that she visited a Labrat-friendly clinic in Glasgow. Friendly enough not to contact the police and inform them of her visit. Nonetheless, we managed to obtain certain records, which show that the rogue growths in her body are accelerating rapidly. She may not live long enough to survive the trip to the *Archimedes.* But I can help her."

"In return for my cooperation?"

Draeger smiled gently. It wasn't the smile of a winner, of someone who believed they held the upper hand. Rather, it was the smile of someone who believed completely in the rightness of what they were saying and doing. Someone who was waiting for the rest of the world to recognize the logic of their actions. It was the smile of a madman.

"Is that why all those men are out there? In case I don't agree to cooperate?"

"I don't need to coerce you, Mr Gallmon. Once you reach the launch facility you'll have no choice but to cooperate. Without my help, you won't get even a hundred feet into the air."

"That's a threat?"

"It's an observation."

"Why me, Draeger? Why not try and persuade Buddy or any of the others?"

"None of them are as important as you. Surely you understand that now? The growths within your body have the greatest affinity with the nanite intelligences on board the *Archimedes*. And now you have been blessed with gifts from the intelligences still residing within the Maze, which will grant you access to the space habitat concerned."

Remember he's crazy. Kendrick didn't want to disabuse Draeger of his delusions, not while there might just be some chance of turning this to his advantage.

He glanced at Smeby, who sat with one leg crossed over the other, his expression as non-committal as if they were sitting in a restaurant discussing the relative merits of the wine list.

Kendrick sat back. "All right, what now?"

"You can tell me now if you accept, on behalf of your friends, my offer of safe escort to the *Archimedes*."

"In return for which, they and I allow you to retrieve any scientific data you like from the *Archimedes*, along with whatever records still exist up there, without our interference." Kendrick was careful to emphasize *whatever records*. He wanted Draeger to understand that he knew there were incriminating documents on board the space station.

Draeger nodded carefully. "That would be correct."

Kendrick smiled back, reached over and clicked the car door open. "No."

"You're making a mistake," Smeby said, a clear warning in his voice.

"Am I?" Kendrick couldn't keep the anger out of his voice. "The way I see it, you need us a hell of a lot more than we need you. You want something that's on board the *Archimedes*, but you can't get it without us. You should know by now that the others would never agree to anything if they knew it was coming from you."

He climbed out into the street and glanced back inside the car. "If we need you, we'll let you know. But, frankly, don't wait around."

He slammed the door shut on them. But Draeger just looked

quietly serene, as if he held some precious secret that the rest of the world knew nothing about.

Kendrick walked quickly back to the compound, feeling the skin between his shoulder blades burning every step of the way. But no shots rang out.

Buddy stirred groggily from his cot. "You're sure about this?"

"Very sure."

Buddy pressed the palm of one hand against his forehead and swore softly, still half asleep.

"I don't know how rational Draeger is likely to be," Kendrick told him. "He's fighting for his survival."

Next he turned to Audrey, who stood, looking worried, in the doorway. "How long before we head off?"

"Took most of the night to take care of refuelling and maintenance. You've come a long way in that 'copter, so it's best to check everything twice so we don't have any nasty surprises after we're airborne." Her eyes half closed as she became momentarily deep in thought. "But give me twenty minutes, tops, and she'll be ready."

"Can you make it ten?"

Audrey nodded hesitantly, then slipped away, looking pale.

"Jesus. So Draeger really is here?" Buddy sounded more awake now. He started to pull on a pair of boots. "How long you think we got?"

"Hard to say. He has a small army with him back there."

Several minutes later they heard the steady drone of choppers approaching, fast.

Kendrick had stepped outside to see if anyone was trying to enter the compound. He turned in time to see Buddy emerge from the doorway, still zipping up his fly.

"The tarpaulin," Buddy urged him. "Help me get it off."

Kendrick nodded, and they unveiled the helicopter, its now-exposed skin gleaming black in the early-morning light. Kendrick saw Audrey staring off towards the east, and glanced in the same direction. Small shapes, rapidly growing larger, were heading towards them in a line across the sky.

Time's up.

Kendrick was surprised that the attack came from the air. Draeger's men, after all, had moved on foot. But then, he remembered, Draeger wasn't the only hostile force they had to deal with. The approaching aircraft could also belong to Los Muertos.

Buddy was now in the pilot's seat. The helicopter's rotors whined into life, producing a steady, deafening wail within seconds.

Audrey was nowhere to be seen as Kendrick pulled himself on board, the rotors beating at the air inches above his head. Buddy mouthed her name and Kendrick jabbed a finger towards the nearest building.

He saw Audrey emerge from a doorway. She was carrying some sort of weapon, a wicked-looking black thing with a snub nose. Kendrick started to climb back out of the 'copter, feeling that he should help her in some way.

Buddy placed a gloved hand on his shoulder and shook his head. Kendrick hesitated, realizing what Buddy was saying: it wasn't likely he'd be much use.

Audrey had slung the weapon over her shoulder on a strap before leaping up in an augmented blur to grab the lower edge of the building's roof with both hands. She pulled herself up effortlessly onto the sloping surface, running up to its apex just as out of nowhere a roar of rotors beat deafeningly down around them.

Buddy pulled back on the 'copter's stick until they were hovering several feet above the ground. There was a flash of light and the sound of gunfire. Buddy took the aircraft higher as bullets streaked through the air around them.

"We have to get Audrey inside," Kendrick yelled in Buddy's ear. "She'll get herself killed."

"You think I don't know that?" Buddy yelled back. "What am I supposed to do, jump out and get her?"

Audrey was returning fire now, her weapon spitting bullets at an astonishing rate. An enemy helicopter jerked up and away, swerving and ducking as she aimed for it.

Kendrick didn't allow himself the luxury of thinking about what he did next. He slammed open the door next to him and fell for several metres, hitting the ground rolling. Keeping low, he ran towards the shelter of a nearby shed.

Something hot zinged past his ear and he found himself taking cover behind a stack of concrete blocks, which looked like they'd been salvaged from nearby ruins. Puffs of dust suddenly spurted from the hard-packed dirt only inches away.

The attack was coming, Kendrick could see now, as a new helicopter appeared from an entirely different direction. He pulled himself up onto the roof, as he'd seen Audrey do. He watched in amazement as she jumped up onto one of the struts of the attacking helicopter and ripped open the door on the pilot's side.

The helicopter rapidly spiralled upwards. He saw a body tumble out, arms and legs flailing. Not Audrey – the pilot.

He saw her leap away from the craft as it spun end over end. Audrey landed back on the building roof, feet first, the movement almost ballet-like.

Kendrick started to move towards her, seeing what she hadn't yet spotted. As the helicopter twisted in the air above her, instinct made Kendrick roll away fast, dropping off the shed roof onto the ground.

The 'copter ploughed down on top of the building, and Audrey vanished in a great plume of flames and smoke that swallowed the structure, turning it into a huge pyre.

Kendrick turned, dumbstruck, just in time to see another helicopter sweeping over the burning roof towards him. He ducked away, ready to run, before he realized that it was Buddy.

He could see the fear etched on Buddy's face through the

canopy. The aircraft dipped close enough to the ground to let Kendrick get on board.

He hurled himself back into the co-pilot's seat and, in the next instant, Buddy pulled back on the stick and they shot upwards.

Below them the ground fell away with alarming speed. "Can we make it?" Kendrick yelled.

"There's six other choppers coming this way fast. That's going to be a problem." Streets of broken buildings flashed by below.

To the east, the sun continued its slow climb into the sky, its rays reflecting off their pursuers and making them look like burning insects.

"They're keeping their distance," Buddy announced, "I don't know why. They could bring us down if they wanted to. We're outnumbered, but they're just following us."

"You know," Kendrick said carefully, "that it's me they want, not just you. They seem to think I'm important."

Buddy looked straight ahead and nodded. "Yeah, you *could* say that."

"If I hadn't come along, if Erik Whitsett hadn't been able to find me – if I hadn't come to Loch Awe that time. Is there any reason why you might not have been able to go ahead with all of this, your launch to the *Archimedes*?"

Buddy sighed, his eyes flickering over the screens that displayed the pursuing helicopters. "Look, it was clear from the start that Los Muertos thought you were important. Maybe they knew something we didn't, something we'd missed somehow when the Bright showed us what they could give us. Then you went to visit Draeger and that made us think, yeah, maybe you were vital to the whole operation in some way that we couldn't figure."

"So really you were hedging your bets. That's why you wanted *me* here."

"Ken, you're one of us – *that's* why I wanted you here. So please don't write us off as a bunch of self-serving pricks like Draeger. Some of us are 'more' like the Bright than others, sure, but in the end I don't know if it makes any damn difference. Ask the Bright – maybe they know."

So much had changed. In the beginning, Kendrick had wanted nothing to do with Buddy's plans: now he understood that the only way to halt the plans of Draeger or Los Muertos lay on board the *Archimedes* space habitat.

And then there was the question of the presumed evidence that could destroy Max Draeger. The thought that Peter McCowan was lying about such evidence – was engaged in some vast deception in which Kendrick had all too willingly played his part – had occurred to him more than a few times.

Yet, despite all his worries and doubts, he found himself believing McCowan. *Or is that just my own guilt talking?*

The landscape below revealed occasional oases of generator-powered activity where the post-Nuke reconstruction work had started. For the first time, Kendrick understood just how much he was prepared to sacrifice to bring Draeger down. More than he might ever have suspected, or admitted to anyone else.

"They're getting closer," Buddy muttered, his face turning stiff and expressionless.

A screen displayed the pursuing 'copters against a blue sky, most of the detail lost in the glare of the sun shining down on the Santa Monica hills. Kendrick studied the screen and saw tiny pulses of light appear from the helicopters, moving fast. Buddy dived suddenly, almost running their helicopter into the ground, and a missile streaked past them to plough into the soil in an explosive burst of flame and smoke.

Buddy twisted the stick again so they were climbing, the ground falling away once more in a rush as more streaks of light came uncomfortably close.

Kendrick's head spun with vertigo. Buddy was pushing the aircraft to its limits.

Buddy grunted in surprise and Kendrick looked up to see a string of tiny lights hanging in the air barely a klick ahead, directly in their path. Something about the way they hovered

291

suggested balloons of some kind – they didn't appear to be moving, so perhaps they were tethered to the ground.

"This could be some kind of trap," Kendrick said. "They might have set it up in advance, if they knew we'd be heading west."

Buddy shrugged. "Yeah, well. Maybe, maybe not. Can't turn back now. Shit."

Bright sparks sailed past them again, and again the helicopter spun to one side. Kendrick hung on as if for dear life.

"Fuck!" Buddy bellowed, gripping the stick with both hands and twisting hard. Kendrick felt his gorge rise and he choked as the aircraft wheeled over. "Okay," he heard Buddy yell, his voice verging on outright panic. "Now *that*'s just too fucking close for comfort!"

The points of light in their path had now resolved themselves into distinct yellowish and cylindrical-looking shapes. They started moving of their own volition, appearing to part in order to allow Buddy's 'copter to pass between them. Tracer fire from one of the pursuing helicopters grazed one of the cylindrical shapes and it blossomed in a ball of flame and tumbled slowly downwards.

Kendrick felt his throat start to close up once he saw just how close the other craft were. They were never going to get away from them.

In an instant, though, they were through and past the hovering shapes. Kendrick caught a fleeting glimpse of one: an unmanned helicopter drone, several feet in diameter, shaped like a fat doughnut. It wobbled in the air and, because it was slightly below and to the side of them as they flew past, he could see that at its centre was a rotor device to keep it aloft.

But what was it doing here? Was it Draeger or Los Muertos who had positioned them? It rapidly became clear that the drones were not floating idly: now they were moving with clear purpose towards their pursuers.

"What the hell *are* those things?" yelled Buddy.

"Absolutely no fucking idea," Kendrick replied. "But – Jesus! – look what's happening!"

Behind them they could see a series of bright flashes, followed by a succession of long, distant booming sounds. Burning shapes tumbled to the earth, trailing streaks of liquid flame as they spiralled downward.

Three of the pursuing helicopters were already down. The three survivors appeared to be playing a complicated game of tag with the remaining unmanned drones.

Buddy's expression was frenzied. "Somebody did that. Somebody helped us get away. Who the fuck *was* it? Who *did* that?"

Kendrick couldn't think of an appropriate reply.

27 October 2096
Over the Pacific

Most of the next hour and a half was spent flying over water, hugging the coastline as they travelled north-west. Kendrick surprised himself by falling asleep, and found that he was actually getting used to airborne dozing despite the constant thundering drone of rotor blades.

He woke – bleary-eyed, stiff-necked and with a bad headache – to gaze out on something very like an oil platform marooned in an infinity of bright blue water. Whether or not that had been its original role Kendrick didn't know but it had clearly gained a new purpose.

Its upper deck housed a gantry supporting a shuttle like those he had seen taking off from the Los Muertos base. The shuttle itself was painted pale blue, with wide strips of a darker blue angling across its body from the nose. Vapour was already emerging from its base in dense clouds before descending to meet the waves licking the platform's supporting columns far below. A ship the size of a large frigate, its upper decks strewn with radar and comms towers, floated in the water only a short distance away. As Buddy circled in towards the ship's landing pad, Kendrick recognized Veliz and some of the other Labrats from LA waiting below.

Kendrick glanced down at his hands where they rested in his lap. They still didn't look anywhere near normal, but at least they were no longer as nightmarish in appearance as when he had recently emerged from the Maze.

Kendrick stepped down from the helicopter and onto the landing pad. The ship's deck stretched out ahead of him, rising to a forest of communications dishes and radar equipment mounted just above the bridge. He enjoyed the sensation of the fresh wind against his face, the taste of salt on his tongue.

When Buddy clapped him on his shoulder, Kendrick could see how much the past several days of stress had taken out of him. A man in a naval-style white uniform stepped up onto the landing platform, followed by several others similarly attired.

"Captain Arnheim," the leading man introduced himself. "Mr Juarez, it's good to see you again. Mr Sabak would like to speak with you urgently."

"Thank you, captain."

Arnheim was a hawk-faced man in his fifties who had a look that Kendrick had come to recognize: of not being sure quite who or what to believe. He could almost read the naval officer's thoughts as his gaze settled on Kendrick. Did he need to be placed in containment? Did he represent a danger not only to the other Labrats on board but also to his own crew and the scientists?

"It looks a lot worse than it feels," Kendrick said evenly. "I'm not infectious. I don't represent any danger."

Arnheim studied him with bright, hard eyes. Kendrick knew that the man would have no hesitation in flinging him overboard if he deemed it necessary to protect his crew and passengers. "You should know that we have a containment facility in case of extreme emergencies. If your condition worsens significantly prior to the launch, we may have to make use of it."

"I understand," Kendrick replied.

They let Arnheim's officers guide them both down below, proceeding along clanging metal corridors where technicians and crewmen swarmed around them. Kendrick couldn't help but notice how Arnheim's men surrounded him at a safe distance, thus effectively isolating him from everyone they came in contact with.

Someone stepped through a door and headed towards them. He shook Buddy's hand with a strong grip. As he turned to Kendrick he faltered, then – in an impressively humane and generous gesture – reached out and shook his hand just as firmly.

"Gerard," Buddy greeted him. Gerard Sabak was one of the owners of the launch facility, and a Ward Seventeen Labrat himself.

"We have a lot to talk about," Sabak began. He was a large, hearty man, the sides of his neck distended and scarred with rogue nanite growth. His accent sounded Austrian or German, via California.

"Mr Gallmon, it's a pleasure to meet you," he said, turning now to Kendrick. "Buddy radioed ahead that you'd need medical attention. Are you able to—?"

"Even if your medical staff could do something about this, I really don't think there'd be time before . . . you know." Kendrick angled his gaze upward to the ceiling. "I think we need to talk about some other things first."

Sabak studied him uncertainly. "Are you . . . in pain? Or—?"

"I know this may sound ridiculous but it's really not as bad as it looks."

Buddy spoke up. "Jerry, this isn't the result of rogue bio-augmentation. It's a lot more like the kind of condition you pick up near the Maze – like the Los Muertos people I told you about."

Sabak sighed. "I guess I'll just have to take your word for it. Let's have something to eat in my office and discuss things there." He turned to Kendrick and studied him with a worried expression.

"To be honest, Mr Gallmon, if we took you into one of the mess rooms I think we'd have a staff riot on our hands."

Sabak took a seat behind a mahogany desk in his office. Fresh food and coffee arrived moments later, and the aroma made Kendrick feel giddy. He wolfed down a steak and salad while listening to the other two and nodding at appropriate intervals. By the time he'd finished, fatigue was tugging at his senses again. He felt as though he could sleep for a thousand years.

Buddy had been telling Sabak about their trip to the Maze. "Look" – Sabak turned now to Kendrick – "what you undertook is . . . remarkable. But I don't understand why you did it. What did you expect to find down there in the Maze?"

Buddy glanced at him as if he was ready to speak in his stead. But Kendrick wanted to explain for himself.

"I've been looking for proof that will link Draeger, absolutely and incontrovertibly, to the Labrat experiments."

"And you found such proof? Down there?"

Kendrick rubbed at his face. "Not exactly. I . . . what I found down there tells me that the proof exists on the *Archimedes*. I don't really want to go into the details now, but I needed to go to the Maze in order to learn where to look for that information once I get up there."

Sabak shot Buddy a look that bordered on the incredulous. "What makes you think that any such information would even be up there?"

"Look, neither Max Draeger nor anyone else can access, not even remotely, any records of his activities, physical or otherwise, that still exist on the *Archimedes*, and I have information that suggests they do still exist. If I can find real evidence against him it would finally bring him down. Completely."

"So you're going to track down this stuff, then join us when we go with the Bright?"

"I'm not sure about that part, no."

Sabak's expression became stony. "I know about you. I remember all the work you did during the Trials. All the shit you dug up. I was impressed. There are one or two people think you're a hero for that. You were in Ward Seventeen, though, so haven't you been seeing the same things as the rest of us?"

"I did see *something*," Kendrick admitted. "But not necessarily the same thing that the rest of you apparently experienced. Not enough to convince me personally of what you and the rest of them believe."

"I guess not," Sabak replied after an uncomfortable pause. "Otherwise you'd know already."

He leant forward, his voice lowering as if inviting Kendrick into a conspiracy. "Are you aware that there are only just over a hundred of us left from Ward Seventeen?"

Kendrick went numb with shock. "A hundred?" He felt his skin flush. "I didn't realize—"

"There were considerably more who escaped the Maze, yes. But it's been a while since then. The ones who didn't survive – well, not many of them died through anything you'd call natural causes. Whether or not you feel we're right in this venture, just remember, Kendrick, there's nowhere else now for any of them to go."

Caroline's eyes glittered, and for one terrible moment Kendrick thought that she might turn and look at him. Instead she stared, unseeing, at the ceiling of the containment unit. Her clothes had been replaced by a blue paper smock that reminded him with a chill of the clothes they had been forced to wear in the Maze. A woman stood at a respectful distance behind him, lips pursed in the centre of a round face. A tag on her jacket identified her as Doctor Maria Numark.

Something had distorted Caroline's skull. The bone around her right ear appeared to be puffed out, thick, rigid lines contorting the flesh there. Her lips were parted slightly, as if she had been about to speak before she died.

Nothing. Kendrick could feel nothing. It was as if his emotions had been sucked out of him, leaving only a shell of semi-organic augmentation that had mistaken itself for a human being.

"I'd like to see her, for real." He turned to Doctor Numark. "Let me in there."

Maria Numark shook her head and gestured at the elaborate precautions set up around where Caroline lay on the other side of the glass. Kendrick wondered if eyebrows had been raised among the non-Labrat crew when Sabak and his colleagues had installed a secure biological containment room. "I'm afraid that's impossible."

Kendrick licked his lips. "When?" he asked. "I mean, when did she . . ." He gestured towards Caroline.

"Just before you arrived on board. We did everything we could." He could see where some of the augments had broken through her flesh, vague shapes that pushed up her paper smock here and there. He looked away, sickened, then stepped back.

"We'll need to arrange for a funeral service," he mumbled.

The doctor glanced at a wall clock. "To be honest, I'm not sure there's time for that, Mr Gallmon. I'm sorry."

"She looked as though she was getting better the last time I saw her."

Doctor Numark nodded sympathetically. "According to the literature, that's often the case. Outward appearances, however, when it comes to this kind of thing, can be extremely deceptive." She stepped forward. "Perhaps . . . I could leave you alone out here for a few minutes, if you wish."

Kendrick pressed his forehead against the glass, feeling numbing waves of exhaustion wash over him. Did he imagine those faint flecks of light where her hands touched the metal pallet on which she lay? As if something metallic extended downwards, from her fingertips. Something threadlike.

He heard Maria Numark step up behind him, gently placing

fingers on his arm. He began to turn and almost lost his balance. He reached out and caught himself on the edge of a table.

"You need some rest now," the doctor told him, her voice firm. "You'll do yourself an injury if you don't get some sleep."

"No—"

"Rest."

Kendrick dreamed.

He opened his eyes. He was back on the *Archimedes*.

A great silver cloud filled the air far above his head. Moments later it broke up into a rippling mist of winged shapes that spiralled down towards him.

The last thing he remembered was Buddy helping him to a spare cabin after being called to the surgery by Doctor Numark. Buddy had looked ashen-faced, having only just found out himself about Caroline's death. If Buddy had said anything of consequence to him, he didn't remember it.

Kendrick had put his head down on the pillow, his mind and emotions still full of the memory of Caroline lying still and lifeless, and now he was here again.

Like he'd always been here, waiting.

The creatures came closer, flitting through the turgid air, their tiny faces ugly and distorted. No wonder it had taken him so long to recognize their origin.

"Robert," Kendrick said at last as a thousand winged shapes hovered in the air around him.

One of them spoke, its voice clear and full, unexpected from something so small.

"You shouldn't be here," the tiny Robert-homunculus said. "We don't want you here."

"I'm coming anyway," said Kendrick. "I'm bringing Peter McCowan with me."

The creature's companions beat chaotic patterns in the air as Kendrick spoke.

"Peter told me you wouldn't let him get free from the Maze," he continued. "You kept him down there, blind and deaf."

The rapid motion of the tiny creatures became even more frenzied as they swirled and dived with renewed vigour. He thought again of shoals of fish darting through deep ocean waters.

"*Peter* is an abomination," squealed the same creature as before, hovering momentarily in front of Kendrick's face. "You must not bring him here!"

"I need to find something that's on board the *Archimedes*. I can—"

"You must not bring him here! You must not bring him here!" another of the creatures buzzed angrily – or was it the same one? It was impossible to tell as they darted around him. "I can see him hiding inside you!"

Kendrick's mouth felt dry. *What did Buddy or Sabak or any of them see and hear in their visions, to think that this thing was sane?*

The creatures all around reminded him of nothing so much as locusts preparing to swarm. He ducked and shielded his face as they buzzed around him in uncountable legions. Their sheer weight of numbers forced him to kneel on the ground, shielding himself with his arms. He spoke again, raising his voice to a yell. "It's you that the Bright use to communicate with us, right? You were the first. You became a part of them. Something went wrong."

They scattered away from him in an instant in a great storm of flapping. The thick, honeyed air felt full of a palpable menace.

They circled him still, their massed voices roaring as one. Kendrick's head filled with so many alien images and thoughts that he crumpled completely to the ground, unable to absorb even a fraction of the information besieging his skull.

But behind the images and sensations he detected something else, something deeper: regular, rhythmic. Almost . . . like singing.

No, not singing – talking. But nothing like any language he had ever heard . . . nonetheless, he felt he might be able to understand it if only he listened harder.

Kendrick summoned the energy to stand again, batting at the tiny shapes now darting towards him, shrieking and flapping. However much he might tell himself none of this was real, instinct said differently.

He moved as if in a dream. The singing-but-not-singing began to build, drowning out even the chaotic menace of the buzzing creatures.

The singing became clearer, suddenly perfectly comprehensible. He understood that this was the Bright, rather than Robert, and that they were now speaking to him directly.

Kendrick found himself floating, caught up in the light now flooding around him. He looked down and saw a grassy plain far below. On it, two men wearing Los Muertos insignia were running for their lives towards the entrance of a low one-storey building.

One of them stopped to point a nozzled device at a vast swarm of Robert-homunculi bearing down on him: flames belched out of it. Kendrick noticed the fuel tank slung over his shoulders.

Regardless of his efforts, the soldier was soon engulfed in gossamer wings. They swarmed around both men in great shimmering masses, eventually drowning and crushing them.

And then, without apparent transition, Kendrick found himself outside the *Archimedes* itself, the surface of the station slipping past beneath him. He recognized there the two shuttles he'd seen taking off from the desert, their hulls jutting out at right angles from a row of docking bays surrounded by an external gantry threaded with access tubes and pressurized pods.

And then even the *Archimedes* vanished. It came to him now that this was what Buddy, and Sabak, and Caroline, and all the rest of them had been seeing.

Whatever Hardenbrooke had put inside Kendrick, it was no longer blocking the Bright's signal.

He floated far above the curve of the Earth, a great half-crescent lit by the twinkling lights of cities still shrouded in night.

He saw clouds lit from underneath by flashes of lightning some-where over the Bay of Biscay.

He watched as the nightline slid across the face of the Earth, faster and faster, becoming a blue-green blur within what seemed like seconds.

Faster, and yet faster.

The stars began to move in their positions. A sensation of utter cold filled Kendrick as he looked towards the broad sparkling band of the Milky Way and saw that it too was in motion.

The universe aged around him. Thousands upon thousands of stars swept past, time flying by at a rate of tens of millions of years every second. He saw galaxies arranged in patterns too regular to be natural, connected by what appeared to be beacons of light strung between them.

In his mind, Kendrick felt the strengthening heartbeat of vast empires, and of invasive hive-minds absorbing countless helpless worlds before themselves fading back into obscurity, half-forgotten legends in less time than it took for his eyelids to blink.

He spun on and on until any sense of his physical body had vanished, reducing him to a tiny mote of awareness racing at ever greater speed through the lifetime of the universe. He saw the final darkness approaching, became aware of a vast intel-ligence surrounding him. And then he understood: they were going all the way to the end.

The end of all things.

The galaxies were crashing together now, and Kendrick imagined that he could hear the cries of worlds dying. He wit-nessed entire constellations surrounded by vast artificial shells of energy that trapped and retained the light of their stars, banishing them from the visible universe. Throughout the mighty expanse of time and space he could sense what the Bright had found when they had first reached out, a hundred billion years into the future.

The intelligence that he had sensed earlier surrounded him totally now, vast and omnipotent, and tens of billions of years old.

It permeated to the deepest level of reality, residing in the weak, hidden dimensions below the quantum soup that constituted the most fundamental level of existence.

The cosmos shrank and darkened and Kendrick was hurled ever onward. All around him the universe rushed towards its conclusion, the galaxies colliding in fiery explosions . . . faster and faster . . .

. . . and then it stopped.

Kendrick sensed that he was not alone.

His cheek rested on damp fragrant grass, soft sunlight trickling down from somewhere far above. He raised his head.

"Sleeping on the job, eh?" Peter McCowan grinned down at him, a cigarette dangling from his stubby fingers.

Kendrick stared at him, stunned. He gathered his wits, then remarked: "So if you're here, I guess this must be Hell?"

Peter laughed, the sound rumbling from deep in his chest. "Nah, it's Heaven – that's why the cigarettes taste like shit." Again, that deep, rumbling laugh; and it was like all those years since the Maze had never happened.

"Where are we?" Kendrick rose, looking up and around him. He found it impossible to react to what had just happened to him: it was too much, too quickly, on a scale he couldn't even imagine. "It looks like—"

"The Tay Hills is my guess," said Peter. "Fucking hell, a realm of infinite possibility to choose from, and this is what your mind picks?" He shook his head and took a drag on his cigarette. "No imagination, you. But yeah, this is it."

Clouds scudded low on the horizon. It was so real, so normal, that it was surreal.

"And this . . . this really is the Omega?"

Peter shrugged. "I guess so."

"You *guess* so?"

Peter raised his hands. "It's not like I've got some kind of special knowledge, Kendrick. I was trapped down there for years by that bonkers son of a bitch. You don't know what it was like:

everything I thought, he heard. Everything he thought, I heard."
He grinned. "Or at least that was the case until you sprang me. As
long as I'm with you, I can help you."

The sky had begun to darken even as they spoke, revealing a
great whirlpool of stars that stretched from horizon to horizon.
The stars themselves rippled, as if invisible shapes were darting
through the atmosphere, distorting and refracting the starlight
with their passage.

A vivid awareness crept into every cell of Kendrick's being.
Everything – the grass, trees, clouds, the stars and even the air –
was alive, sentient. It was God, after a fashion, but a God born of
science and knowledge.

During his long journey here, Kendrick had seen flesh and
silicon merge into an intelligence woven into the fabric of the
cosmos itself. He could sense it all around him. It enervated him,
overwhelmed him.

"The *Archimedes*," he managed to say. "What are you going to
do when we get there?"

"You'll see," Peter replied. "We won't be speaking again before
we arrive. I need to prepare." He paused. "I'm sorry about
Caroline."

"Yeah," Kendrick mumbled. "Me too."

"You've not quite taken it in, have you?"

"Not really, no." Kendrick looked back up. "I've seen too many
people end up dead over the years."

"Including me."

Kendrick allowed himself a small smile. "Including you.
Though it feels really weird to say it with you standing right
there."

"You mean you're getting used to it."

"Christ, I hope not." Kendrick let out a bitter chuckle. "Numb
to it, more like." The image of Caroline lying dead in the containment room wouldn't leave his mind's eye. He couldn't stop
himself imagining what it must have been like for her in her last
moments. "Listen, I need to know something," he went on

quickly, hoping to banish those thoughts. "Where do I go once we're on board?"

"The main research facility," said Peter, his voice fading. "In the second chamber."

There was still more that Kendrick wanted to ask. But now he could almost sense the confines of the ship's cabin around him again, the hillside fading like little more than a particularly vivid dream.

He woke in the small cabin as klaxons filled the air with a loud whooping that sent dull vibrations through the frame of his bunk.

He glanced at the clock mounted on the wall, his mind still reeling from revelation and mystery. Only six hours to launch time.

Twenty minutes later, Kendrick found Sabak up on the ship's bridge, conferring with Arnheim. Buddy and Veliz were there too. The sirens had finally shut off several minutes before, but Kendrick hadn't failed to notice the strained expressions on the crew members he'd passed in the narrow corridors or the way some of them glanced away at his approach. He hadn't had time to check in a mirror, but he reckoned he could assume that he still looked pretty gruesome.

Buddy glanced over when he arrived. "Looks like we're under attack." A look of concern crossed his face. "Look, you've just lost someone important to you. Are you sure you—?"

"I'm fine. I'm not an invalid." Kendrick glanced over at Sabak. "What sort of attack?"

Sabak looked at him as though he was about to tell him that he shouldn't be there. "Hard to say," he finally said, shrugging. "They're holding off for now. But it's not looking good." He turned to look back out towards the horizon.

Kendrick stepped up beside Sabak. From here he could see across the whole of the ship and a large expanse of the ocean beyond. At first he thought the dark line separating sea and sky was a distant shore. Then he saw that it was in fact another ship, but one that apparently stretched across a daunting expanse of the horizon.

Next he glanced over at the launch platform, a hundred or so metres away. Four helicopters were hovering around the shuttle, keeping their distance but clearly presenting a considerable threat. Kendrick could see the missile tubes bulging from their under-carriages.

"Draeger," Sabak informed Kendrick sourly.

"How can you be sure?"

Sabak looked over at Arnheim, who nodded to a bank of screens displaying high-res images of the ship on the horizon. Kendrick could see it was an oil tanker, and it didn't take much to guess that this was where the 'copters had come from.

"We've checked the records," Sabak explained. "The tanker is owned by one of Max Draeger's subsidiary companies."

"Okay, so do we know what he wants?"

Buddy stepped up beside Kendrick. "You were the last one to talk to him. If anybody knows the answer to that question, it's you."

"I told you, he says he wants us to take him or his men up there with us when we go."

Arnheim stabbed a finger out at the four aircraft still buzzing around the shuttle. "Or what? He's going to blow us up? Is that what he wants?"

"He offered us some kind of protection from Los Muertos."

Arnheim turned to Sabak. "Is it worth considering?"

Kendrick stepped towards Arnheim. "No, it's not. Not under any circumstances."

"Sir." A young man stepped over from a bank of terminals on the far side of the bridge. "We've got a message incoming."

Arnheim turned to him. "Is it from the tanker?"

"Yes, sir, they want to talk to the, uh . . ." He glanced nervously at Kendrick and the other Labrats. "To the passengers."

"That's fine, Stan." Sabak spoke to Arnheim. "Re-route the signal to the back-up comms room and we'll take it in there."

Sabak stepped over to join Kendrick, Buddy and Veliz while gesturing towards the exit.

"If you please," he said quietly. "It's just on the next deck down. No reason to get the crew or the launch staff any more worried than they need to be."

A few minutes later they found themselves in a long low-ceilinged room furnished with office chairs and banks of terminals similar to the ones that Kendrick had seen on the bridge itself. A crewman glanced over his shoulder as they entered, his gaze lingering on Kendrick for a little longer than might have been considered polite under normal circumstances. Kendrick watched as the crewman finally remembered how to close his mouth. Sabak dismissed the man and slid into the vacated seat. He began rapidly tapping at a touch-screen.

As Kendrick and the rest stepped up behind him, a variety of views of the surrounding ocean sprang to life on the wall-mounted screens. Kendrick could see that the tanker had drawn nearer, approaching the launch pad at an angle. It had probably been braking for some time.

Another screen sprang to life, fizzing with static before resolving into an image of Max Draeger talking to someone off-camera. He turned, his eyes looking slightly to one side as he focused on the lens of his display screen.

Sabak addressed Draeger's image. "Mr Draeger, we have you on a secure line. You're speaking directly to me and some witnesses here aboard the launch-control vessel. I'm a director of the company that owns this facility. Is that approaching tanker yours?"

"Yes, it is." Draeger's voice sounded calm. "I have a proposition to make to you."

"Just a minute," said Sabak, shooing Buddy away with a wave of his hand as he leant forward to speak. "I have to ask, are those helicopters around our launch pad also yours? Because if they are, you're currently in violation of enough internationally recognized regulations to bury you in a ton of shit from now till doomsday.

Those 'copters are armed, and that in itself is considered an act of piracy."

"The helicopters are there for your own protection," Draeger replied. "You have only a few hours left before your launch window closes. I'm offering my own security services as a protection against interference."

Kendrick bent forward towards the screen. "What do you want now, Draeger?"

Draeger smiled tightly. "Were you aware that a squadron of Los Muertos-piloted fighter jets is currently flying north-west from Panama to blow you out of the water?"

Kendrick blinked. "I don't have any reason to believe you."

Draeger shrugged. "In that case, maybe you should wait until they arrive."

Sabak put a hand on Kendrick's shoulder but he shrugged it off. "Stop fucking around," he said to the screen, "and just tell us what you want."

"If you agree to carry a selection of my own men on board the *Archimedes*, I will guarantee to use all my available resources to prevent any hostile attacks on your ship and facility during and after the launch itself."

Sabak motioned silently to Kendrick and they stepped away from the screen.

Sabak spoke in a low voice. "You're supposed to know the guy inside out. That's what Buddy told me. Is he telling the truth?"

"Probably, but no guarantees. He's likely bluffing us at the same time."

"You're going to have to explain that to me."

"I don't believe for one moment that he'd just stand by and let us be wiped out by those supposed jets if we refused his help. We're his only ticket on board the *Archimedes*. If we wait long enough, I'm sure he'll give us protection regardless of whether or not we accept his offer, even to have the slimmest chance of persuading us to help him get on board."

"What if we accept his offer anyway?"

"Remember who this is," Kendrick said. "This is Max Draeger. We don't have any proof that those fighter jets even exist – or, if they do, that they aren't *his*."

"Shit." Sabak stared into space, thinking hard, then shook his head. "Look, *assuming* he's telling the truth about those fighter jets, then turning him down still means taking an enormous risk, whether or not he's bluffing. If he really did stand by while we came under attack, then hundreds of lives that myself and Captain Arnheim are supposed to be responsible for would be put at risk. No." He shook his head again. "I'm not taking any more chances if I can possibly help it."

Kendrick felt a wave of defeat wash over him. "If we come to any agreement with him, we're going to be sucked into something we're going to regret. We're dealing with the devil here."

"Look, I need all the advice I can get, I admit. But if there's any truth in what he's saying I don't have any choice but to agree to his terms."

Kendrick shook his head angrily, fighting to keep his temper. "That's your decision," he said tightly. "Just remember, he's as responsible for Caroline Vincenzo's death as if he'd put a gun to her head and pulled the trigger."

"I know that," Sabak said. "Just don't make the mistake of thinking that I like this any more than you do."

Sabak stepped back over to the monitor and addressed Draeger. "We're going to need evidence before we accept anything whatsoever from you. Can you prove any of what you've told us?"

An icon flashed on the screen below Draeger's image. "I'm uploading the information you need right now," Draeger stated.

Buddy leant over Sabak and tapped the icon. "This is a live satellite feed," he explained. He nodded at Draeger's image. "Can he hear us?"

Sabak tapped another icon. "Not now, he can't."

"Look, this is the same kind of sat-recon info and telemetry we used to get back in my army days. Live feeds of plane and ship movements and likely intercept points."

"I know about these things just as well as you do," said Sabak. "They can be faked."

Buddy shook his head. "No, not these. Look at the satellite ident information. That's coming straight from pre-war orbital platforms that can't be hacked into. You'll never, ever get those idents on any kind of civilian GPS networks. At the most, Draeger might have hacked into a transmission from one of the sats in order to siphon off this information, but it's legit all the same."

"So you're saying we have to take this stuff seriously."

Buddy nodded emphatically. "I am, yes."

Numbers scrolled up on the screen as Kendrick watched. Latitudes and longitudes, air speed and distance. Buddy tapped a finger on a series of tabled figures. "And if this is anything to go by, those fighter jets will get here just about the time we're due to launch."

Sabak put out a finger, letting it hover over the voice icon for several moments before touching it. "Mr Draeger, you believe that you can't get on board the *Archimedes* without us. Correct?"

"Every salvage expedition carried out by myself – or by others – has always ended in disaster. That's a matter of public record."

"What makes you so sure that you'll succeed with our help, then?"

"I know about the Bright, Mr Sabak. Indeed, I know as much about what is happening here as you do, except I haven't shared the . . . *experiences* that you and the other Augments have. Besides, once I get on board the station I will require only a limited amount of time to extract the information that interests me. It's my belief that I have a much greater chance of success if I accompany those with whom the Bright clearly share a powerful affinity."

"What's on the *Archimedes* that you want so badly?"

"I created the Bright, therefore I should be the one to communicate with them. There is certain information on board the station that is wired to my direct command, meaning that it can only be accessed by me in person. I wish to retrieve it." Draeger paused. "The benefit to humanity of the knowledge harvested by

the Bright may be immeasurable. That alone justifies my participation in this expedition."

Draeger turned his attention to Kendrick next. "Mr Gallmon,
do you remember when you left Los Angeles and came under fire?
Do you remember the aerial drones that attacked your pursuers?"

"So that *was* you," Kendrick heard Buddy behind him.

Draeger nodded. "Think of it as a goodwill gesture. If not for
that, neither of you would be here today."

"Is this true?" asked Sabak, addressing both of them.

"We did come under fire as we left LA," Buddy confirmed.
"Something got in the way of the 'copters chasing us."

"Remember, without me you won't get off the ground,"
Draeger stated. "Will you accept my offer?"

"We'll be back in touch," Sabak replied. Then he looked around
at the others. Nobody said anything, so he reached out and
touched the screen. Draeger faded to black.

"Now that is one slippery bastard," said Sabak. But he sounded
impressed.

"There's something about Draeger actually saving our lives that
makes me feel ill," muttered Veliz. "He doesn't even try to deny
he's manipulating us to get his own way."

"We don't have long now before we go up," Buddy reminded
them. "This late in the game, I don't know if we have any choice
but to accept his terms." Sabak nodded his agreement at this.

Kendrick felt a cold horror creeping into his belly. This was
wrong, all wrong. "Don't ever make the mistake of taking him at
his word. Once we're up there, that'll be another matter entirely.
If he tries anything, it'll be him against us. But we're Labrats –
We'll still have *that* advantage."

Kendrick found his way to the deck, unable to remain in the
comms room while Sabak contacted Draeger to agree to his terms.
He wondered if Draeger intended to return to Earth with whatever information he gained. Or was it possible that he believed he

could travel through the wormhole to the Omega along with the rest of the Labrats?

Once Kendrick was out in the open the sea air made him feel light-headed. The waters, as expected, were calm: if it had been otherwise the launch would have been disastrously delayed. The sky was cloud-free, the ocean in front of him disappearing into limpid blue depths as clear and smooth as crystal.

He looked over to the tanker, which had now stopped moving. Its upper decks looked as though they had been modelled after an aircraft carrier, and a dozen sleek-looking military-style jump jets stood alongside more missile-carrying armoured helicopters. Dozens of figures, insect-like at that distance, moved across its acres of steel. Kendrick thought again of Angkor Wat and wondered if the huge vessel was some kind of mobile secondary base of operations for Draeger.

He gazed up at the early-evening sky, the first stars revealing themselves as the light began to fade. The *Archimedes* was orbiting somewhere far above his head, and the reality of his decision to go there was only just beginning to sink in. He turned his attention to the shuttle, sleek and powerful-looking, resting on its launch platform. As he watched, Draeger's helicopters moved away from the platform, returning to the tanker. Clearly, Sabak had come to an agreement with Draeger.

Buddy came for him a while later, clapping him on the shoulder.

"This is it," he said. "You ready to go?"

Kendrick turned and looked at his old friend. "Are we really going to do this?"

"Sure we are. Still full of misgivings, aren't you?"

Kendrick looked back over the sea. "Can you really leave all this behind?"

"I probably wouldn't survive more than another few years here before my augments killed me," Buddy said calmly. "You seem different – care to share?"

"I experienced something like a vision, Buddy. I think it was what you saw. As though I was taken on a carnival ride through the history of the universe."

"All the way?"

Kendrick nodded. "All the way."

Buddy cocked his head at him. "But you still don't really believe it, do you?"

Kendrick sighed and turned away from looking at the launch platform. He remembered his conversation with McCowan. "Not like you do: no revelation, no firm sense that this is absolutely the right thing to do."

"Kendrick, for most of the people going with us there is no other way. Even if they felt they were just taking a chance they'd still take it. It's either that or stay here on Earth, hated and despised, and wait for a long and lingering death. It's not much of a choice. Remember, I hate Draeger just as much as you do. I want you to find the proof you're looking for. I just don't like the thought of staying here and dying slowly, maybe locked up in a secure ward somewhere."

Kendrick shook his head. "Look, the one thing I know about Draeger is that he doesn't lie. He could stab you in the back, but he's too proud of his achievements to ever make claims that are unsupportable."

"You're talking about that cure he offered you, right?"

"I met someone out at Angkor Wat who assured me that his rogue augments had been stabilized by Draeger's treatments. The same treatments that I was receiving from Hardenbrooke."

Buddy regarded him sceptically. "So you're saying that you'll return from the *Archimedes* with evidence to incriminate Draeger, but then you'll still take his cure?"

"If Draeger's really found a way to control the Labrat augments, then other people can develop the same techniques. But even if there were no cure *yet*, I'd still want to come back. There's always hope."

"Maybe for you, Kendrick, if you want to take that chance." Buddy shook his head. "But I already told you, I've got more faith in the Bright than I have in any number of spurious claims about curing something that I don't believe *can* be cured."

The funeral service never happened, because Doctor Numark had felt constrained to incinerate Caroline's remains immediately as a precautionary measure. Kendrick felt his temper rise when she told him that he couldn't even keep the ashes for a ceremony later as she wanted to keep them isolated. To Kendrick, the need to mark Caroline's passing in some way felt vital, necessary.

It was in case, Doctor Numark argued, there was even a slight chance of a containment breach. Kendrick almost laughed in her face, insisting that since he himself constituted a walking containment breach it wasn't likely to make much difference to him. She replied stonily that unfortunately there wasn't much she could do about *him*.

In the end, he dragged Buddy back out onto the deck, since he was the only other Labrat still alive who had really known Caroline. They took sips from a bottle of whisky that Buddy had acquired from a crewman and stared silently out to sea. There really wasn't much either of them could bring themselves to say.

Within the hour they were ferried by boat to the launch platform and each of them was given a lightweight spacesuit to wear, marked with the colourful logo of Sabak's private launch company. A hundred or so Labrats trooped onto the platform, looking not so different from the kind of rich tourists who'd spend an afternoon orbiting the Earth as an alternative to skiing in the Alps.

Kendrick soon found himself inside a steel-walled hut set high up in the gantry, from where he and the rest could look down the length of the shuttle, to its engines far below.

27 October 2096
Cocha Canyon offshore launch platform

The evening skies above them were still clear, the sea still calm. Ancillary launch technicians wearing jumpsuits and hard hats carefully inspected each of the spacesuits three times. Kendrick could hear continuous, incessant systems checks crackling over a nearby intercom.

Just as the checking procedures were completed, the attack finally came.

First, there were dark spots on the horizon. Then, just as Kendrick and the rest were being guided through the gantry and along an elevated platform towards a door set in the side of the shuttle, three sleek silver shapes rocketed past the platform, moving over Draeger's ship in a flash and continuing onwards in a long, curving trajectory.

At the same time, Kendrick noticed a helicopter lifting from the deck of Draeger's ship. It landed on the launch platform's landing pad barely a minute later and he watched as several small figures stepped out and looked around, half bent over under the whirring blades, before stepping quickly to one side. He could see Draeger among them, and the others, he was sure, were the men he'd seen waiting in the shadows of the ruined buildings of LA. They all wore spacesuits modified with black Kevlar body armour.

A moment later another figure stepped out of the helicopter just before it lifted to return to the tanker. This time it was Smeby.

"Jesus Christ," he heard someone mutter. Kendrick turned to see Sabak standing nearby. "Will you look at that?"

They all turned to look as one, as three simultaneous explosions of light shot upwards from the main deck of the tanker. Something flared, arrowing in towards the three jets which were now twisting round in their trajectory to take another pass over the launch platform. This time, Kendrick was sure, they would fire on it.

He glanced around, seeing how utterly exposed they all were on the gantry. There would never be enough time to get them all inside the shuttle, and even that was far from the safest place to be.

Then he saw the jets veer in a curve that would bring the shuttle directly into their line of fire. A moment later two of the aircraft twisted away in a high-speed manoeuvre as the missiles launched from Draeger's ship rapidly closed in. Kendrick felt his heart crawl into his throat as two of the pursuing missiles sped into the ocean in an explosion of salt spray.

The third missile, however, zeroed in on the third jet, whose pilot had veered too close to the waves, and as he pulled up and away from the ocean the missile gained on him. The two met in a blossoming ball of fire a few hundred metres away from the launch platform. People yelled and screamed around Kendrick as shredded pieces of the jet's fuselage shot overhead. A deep shudder ran through the platform's structure.

He gazed, dry-mouthed, at the shuttle. That had been far too close.

"We've got to launch now," Kendrick yelled at Sabak who was standing just a few feet away. "For Christ's sake, get everybody on board!"

Sabak shot him an angry look. "What the hell do you think we're already *doing*?"

Kendrick looked around to see the remaining two jets swoop off into the far distance, half a dozen of Draeger's choppers in pursuit of them.

There was a sudden altercation at the head of the line. Kendrick watched silently as an elderly couple, their faces distorted and ugly from runaway augmentation growth, refused to get on board. He could easily understand, since he had his own doubts about boarding a flying bomb while it was coming under attack. He watched as they hurried back past him: the old woman weeping, her partner stony-faced but clearly frightened. Kendrick turned and watched one or two people at the rear of the line break away and go towards them, presumably to attempt to persuade them not to turn back.

"Is this going to be safe? Are those planes going to come back?" asked the woman standing in front of Kendrick. She was wide-eyed with fear. Like the rest, she carried her helmet in a knapsack over her shoulder, but she wore an incongruous brightly coloured scarf that covered most of her neck where it was exposed under the heavy rim of the spacesuit's neck ring.

"I think we'll be just fine," Kendrick lied, his voice tight. "We'll get on board, and then . . ."

She nodded. Kendrick could see how badly she was trembling. He looked up and down the line, shocked by how many of those around him were obviously in the later stages of rogue augment growth. These, then, were the ones who had nothing to lose, who possessed only the belief that, in some far-future place, they might have everything to gain.

Kendrick looked again towards the horizon but could see nothing from where he was standing. If the choppers were still in pursuit, they were far away on the other side of the platform.

Kendrick duly arrived at the front of the queue where a technician guided him speedily on board through an airlock inserted into what had originally been a pair of cargo-bay doors. He turned around just before he entered to see that the high-capacity elevator that had lifted them into the gantry was rising again. Draeger stepped out, dressed in a grey-blue spacesuit with racing stripes on the arms, a lightweight helmet tucked into the crook of his arm. Marlin Smeby appeared by his side, followed by the rest of Draeger's entourage.

Kendrick spoke for a moment to the technician who was processing everyone on board, then waited until Draeger and his men, queuing dutifully, reached the shuttle. Sabak was talking quietly to Draeger, and he glanced over at Kendrick with a wary expression when he noticed him waiting. Everyone else was already on board.

Draeger studied them both in turn with dark, hard eyes before smiling tightly. "I appreciate your help in this matter," he said to them both. "There are wonderful things happening just a few thousand miles above our heads. We may soon be witnessing things that very few people are ever likely to, at least in this life."

Kendrick glanced over at Smeby who gazed back levelly. Smeby, he knew, was the one he really had to worry about. Smeby was Draeger's right hand.

Draeger smiled disingenuously. Kendrick turned away from him to enter the shuttle.

Three more technicians guided them into a tall vertical bay filled with seats, all facing upwards. Kendrick tried to ignore the feeling of vertigo but with minimal success. He was led to his seat via a complicated array of ladders and strapped carefully into place. Buddy was positioned nearby. They nodded to each other.

"I'm sure there were more people than this," Kendrick called to Buddy over the tumult of voices. Some others nearby were weeping, not without reason. One or two were even praying, although Kendrick couldn't help but wonder to what or to whom their prayers were directed.

Buddy looked pointedly over his shoulder at Draeger and his men who were being helped into seats at the very rear of the passenger bay. It occurred to Kendrick that the only reason there were any seats for them was because of the Labrats who had turned back or who had died before they could make it here. He thought of Erik, dying by a frozen northern shore, and of Audrey, back in LA. And Caroline. He stared over again at Draeger and nursed the hate that burned deep within him.

Then, finally, even the technicians were gone and the passengers were alone. The air was filled with nervous muttering and the incessant litanies of the few people who were praying.

The same image played over and over in Kendrick's mind: the third Los Muertos shuttle barely getting off the ground before exploding, its sides rupturing and splitting, liquid fire spewing out, anything alive inside it obliterated instantly . . . he gripped the armrests of his seat so hard that sharp spikes of pain radiated through his hands.

Instinct told Kendrick to get himself out of the shuttle, to run, to throw himself into the Pacific and start swimming. But just then a deep pulsation rattled through the craft, building to a powerful and steady roar. The craft lurched violently, and he let out a yell. People around him screamed, clearly believing as he did that the attacking jets had returned, or that the whole platform had been holed and was sinking. For a moment he imagined that the shuttle had been blown free from its gantry and was falling towards the ocean. Powerful vibrations made his teeth rattle.

Very gently, the shuttle swayed. Panicked, Kendrick glanced over at Buddy, and to his consternation saw him grinning happily. Turning in Kendrick's direction, Buddy gave him a thumbs-up.

Next followed a terrible lurch, and the whole craft began to tremble with furious energy. An enormous invisible hand seemed to press down on Kendrick's face and chest and he writhed desperately.

"When are we taking off?" someone shouted over the tumult.

"We already have," Kendrick heard Buddy yell. Barely audible, there were a few half-hearted cheers and whoops.

They were off.

Fifteen minutes later Sabak unstrapped himself and floated over to Buddy, conferring with him briefly. Kendrick gripped his armrests, convinced he was falling, knowing it was only the lack of gravity that made him feel that way. Most of the other passengers would remain strapped in for the duration of their short flight to the space station. He still couldn't quite believe they had not been blown out of the skies.

He found it wasn't quite so difficult to adapt to free fall as he might have expected. In fact, once he was out of his seat it was kind of fun.

Buddy unstrapped himself next and floated over to Kendrick. "We need to talk further with Sabak about Draeger, and we don't have much time to figure out what we're going to do once we get to the *Archimedes*."

"All that really matters is that nobody makes the mistake of trusting him."

"Those guys with him . . ."

Kendrick glanced carefully to the rear of the cabin where Draeger had unstrapped, as had Smeby and the rest of them. They still remained carefully apart from everyone else.

"You might want to assume that his men are Augments, too," Kendrick replied.

Buddy looked at him quizzically. "You mean Labrats? They don't look—"

"Not Labrats. Black-market work – at least one of them. I've met others, too, including a woman employed by Draeger. She was also an Augment but I'd be surprised if she was ever within a thousand miles of the Maze."

Buddy frowned. "There's a shitload of international laws against . . ." He stopped, and pressed one hand against the side of his head. "Jesus, just listen to me. So you've dealt with these guys before?"

"Only Smeby." Kendrick nodded at the man in question. "He's not to be trusted under any circumstances."

There was a commotion, and they glanced over to see that Sabak had opened a hatch. Behind it lay a tiny porthole, and Draeger had floated over to stare out through it.

Looking around at the other passengers, Kendrick could see from the consternation and anger on their faces that they were now well aware who their unwelcome guest was.

Sabak floated over and put a hand on Kendrick's and Buddy's shoulders. "Gentlemen, I want you to come and see exactly where we're going."

As he guided them forward, Kendrick flailed about uncertainly for a moment but Buddy kept a firm grip on his shoulder as they eased through a pressurized door into the cockpit area.

There was a crew of four, and Kendrick suspected that one or two of them might turn out to be Labrats. But it was impossible to tell since they were all wearing spacesuits.

Beyond them he could see stars, the bright curve of the Earth visible over to one side, and something else in the far distance: a dark grey cylinder floating against a sea of black velvet.

Sabak moved forward to chat to the pilots. They all looked relaxed and happy, and Kendrick wished that he could feel the same.

Sabak returned to their side shortly. "We're coming in for an approach pretty soon."

"How close did it get down there?" asked Kendrick.

Sabak raised his eyebrows. "Pretty close. I find this difficult to admit, but Draeger's the only reason we got this far." He shook his head. "I think he must be obsessed with the *Archimedes*, wanting to come here in person. That does take a certain kind of guts."

Buddy nodded. "Yeah, but he's only going to stay friendly for as long as we serve his purpose. We've got to start being real careful."

"Sir?"

Sabak glanced over at the crew member who had spoken.

"We've got visual contact with the two Los Muertos shuttles."

Kendrick peered forward intently to where the *Archimedes* was growing visibly larger. He saw a rough-hewn tube covered in fragile-looking gantries and docking facilities. Kendrick noticed that one of the shuttles was still locked into an external gantry, its nose pointing inwards towards the main body of the station. The other shuttle, though, appeared to have ripped itself free and only dozens of powerful-looking cables kept it connected to the station. They were twisting and writhing slowly like snakes, and the hull of the shuttle looked battered and broken, presumably from repeated impacts with the hull of the *Archimedes*. As they came even closer, they could see an intermittent sparkle of light inside a deep wound in the shuttle's structure.

Sabak spoke up. "Looks like they've got something burning inside. Wouldn't be possible unless something was feeding it – probably broken fuel and air lines. Can we get a zoom on that?"

"Sure," said one of the pilots, and a screen displayed a close-up of the damaged shuttle.

"It looks like one of its engines exploded," said Buddy. "Something blew up on the inside and ripped through the hull."

"What the hell could do something like that?" Kendrick asked.

"There's no other ships in the vicinity," replied the pilot, turning a little in his seat to give Kendrick and the rest a significant look. "If I didn't know better, I'd say it looks like they tried to get away from it."

The second pilot glanced over her shoulder with an expression clearly saying *Tell me what in God's name is going on here*. Kendrick caught her eye and shrugged feebly. She frowned at him and turned back.

Kendrick continued to study the *Archimedes* with interest, as Sabak consulted with the two pilots about docking strategies. After a few minutes' discussion they settled for another gantry that was positioned a little further around the circumference of the station. They were closer now to the exterior of the *Archimedes* and Kendrick gazed at the ripped-apart shuttle in horrified fascination. *Nobody could have survived that sort of damage*, he thought.

Their view changed further as they approached their selected gantry, the *Archimedes'* speed of rotation slowing to an apparent nil. Sabak guided them both to the rear of the cockpit where a row of tiny plastic seats were attached to the bulkhead.

They buckled in and waited. Soon a heavy, clanging reverberation rattled through the hull, as gravity returned.

The sudden change was jarring. Kendrick pictured the shuttle being whirled around now by the station as it rotated, providing artificial gravity as it tried to fling the incoming ship loose. They'd docked with the shuttle's underbelly facing outward, allowing them to walk around inside the shuttle without feeling as though they were the wrong way up.

Sabak unstrapped himself and motioned to Kendrick and Buddy

to do likewise. Then he led them back into the short corridor connecting the cockpit to the main passenger bay.

"Wait just one second," Sabak told them, pulling open a section of the wall to reveal a deep cabinet. There were weapons stored inside – rifles, pistols and what appeared to be grenades. There were also bricks of plastic explosive.

Sabak extracted a pair of side arms and handed one each to his companions. Buddy handled his with practised efficiency, nodding with apparent satisfaction.

Kendrick stared down suspiciously at the gun in his own hand.

"Just hold on to it," Buddy advised him. "I don't think it's likely that you'll have to use it. Give it here." He took the weapon from Kendrick and slotted in an ammunition clip. "This catch here on top is the safety, so just leave it where it is unless you feel you need to use the gun. Got that?"

"I think so."

"Meanwhile keep it out of sight. We don't want Draeger's men knowing that we're armed. Any small advantage we have can only be good for us."

Kendrick caught Sabak's eye. "Draeger and his men – did anyone check them for weapons?"

"There was neither the time nor the opportunity," Sabak replied sourly. "Which is another good reason for making sure we're ready for anything."

The flight crew caught up with them and Sabak doled weapons out to them as well, keeping a cautious eye on the door to the passenger area. Several Labrats – the only one Kendrick recognized was Veliz – slipped through from the passenger bay, and Sabak armed them too.

"What about all the rest of them?" said Buddy, nodding towards the door. "None of that lot came up here expecting to be combatants."

"I'm well aware of that," Sabak replied darkly. "We should split into two groups once we're further in. Some of us will move ahead and deal with any Los Muertos who may have been left behind.

The other group can stay near the docking area and guard the rest of our lot."

"And Draeger?" asked Kendrick.

"The question is whether he's likely to try anything once we're inside."

"I'm sure of it. But then there's the matter of whether we're really going to let him have what he wants." Kendrick looked at Sabak questioningly.

"I didn't expect we'd have to deal with Draeger when we got here. Which may have been a glaring mistake on our part." Sabak turned to Buddy. "You've got as much military experience as I have, so when we're in there I want you to help us keep an eye on Draeger and his goons. The question remains: are they likely to be armed?"

Buddy shrugged. "Heavily, I'd be inclined to guess."

Sabak nodded in agreement. "Okay, let's go ahead on the assumption that we'll be dealing with opposition at some point. If we find no survivors from the Los Muertos shuttles, maybe we can step things down a little, except where Draeger is concerned."

"Draeger's going to be searching for the same records that I want," Kendrick reminded them.

Sabak squinted. "The *Archimedes* is a big place. You'd need a couple of weeks to find something that specific. And a couple of weeks is what you don't have."

Kendrick shook his head. "I need to locate a research facility in the second chamber. That's exactly where I'll find what I'm looking for."

Sabak shook his head slowly. "A research facility?"

One of the flight crew spoke up. "That's where all the station's functions are centrally controlled, sir. The computer systems are evenly distributed throughout the entire shell so that the station can continue functioning in case of serious trauma. But the research facility is the central point where you input data directly and get collated feedback."

"We can't rule out sabotage either," said Buddy. "We don't

know what Los Muertos have managed to do while they've been up here ahead of us."

Kendrick was unable to avoid a deep sense of dread about what they might actually find once inside the *Archimedes*. Everything they knew so far had been filtered through the lens of Robert's fractured, dead mind. When it came down to it, none of them had any idea what they were up against.

They headed through to the passenger area, which had transformed from a vertical cylinder to a long, low-ceilinged room. Buddy, Sabak, and the flight crew checked everyone in turn, making sure they were fully suited up.

By some mutual unspoken decision they left Draeger and his men to take care of themselves. Within minutes, the external airlock opened to connect with a long, flexible tube linking to the *Archimedes* itself. The tube looked surprisingly flimsy and delicate.

Once Kendrick had his helmet on, the voices all around him were reduced to distant electronic squawks. He joined the queue and was guided by one of the pilots onto a platform with plenty of handgrips, obviously designed to carry them through the tube and into the station.

It took about twenty minutes to get everyone on board via the access tube. Kendrick and the rest found themselves in what had clearly been designed to be a reception area, full of desks and long, low couches. Kendrick studied some of the safety warnings and information posters still mounted on the pastel-coloured walls.

Sabak and his flight crew had gathered by another airlock door at the opposite end of the reception lobby. According to a nearby sign, this gave access to the interior of the main station proper.

Kendrick studied the screen built into the arm of his spacesuit. He played around with the menus, finding something that informed him that the atmospheric pressure outside his suit was currently zero. He wondered how this section of the station had come to lose its air, and if this meant that they were going to find the whole station depressurized.

He rejoined Sabak by the airlock door. One of the pilots had a panel open in the wall next to it and had attached a small device to some wires protruding from the interior. Kendrick wondered briefly why they didn't ask him or some other Labrat to magic the door open. Then he remembered that no one had ever tried that while wearing a bulky spacesuit.

After a little more effort, the airlock slid open to reveal a series of corridors branching off into the distance. Immediately ahead of them lay a wide-open space furnished with low pastel-coloured couches.

"No air, but the lights still work," Buddy observed through his spacesuit's intercom.

"Power runs through solar arrays on the station's exterior," Sabak explained. "Means we don't have to find our way through the dark."

Buddy laughed shakily. "Don't remind me of all *that*," he said.

A small crowd of Labrats had gathered nearby and one of the flight crew was briefing them, trying to keep them from either wandering off or getting in the way.

Sabak approached Kendrick. "Do you know how to switch over to a private channel? No? Okay, you're broadcasting on a general channel now. If you want to keep the conversation private, just do this."

Kendrick watched as Sabak led him through the necessary submenus on his suit's arm-mounted screen.

Draeger and his men were just arriving in the reception area behind them. Kendrick caught the attention of one of the pilots whose suit's name tag read Roux.

"I need to ask you something," Kendrick began over a private link.

"Wait a second," said the pilot. "Okay, we can talk one-to-one now."

"I'm heading back down with you," Kendrick told him. "So when are you flying back – now or later?"

"We're waiting long enough to know that everyone's safe, then myself and one other will pilot the shuttle back home. We're going back to wait on board in just a few moments. Care to join us now?"

Kendrick shook his head. "I've got some things to take care of first."

Roux's face betrayed his feelings: a touch of bewilderment at whatever was happening here, something he couldn't understand even if he tried. Kendrick felt a brief stab of sympathy for the returning flight crew. They must have felt as if they were helping to orchestrate a mass assisted suicide.

"Okay," Roux said. "If we don't see you later you're stuck here. Just remember, we're not sticking around for more than a couple of hours at the most."

"Thank you." Kendrick smiled briefly and stepped away from him. He felt filled with a kind of numb desperation, finding it impossible to convince himself he wasn't indeed committing suicide. There was a very good chance that he wasn't going to get back home at all – and the thought terrified him, to the very core.

28 October 2096
On board the *Archimedes*

A map of the station was mounted on one wall. It showed several levels, or decks, interrupted by two enormous artificial caverns – one of which Kendrick had already seen, after a fashion, in his augment-induced visions. Near the map were a variety of panoramic photos of the interiors of the caverns. These showed technicians with the good looks of models taking soil samples or carrying out experimental procedures under the vast mirrors designed to reflect sunlight into the station's interior.

This, thought Kendrick, would be what the station's

administrators wanted their prospective investors to see as soon as they arrived here. They would be brought to wait here before each tour started.

He began to wonder if the depressurization had been due to some kind of life-support failure. If that were the case, the electrical systems, at least in this part of the *Archimedes*, hadn't been affected. Panels set along the ceiling and walls around them glowed softly with diffuse light.

Kendrick glanced over at Draeger and his men who had continued following behind everyone else at a careful distance. Smeby returned his inquiring look with a hostile glare.

Sabak moved to the centre of the large room and raised his hands for everybody's attention. He swivelled around to look at all of them, while pointing a finger exaggeratedly at the panel on his spacesuit's arm. He was asking them all to switch to the public channel. As Kendrick tapped at his own screen, his ears were filled by a tumult of voices from all around him.

"We made it," Sabak was announcing, his grin just visible through his helmet visor. "We made it here, thanks to the Bright." There were several whoops and a lot of cheering.

"If any of you have started to have doubts, if you've decided there's too much for you to leave behind, then now is the time to say so," Sabak continued. "Nobody will think the worse of you. This is something monumental, but we're only human. If you want to go home, then do so with our blessing."

He turned to scan all the faces around him, but no one spoke out, no one stepped forward. Even the ones Kendrick had seen earlier in floods of tears remained resolutely silent.

"What about him?" somebody called out, pointing at Draeger. Kendrick glanced over at the billionaire, whose face remained impassive behind his visor.

"Mr Draeger has helped us get here in one piece," Sabak explained carefully. "If it wasn't for him—"

"If it wasn't for him," somebody else shouted, in a voice crackling with static, "we would never have got into this shit in the first place! What the hell is he doing here, anyway? We didn't invite him!"

In an instant the mood turned, with more shouting and accusations blending into a tumult. It was clear that Sabak was on the brink of losing control. Draeger and his men numbered barely more than half a dozen, and there were many more times that number of angry Labrats.

Someone suddenly ran at Draeger, their movements clumsy in the low-g environment. Kendrick watched in horror as Smeby reached into a deep pocket and produced a snub-nosed weapon that he then gripped tightly in both hands and aimed.

Kendrick began to move forward, seeing a way in which he might calm the situation. Through the protester's visor he caught a brief glimpse of a middle-aged male face, the marks of long-term rogue augmentation extending across the forehead.

As if by magic, holes appeared in the assailant's spacesuit. Kendrick watched as the Labrat spun around, almost in a parody of a ballet twirl. He collided with a nearby couch and fell into a lifeless heap.

Kendrick opened his mouth to yell something, but his words were lost even to himself as his ears filled with the distorted sound of people screaming.

"Stay back!" Smeby was yelling over the public channel. The rest of Draeger's men now stood brandishing identical black weapons.

Kendrick stared in horror at the body of the dead Labrat. The man's face had ceased to exist below the nose, and an ocean of red fountained from the ruin of his jaw, spilling out of the shattered remains of his helmet.

Kendrick turned away, sickened. They were heading for a massacre. He found his own weapon and gripped it in one hand, all too aware of the terrible special dangers of getting shot in a vacuum. Sabak's men had produced their own weapons and now faced Smeby and the rest of Draeger's men in a deadly stand-off.

"We're going ahead," Smeby announced tightly. "Anybody tries to follow, we'll shoot to kill. All of you got that?"

Sabak stared past him, looking Draeger in the eyes. "The Bright will kill you all. You know that, don't you?" he warned.

As Draeger gazed back with glittering eyes, Kendrick felt a tingling in his hand, as if a faint electric current was running through it. He felt an overwhelming urge to touch something: a wall, a floor, anything.

"We're going to head through that door," Smeby announced, his voice distorted with static. "Nobody else comes through it for at least another twenty minutes, do you understand me?" Draeger himself remained mute.

There were only four internal exits from the reception area they all stood in, three of them corridors winding out of sight as they followed the curvature of the space station's hull. The fourth exit remained sealed by a pressure door beside which two of Draeger's men were now huddled. The other three, along with Smeby, faced the Labrats, weapons at the ready.

An intensely bright flash briefly blinded Kendrick and the pressure door jerked open, revealing the corridor beyond. Draeger and the rest of his party hustled through, all the while keeping their weapons aimed at the Labrats. The door slid shut again, cutting off Draeger's party from sight.

Sabak ran forward as soon as the door had closed. Others rushed up behind him, one reaching for the control panel. "Stay back!" Sabak yelled. "Don't try anything until I tell you to. Give them time to get away. Everyone, stay back!"

Kendrick thumbed his suit panel until he was on a one-to-one channel with Sabak. "Nobody's letting them get away."

"We have priorities, do you understand me?" Sabak's voice was angry. "At least this way we don't have to watch them the whole time."

Kendrick pushed closer. "What the hell do you think he's going to do in there? Have you even thought about the damage he could do if he finds what he's looking for?"

"Assuming he gets anywhere" Sabak replied. "The Bright haven't shown any lack of aptitude where repelling boarding parties is concerned. And, besides, he can't get back down to Earth without our help."

"Unless he finds a way to reach that one intact Los Muertos shuttle. There's no reason to assume it isn't still functioning. I just don't believe that Draeger would have come up here unless he was pretty sure of finding a way back down again."

"The Bright will take care of him," Sabak replied confidently.

"Or maybe we've all been seriously underestimating him for too long. He could have something planned that we haven't been expecting. Don't you understand yet what's at stake here? Look, myself and a couple of others, we can go in and scout ahead. That'll give the rest of you an opportunity to move somewhere more secure in the meantime."

Sabak looked ready to explode behind his visor. "Jesus – fine, do whatever you think you have to do. But if anything happens I'm not sending anyone to look for you."

Buddy stepped up and broke into their conversation. "Gerry, quit arguing. We need to find somewhere properly pressurized before people start running out of air." He caught Kendrick's eye. "Right now that's our first priority, and we're going to need every hand."

Sabak made the decision to follow a passage leading directly to one of the main caverns, in the hope that they'd find somewhere along the way where they'd be able to breathe without depleting their tanks. Kendrick still felt that overwhelming urge to take off a glove and just *touch* something.

But that, of course, would result in a fatal loss of air. He'd found himself wondering if he could try repeating his experience in the airbase, when he'd found he had stopped breathing completely, but decided he'd rather not experiment. Not if it ended up with him writhing on the ground, desperately trying to get his helmet back on.

As they entered the wide passage Kendrick noted that wand-nodes were mounted along the walls every several metres. These old-fashioned devices dated the station, giving it an oddly quaint edge. He was suddenly glad he'd retained the wand that Buddy had given him back at the Maze.

As he pointed it at the nearest node, the wand's little screen blinked rapidly, informing him that it had downloaded a station guide. This turned out to include a 3D version of the map he'd first noticed back in the reception area.

Here he was in the middle of a crowd of Labrats, most of whom looked fairly subdued following the death of one of their number. He glanced around, studying the faces visible behind the visors: nobody seemed particularly heroic or brave or adventurous. But the *Archimedes* had cowed almost all of them, and Kendrick could feel its vast bulk weighing on him too.

This was the place where microscopic monsters lived, a place where the messengers of gods walked in their dreams, a place of empty echoing corridors full of dark, inchoate mystery. Just the fact of being on board the *Archimedes* was enough to still anyone's tongue, for a while at least.

Kendrick felt a sensation akin to jealousy. The people around him knew what they wanted, had given up everything for one last chance at survival. They had willingly boarded that shuttle, never expecting to see home again.

So what's so different about me? Suddenly he not only wanted to believe too – he felt that he *could* believe. He'd witnessed the end of everything, and the beginning of something he couldn't even start to comprehend. One tiny corner of something that might, just might, be Heaven.

And, almost in the same instant, Kendrick understood why he found it so hard to believe. He was scared, that was all. Now that he'd felt at least a part of what filled Buddy and the rest with such unwavering conviction, he was scared that it might not turn out to be true, that it was in fact a false dream born of technology. So it was easier, then, not to believe.

He studied further the map of the *Archimedes* displayed on his wand. They'd be reaching the first cavern soon, and the idea terrified him. Would tiny winged shapes come diving down at him, through air as thick as soup with them?

Buddy came up beside him again, jabbing a finger at the read-out screen on his own suit. Kendrick realized he had his own map displayed there.

"Pressurized area up ahead," Buddy informed him over a private channel.

"How do you know?"

"Green means pressurized, red is depressurized."

Kendrick glanced at his own map and saw the same colour-coding.

The corridor terminated in another airlock. He could see tiny sparkles of light flitting across the several metres of passageway just in front of it.

Tiny silver fibres? A chill gripped his spine. He looked around and saw that he wasn't the only one to have noticed them. His skin crawled with horror as several others reached out with glove-encased hands to touch them. He imagined those threads finding their way through the material of spacesuits, invading the augment-riddled flesh beneath.

Sabak led the way, surrounded by the half-dozen Labrats he had armed on board the shuttle. From the way they huddled together Kendrick guessed they were communicating over a private conference band.

They stopped at the airlock and Sabak appeared to have a heated discussion with some of them. Then he reached forward and touched a panel. The airlock door swung open, revealing a high-ceilinged room beyond, big enough to hold them all. Kendrick trooped inside with the rest, noting a second pressure door on the opposite wall.

The first door closed, sealing them all inside. After several moments a faint but increasingly audible hiss became evident as the chamber began to pressurize. A light flashed above both doors, and Kendrick watched as Sabak took off his helmet to speak. His voice echoing dully in the chamber, he was urging them all to take off their helmets too.

As Kendrick removed his own, the other chamber door opened to reveal light seeping through.

Beyond it he could see trees, and grass.

They crowded through and found themselves in the rear of a very spacious low-ceilinged gallery, with panoramic glass windows overlooking a wooded area. The trees seemed a little too regularly spaced to be natural. The soil outside had been arranged carefully in little hillocks, again attempting to trick the eye into thinking it saw a natural environment. Further beyond the glass, the ground curved steeply upwards.

By now most of the people who'd entered behind Kendrick had removed their helmets.

Kendrick sucked the air deep into his lungs. It smelled so fresh – he'd more than half-expected to find it as polluted as in the Maze. Although the nanite threads had already made their presence known here, there wasn't yet anywhere near the same degree of infestation. He stepped closer to the glass wall and gazed out at the greenery beyond.

Buddy soon joined him, helmet held loosely in one hand. He was positively glowing, his smile radiant, looking happier and more content than Kendrick recalled seeing him ever before.

A sudden, unexpected sound . . .

Kendrick glanced sideways along the front of the building where a path was visible, winding its way through the trees. "Did you hear that?"

"No, I—"

Something whirred – a machine sound that stirred up deep memories. Kendrick stepped away from the window and headed along until he was about halfway between the airlock exit and the building's entrance.

Out there, something glinted in among the trees. There was something hauntingly familiar about the noise he'd just heard.

Kendrick moved closer to the far end of the huge room, to look further between the building's exterior and the trees beyond where gardens once carefully maintained had grown wild. He cocked his head, listening hard, and heard a series of rapid staccato thumps. At the same instant he glanced over his left shoulder – in time to witness the main entrance of the building explode inwards in a shower of glass.

Kendrick fell to the marbled floor, covering his head with his hands as the windows nearby shattered almost at the same instant. He half-crawled, half-scuttled towards the relative safety of an expanse of wall that separated one large glass panel from the next. There he pressed himself flat against the floor while bullets whined through the air above him. They made a dull thudding sound as they impacted with the inner walls opposite the windows.

Peering down, Kendrick saw a fine tracery of nanite threads rapidly spreading across the marbled tiles under him. The tingling in his hands became urgent, almost unbearable. He longed to scratch his palms, to—

In an instant he understood what was required of him. Rolling slightly onto his side, he started to pull a glove off. Throwing it to one side, he gazed down at the palm of his uncovered left hand, noticing the faintest pattern of gold still etched into his flesh.

Only a few days before, he had witnessed all-out war raging at the molecular level, deep underground. Perhaps this time things would be different.

Kendrick spread his fingers out wide and laid his bared palm flat against the tiles beneath him. He screamed as his flesh united with the cool stone. Searing pain shot into his brain while bullets continued to zip through the air just inches above his head.

He could hear people shouting, and yet more screaming.

Through a haze of agony he became aware of the corpse lying several feet away from him, its head and shoulders reduced to a crimson pulp. He still couldn't prise his hand away from the tiles, so he twisted his head around, trying to see what was happening behind him. Most of the other Labrats, he saw, had retreated to the relative shelter of the pressure chamber.

The walls of the gallery were constructed from alternate panels of glass and columns of concrete: perhaps twenty Labrats had managed to find shelter behind the safety of the concrete. At least a dozen more lay scattered in the stillness of death.

Kendrick gripped his wrist, still trying to pull his hand free. He felt a fresh stab of icy pain as the skin of his palm ripped. While he watched, golden threads crawled out from under the flesh, seeking out the nearest silver filaments. The silver turned to gold within moments.

He finally realized that the firing outside had stopped. "It's me – Kendrick!" he screamed into the sudden silence. "Can anyone hear me?"

"Ken!" It was Buddy. "I thought you were down!"

"Those things are gun turrets," Kendrick yelled. "The same as back in the Maze."

"Stay tight, Ken. We did notice that."

Kendrick twisted his head around enough to catch sight of Buddy crouching low behind a long concrete bench near the centre of the gallery.

He managed to work his hand free at last, leaving a disturbing amount of blood and skin on the tiles. Keeping his injured hand cradled, he worked his way to the edge of a wall column and peeked around it.

He saw a sliver of grassland, then spotted something shiny and man-made visible to one side of a tree ten or twelve metres away, deliberately positioned so that it covered as much of that side of the building as possible. He slowly pulled his head back again.

They *had* to do something now. Draeger was still somewhere out there.

Moving very slowly again, Kendrick shifted closer to where the window had been, and lifted his head.

"Hey!" a voice yelled. "Hey, stay back!"

He saw Veliz peeking out from the door leading into the pressure chamber. One of the turrets whirred and Veliz dodged back out of range. Another volley of bullets spat into the building's interior.

Draeger could be downloading reams of lethal information and transmitting it back down to Earth while they were trapped here. Or else erasing the proof of his guilt for ever.

Kendrick allowed himself no more time to think. He stood and ran out through the shattered window, still cradling his injured left hand against his chest. He headed towards a copse only a few metres distant. His movements were restricted by the suit he was wearing, making him feel clumsy and slow.

The turret whined again and dirt was kicked up in tiny spurts, tracking after Kendrick as he threw himself into the shelter of the trees. Bullets ripped through the branches above him. He shielded his head as leaves and twigs rained down.

The gun whined into silence as its target disappeared from its sensors.

"Kendrick! Are you there?" Buddy again.

"I'm okay," Kendrick shouted back. "I'm outside here. There's a turret just ahead of me."

He heard a muted argument from somewhere inside the building. "Stay where you are," Buddy yelled back.

Then came the sounds of running feet and more bullets whining and ricocheting. Glancing back quickly towards the shattered window through which he'd exited, Kendrick saw Buddy take cover in the same place he himself had. Buddy gave him a one-handed thumbs-up before ducking back out of sight.

The reality of what he had just done began to hit Kendrick with the force of shock. He could very easily have died. He rolled onto his back and gazed up through the copse's branches.

Buddy called out to him again. "Kendrick, I'm throwing something over."

A small brick-like object landed not too far away, compact enough to fit into the palm of Kendrick's uninjured right hand.

The turret whined briefly in response, spitting a few bullets into the air near where the object had landed. Kendrick reached out for it with tentative fingers, ready to snatch them back behind his cover, but the turret didn't respond this time. He picked the object up and recognized it as one of the grenades that Sabak had taken on board the shuttle.

"Do you think you can hit that thing from where you are now?" Buddy yelled.

"I can *try* – but do we have any more of these if I miss?"

A pause. "Just try and get it first time, okay?"

Great. "How does it work?"

"Touch the screen. Press where it says 'arming'. Got that?"

"Got it."

"When you're ready to throw, press down hard on the plastic button on the reverse side, and then for God's sake just throw the damn thing. You'll have maybe seven seconds before it detonates."

Kendrick nodded. Then he dragged a branch from the soil and tossed it high into the open air. The turret whined, and the chunk of bullet-splintered wood jerked in the air before hitting the ground.

"Listen," said Buddy. "I'm going to draw its fire, then you throw. You got me?"

"I don't know if that's such a good idea. That thing's got a much faster response rate than—"

Buddy moved in an augmented blur, heading for another tree several metres away from where Kendrick sheltered. The turret whirred in response, tracking Buddy's path with fire as he ran.

Damn. Again there was no time to think. Kendrick pressed down on the grenade's activator and stepped out from behind his own tree, hurling the device as hard as he could in the direction of the turret.

As he'd stood he'd glimpsed Buddy diving towards the meagre shelter of another tree. None of the trees on board the station could possibly be more than nine or ten years old but they were already tall and gnarled, with thick trunks. It occurred to him that they'd have been altered genetically to grow much faster than nature intended. They also, he dimly recalled from some documentary, served a vital function in the station's complex artificial ecology.

Far more importantly, they at least provided more shelter than natural-grown saplings.

Buddy dropped down out of sight again and the turret rapidly swung back towards Kendrick. The grenade had landed just a foot from its base.

Kendrick threw himself back behind the tree and stumbled. As he started to pull himself up, he realized that he was still in the turret's line of sight.

He could see the turret zeroing in on him. Desperately, he reached behind himself for the knapsack in which he had stored his helmet. As he flung it away from him the turret's sensors picked up the sudden movement. Kendrick caught a glimpse of the knapsack dancing in the air, giving him the opportunity to slide rapidly back behind the tree.

A moment later the air was filled by a noise like a giant hammer blow. Dirt and splinters rained down on Kendrick's head. He lay exhausted, trembling from the adrenalin still pumping through his veins.

But the turret was dead.

Over the next several minutes, similar blasts were audible from further along the side of the building as Sabak's men managed to take out the remaining gun turrets. As Kendrick lifted himself up and peered towards the one he'd managed to destroy he half-expected it to spring back to life.

He climbed up on unsteady feet and went to retrieve the knapsack. The helmet, he found, was ruined. If he wanted to escape from the station he'd have to find another.

Buddy looked haggard and pale, and Kendrick assumed that he himself probably looked just as bad. He glanced around at the grass and trees, shimmering here and there with familiar pale silver threads.

Buddy followed the direction of his gaze. "Same as the Maze," he muttered.

"Not quite, no." The flesh of Kendrick's hand was still torn and bleeding. The pain felt even greater now that he was less pre-occupied with just staying alive.

Kendrick looked back to the building, where the survivors were only just beginning to emerge from hiding. Its walls sparkled here and there with silvery light, but the longer he watched the more the silver took on a distinctly golden hue. He visualized the same change spreading through the entire station, through the soil under his feet, through all those circuits and corridors.

All around them a war was taking place – in absolute silence.

Fourteen people were dead. They were laid out in rows in the centre of the gallery. All around Kendrick the tiles were red with blood where the victims had been caught in a massacre.

Kendrick spotted Sabak and approached him. "Look, time's running out. I'm going after Draeger now and I need your help. I know I can't manage this alone."

Sabak shook his head firmly. "Nobody's going anywhere. None of us are taking any more chances than we have to. So we stay right here. Not one more life is going to be wasted before the wormhole opens."

Kendrick stared at him, his expression revealing his sudden anger. "And Draeger? You're going to let him get away with this?"

Sabak chuckled long and low, glaring back at Kendrick with something like hatred. "You don't get it, do you? You're not in charge of this operation. I know you think we're all crazy. Well then, fuck you. Fuck you and Draeger both."

Kendrick stepped away, appalled. "I can't believe I'm hearing this. You're a Labrat, and you—"

"I'm a *human being*, Mr Gallmon. I want to be able to choose my own destiny – and this is what I choose. I'm not here to be a hero or to save the human race." Sabak jabbed a finger into his own chest. "The human race can take care of itself just fine."

Kendrick licked his lips. He opened his mouth to speak, then closed it. He looked around and saw that other people had been listening. But none of them would meet his gaze.

"This isn't right," he said, for the benefit of all of them. "There are people down there who— Ah, the hell with it."

He turned from Sabak without another word and stepped back outside the building.

Kendrick wasn't sure how long he'd been out there in the open when he realized that Buddy was standing near him. No more than a couple of minutes, probably.

"I saw the way you were looking at these threads. I can see they're changing colour. You're going to tell me what's happening here, aren't you?"

"I don't know," Kendrick lied. How could he explain? He was far from sure that he could go out there and find Draeger on his own. He needed Buddy's support – even Sabak's.

Buddy shook his head slowly. "There's something you're not telling me. First that trip to the Maze, now this. It's not right to keep me in the dark."

Kendrick sighed and looked away. "I need to find Draeger. Are you going to help me?"

Buddy glanced back into the building where they could see Sabak in heated conference with several of the Labrat survivors. Things were not going nearly as well as most of them had hoped.

"I'm not sure," Buddy admitted. "We need to take care of things here. Sabak—"

"You heard what he said! This is as far as the rest of them are going. But this isn't the time to discuss or negotiate. We go *now*, and we find him. I need whatever help I can get."

Buddy rubbed at his face with both hands, gazing off into the middle distance. Meanwhile Kendrick studied his suit's read-out. Nearly an hour and a half had passed since they had disembarked from the shuttle, so his time was running out if he was to have any hope of escaping from the *Archimedes*.

But did you ever really believe you were going to be coming back home from this?

"See things from my point of view," Buddy pleaded. "There are injured people back there. I'm needed."

Kendrick shook his head in disgust and began to walk further away from the building and from Buddy. "You know why I'm here," he called over his shoulder. "You know what's at stake."

"Ken—"

Kendrick stopped and turned. "Doesn't what we went through matter to you any more? Or do you really want to stand by while Draeger gets away with everything?"

A few moments passed but Buddy still didn't answer. Kendrick turned and resumed walking.

"Wait!" Kendrick slowed his pace and Buddy fell into step beside him. "Okay. Look, we've come this far together, so fine. I'll come with you. Everyone's badly shaken, is all. Nobody was expecting to have to deal with any of this."

Kendrick merely nodded and glanced back over his shoulder. He could see the building behind them rising above their heads now as they moved further up the curve of the cylindrical chamber. He quickened his pace to a trot, and Buddy moved to keep up with him.

There were other buildings hanging above their heads now, open-air offices among gardens that had grown wild. None of it looked as though it had been really designed for people to live in. These vast chambers, with their artificial forests and machine-controlled environments, were really little more than a showcase not just for Draeger's technological achievements but for the sheer amount of money President Wilber had been happy to pump into constructing them.

Kendrick dug out his wand and studied the station map. It

would have been a lot easier if they'd been able to use whatever the station's erstwhile occupants had used to move themselves around its interior. According to the map there was a transport system buried in the hull, but its nearest entrance was next to the place they were heading for anyway.

"Here." He jabbed his finger at the map display and turned to Buddy. "This is the research facility that's in the next chamber. It's where Draeger's heading because he can access the central AI memory core from there. We keep moving this way, we should reach an airlock leading to a connecting corridor pretty soon. You got any more of those grenade things?"

"Just a couple," Buddy replied.

Kendrick had the illusion that, even as he walked, he was in fact staying rooted to the spot while the ground rotated under him. The building where Sabak and the others were still sheltering now hung way down behind them. He looked back and saw small figures milling around outside it, perhaps looking for them. All they needed to do was look up.

They found their first corpse by the airlock complex that led into the second chamber. The male victim appeared to have been flayed alive. The stink reached them long before they even set eyes on the ghastly remains. There were enough scraps of clothing left to identify him as one of Los Muertos.

Equipment lay scattered around the grass near the body and Kendrick stepped forward to find weapons or anything else they could use. He tried hard to ignore the overwhelming stench of death in his nostrils but failed completely.

"Jesus," Buddy muttered as he went to help him. Then he turned away, his hand clamped over his nose. Kendrick suddenly remembered the vision he'd had of Los Muertos soldiers torn apart by the creatures with Robert's face.

"He was in the middle of doing something when he died," Kendrick suggested, noticing a heavy backpack nearby that had some oblong metal object sticking half out of it. Fingers half-stripped of their meat reached towards a rifle that lay a few metres away. Buddy pulled the oblong thing free of the backpack before retreating out of range of the reek of putrefaction.

"What is it?"

Buddy didn't answer. He just stared at the box in his hands before lowering it to the grass, his face pale.

The metal casing featured an inset LED display on which a series of numbers appeared. It looked like a countdown, but the display was frozen. Kendrick imagined that the dead soldier had been configuring it in some way but had died before completing his task.

"What is that thing?" he asked. But Buddy simply closed his eyes and gave no answer.

"We don't have *time* for this shit. What the fuck *is* it?"

Buddy's eyes were full of pain as he opened them again. "It's a nuke. Those fucking idiots brought *nukes* on board." He stared down again at the oblong device and shook his head. At first Kendrick thought he might even be weeping. "I hadn't expected this," Buddy whispered.

Kendrick almost didn't catch these hushed words. But he sure felt the urge to say something – like *So what exactly did you expect?*

Instead he stepped on past the corpse towards the chamber airlock.

According to Kendrick's map, the other side of the airlock was pressurized. Ashen-faced and silent, Buddy followed his comrade into the pressure chamber.

Kendrick asked himself just why Los Muertos would have brought a nuke on board, the obvious conclusion being that they intended to destroy the station. Which led to the next question: why?

But even if that were the case, could just one nuke do the job? Kendrick couldn't begin to guess. Buddy muttered quietly from somewhere behind him, conferring with Sabak over his suit comm, telling him about the nuke.

"Buddy, tell him that the guy carrying the nuke died before he could set a detonation time. The bomb isn't going to go off."

"Yeah," said Buddy, "I already told them that. They're going to come and take a look at it."

He caught Kendrick's expression and shook his head. "Listen, they're not too wild about us heading off on our own like this, but right now they're more concerned about the nuke. We should get moving."

They passed through the far exit of the pressure chamber and into another series of interconnected corridors. They soon found themselves at a second airlock complex, which in turn opened into the second cavern. Buddy said little as they cycled through, for which Kendrick was grateful since he needed to organize his thoughts. The closer they came to the second chamber – the one he'd seen in his visions – the more prevalent the silver threads became.

They found themselves next in a building identical in construction to the one that had led into the first chamber. They moved with extreme caution, but after a few minutes it became clear that Los Muertos had not had a chance – or the desire – to plant gun turrets or rig booby traps.

This was, indeed, recognizably the chamber that Kendrick had seen in his visions – but it had been transformed into something simultaneously wonderful and terrible.

It looked as if the whole interior had been liberally coated with silver fairy dust so that it twinkled like a vast bejewelled grotto. Kendrick stepped forward to see the same wide plain he had found himself standing on during those strange dream-like but utterly convincing episodes. Great ragged-edged columns of compacted silver threads stretched right across the circumference of the chamber, looking as if a million spiders had spent a thousand years spinning them. Every surface was coated in thick layers of glistening silver.

"Oh, my God," Buddy breathed, staring around them as they passed through into the chamber proper. "Oh, my God."

Kendrick looked at these innumerable multitudes of threads and felt as if he were passing through the living, beating heart of some enormous beast. They didn't now need to search for the Bright – they were already *in* the Bright.

"Buddy, this isn't anything like my visions."

"Mine neither." Buddy grinned like a child who'd just stumbled into Wonderland. "But it's wonderful, isn't it?"

Kendrick remembered his recent ordeal in the Maze and said nothing. He consulted the wand again, trying to ignore how badly his hands were shaking.

Had he . . .? *No.* He closed his eyes and felt a surge of relief. For a moment he thought he'd left behind the glove that he'd removed to release McCowan into the body of the station. He dug out both gloves from a thigh pocket and pulled them back on, wincing as he pulled them over his injured flesh. They looked odd, oversized without the spacesuit they usually went with.

"You know what this means, don't you?" He glanced over at Buddy.

"Nope."

"If this is nothing like what we had visions of before we even got here, then there's no way to be sure that anything else the Bright have shown us is true."

Buddy laughed nervously and shook his head. "C'mon, Ken, that's bullshit reasoning."

"Why is it? All that's happened till now is that we've seen pictures in our heads. There's no reason to assume what we see in our mind's eye might be anything like the reality—"

"Kendrick." Buddy stepped in front of him. "Listen to me. What *you* saw clearly isn't the same as what the rest of us saw. We've been over all that already."

"I saw the whole thing, the . . . the history of the universe, and I felt every second of it. Peter warned me—"

"No. McCowan was never part of it. Robert—"

"*Robert* is insane. He lost his mind long before we even got ourselves out of the Maze."

"No, Kendrick, shut up and *listen* to me. I *touched* God – do you understand what I'm saying? Whatever you saw, whether it had McCowan's face or whatever, it was standing between you and . . . and the things that I experienced, and that the rest of those people back there experienced.

"Look. If you've never seen before, or . . . no, if you've spent your *entire life* locked in a box, where you can't see anything, hear anything, do anything, and then one day someone opens the box and you're in the middle of the Rio Carnival, then maybe you'd have some idea of what it was like for the rest of us – maybe just an inkling. And if you can't understand that, then try to accept that that's how the rest of us see it. You're in the minority here. You *can't* understand."

Kendrick found that he couldn't think of anything else to say. As he glanced to one side he noticed the gold had already made its way to this part of the *Archimedes*, too. He could see faint yellow flecks where there had been none only seconds before.

They came to a small clearing and discovered two more bodies as badly mauled as the first. They too wore the remnants of Los Muertos uniforms. Their jaws, stripped of their flesh, gaped upwards.

"Draeger's been through here," said Buddy, sniffing at the air.

Kendrick was incredulous. "You can *smell* him? Over this carnage?" The stink of putrefaction wasn't any better the second time around.

Buddy grinned and tapped the side of his nose. "The augments whacked my olfactory sense up a couple of notches a year or two ago. Now I can pick up certain scents." He shrugged. "Well, from time to time, anyway. It's a facility that has a bad habit of coming and going. Sort of useful, though."

"That's why that first corpse affected you so badly when we found it? The stench of it must have been overwhelming."

"Yeah, but I can barely smell these guys now. Guess my augments are already filtering it out."

They had been following a narrow path winding its way through silver-draped trees, aware of the sound of thickly layered filaments crunching underfoot. Kendrick kept a close eye on Buddy, but whatever had affected him during their trip inside the Maze seemed not to be affecting him here.

Kendrick kneeled to peer more closely at the corpses, still managing to keep his distance. "Look – they had backpacks like the last guy, except these are empty."

He stood again and looked around him, then up at the land surface curving away above him, wondering if Draeger and his men might be up there looking down on them.

In the soil just ahead stood a wide concrete cap with a circular door set into its upper surface. Kendrick consulted his wand map again and waved Buddy over to look at it.

"See this?" He pointed to a group of coloured lines.

Buddy nodded. "Yeah, that's where we came on board."

Kendrick tapped the minuscule screen with one finger. "And *this* is where Draeger and his men split off. There's more than one way to get from there to here. I think they took another route, probably bypassing the first cavern altogether." He gestured at the concrete cap, clearly an access point to the tunnels and corridors riddling the station's hull. "They'd have seen these bodies once they emerged."

"What makes you so sure they didn't go the same way as us?"

"A distinct lack of dead thugs around those gun turrets we ran into."

Buddy looked embarrassed. "Yeah, good point." He nodded towards the two corpses. "So . . . do you think these two were hauling nukes around as well?"

"Maybe. Maybe not. Probably best to assume the worst, though."

"And if they were, and then Draeger and his men came out and found them lying here . . ."

They looked at each other. Suddenly things were taking a much worse turn than any of them could have anticipated.

They moved on, spotting another group of buildings up ahead: the research facility. Buddy tapped Kendrick on the arm and pointed to the ground.

"Something's happening," he muttered.

The silver fibres beneath their feet rippled as if a sudden wind had whipped swiftly through the chamber. Except, of course, there was no discernible movement of air beyond a barely perceptible breeze produced by the natural circulation of atmosphere through the huge chamber.

"Forget about it. We need to get moving." Kendrick was trying not to let his fear show. They started forward again. As the facility moved slowly down the giant curving wall to meet them, a great twisting column of threads rose high above them, rooted in the soil nearby. It stretched across the width of the cavern, joining itself to the opposite side of the hull.

Their gaze picked out glistening bulbous shapes on the silver column's surface as they approached. Kendrick didn't want to wait around and see what might emerge from them.

As they came closer they heard a high-pitched scream from the direction of the facility itself.

"Ken, that sounded like—" Gunshots now: several noisy detonations, one after the other, in rapid succession.

Something rumbled through the hull under their feet. Cold sweat sprang out on Kendrick's skin as he imagined someone detonating a nuclear device – perhaps in the previous chamber, perhaps somewhere outside the station. It was far too easy to speculate on the hull ripping apart beneath them, sending them both spinning out into the endless cold vacuum of space.

But the rumbling faded a few moments later. Kendrick glanced down at the read-out on his arm and found a message icon blinking up at him.

He lowered his arm and headed rapidly towards one of the buildings directly ahead. A sign mounted in front identified it as the primary section of the research facility. Draeger was in there somewhere. He had to be.

"Kendrick, wait. Before we go further we should check back with the others and see if they have any idea what just happened."

"Bad idea. Whatever they say won't make any difference, so let's just get this over with."

The low-roofed buildings making up the facility had been tastefully designed from glass and wood. A wide balcony overlooked a pool fringed with pebbles, the water overgrown now with pond scum and silver filaments. It looked like something from an eerily deserted university campus.

Kendrick slowed, wary of running straight into Draeger's men. But there were no more screams and no more gunshots. Buddy kept pace with him, reluctantly.

"Listen, Kendrick, I've got an idea. We're heavily outnumbered, right? We can't just walk right in there among them."

"I know that, but there isn't time left to try anything else. We'll just have to work it out as we go along." He carried on towards the entrance.

"If you march in and they see you they'll have no compunction about killing you. Look, let *me* talk to Draeger."

Kendrick stopped and faced Buddy. "Talking to him isn't on the agenda. He used us to get here and the instant we looked like showing him any resistance he ran – but only because he couldn't kill all of us."

"Those men in there with him are professional soldiers, maybe Augments. You don't stand a chance against them. Negotiation is the only way."

"Someone is already dead, thanks to Max Draeger's negotiating skills. All I'm saying is, if we don't try and stop it now—"

"Maybe we *can* find a way to reason with him."

"*Reason* with him?" Kendrick glared at Buddy. "What exactly is your problem? When he blew that guy's head off, did that strike you as reasonable?"

Buddy's mouth worked silently for a moment. "I suppose what it comes down to is that – I don't trust you as much as I thought I did."

"Meaning?"

"Meaning maybe I had you wrong. I thought that once you were up here with us you'd understand."

"What, you're worried I might jeopardize things for you?"

"Look, ever since we found those bombs I've been thinking that if Draeger *does* have one the last thing we want to do is give him any excuse to set it off. Right?"

"Well," said Kendrick. "That depends."

Buddy looked incredulous. "On what?"

"On whether or not that means we let him get away."

Flinging his hands out in a gesture of despair, Buddy made a strangled sound. "You *see*? Can't you hear yourself? How fucking monomaniacal do you have to *get*? One way or another, if Draeger has one of those nukes, he's also got us by the balls – or can't you understand that?"

Kendrick spoke quietly and carefully. "Buddy, let me explain something. He's got *you* by the balls. He's got *Sabak* by the balls. But he hasn't got *me*, because I don't care about his threats. I'm going to nail the fucker. I want the world to know what kind of man he is. Otherwise everything that happened to us down there in the Maze isn't going to mean a damn thing.

"And it's not even that which really worries me. I don't know how he's going to do it, but I'll bet every last penny that he's had a way out of here figured for a long time. And if he does somehow manage to find something on those computers that he can take back down with him, then I don't believe anyone back home is going to thank us for letting him get away."

Buddy's face looked as though it was carved from stone. "Fuck *them*," he said quietly.

They were standing almost face to face now, and Kendrick started to turn away. From out of the corner of his eye he saw Buddy move towards him, reaching out to grab his arm.

Kendrick swivelled rapidly, taking hold of Buddy's wrist and punching him hard in the face as he did so. Buddy reeled back in surprise, then slipped and fell to the ground. Kendrick stepped over and clouted him a second time – unable to halt the sudden terrible anger that threatened to overwhelm him.

He became distantly aware that the air around him felt chillier than it had only seconds earlier. A sudden wind rippled through his hair, becoming stronger. Something was happening to the atmosphere in the station.

Buddy still lay flat on the ground, gasping and cursing.

"Don't get in my way," Kendrick yelled at him. "Don't dare come after me." He stepped away, panting. "I wish it didn't have to work out this way."

Buddy stared up at him with angry pain-filled eyes. But he didn't try to move from where he lay.

Kendrick retreated for a couple of metres, keeping Buddy well in sight. Then he turned and ran for the facility entrance. He turned a corner and stopped to make sure that his pistol was loaded.

Buddy was right about one thing: just charging in after Draeger would be like committing suicide. Kendrick had felt sure that by now some plan would have come to mind, some way to thwart Draeger without placing himself in such immediate danger. Unfortunately, his mind remained obstinately blank.

The screaming started again, a ragged and terrible animal sound, drifting from somewhere deeper within the building.

Kendrick was far from surprised to find more bodies inside, lying next to a pair of wide doors at the far end of a hallway. Kendrick gagged again at the stench of blood and viscera until his senses could adjust to filter it out. He noticed that both doors had been partly blown off their hinges.

Stepping closer to the corpses, he recognized them as some of Draeger's men. Marlin Smeby was not among them. At first Kendrick assumed they had been blown apart by the force of the explosives after having made a dangerous error in trying to blast their way into the facility interior. But closer inspection revealed that their flesh had been torn and ripped as if by claws. He nudged one body with his foot, trying very hard not to think about what these injuries signified.

The corpse cradled something in its arms. Another nuke, Kendrick realized, shuddering. It had almost certainly been retrieved from one of the dead Los Muertos whom he and Buddy had come across earlier. Two nukes now located, but still with the possibility of another.

Kendrick passed through the ruined doors into a wide office space scattered with the mouldering corpses of yet more Los Muertos. One even appeared to have raked his own eyes out of his skull, while another had clearly blown his own brains out with his rifle. The wall against which he had propped himself was still liberally smeared with the resulting gore.

Kendrick heard another sound, neither screaming nor gunshots this time. More like a bell gently tinkling, as if far away. He stood stock-still, trying to work out what this was, but it faded away to nothing after several seconds.

As far as he could tell, most of the corpses around him had engaged in what looked like mutually assisted suicide. Some lay twisted together in a deadly embrace, knifes still clutched in their fists. Kendrick could not imagine what demons had driven them to such deaths.

He moved on, through another door and into a room filled with racks of delicate-looking computer equipment. He halted, tensing up, at first thinking that something living was in there with him. He relaxed again on seeing that it was another body, a woman's.

He stepped closer and discovered, shocked, that it was his erstwhile interrogator. Leigh squatted in a corner, her combat rifle propped between her knees, its barrel placed under the shattered remains of her jaw. Kendrick looked away quickly.

He glanced around the room and, though he was no expert, he was prepared to bet that she'd raked the banks of machinery around her with automatic fire before ending her life.

He froze on hearing movement nearby. Then, holding his gun out in front of him, he stepped through a further door into a darkened corridor.

"Hold it right there."

The voice came from an adjoining doorway. Kendrick stopped dead, feeling cold metal press into the side of his neck.

"The gun. Drop it, kick it away."

Kendrick reviewed his options and discovered that he had none. He let the pistol slip from his fingers, then pushed at it with his foot. It skidded across the floor and stopped near a wall.

"Turn around."

He'd expected Draeger, or even Buddy. Instead it was Sabak, accompanied by two armed Labrats.

Kendrick was stunned. How had they got here so quickly? They must have gained access to the transport system. That was surely the only way.

"Whatever you're intending, you're not going to do it." Sabak sounded calm, in control.

"I haven't done anything."

"I was at the door of the transport terminus. I saw you beat the fuck out of Buddy."

"I can explain."

Sabak shook his head. "Forget it. I wouldn't believe you anyway. You're working for Draeger, right?"

Kendrick blinked at Sabak, standing with two tough-looking types immediately behind him. He laughed.

"Me, working for Draeger? That's rich."

Sabak bristled. "You've been very vocal against our whole

operation from the start. Did you kill those other men back there?"

Kendrick stared at him, incredulous. "Now you're out of your mind. Most of them have been dead for days."

"I still don't feel convinced."

"I'm *not* working for Draeger. For Christ's sake, I—"

And there it was again: a sound like wine glasses tinkling gently together. Or moths beating against a light bulb.

They all turned as one. Light flickered at the far end of the darkened corridor, briefly illuminating the outline of a doorway that until now had been lost in shadows. The strange sound grew louder before fading again.

And then they appeared: tiny, frail, dream-like bodies, all with the face of Robert Vincenzo and each of them wrapped in an eerie halo of light. At first just a few, then a dozen, then yet more emerged from the darkness.

Kendrick turned to Sabak. "*Those* are the things that killed all these people."

But Sabak wasn't listening to him. "I didn't think . . ." Clearly frightened, he turned to his men. "Get hold of him."

Kendrick was gripped by both arms and dragged back the way he had come. Now he was hustled along a corridor he hadn't yet explored, to a room at the far end. To Kendrick's despair, Sabak had meanwhile confiscated his pistol.

"What do you know about this?" Sabak was pointing to an untidy pile of electronic junk lying in the far corner of the room. Racks of equipment filled the surrounding walls, stretching into unlit gloom.

As Kendrick looked closer, the junk resolved into something else altogether.

He recognized the tiny read-out and the oblong box it was attached to. Plastic explosives were carefully packed around it, and myriad wires linked it all like the serpent-hair of a cybernetic Medusa.

The third and previously unaccounted-for nuke, which he'd been so sure that Draeger had in his possession.

Kendrick licked his lips. "It's a nuclear bomb."

A woman knelt by the device, lost in contemplation. She started gently probing it with some hand-held device. He just hoped she was an expert who knew what she was doing.

She spared Kendrick's arrival the briefest glance before leaning over until the side of her head touched the floor, peering into the narrow space between the nuke itself and the wall against which it was placed.

Sabak spoke to her. "Shirl, is that definitely what he says? No chance it's a decoy or something else altogether?"

She shook her head without even looking at them. "It's the real deal: a field nuke – backpack tactical weapon. Normally used for high-yield radiation effect, but still powerful enough to blow at least a hole in the hull." She paused, as if in contemplation. "No, make that rip the place to shit."

"Okay, then, can you disarm it?"

"Most of these wires have nothing to do with the nuke itself," Shirl explained. "It's all to do with booby-trapping. If we so much as move this thing from where it's currently sitting, there's no guarantee it isn't just going to blow immediately." She shook her head. "We need somebody who knows more about these things than I do. I'm out of my depth."

"Is it on any kind of timer?" Sabak demanded.

She shook her head. "Timer's not working. I think maybe they were about to set it, but then . . ." She shuddered. "Something happened. You saw those other people back there?"

Shirl stood up, wiping dusty hands on her suit. "These things always come with some kind of a remote detonator, a back-up in case the timer fails or you want to blow it ahead of schedule, or at a safe distance. Something hand-held – like, stick a nuke under a dam or someone's presidential palace, drive a long way off, then hit the button."

Sabak started. "You mean there might still be some kind of trigger round here somewhere?"

Leigh's face sprang into Kendrick's mind. He remembered Buddy telling him that she ranked pretty high in Los Muertos. If anyone had been in charge of their expedition here, it might well have been her. So, perhaps any such trigger would be on or near her body . . .?

Of course, Sabak wasn't necessarily aware of this. "We're going to have to search all these corpses," Sabak was even then saying with obvious distaste. "And carefully."

"Just listen to me," Kendrick insisted. Sabak gave him an annoyed glance. "Draeger is around here somewhere, and I'll bet you anything he's looking for that detonator, if he hasn't found it already."

"Bullshit," Sabak sneered. "Los Muertos is one thing, but Draeger doesn't have any reason to blow up the *Archimedes.* He'd be killing himself along with the rest of us."

The sound of screaming resumed, sounding closer now. Sabak stepped away, listening, his face suddenly pale.

"Keep a hold on him." Sabak nodded towards Kendrick. "And bring him along. Shirl, keep working on that thing and let me know if you can figure anything out. Just . . . be seriously fucking careful."

"Really? I thought maybe I'd just cut the blue wire and see what happened," she deadpanned.

Kendrick's two guards pushed him along immediately behind Sabak as they made their way towards the source of the screaming. The sound, an unending ululation like nothing he had ever heard, raised the hairs on the back of Kendrick's neck. He wondered how anyone could have the physical ability to scream so consistently, and for so long.

They turned a corner and found two more of Sabak's men waiting by an open doorway, their weapons at the ready. Kendrick couldn't yet see what lay beyond.

"They're in there," said one of the men. Kendrick could see

how frightened he was. He felt a sudden tightening in his own chest, and didn't want to see what was in there.

As Sabak stepped forward the screaming stopped, to be replaced by a fit of coughing, then by the sound of someone gasping for breath.

Sabak stood for a long time at the doorway, staring at whatever lay beyond.

"Sabak." No response. "*Sabak*," Kendrick called to him again.

The man finally turned to look at him. "Bring him forward," he ordered, almost under his breath.

Beyond the doorway lay an area that had clearly once served as a canteen. Plastic chairs and tables had long ago been neatly stacked in a corner.

In the empty centre of the room two of Draeger's men were in the gruesome process of killing themselves. One had torn off his spacesuit and was gouging deep gashes in his bare chest with a knife. His shirt hung around his waist in tatters. He appeared unaware of his audience.

The other, however, untwisted himself from the foetus position he had assumed, staring back at Kendrick and Sabak. Then, as they watched, he crouched down on all fours and proceeded to slam his forehead repeatedly and violently against the gore-sticky tiled floor in an apparent attempt to bash his own brains out.

Kendrick saw the bodies of two other of Draeger's soldiers lying nearby, in the shadows. They looked like they'd been shot at point-blank range.

"Listen to me," Kendrick said. "Robert is doing this, do you understand me?"

Sabak shook his head violently. "No, the Bright are – they're just protecting themselves."

"*Protecting* themselves? Whatever the Bright may be, in essence they're just machines. And machines don't go out of their way to play sadistic games like that." Kendrick could see the uncertainty in Sabak's eyes. "Your mind's been twisted so that you can't see the truth any more."

The soldier smashing his head against the tiles finally slumped over and lay still. His companion sat exhausted, watching his own blood spread across the canteen floor in a widening pool.

"Look," said Kendrick. "Do you see that?"

Sabak stared, mute, as more of the winged shapes emerged from the shadows. They darted here and there, their tiny mouths opening in a piercing ululation that sent spasms of pain shooting into the back of Kendrick's skull.

Suddenly Sabak's henchmen weren't paying so much attention to their prisoner.

"Is this what you came here for, Sabak? Do you think *they*'re going to lead you into Heaven?"

"Just shut up," Sabak snapped back at him.

The ear-splitting wails emerged again from the creatures' throats. Now it felt as though someone had opened up Kendrick's skull and was tossing burning coals inside. He felt the grip on his arms loosen and instantly took the opportunity to pull himself free and run for the shadows and the outline of a door there. Tiny shapes darted at him as he reached it and something soft brushed against his face, feeling like dry cotton sheets. He heard a faint whispering, the kind of sound young children might make when hiding from a playmate in the dark.

Automatic fire thundered behind Kendrick as he pushed through the door and out into a connecting corridor. Angry voices reverberated behind him as he stumbled down a steep stairwell.

When he'd first entered the facility he'd been at ground level. If he was now descending, then he was penetrating the very hull of the *Archimedes*. Even so, there might be quite a few floors to negotiate before he reached the hull's exterior.

At the bottom of the steps Kendrick found a vast room filled with row upon row of gleaming metal cabinets. He ran on past them to find a stairwell that took him even deeper. He could hear voices clamouring somewhere behind him. He kept going.

Smeby came howling out of nowhere.

Kendrick yelled in surprise as a blade slashed through the air towards his cheek and Smeby slammed into him with his full weight.

Kendrick almost faltered when he saw the other man's face. Smeby had sliced lines into his cheek and brow, turning his features into a demon's mask.

"It's you!" he screamed into Kendrick's face. Then he backed away, tears running down his cheeks, before folding up, his trembling hands pressed against the sides of his head. A high keening noise poured from his lips.

Kendrick's gaze flicked to the doorway from which Smeby had emerged. Dozens of the winged homunculi fluttered in the shadows beyond it.

Now they came spilling through to surround both men, once more filling the air with their howling. Kendrick screamed too, gripping his head as they surrounded him in a vast, flapping storm. His skull was filled with unimaginable pain as incipient madness bubbled up somewhere deep inside his mind.

He stumbled back into the room filled with cabinets, found another door to stagger through and slammed it shut behind him. He was now in a side office with a window overlooking the room where Smeby still crouched helplessly.

More of the malignant creatures poured in from the stairwell till uncountable thousands muffled Smeby's screams with the sheer density of their numbers.

Kendrick stepped away from the glass, sickened. *Not real*, he reminded himself. Aural and visual hallucinations that burned the sanity out of their brains. Anyone without augments would see nothing.

Of course, that didn't explain the corpses he'd found. But it was easier not to think about that aspect.

Kendrick watched in horror as some of the creatures swirled in the air like living smoke, then rushed forward to smack into the glass that separated them from Kendrick. As the glass began to star, he gaped numbly, unable to accept the reality of what he was seeing. Then he looked desperately around the office. There were other doors at the far end: a sign on the wall announced that one of them was an airlock leading out to the station's exterior. The other door seemed to be an elevator, leading back up to the interior of the *Archimedes*.

On a metal desk stood a computer terminal. It was active, with several windows of information displayed on the screen. Kendrick stepped towards it, noticing that the dust covering the table had been disturbed recently.

He glimpsed a shadowy movement and heard the click almost too late. Draeger was crouching behind the desk, a gun gripped in both hands. He yelled when he saw Kendrick and fired at him wildly.

Despite the close quarters, Draeger managed by some miracle to miss. Kendrick stumbled away while Draeger, shrieking like an animal, fired indiscriminately into the air before pulling himself upright and fixing Kendrick firmly in his sights.

"What . . . what the fuck *are* those things out there?" Draeger shouted, wild-eyed and shaking. His spacesuit was smeared with blood, but somehow Kendrick didn't think it was the man's own.

It was difficult for him to accept that the homunculi were physically real. But if Draeger could see them, and he had no augmentation biotechnology . . .

"Robert Vincenzo," Kendrick replied. "They're all Robert Vincenzo."

"Who the hell's he?"

"He was down there in the Maze with the rest of us," Kendrick told him. "That's what your augmentations did to him."

Draeger stared at Kendrick with an expression like a floundering fish. "I want to make a deal," he said finally. His voice was cracking.

A deal? Did this man never give up? Kendrick let out a laugh that sounded halfway to a hysterical sob. "It's far too late for that, you stupid bastard."

"I want you to understand something. You do not belong

here." Draeger waved the gun at Kendrick. "*You do not belong here.*"

"If that's the case, then neither do you."

Draeger shook his head defiantly. "Move over there and turn around. Put your hands against the wall. I don't know what those damn things are, but nobody's going to have to worry about them much longer."

Kendrick complied, having little choice. "Now stay there," said Draeger.

Kendrick heard Draeger step away behind him.

He twisted his head around slowly and saw the other man move over to a wall panel set next to the airlock. Shadows fluttered beyond the window glass. Kendrick didn't think it could hold for much longer.

Draeger's fingers danced across the panel and the door opened, sliding into the wall. He stepped through, the door immediately sliding shut behind him.

As soon as he was gone, Kendrick went over and studied the same panel. He could try using his augmented abilities to get it open but that might take too much time, judging by the sound of scores of small bodies slamming into the glass just behind him. He tried hitting random buttons in the meantime, but – not surprisingly – that didn't work.

Perhaps there was another way to get out of the station . . .

His wand crackled into life. "Kendrick? Kendrick, it's Buddy here. I want an explanation." The other man's voice sounded harsh and brittle.

Kendrick slammed open the door of the surface elevator. He could only pray that the thing would work. "There isn't time," he yelled into the wand.

"Tell me now, Kendrick, before it's too late. Tell me you aren't going to—"

Kendrick broke the connection and put the wand back in his pocket. Then he hit a button and the elevator began to crawl laboriously upwards.

Another great shudder ran through the hull around him, much more violent this time. From somewhere not so far away, he could hear a rushing sound again. He glanced at the display on his space-suit's arm, which told him that the atmospheric pressure in the chamber above him was dropping rapidly. It seemed that the station was venting its air supply.

The rumbling noise grew stronger, rattling the teeth inside his skull. Kendrick had no idea if he'd be able to survive once all the air had been voided.

He pulled out his wand again and hit a switch. "Buddy, did you feel that?"

"Of course I fucking felt it." Buddy sounded distant, distracted. "Someone just blew one of the nukes."

"That's not possible. If one of those nukes had been blown, we wouldn't still be standing here."

"Not if there were other nukes, apart from those we saw." Buddy's voice became very thin, as if he was getting farther away. "Think about it. A station this size, if you wanted a real demoli-tion job, you'd have to plant several of them externally at different points around the hull. You'd need more than one to be abso-lutely sure the station was fully destroyed, if you were relying on low-yield tactical nukes like those."

"Draeger must have figured that out and found one some-where. If I can only find him—"

Buddy laughed shakily. "For what? To blow the thing up your-self? It's too late, Ken. It's time you . . ."

Kendrick stared down at the wand in his hands. *Never too late,* he told himself.

The elevator ground to a halt with a barely audible electronic *ping*.

He slammed the door open and stepped back out into the main facility building, immediately breaking into a run. His wand map would tell him where the other external airlocks were.

"Kendrick!"

He gazed down at the wand, his thumb hovering over the

button that would break the connection. "Goodbye, Buddy," he shouted into it.

If the air was venting he needed to find a spacesuit helmet soon or he'd suffocate before he could track down Draeger – unless survival without breathing was a real possibility for him now. But how long could he manage? Five minutes? Ten? An hour? Better to get himself a suit and take no chances. Still gripping the wand in his gloved hand, Kendrick stumbled back the way he had come. The winged creatures had vanished, at least for the moment.

"Wait, listen!" Buddy yelled to him.

"I've heard enough."

"No, just listen! There's a satellite array fixed on the outside of the station. If Draeger intends to upload any information to Earthside, he'd need to access that array directly – since the power for half the facility is shorted out. Do you follow me?"

No wonder, then, that Draeger had opted to find his way to the station's exterior. Kendrick suddenly realized that he was starting to hyperventilate, his lungs attempting to suck in air that was no longer there.

"How do you know he has anything he wants to send?" With that computer terminal deep down inside the facility Draeger could have already downloaded everything he needed.

"I don't know. But if he's heading for the array that kind of answers the question."

"I'm still sorry for the way things worked out, Buddy."

"So am I, believe me."

Static began overwhelming the wand, making it nearly useless.

"Can't you hear it?" said Buddy's voice, but it was hard to be sure he was actually addressing Kendrick and not someone else.

"Hear what?" Kendrick yelled over the static.

And there it was. He heard the *singing* – was that the right word? – which he'd heard while standing on a hill and talking to Peter McCowan somewhere in the far distant future. It sounded as though everything that ever was or ever could be had been condensed and refined into a simple cadence of unearthly beauty.

Part of Kendrick wanted simply to stand and listen to it. Instead, he finally cut the connection and ran along the corridor to find a door that led back into the cavern.

He pushed through to find that the cavern itself had become filled with a commingling of dust, leaves, grass and filaments. Many of the threads were now distinctly golden. He bent himself into the howling wind that had arisen out of nowhere and looked up to try to locate the breach in the hull.

Amid so much chaos it was almost impossible to see far ahead. More people, Kendrick was now certain, were going to die. He wondered how much abuse the *Archimedes* itself could take before it lost its structural integrity and simply fell apart.

Heavy vibrations rolled through the hull beneath his feet.

Something about the light in the chamber had changed. It was getting *brighter*.

Everything was getting brighter.

Kendrick saw that this light came from the filaments, which had by now lost most of their silver lustre. They were glowing with a kind of internal radiation. The light had a pale, translucent quality to it.

A *golden* light.

He ran through the door by which he'd first entered the facility. Something flew past his head, carried in a swirling maelstrom of air that lifted him off his feet before slamming him into the ground again. He watched as a twisted rope of filaments, as thick as a giant redwood tree, tore loose from the soil outside and smashed itself against the foyer windows, sending the glass exploding inwards.

All this happened in an eerie half-silence as Kendrick's ears popped painfully and his lungs laboured to draw in what little air remained.

He scrambled up and ran into the foyer, past some of Sabak's men who had suited up and were now trying to help one of their number whose helmet had been smashed open. They barely glanced Kendrick's way.

He pounded through the far doors of the foyer, heading for the canteen where earlier he'd seen two of Draeger's men slaughter themselves.

He reached frantically for their blood-slicked suit helmets, pulling each one in turn over his head before discarding it. Neither would fit onto his suit. He ran back to the room where Leigh's corpse lay slumped. But her suit was torn, her helmet lying nearby with its visor shattered.

Despair and hopelessness finally settling over him like a great black cloud, Kendrick ran back into the corridor, almost colliding with Buddy who stared back at him. He'd never be able to find a usable helmet in time.

But then, as he reminded himself, perhaps he no longer really *needed* to breathe. The idea that breathing might be something he could switch off or on at will had simply never occurred to him.

As if responding to this thought, something heavy, wet and translucent slid down over Kendrick's pupils from under his eyelids. He jerked his hands up to his face and touched the membrane, probing gently with his fingers.

What's happening to me?

Now he felt as if he were viewing everything through a very faintly tinted screen.

Touching the skin on his face, Kendrick realized that the ridges left there from his visit to the Maze had now mostly faded. But the skin itself felt hard and smooth in a way that it never had before.

How long could he survive like this? Was there a limit? Or would he be able to survive like this indefinitely? *Son of a bitch, I'm still alive.*

Where did the energy come from, he wondered, to keep him going without the constant replenishment of oxygen in his bloodstream? Had some kind of internal reservoir of energy, perhaps some new organ that hadn't been there before, appeared inside him? He had a sudden mental image of his stomach muscles peeled back to reveal large copper-coloured batteries where his heart, liver, kidneys and lungs should have been.

Buddy was still staring at him, his mouth working uselessly behind his visor, as if Kendrick could somehow hear the transmissions through his comms channel.

Surrounded by this vacuum, Kendrick experienced a silence more absolute than he could ever have imagined. He pushed his way past Buddy, the glow that filled the cavern now patterning the walls around him with a pale gold light.

Kendrick wrestled himself out of his spacesuit. If he didn't need it he could move a lot quicker without it. He looked down at his wand, checking which way he had to go.

He stepped into a side room to find what he was looking for. Wrenching open a floor hatch, he hurriedly pushed himself down the ladder bolted inside the narrow shaft below. A few minutes later he came to a passageway with a ceiling so low that he was forced to crouch. He moved like a ghost past walls bearing rack after rack of semi-organic circuitry prominently labelled with warnings about contamination.

A sign informed him that he was now in the central AI core. He saw a door ahead and quickly stepped up to it. He'd found his way inside the internal transport system. Stepping through, he found a narrow tunnel and a rail-mounted platform like an old-style railway handcar.

The door that Draeger had disappeared through earlier led directly here, so he *had* to have come this way.

Kendrick's wand informed him that the tunnel connected to the external endcap of this chamber. He climbed on board the car and found several handholds, mounted with safety buckles, but no seats – passengers were obviously required to stand. He tinkered with the small control panel mounted on a short pillar and after a few moments the car moved off.

A minute and a half later Kendrick arrived at the terminus and found himself facing yet another airlock door. He hit the "open" button and, to his surprise and great relief, the barrier swung wide open without further effort.

He looked inside to see fine golden threads everywhere, pulsing gently with ethereal light. As he sensed something moving behind him he turned and saw the rail car automatically returning to its point of departure.

Kendrick's bare hand still rested on the keypad, also coated in golden threads. He felt a faint sting as—

Cool blades of grass touched his skin, his fingers digging unexpectedly into damp soil. He was back in Scotland, back in the Tay Hills. He clung to the soil desperately, initially unable to comprehend the sudden transition from the *Archimedes*. The shock of it had dropped him to his knees.

A few moments later he managed to raise himself onto unsteady feet. Beyond the familiar damp hills, covered with gorse and rough grass, the land stretched on quite literally for ever, broken by unfamiliar rivers and forests. Distant mountain ranges became hazy with sheer distance, rather than disappearing out of sight beyond the curve of the horizon.

Kendrick turned and saw Peter McCowan waiting there beside him.

"Kendrick, I want to thank you for getting me here." There was a slight smile on McCowan's lips. "Buddy and the rest of them might not appreciate it, but I'm the only reason the Bright will be able to successfully negotiate the opening of the wormhole." A familiar grin spread over his face. "It's been bad enough as it is with that mad little shit running fucking riot with hobnailed boots over the Bright's collective intelligence."

"I'm glad for you, Peter, I really am. But Draeger's already detonated a nuke, and if I don't go after him right now he's going to get away from us."

McCowan nodded slowly as if this were old, old news. "You don't really imagine that Draeger would blow the station up out of mere spite, do you?"

"For Christ's sake, he already has!"

McCowan smiled, then shook his head. "Ken, you clearly don't get it. That wasn't Draeger. That was Robert Vincenzo."

Kendrick shook his head, appalled. "Robert?"

"He's dying. The nuke was on board one of the Los Muertos shuttles. Detonating it was a tactic born of his desperation. My biggest worry right now, however, is you."

"I don't understand."

"You figured out that Draeger had got his hands on one of the remote detonators, didn't you?"

"We found three nukes, but no detonators. The only possible reason for that is that Draeger picked up at least one of them."

"So what are you going to do – assuming you ever catch Draeger? What do you reckon is going to happen next?"

"I'll find a way to contact the shuttle. Then I can get home."

McCowan cackled, shaking his head. "I can see, even better than you can, how you're thinking. You're like an open book, you know that? With all those things you won't even tell yourself laid bare."

"Okay, then, just tell me whatever it is you're trying to say, then let me find Draeger." Kendrick bunched his hands into fists in frustration. Whatever McCowan now told him, in whatever cybernetic realm he currently inhabited, it still felt to him like they were wasting valuable time.

"You're going to try and destroy the *Archimedes*," McCowan stated flatly. "You can't even admit to yourself that you never intended anything else."

"That's ridiculous."

"All these years, you've let your hatred for Draeger carry you along. Now here you are, with the chance to destroy the focus of everything he's been working towards. Are you telling me that if you now had such a chance to hurt him, you wouldn't take it?"

"This is me you're talking about!" Kendrick shouted. "I'm not a murderer like he is! This is bullshit!"

"But do you really understand what's happening here? You've doubted everything you've seen all along, regardless of how many others shared those same experiences. But now you think that you have the opportunity to destroy everything dear to the man you hold responsible for the death of your family. It's not like I blame you for that, but that doesn't mean what you're intending to do is right."

Kendrick ran towards him. McCowan stood only a few metres away but somehow that tiny distance became an uncrossable chasm. Kendrick threw himself towards McCowan but landed in exactly the same spot where he'd already been standing. He shrieked with pure rage and began beating at the ground with his fists.

"Ken, stop that."

"Let me go!" Kendrick tore at the stony soil beneath his fingers till shards of pain ran up his wrists. But it still wasn't enough, and he drove his fists harder into the earth, to feel the spike of shock and pain that he knew he should be sensing, to see if he could somehow pry himself away from this hallucinatory place and back to the station, back to Draeger.

"People who've suffered unjustly don't automatically go out into the world to do good deeds," McCowan continued. "They go and do to others what was done unto them, and the whole shitty carnival rolls back to the beginning and starts again. Yes, the worst thing you could do to Draeger is to destroy the *Archimedes* even before it goes through the wormhole, even with all these people on board, even with me here. But I'm asking you to just think, Ken."

You're already dead, Kendrick thought silently. *You died a long time ago.*

"The station will enter the wormhole in only a few more minutes," McCowan continued. Now Kendrick tore at his own eyes, feeling blood trickle down his wrists. It wasn't real, none of this was real, so what did it matter? "There won't be any technology for Los Muertos to steal, or anyone else either. Stopping Draeger is one thing, but what then?"

"If you thought I was so dangerous, then why did you bring me all the way to the *Archimedes*?" Kendrick shouted back.

"Unfortunately," said McCowan, from a thousand miles away,

"I did not anticipate that someone would also bring a truckload of nuclear fucking bombs on board."

Kendrick began to smash his head against a rock, cool icebergs of agony crashing behind his eyes with each impact. There was a hard, unpleasant numbness behind his teeth. But what did it matter? What did it matter? What—?

—cheek pressed against the wall next to the airlock, and he was back, he was back. He tore himself away, pain still coursing through him.

It faded after a moment, like suddenly waking after re-experiencing a terrible accident in a dream. Like so much else, a lie, an illusion.

Breathless, his skin smooth and hard, eyes semi-opaque under their nictitating membranes, Kendrick stepped through the door. He pulled it closed behind him and ran the depressurization routine. There was no air to suck out, but still the outer airlock door wasn't going to open until the routine had run its course.

Then he pushed the outer airlock door open and stared off into empty space with naked eyes. He was now at the far end of the station, looking out across the exterior of the chamber's cap. The Earth slid past his view as the station spun on its axis.

Kendrick could see rails on which small platforms were mounted and rungs radiating out from the centre of the endcap. Also at the centre of the endcap was a raised area bristling with communications equipment. The airlock doorway in which he stood was positioned roughly equidistant between the endcap's centre and its rim. The station's spin made the endcap appear to his senses like a vertical cliff. He stepped quickly back from the lip of the airlock, feeling the sudden onset of nausea.

A terrible cold had begun to creep over him and he wondered just how much his body would be able to take of what he was about to put it through. Even though he knew he was running out of time, this gave him more than a moment's hesitation.

Kendrick reached for a handhold positioned just outside the air-lock door and pulled himself further out onto the *Archimedes'* hull. Then he gazed upwards towards the comms array at the centre of the endcap. In the distance he saw a figure in a spacesuit.

It had to be Draeger.

Kendrick gripped on to the rungs and pulled himself slowly upwards, working against the station's spin. He imagined himself as a machine, an automaton incapable of feeling fear or any other emotion. All he had to do was hang on to those rungs and not let go.

All the while a painful numbness gnawed at the edge of his thoughts. There were limits to how long he could survive like this. He kept on climbing, concentrating solely on the rhythmic flexing of his muscles, ignoring the gathering pain as he pushed himself on. Chunks of metal and concrete became visible around him in the inky blackness, some of them spinning wildly. Pieces of the shattered hull, he presumed.

He glanced towards the comms array and saw that Draeger had almost reached it. Kendrick yelled soundlessly, his lungs empty and useless, then pulled himself along faster. Draeger appeared as yet unaware that he was being pursued.

When a shadow passed over Kendrick he almost lost his grip. He managed to hold on and stared up at the underbelly of a shuttle with unfamiliar markings. The craft moved on, disappearing from sight beyond the curved rim of the endcap as it performed a docking manoeuvre.

He'd been right. A man as cunning as Max Draeger would never have come all this way without a carefully planned strategy of escape.

Draeger finally turned his way, perhaps catching sight of the shuttle as it passed overhead. His face was invisible behind the faceplate of his helmet, but it was clear he could see Kendrick.

Now Kendrick knew that he'd become everything Sieracki had intended for him to be: a man-machine built for killing. He felt a distant, almost inhuman sense of satisfaction as he clambered rapidly up towards the spacesuited figure ahead of him.

On the side of the communications tower Draeger had opened a panel behind which lay a display screen showing status lights. As Kendrick rushed towards him, he tried to scramble out of the way and, in doing so, something slipped from his gloved hand. Draeger reached out for it frantically.

Kendrick caught it easily with his uninjured hand and realized that it was a datachip. He could guess only too well what information was contained in it. Though his numb fingers held it clumsily, he continued squeezing it until the brittle plastic snapped and disintegrated.

Now Draeger was trying to get away from him. As he turned for a handhold, Kendrick let the fragments of the crushed datachip spin away. Then he reached out for his adversary.

When Draeger kicked out frantically with one boot Kendrick lost his grip for a moment before grabbing the other's leg and hauling himself on top of him. Draeger struggled and twisted beneath him, letting go of the rungs. He floated away for a moment before returning to hit the surface of the station with a thump after his safety cord had reeled out to its full length.

Kendrick ignored the gloved hands that beat frantically at his face as he reached for Draeger's helmet and released the clasps holding it in place. Draeger continued to struggle desperately for his life but was clearly finding it difficult to manoeuvre inside his bulky spacesuit. Kendrick could see the man's mouth working uselessly behind the visor, his eyes wide and full of terror. Then Kendrick twisted Draeger's helmet off its retaining ring and wrenched it away, careful even so not to let go of it.

He watched Draeger's features become puffy, the man's mouth moving soundlessly, his limbs still flailing. After several seconds he grew limp, his lips ceasing to frame dying words that would never be heard. Draeger's face became frozen for eternity in an expression of shock and dread.

Watching an unaugmented human undergoing implosive

decompression was far from pretty. Kendrick tried to register some kind of emotion. But he only felt empty, used up. Draeger was dead, but he himself didn't feel any different.

As blackness began to creep across his vision, a desperate, all-consuming need to survive now drove him on. He thought of his wife and daughter, disappearing from the world for ever; of Caroline and her slow, terrible death; then of Peter McCowan.

There were no guarantees that Draeger's spacesuit would fit Kendrick but the two men were of a similar height and body type. Kendrick pulled the suit open and manoeuvred Draeger's corpse out of it. It spun away from him slowly, tumbling end over end.

Carefully, he slotted himself into the suit, first wedging the helmet as best he could between two rungs and praying that it wouldn't work its way loose. The suit felt tight and uncomfortable, but Kendrick suspected that he only had seconds left before he lost consciousness. Then he gripped the helmet with both hands and pulled it on quickly.

With the last of his strength he tapped at the panel on the spacesuit's arm and was rewarded with the sound of hissing air. Overwhelming nausea filled him as his lungs shuddered back into life. He twisted helplessly on the end of the safety line as agonizing spasms racked his body.

After several minutes the worst of it had passed. Kendrick reached into the pockets of the spacesuit – and finally found what he was looking for.

28 October 28, 2096
The Edge of Infinity

Kendrick only realized that he had indeed lost consciousness when he awoke some minutes later.

As he held on to a rung he felt the entire station tremble under him. The stars twisted and flickered as if distorted by a vast lens. A sudden powerful spasm rolled through the hull and finally

Kendrick lost his grip. He spun away, the spacesuit's safety cord snapping out to its full length but holding firm. Slowly he drew himself back and took a firm grip again on a couple of rungs. He didn't even want to begin to think of the damage already done to his body tissues during the time he had spent in full vacuum.

Kendrick looked out to the distant curvature of the Earth as it slipped past his point of view and saw a blaze of light appear at the edge of its globe. Sunlight scattered across the *Archimedes*, and the suit's visor darkened automatically.

"Kendrick, listen to me. Where are you?"

He recognized Buddy's voice coming over a private channel. "I'm outside," he said weakly. "Draeger is dead."

"Jesus, I can't believe you're still alive. I mean . . . no, I don't know how you did it, but I can see you."

"I've got the detonator, Buddy. And I'm pretty sure Draeger didn't manage to send anything Earthside."

"Just a minute, you've got the trigger? The *nuclear* trigger? Christ. I . . . no, wait, Kendrick, listen to me. You're not thinking of doing anything, are you?"

Kendrick floated in the silence of space. Had those cracks visible in the side of the station been there before? *No, of course not.* Black lines now extended far and wide across the surface of its vast cylinder. He pulled out the detonator and studied it, remembering McCowan's words.

A ghostly light burned from deep within the cracks.

"Buddy?" he said. "Buddy, what's happening inside there?"

Buddy laughed. "You didn't see any of it, did you? I can't begin to describe what it's like . . . just light, everywhere." Buddy was gasping hard, as if he'd just run a couple of miles. "You can't begin to imagine. Everyone else is safe in a pressurized area, and all we can do is hope it stays that way until we're through. Look, just stay where you are. I'm almost there. I—"

Static crackled across the sound of Buddy's voice, like waves crashing upon a shore, and washed the last of his words away. Kendrick gripped the detonator a little harder, looking back the way he had come. He saw another spacesuited figure moving rapidly towards him across the rungs.

Great chasms of light flickered from deep inside the *Archimedes*. A gantry broke loose and spun outwards from the space station, trailing fragments of metal. Kendrick pulled himself closer to the hull and watched as the debris spiralled away into the darkness. There was now no sign of Draeger's shuttle.

Space rippled again, and the light from stars older than the universe itself spilled across the hull of the *Archimedes*.

Buddy pulled himself speedily over the rungs until he and Kendrick came face to face. Visor to visor, Kendrick could see the sweat on the other man's brow. He held up the detonator so that Buddy could see his finger poised just above the button.

"You're not going to do it," said Buddy, more a statement than a question.

"Here's what I've been thinking." Kendrick gripped the detonator hard, terrified of letting go of it. "The Bright were contaminated with Robert Vincenzo's deranged thoughts. Correct?"

"You tell me, Kendrick."

"Then bear with me. Robert's contamination damaged the Bright's chances of successfully passing through the wormhole leading to the Omega."

Buddy waited, mute. Kendrick continued. "McCowan came to me one last time. He knew what I was thinking, what was running through my mind. And, you know what? I thought I was imagining it at first, but I knew what he was thinking too. It wasn't telepathy or anything supernatural. Along with Peter McCowan, I was inside the machine that calls itself the Bright, and I could read McCowan as well as he could read me – maybe not with as much skill."

Buddy waited while Kendrick continued. "The Bright were infected with Robert's insanity. When I looked into Peter's thoughts, what I saw told me that it might be too late."

They rode on a mountain of steel and rock into a great shining chasm of light. The wormhole was preparing to suck them through.

"You can see that it's happening," Buddy implored him. "We'll be there soon. Doesn't that mean *anything* to you?"

Kendrick laughed shakily. "I only want what's *real*."

"You could let go of the detonator. You don't need it anymore."

Kendrick looked back towards the Earth. "The *Archimedes* might not go through. Until we know one way or the other, I'm hanging on to this."

Buddy made a move forward and Kendrick jerked away, holding the device out between them.

"The *Archimedes* will go through," Buddy insisted, his voice hoarse. "For Christ's sake, Kendrick—"

"No, listen to me. If the *Archimedes* goes through, then that's it – it's gone. You'll have got where you wanted to be, thanks to a man complicit in one of the greatest acts of mass murder of our century, but I guess you aren't worrying about that too much." Buddy's eyes were filled with desperate panic while Kendrick continued. "But if it doesn't go through – if you've got it wrong and there's any chance that Los Muertos or any other pack of lunatics could come here and grab something powerful enough to destroy a solar system, then I hit the button. Do you understand me? *I hit the button*."

"Fine, okay." Buddy nodded, his expression tense. "But it *will* go through."

Kendrick laughed, surprised at how ragged the sound was. "Maybe it will, Buddy. Maybe it will."

He pushed himself back a little until he bounced against one of the lower girders of the satellite array, wedging himself there into a narrow space. "Come near me meanwhile," he insisted, "and I'll blow the station anyway. Better that than risk the alternatives, don't you think?"

Buddy stared back, his expression unreadable.

Kendrick glanced towards the Earth, wondering if that view of it would be the last thing he would ever see. Half a dozen tiny lights burned now between the *Archimedes* and the world below. *More shuttles on their way*, Kendrick thought, *hoping to salvage whatever's left – if there is anything left.*

They waited there, suspended between Heaven and Earth.